Beach House Views
Ruan Willow
Writing as
R.U. Ann

# Table of Contents

HUMAN
AUTHORED

# Dedication

This book is dedicated to lovers who play in and out of the bedroom, those who never stop playing, and those who desire to please their partners and get off on getting their partner off, plus celebrate who they truly are because that's how it should be. Mutual pleasure is mutual bliss. Aftercare matters. Before care matters. During care matters.

Communication is key.

This book is an open door spicy dark romance, please read and enjoy it knowing this is the subgenre of romance it is in.

Marinate in your sexuality daily.

Enjoy and never stop seeking pleasure.

Pleasure is your birthright.

Passion is beautiful, unless it's an obsession that shatters.

# Chapter One

Juniper Clovis knows this beach house will change her life. She knows it with absolute certainty. If she didn't believe in premonitions, she'd be someone who ignores her gut feelings. That's not her. But the promise has already settled in the center of her bones, and without a doubt, it will most definitely be epic. She watches the wind tease the tree branches and imagines how they'd tickle her hands if she places her palm beneath the fronds. A change like this could be unnerving, but it is also exciting to contemplate.

She shivers as prickles travel her spine as she and her husband, Bridge, pull up snug to the four-car garage doors of the large one-level beach house. Its whiteness shines brilliantly in the sun as if it's a mirror to the cloudless sky. It's the kind of house she had dreamed of living in her entire life, and here it looms in front of her like a real possibility, something legit, plus, it's on the beach.

This is the kind of dream house she never expected she would be able to ever touch, let alone call her own.

But this carrot is in front of her, ripe for the taking.

She gives a little squeal as she slams the door of the SUV and shimmies her shoulders at her husband, who grins like a thousand smiles at once. He's excited, too, and she loves it. She drops her eyes to his crotch, where she had worked on him on the drive over, and his arousal is beautifully on display. It doesn't embarrass him a bit as he walks around the vehicle to join her at the base of the front steps. He's never embarrassed by his truth. And his confidence is a total turn-on, every time.

She bites her lip and flicks her eyes at him, her desire twitching with brightly raging lust. She wants to ride that thing of his right now, but unfortunately, their appointment takes precedence. However, she'd not have turned down a car quickie on the side of the road, had he asked. Standing before the house is not the time to bring that up.

He raises an eyebrow at her with a deliciously naughty expression. She hesitates before moving, contemplating grabbing him and dragging him back into the vehicle before the tour, but she knows the agent is waiting. She must defer her passion...for now. Politeness and courtesy wins. This time.

"Do you know whose house this is?" asks Juniper as she slips her slender hand into her husband's large one, stroking his palm with her index finger. They climb the wide cement stairs together with their hands joined, an act of solidarity she hopes the agent sees.

Juniper takes in the front. It's beautiful. Two large ivory vases shaped like giant tulips flank the dark blue front door. Elegant ivy vines spill down their fronts with red, white, and purple flowers filling the pots. The colors against the white background make the pop of colors burst.

Bridge grips the chrome handle of the door and pulls it open, offering for his wife to enter before him with a swish of his arm. Juniper loves Bridge's bold approach to living his life, as evidenced by his not knocking but claiming the right to enter. It makes her proud to be by his side. He rarely waits to be invited.

Their new real estate agent, Max, greets them with a wave as they peer into the gorgeous beachfront home. He looks his usual mousey self with a hurried, anxious look. He doesn't greet them, which is odd. Juniper's eyes drift away from him.

The house's aura fills her with an immediate comfy, posh, yet homey feel. The brilliant sun streams in as if the place is blessed by the heavens. Seriously, it's perfect. This could be her home! It would be a dream, though living with Bridge anywhere is already her dream come true.

She meets Bridge's gaze as he watches her, as he so often attentively does. She shakes her hands with excitement as they stride further into the stunning house.

Bridge finally answers her question, which she had almost forgotten she had asked, "No, I was in the bathroom when you two talked about the previous owner. Remember?" He smirks, adjusting his shorts to cover his swollen rod, but to no avail because it's still obvious.

They needed another two minutes in the vehicle, and he would have been much more comfortable. No matter. He'd get to use it on her soon now. He's creative; he'd come up with a plan. She has zero doubts. He steps closer and presses his swollenness against her firm butt, brandishing his lust.

She giggles, as if it weren't already as evident from a quick glance. What must the agent think? Bridge is a horn dog, so he wouldn't be wrong if he assumed so.

Juniper gives him a slight wiggle of her bum as she glances back at him. "Oh, yeah, that's right," she says with a swipe of her hand to flick her golden locks off her forehead.

His bold move proves his arousal, which only serves to flare the opening of her wanton core even more. Her libido is legit begging her to sit on him, regardless of present company. She hates putting off exercising her desire for Bridge.

"You missed the best part of the conversation. It's the famous writer, John Penn."

Bridge hangs his head to watch his wife's sashaying walk through the foyer. "No, kidding. Huh? Wow. That's crazy," he says, dragging his eyes up from Juniper to meet Max's, who is still silent, watching their seductive entrance.

The poor man looks sex starved.

Juniper clutches her small light blue satchel to her large bosom. She's so excited to even be in the same space the writer has occupied, let alone considering that she might get to live in it. "I know, right? That really excites me." She slowly scans the space, taking in the famous author's home, imagining him sitting in every spot with an open laptop on his knee.

This is like a shrine to his epic writing, and she's luxuriating in the atmosphere that helped him write all those incredible books. She needs to be pinched. This doesn't feel real!

The floor plan is open, which she likes very much. The kitchen is just beyond the foyer to the left, and the house opens up into a huge rectangular shape overlooking the ocean. The waves glisten in constant motion, serving as the backdrop to the modern-looking steel-gray deck. Four alternating-direction triangle windows fill the space above both sliding doors, stretching their glass faces upward to the ceiling. The views from all of them are spectacular. She draws in a deep breath and then slowly releases it.

"Wow," she murmurs.

There are five doorways off the main room rectangle. A large fireplace sits between the sliding doors, which leads out to the massive deck speckled with chairs. The whole room is a beautiful dream to Juniper, a mirage of white, dark, and light gray with accents of scarlet and golden yellow in the form of overstuffed throw pillows. The covers vary, some with coarse upholstery and some with smooth fabric. A few aqua throw blankets, a fluffy white floor rug on the hardwood, and abstract artwork in matching hues artfully adorn the walls. They fit the décor for what she'd expect in a beach house. An elegant nude statue of a curvy woman with long flowing hair, ironically, a striking resemblance to Juniper herself, stands in the right corner near the sliding glass door. The whole statue is about two feet tall and sits atop a white, curvy, pockmarked stone pedestal.

She doesn't think she'd change a single thing about this lovely décor.

Juniper widens her bright blue eyes, smooths an eyebrow with her slender finger as she says, "It's like a museum in here. I absolutely love it." She swivels to look at the men. "Why is he selling this so cheaply again?" Her arm falls gracefully to her side as she takes a few steps away. Both men stare at her.

Max rubs his stubbly chin and cocks his head before saying, "He wants to move and quick, so he's trying to unload it fast."

She smirks. Finally, he speaks. He continues to take in Juniper with hungry eyes. She watches Bridge smirk. He loves showing her off, and loves it even more when men look at her with lust, because he's the only one who actually gets to be with her. She loves that he's never jealous, no matter how another man looks at her. Instead, he says it confirms for him he's the luckiest man on the planet.

She smiles at both, enjoying the lavish attention.

"Wow, is right." Bridge follows his wife as they step forward to survey the room further. "This really is a steal at that price you quoted. Unreal." Bridge furrows his brows. "So, what's wrong with it?" He releases a guffaw.

Max nods, approaching the kitchen counter. Once there, he opens a folder and scans the paper inside. "Yes, it sure is. There's not a single thing wrong with it. It's been fully inspected. It's a true gem. A steal. You won't find this kind of thing happening very often. Or ever. You two should think hard. And fast." His eyebrow remains raised long after he stops talking. "This place will not last the day without selling."

Glee fills Juniper. "This is amazing," she says as she walks toward the brightly lit, crisp modern kitchen. She runs her hand along the steel-gray granite countertop, its smooth face flecked with red and banded in scattered streaks of white, like lightning fighting the dark. "Gorgeous granite." Her eyes soften as she strokes its smoothness. "This place is surely a dream."

"Yep. All custom. Best granite from Italy." Max pats the smooth, shiny countertop. "Only the best for Mr. Penn." The man's eyes fall to her cleavage and remain there.

Juniper giggles, imagining him talking to her breasts. It doesn't bother her a bit. They are a part of her superpower. "I've always wondered if that's his real name. It sounds like a pen name. I mean, a writer with the last name of Penn? Come on." She laughs like it's funnier than it is. Bridge smirks; he never minds her dumb jokes.

Both men smile at her; it's a gift of being sexy, she supposes. She gets granted what she wants by the male gender more often than not. Pausing to pose for them, she snickers inside. Lightly pressing her lips together, she runs her finger along the top of the wine fridge below the countertop. She flicks her eyebrows up, widening her eyes at her husband as she nods. "I really like it."

Bridge grins at his wife, his full ruby red lips play into a devilish smirk. He always looks at her as if she'd still be fascinating if she were reading the ingredients of a plain old oatmeal cookie package.

"I know, right, babe? Nice fridge there. That will come in handy for happy hours." He comes behind her and gives her a bear hug, which causes her to swoon as he mashes his still raging hard-on between her buttocks. She can't stop giggling as she leans slightly forward into the circle of his hug, as if he's ready to bend her over the counter.

She glances back at Max, who grins lewdly at their display of affection, and rubs his throat, looking like he wants to throw her on the counter himself, lift her flowing skirt, and get lost in there.

The man clears his throat. "Right you are. I don't know, about his name being a pen, I only know him by that name. He approached me a few days ago and told me he wants to unload his house quickly because he found another he really wants." He clears his throat again and sucks his lower lip into his mouth as he watches Bridge snuggle Juniper from behind, pulling her against his body snugly, as if they were alone. Instead of looking uncomfortable, his eyes flash to Juniper with want.

This pleases her, but she's getting a bit too aroused. She bumps Bridge with her butt, and he groans, but steps back. She moves away and runs her hands along the white cupboards. Her French manicured hand rests on the simple, smooth pewter handle of the last cabinet before the fridge.

She glances at Max. "May I?" As she cocks her head, a strand of blond hair falls off her shoulder and lands in front of her right breast, a motion apparently not wasted on either man. Both of their eyes are glued to her every move. She can't help but relish it. She could cut the sexual tension in the room with a knife. Part of her wants to suggest a threesome with the looks on both men's faces, but she knows Bridge won't go for it, so she swallows the wish.

"I mean, it's not too forward to look inside the man's cupboards when we are considering buying this place, is it? It seems kind of like I'm invading his privacy."

"Go ahead," says Max. "That's what a tour is for."

Bridge walks closer to the living room and scans it, glancing back at Juniper. Their eyes meet in an exchange that promises an impending union. She knows that look; he's very horny.

"Sure, go for it," Max repeats. "Whatever you want. That's what we're here for. Don't think he will care anyhow. It's expected of buyers to snoop." Max chuckles. "Gotta look under the hood if you're gonna buy something," he says, his words full of sexual suggestion. He holds a hand over his mouth and whispers to Bridge, "Or under the skirt. Right?" He releases a dirty chuckle.

Bridge heckles a guffaw. "Right."

"I heard that," Juniper says offhandedly as she raises up on her tiptoes to peer into a high cupboard. She knows both men are eyeing up her ass as she firms it up to stretch. She's determined to peer into the hard to reach spot and extends her neck. "Dang, I'm not a short woman, but I will need a stool for these top shelves."

Bridge glares at the back of Max's head, and Juniper suppresses a laugh. She knows exactly what's going through her husband's mind. Mr. Max Holden desires her but will never get with her, while he gets to fuck her every damn day. She sees his urge to smack the back of the agent's slimy, lecherous head, but he resists, grumpily. She'll reward him with sexual favors later. Maybe that jealousy isn't so elusive after all.

A gleam of a sudden thought erupts on Bridge's face. "Hey, Juniper, let's check out the bedroom. We haven't seen it yet, and it's the most important room in the house." He approaches her and rubs her ass cheeks from behind, running his hands from her waist to her thighs, in full sight of Max. A deliberate display of his ownership, which she secretly loves. "Because you know we will be spending hours upon hours in there." He grunts. "Baby making." He whistles.

Juniper smirks. He's such a brute, but not wrong. She reaches for something high in the cabinet. She's so busy on her mission that she forgets to blush from Bridge's bold touches in the presence of Max.

"Ugh, I can't reach this little drawer," she grunts, and Bridge leans into his wife's ass, cramming his meat into her as he reaches over her head to open the little drawer in the cupboard.

"Here, baby," he says softly into her hair.

"Thanks," she says. If she wasn't turned on before, she's now livid with want. She feels around inside the little drawer, trying to figure out what she's touching inside.

She meets Bridge's gaze with a knowing smile. His hand moves to his waist. Cradling his chub against the waistline of his shorts with his palm, he grabs his wife's hand and pulls her toward the bedroom off to the right.

Oh, he's got plans, alright.

"This is the master bedroom?" he asks Max.

"Yup," he replies as he drops his gaze to his phone.

"Wait, I felt something up there. I want to see what it is first." She hurries back to the cabinet. "I think it might be a key." She goes up on her tiptoes and reaches into the little drawer. Her fingers grace it, and she snags it. "Yeah. This little drawer has a key in it." She holds the little metal cylinder and lowers herself back down. She turns the key over and over in her hands, examining. "I wonder what this is for. A secret room?" Her eyes go wide as she scans the house. "That would be exciting."

"Like a secret sex room? Like a dungeon?" Bridge chuckles and runs his fingers down his strong chin. "Sold. Where's the paperwork?"

Max joins in his laughter. "Right?" He is chuckling a bit too heartily, causing Bridge to frown.

Juniper grins as she likes the idea of a sex room too, then asks, "Ask him, please, Mr. Holden? Mr. Penn, I mean. Will you ask him what the key is for?" She blinks as she watches his reaction.

"Yes, of course I will. And, please call me Max." He nods and runs his hand down his slight beer belly as if that somehow flattens it.

Juniper grins as she tries not to laugh. "Thank you."

Bridge walks toward the bedroom. "This place has a security system, right?" he asks from the door of the master bedroom suite as he waves Juniper over to join him. Bridge takes up most of the doorway with his broad shoulders, which complement his six-two height, fitting, being he had been a football star in college. His career had been abruptly cut short his junior year due to a devastating knee injury that rendered him unplayable for college football—and, unfortunately, for life.

His football career died from one seemingly harmless injury that wasn't so harmless after all. So, he used his degree and became a manager in the engineering department of a top medical device company instead. It had been paying off well, beefing up their bank account to a nice fat sum.

"Yes, well, not sure. Mr. Penn lived here alone, though." Max writes a note in his folder. He looks at the papers. "Yup, top-notch security system. All the bells and whistles."

Juniper's eyes widen as Bridge raises an eyebrow at her. He grabs his wife's hand and pulls her through the bedroom door. He's brandishing some serious bedroom eyes.

She falls into the room from his pull with a gasp and says, "Oh!" as Bridge shuts the door behind them.

"Wow, right now?" Juniper gazes about the room before returning her eyes back to Bridge, where she sees the depth of his hunger lingering like the hot belligerence of a bull. That's something she loves because he just devours her when he looks like that. She allows her gaze to fall to his groin. His boner is riding a wet spot on his shorts.

"Mmm," she purrs.

He grins at her with lascivious intent before her eyes fall back on his crotch. He runs his hand up his ready cock.

She naughtily grins. "Really?" she croons as she saunters closer to her husband. "Seriously? Here? Now?"

"Well, like he said, you can't buy something without looking under its skirt first. I need a peek. And the best way to do that is to fuck in the bedroom space to see if it feels right." He wraps his thick, muscular arms around her and hovers his mouth above hers. "Wanna fuck, baby? Let's make a baby right here, right now."

She squirms with delight as he sucks her lower lip in between his, then she slips her tongue into his mouth, riding the length of his tongue back and forth until he grips hers for a hard suck. Her hands climb his biceps to his shoulders. She's so ripe, so ready. Her heart pounds.

"Mmm, I love this idea."

He gropes her ass with a claiming squeeze. "Me too."

She moans. "Oh, you know I want to," she whispers into his open mouth. She rubs her tongue against his, then whispers, "Should we invite Mr. Max Holden to join us? He seems like he's pretty ready to fuck me, too."

Bridge frowns. "Nope. I ain't letting that slimy ass hairy dickless wiener anywhere near you, baby."

Juniper sighs and releases a curt laugh. Again, she wishes her husband weren't so picky so they could have a threesome sometime. It's been on her bucket list forever. "You're no fun," she says, but with a big, sexy, suggestive grin. "Zero."

"Oh, I'm fun, alright," he says as he spins her masterfully onto the bed and presses her face down into the plush comforter. He flips up her skirt to bare her ass. "Gotta check under the skirt here to be sure. Agent's orders."

Juniper laughs with relish, then writhes on the bed, wiggling her butt, anticipating his touch. She grabs the comforter with a massive sigh, readying to stabilize herself against his thrusts.

Bridge's cock grazes her rear as he hovers above her ear to say, "So far, I like the underskirt view of this room." He rubs her lower lips and slips two fingers in her wet hole as he trails kisses down her spine. "I want it. Let's take it."

Juniper shifts on the bed and coos, "Mmm. Yes. I'm in." She settles her face into the soft white comforter.

Bridge tickles her labia lips with the tip of his boner. Her fire is now fully thickened, her naked folds practically screaming as they beckon him to taste her depths.

"Yum, yes please," she murmurs, writhing with pleasure. "Penetrate me hard and fast, you bastard." It's so hot he's making this move to fuck her with Max outside waiting for them. It's freaking delicious.

"Aw, this is hot to you, huh? Me fucking you in an author's private bed? With the agent out there knowing. You're very wet, my baby," he croons it from deep within his lungs in a gruff, raspy voice.

Juniper nods with a little smile on her lips. "Yep. Mega hot. Like raging forest fire hot."

Bridge rubs his cockhead against her very slick flesh, causing her to moan and ride the bed in impatient squirms. He fondles her hip with his other hand, then squeezes her ass cheek. "I want you so bad. Right now. Can't wait."

"Same," she mutters, her need for him blazing.

"I wonder if he wrote one of his bestsellers in here," wonders Bridge aloud as he manhandles Juniper's sides up and down, feeling her up nonstop.

Juniper adores the sunlight hitting her flesh from the skylight above. She does indeed like this bedroom, and she very much loves Bridge's show of passion.

"Yeah, like that sexy thriller about the couple who lived on the beach, you know, the one with the famous sex scene in..." Juniper stops as Bridge pushes his hard-on into her pussy. She moans and grips the comforter harder as Bridge slowly increases his pumping. "Ummmm...fuck," is all she gets out.

He flicks on the little sex toy he keeps in his pocket, and it buzzes. She adores how he always takes it along when they leave the house, just in case they can do a quickie. He pumps himself hard into his wife's pussy, slamming her ass with his abdomen the way she likes. Her ass cheeks jiggle from each pound, and their skin deliciously slaps together.

"I'm gonna make you cum hard on a famous author's bed, baby," he whispers, pressing the vibrating toy to her hip.

She moans out a slurred, "Yes, fuck me, fuck me good here." She sighs as he pumps. "Please. Fuck yes." Her eyes are rolling back, and her mouth falls open as she moans. She adores that he loves to play sexually in unusual places, and his bringing out the toy is a top seduction move he never misses.

Bridge leans back down and rubs the small vibrator on his wife's clit, causing her to moan and whimper loud enough for Max to surely hear. He slows his pounding as he holds the vibrating sex toy to her and increases the pressure; he knows exactly how to drive her wild.

She moans, not hiding her pleasure one bit.

He lets out a manly growl, pressing the toy more firmly. She responds by lifting her perfect, round little bubble butt up, presenting it to him. She takes over, pressing the toy, freeing him up to grip her hips. He firmly pounds into her as she whimper-groans, making the sounds she often makes before climaxing. He continues to fuck her as her arms draw tight to her body, her knees bend more against the bed as she shakes, her shoulders curling, her pussy clenching his cock as it contracts. Her body slumps against the bed as she's overcome by climaxing.

Once she's stopped twitching, he releases his load and comes full bore inside her pussy. She smiles. This is great because they are on a quest for a baby, and here's another shot in the bucket. It would be incredible to get pregnant on the day they toured and found their new home.

They both lie still on the bed, his body draping hers for a few moments of recovery as both come down off their highs. The little hum of the egg is the only sound besides their panting.

"Um...that was yummy. Really strong. Delicious." Juniper feels up the comforter with repeated squeezes of her hands, squirming and stretching against the mattress. She lifts her head slightly, making the veil of her hair gently fall back. "I like this bedroom setup. I wonder if he'd consider selling it with the house. I kinda hate ours."

"Let's ask. I like it too, baby." He pumps into her a few more times, even though his dick is going flaccid.

Juniper looks over her shoulder and grins, then drops her head back to the bed. Her hair falls, shrouding her face. "I wonder if Max heard us."

"You mean heard you?" Bridge chuckles. "It was all you, baby. I barely made a sound."

"Liar. I heard you make your man growl sounds." Juniper reaches under her pelvis and grasps the small vibrator in her hands. "My little friend," she says as she hands it over to him, the toy still vibrating. "This belongs to you."

"Nope, I'm pretty sure it's yours." Bridge shuts it off and slips it into his pocket. She knows he wants to lick it, but he resists until he can't. He pulls it back out and licks it like a sucker.

Juniper rolls to her back. "You're always obsessed with tasting me, aren't you?"

He nods as he continues to lick. "I am. I love the smell, taste, and flavor of you, and I can't ever get enough." He rubs her bald pussy. "Thanking God you go commando, baby. Makes for easy quickies. And makes your scent waft off you." He grins. "I can almost always smell you."

She puts her hands behind her head with a grin. "Right?" It's true, being commando makes her scent more evident, she can smell herself most of the time, too. It's arousing even to her. She slides back on the bed, bare assed. "You think he minds my bare ass on his bed?" She gives him a saucy look.

"Doubt it. You've seen your perfect ass, right? What man would say no to that booty?" He pulls up his shorts and buttons them.

"A gay man." She runs her index finger over her lips.

"Nope. I think even a gay man would agree you have a great ass." He chuckles. "They have good taste in asses."

Juniper throws a pillow at his face. "Talk nice, you pervert."

"You like me being a pervert," he says with a laugh as he takes a picture of Juniper half-naked on the bed. "We need a picture of your naked, spent pussy on a famous author's bed."

She spreads her legs wide open for his camera. "Is this better?" She opens her labia lips to reveal her pinkness. "This could be our bed."

He clears his throat. "Um...yes. You keep this up, though, and I'm going to need round two. Or my tongue will need round one."

Juniper grins. "You going to fuck me in every house Max brings us to today?"

"Hell yes. We need to try out the fucking vibes of the space to be sure. But, I must say, this house feels so right, I don't know that I even want to keep looking. You?" He stares at his phone. "Damn, I could sell these pics of you and make a mint, you're so damn fucking sexy hot."

Juniper smirks and throws another pillow at him. "Don't you dare, mister." She shimmies her skirt down while still lying on the bed and then hops up. But wait, that sounds kinda hot, she ponders the thought of other men looking at her with a grin. "Let's see the rest of this house so we can know if it's the one. I'm kinda right with you on this. I'm loving everything so far." She winks. "Everything. Including the obvious luscious bedroom fucking vibes."

He nods, mirroring her smirk. "Okay. Let's go find Max. I bet he's got a load coating the front of his pants after that loud verbal porn you just belted out." Bridge cups his wife's ass as she opens the bedroom door. "But he only gets to listen, I get the pound," he whispers in her ear.

She nods and gives him a naughty look with an eyebrow raise, her eyes flashing with brilliance. She glances around the living room and spots Max on the couch, typing something on his phone.

# Chapter Two

"Like the bedroom, huh?" Max doesn't look up from his phone, but his grin is about as giant as one can get.

"Out of this world," Juniper says, still savoring the aftereffects of her orgasm. Yep. He heard them. How could he not? She'd blush if he looked at her right now, but thankfully, he doesn't. She's not so sure how she feels about another man knowing how her moans sound during sex, but he sure got an earful. And truthfully, it's starting to make her hot to know he clearly heard. She scans the room again. "Can we see the rest of the house now?" She pauses as he looks up. "And you said there's no basement, right? But there's like a sort of patio entertainment area underneath the house or something?"

"Yes. That space is a huge selling point. I call it the open-air entertainment room. I'll show it to you after we walk through the rooms here." He stands up and shoves his phone in his pocket, then runs his hand through his gray-speckled dark brown hair. "I...um...don't need to show you the master bedroom, you've seen that." The sarcasm drips from his words as his expression grows lecherous.

Juniper blushes deeply as he stares directly at her, but she grins regardless and gives him a nod with her left eyebrow raised.

He snickers, then points to the corner of the house. "Let's go into the exercise room off the kitchen first. This way." He lightly touches Juniper's arm, ushering her toward the room.

She glances at Bridge, who is frowning. She raises her eyebrows and gives him a pleasant look. He's going to let the touch go, she hopes.

He leads them past the kitchen and into a decent-sized exercise room. One wall is lined with mirrors, another with windows overlooking the wraparound porch walkway, and the other has a ballet barre, with another wall of mirrors. There's a treadmill, an exercise bike, two exercise balls, an elliptical machine, plus a weight-lifting area.

"Wow, this is amazing. Like his own personal decked-out gym." Juniper touches the elliptical machine; she's always wanted one. "Lucky man."

Max clears his throat, his expression expectant. "These come with the house, by the way, so you're now the lucky one." He smirks, seeming to enjoy his own pun. "He doesn't want them. In fact, he doesn't want any of the furniture at all, so it's all yours to keep or sell or donate or whatever."

Both Bridge and Juniper swivel their heads to view Max. They look at each other in shock.

"Are you serious?" Bridge asks, his jaw remaining open. "Who is this man anyway?"

"Really? Oh my gosh. This is…decadent." Juniper rubs the elliptical machine's arms as she imagines herself using it daily. "Wow. That's beyond amazing and generous. I really can't believe this."

"This really is way too good to be true." Bridge meets her gaze again, his shocked face switching to happiness.

They've won some kind of lottery.

"Yeah, he said this stuff fits this space, so he wants his designer to fill his new space properly rather than fit this stuff in. I guess when you're as rich as he is, you can do that kind of thing." Max waves his arm in a circle. "That includes everything in this house. He will only take his personal items, computer, etc."

"Unbelievable." Bridge crinkles his nose. "Someone didn't die here recently, did they? I mean, if that happened, I could see why he'd want to hightail it out of here."

"Nope. No deaths occurred here. He just found something he wants more." Max picks up a barbell and does a few curls with it. "Again, like I said, when you're rich enough, you can do that kinda shit at your own whim."

"I can't even imagine," Juniper muses softly, shaking her head.

"Man's fleeing like he saw a ghost. Any paranormal weird shit? Ghost spottings?" Bridge eyes up the collection of weights and the vast selection of barbells he's always wanted, but only ever got at a gym. "We won't need a gym membership anymore with this."

"Not that I know of," says Max with a raised bushy eyebrow. "Guy seems legit, just wanting to move on."

Juniper runs her hand along the bar. "This will be amazing for steadying while doing yoga." Her wanton eyes widen as she caresses the entire length of it.

"And fucking." Bridge chuckles deeply. "We could put a pole for you right there in the corner, too." He motions to the area with a swipe upward of his arm.

Juniper drops her jaw. Of course, his brain goes there. "Oh, behave, Bridge. Seriously. What will Max think?" Juniper swats the air at him as she catches a knowing smirk on Max's face. She loves that her husband is always thinking about sex, though. To hide her blush, she walks over to the wall of windows. "So, this porch is a wraparound one that goes around the entire house, or just this corner?"

"It goes around," Max says as he approaches the window where Juniper stands. He looks at her with hungry eyes as he waves his hand toward the outside. "We'll go out there too, but it goes around the entire house and connects on both sides to the deck by the ocean. Both bedrooms have a sliding glass door access to the porch, not sure if you two noticed that when you were...um...visiting the master bedroom. You sounded kind of busy." He chuckles. Juniper bites the insides of her lips to keep from laughing as he continues on, "Then there's a spiral staircase off the deck to the patio entertainment area underneath, too. It's large and really quite a stunning use of space. He had an architect design this home, a top-notch company."

"Don't seem to see many spiral staircases these days," Bridge says with a rub of his upper lip. He looks as if his brain is working overtime.

"No, not really. I mean, you could easily put in a regular staircase if you wanted to." Max motions for them to leave. "Next room?"

"Yes," Juniper says after running her hand along the barre's length again, deliciously imagining herself holding it while Bridge fucks her from behind—or him holding it, trapping her to it. She gives off too much of her thoughts, apparently, as Max's lewd grin deepens. She turns away from him quickly, so he won't see her cheeks redden deeper. He doesn't need further confirmation.

"This is basically the sex room," Bridge declares with a cock of his head.

"Isn't that every room?" Juniper asks with a smirk.

"Yeah," Bridge says, nodding. "True."

Max shakes his head as he leads them out of the room. "Lucky motherfucker," he mutters under his breath. He leads them to the next room. He returns back to his all-business persona. "This spare bedroom bathroom here has two doors, one for access for guests in the living room, and one door to the spare bedroom."

He points into the bathroom, and Juniper peers in. It's nicely decorated in a nautical and beach theme in beiges and pinks, light blue with a bit of light purple. Pictures of ships on the sea adorn the walls. Shell-themed towels are perfectly aligned on the towel rack. They look crisp and pristine. It has a shower in a tub, two sinks, and the rest is a standard bathroom display. This bathroom has no evidence of being used.

"It's a very pretty bathroom. I love how his decorator decorated this whole house. I don't even think I want to change anything I've seen yet." Juniper's voice comes out strong and pure. *How did we get this lucky?*

Max leads them on to the next room. "Only one spare bedroom here, though. That's the downfall of this house. It only has two bedrooms, so it won't work for families very well. Maybe a single-child family, but then there's no other spare bedroom. So, it's ideal for childless couples like you two." He shrugs. "But you could also convert the entertainment room below into actual house space if you want more rooms someday, I mean, if you two ever have kids or something." He grins. "Speaking of fucking."

Juniper startles at his words. Did he just say that out loud? She winces at his mention of kids. It's a sore spot in her heart. They've been trying for five years and still no baby, and certainly not from lack of fucking, they have sex every damn day, sometimes twice. Juniper hugs herself and tries not to let it bother her.

Bridge's face softens as he puts his hand on Juniper's elbow. "Yeah. We could easily do that, I bet, babe," he says in a soft, comforting voice. He gives her arm a squeeze. "We could make it work. Easy."

She gazes out of the large window at the ocean. All she wants in this world is a baby. It wasn't supposed to be this tough to get pregnant.

"This would be a nice space for guests, for like when your parents come to visit, too, Bridge, or your brother's family." It hurts to be too hopeful and imagine it as a nursery. She blinks her tears away as she walks further into the room. "It's really just lovely for guests." She runs her hand along the king bed as she walks, savoring the lush softness of the sage green comforter. "I really like how both bedrooms face the ocean to get that spectacular beach view." She scans the room again. "I just never thought we'd ever be able to afford a beachfront house, let alone one like this. The extravagance is mind-blowing. This is like a dream, but please don't wake me!" She giggles delightfully. It helps her sour mood lift a little. "I think this is my dream house of all time." She walks over to the window and touches the glass with one hand, as if she's trying to feel the ocean through it. To be holding a baby while looking out at the water, with Bridge by her side; life surely couldn't get any better than that.

Bridge clears his throat. "Again, we'll take it, Max." He walks over to Juniper and wraps his arms around her, hugging her from behind. "I want this for you if it's your dream home. I want to give you everything your heart desires." He nuzzles his lips into her neck and sucks her skin lightly.

She nods but doesn't speak. His arms wrapped around her are comforting. "I want it, too," she whispers as he kisses her neck and fondles her belly. As she stares out over the rolling sea, she asks, "Can we see the rest of the house now, Max?"

"Of course, Juniper, of course." Max jumps and lunges toward the bedroom door as if they are about to start fucking again. He almost runs out, which makes Bridge snort.

Juniper swivels in her husband's arms and smacks his shoulder, giving him a 'you behave' look.

Bridge smirks and touches his wife's cheek. "What? I can't ever resist you." He gives her a kiss on the lips, then releases his hold on her as she breaks free to follow Max, who is now completely out of sight.

She laughs, shaking her head. She knows Bridge, and he is surely ready to go again, and would not hesitate to do so, Max present or not.

"Poor Max," she whispers as she meets her husband's wanton gaze.

Once she reaches Max, he's got his agent hat back on again. "Let's head out to the wraparound porch and then down to the entertainment area. I can't wait to show you it." Max leads them out onto the deck.

The big waves are crashing into the shore. To Juniper, it's surely the most luscious sound, wholly unmatched on this Earth.

She grins. "I seriously can't believe I'll be hearing that sound all day, every day, and on weekends, too." She shrugs her shoulders as a look of gleeful joy spreads across her face. "This is my heaven."

Bridge returns her smile. "Yes, it will be wonderful. My heaven, too, but only with you in it." He chuckles as he grabs for his wife's ass as she crosses the deck to the railing.

She shoos his hand away. "You won't stop, will you?" she asks in a teasing voice.

"Never," he retorts in an equally flirty tone.

Juniper watches Max's look of bewilderment; he's likely never had such a horny couple as them on a house tour before. Bridge can't keep his hands off her.

She turns her gaze to the vast face of the sun-soaked ocean. She raises her cheeks up to the massive run of blue sky. The wind lifts her golden hair in sheets, then it falls down in a lush veil to her shoulders. The damp breeze is blissfully sea-salted; it caresses the three of them into a motionless trance of silence on the deck.

"This is truly some kind of heaven on Earth," she murmurs to no one in particular, and maybe to the ocean itself. "It's like the ocean is alive, breathing, taking and giving, rolling herself along in her travels, devouring herself in continual waves. The Earth feeling her up wherever he can reach his hungry fingers against her."

Bridge hugs his wife from behind and kisses her neck, slightly swaying her in the breeze.

"Beautifully poetic, Juniper." He cups her breasts and rubs his thumbs over her hard nipples beneath, then pinches her thick peaks as he nuzzles her neck. He grunts in her ear, "Made me horny."

"You were already horny," she teases.

Max leans against the deck rail, gripping it firmly as if to steady himself. "Holy shit," he mutters. "This tour is like I'm in porn."

"I can deliver that," Bridge says smoothly while heckling.

Juniper chuckles as she stares off over the ocean, feeling like she's in a dream, leaning back against Bridge as his right hand travels down her belly. He slips his hand into her skirt, finger-crawling along her mound and ending at her pussy lips. He moves with his wife's body back and forth to the sound of the crashing waves as he finger fucks her. She moans, forgetting where she is, and she lets out a massive sigh.

Max clears his throat. "Wow. Um, uh, yeah, that's so poetic and beautiful, Juniper." He clears his throat again. "Did. Did. Did you guys want to see the entertainment area?" Max hurries away from them and stares off into the distance.

She startles and tries to pry herself from Bridge's hold. "Yes. I mean, yes. Of course, Max. Coming." She whispers to Bridge, "We need to quit tormenting the poor man." She caresses his arm as his hand is still inside her skirt, and she giggles. "Oops," she whispers as she pushes his hand away. She swivels to face her husband. "I guess we got a bit carried away. The ocean is so romantic, though, right? I lose myself."

Bridge tucks her hair behind her ear. She can smell her pussy on his fingers. "I'm looking forward to lots of you losing yourself here," he says soothingly. He grabs her hand and pulls her along to join Max.

Juniper walks, enjoying the feel of her hand in Bridge's. "Yeah, I love how private this house is, too. I know there are neighbors on each side, but you can't really tell with the fences, terracing, and the vegetation."

"Yeah, in this area, that's pretty much by design," says Max with another clearing of his throat. "For privacy."

For privacy for beach fucking. Juniper scoffs as she notices Max has a raging hard-on. After what she and Bridge just did, she can't blame him. She averts her eyes from his crotch, only a bit too late. He grins sheepishly at her.

She wishes his erection could be put to better use than high and dry in his pants. "So, Max. Can we walk the wraparound porch first?" She loves how the ocean breeze plays against her skin as she walks. "I think I would just walk around this house on this porch for hours; it's so hypnotic here. Almost seductive."

"Very seductive," agrees Bridge.

They roam around the wraparound deck, three in a single line.

Juniper walks along, trying to quell her arousal. She turns her attention to looking in the windows intently, taking in the amazingly unbelievable fact that this will really soon be their home. The short jaunt takes them past the spare bedroom, the guest bathroom, and the exercise room before they reach the front corner of the house, where she pauses.

Juniper touches the wall of the house. "Something seems weird right here, like the exercise room ends, but yet there seems to be more house than the kitchen doesn't seem to have. Is there another room in this corner?" She grins. "Maybe that's what the secret key is for."

Bridge comes up behind his wife, his full body touching hers.

"Well, darlin', you're quite right. There seems to be something off here. The space isn't adding up." Bridge looks back and forth along the wall. "Max, did the owner say anything about a hidden room? Like a safe room or a wine cellar or something?" He clears his throat. "Maybe it's a sex room? Please say yes." His voice is low and hushed.

Max chortles and smirks. "No," he says, surveying the house layout himself. "It indeed seems off spatially, though. I will ask him about it. Perhaps it's like you said, a safe room, or something. I feel like he would have told me if it were a wine room, because that would be a major selling point for the house. If it is indeed a sex room, it's brilliantly hidden from the eyes of guests, and that's a damn genius design right there." He bobs his head.

"Right," Juniper says as she cocks her head. "But kinda weird that he didn't mention it. Must be nothing. Just wasted space."

"Maybe it is a sex room. Or could be one." Bridge sounds quite chipper about that. He spreads his arms wide. "Did I mention we'll take the house?"

Juniper elbows Bridge. "Stop. You're awful, we're making poor Max all hot and bothered enough as it is with how we can't keep our hands off each other."

"Oh, don't stop on my account. I only wish my wife would let me do half of that stuff to her." He chuckles and runs his hand through his hair. "Even if only in private." He grimaces, then raises an eyebrow. "You two don't stop on account of me." He turns around and leads the way along the rest of the porch until they end up back at the beachfront deck again.

"I love that design so much. A big deck is not a waste of space in my mind. I could just roam and roam it all day and night." She touches the soft cushions on the deck couch. "These come with the house, too, then?"

"Yep, Juniper, everything. He said all he's taking are his clothes, personal items, books, pictures, his bike, his extra car, some stuff from the garage, and things like suitcases, computers, and other items. But all the furniture, decorations, and everything in the kitchen, including dishes, pots, pans, and all the stuff in the exercise room, are being sold with the house, too. Most of what you see is what you get." He shakes his head. "This is a steal. Unheard of. You'd be stupid not to take it, honestly. I never see this, and I've been doing this for thirty years."

Juniper shakes her head, causing her fine hair to float back and forth. "Unbelievably generous of him." She purses her lips, then says, "We'll have to sell our stuff or donate it all. It won't fit here."

"Indeed," says Bridge. "Now, let's see this entertainment area. You said it has a small pool and hot tub too, right?"

"Yes, the pool is a small, kidney-shaped pool that's heated. The pool and the hot tub share the same heater." Max leads them down the spiral staircase from the deck down to the giant entertainment area, which is spread out to encompass the full space of the house above.

It's partially walled off, three-quarters of the area is flanked with walls, and the remaining quarter is open to the seaside. There is a patio area facing the beach that houses the hot tub and the small pool. Behind the hot tub is a square tiki hut-type bar with stools placed all around it. Behind it, there is a pool table, a foosball table, a dart board machine, plus a sitting area with plush cushioned outdoor couches. There is a giant TV on the far wall with three rows of stadium-type seating with reclining chairs.

"This is incredible," Juniper coos.

Bridge nods over toward the back. "Ah, there's the movie theater area. I love it. That will be perfect for football games, too."

"Yes, absolutely perfect. The chairs are embedded with their own heaters, like car seats, and as you can see, there are heaters scattered about for those cool evenings." Max points at them scattered about the space.

"He's thought of everything." Juniper gazes about the area with wide eyes. "Well, I guess his interior designer did." She walks over to the bar and touches the bamboo on the sides. "It's unreal what unlimited money can do. And, I seriously love this bar. We're going to have so much fun here, Bridge. With family and friends, and ourselves." She imagines their little ones frolicking around, enjoying the area as well. "And hopefully, more." She pictures a little girl riding a trike and giggling. She smiles. "Yeah, definitely more."

Bridge grunts. "Yes, we will." His confidence is addictive.

Juniper looks out at the ocean. She knows she looks wistful, but she can't help it. She wants that vision of the future so badly. She grasps for something positive to rescue her from her sad thoughts. "Mags will love to sit here and lounge for hours, I bet."

Max looks up from his phone. "Mags?"

"Our cat," says Bridge as he joins his wife and wraps his arms around her once more.

Juniper swoons in his arms as he sways them.

"Ah," Max says, looking in a rush as he starts for the staircase. "I'm just going to go out to the car and work while you two have a full look around, give you some alone time to…you know…to fully consider the place. Come out when you're done. I'll let the seller know you're interested in the meantime, and we can get things rolling." He catches Bridge's eye with a knowing look. "Take your time."

Bridge nods, the typical guy nod, the knowing nod, the fuck yes, I'm gonna fuck her right when you leave nod. And thanks, bro.

Juniper smirks. They're so obvious. "Bro code paving the way for sex?"

Bridge scoffs. "Yeah, it's either get that or jealousy."

Max climbs the stairs and dares a peek back. Bridge gives him an affirming head nod as he shoves his hand up the back of Juniper's skirt. Talk about getting permission to fool around from the agent, indeed.

Maybe she should be embarrassed having Bridge access her in Max's sight, but in truth, it turns her on. She kind of wishes Max would stay and watch, but that's clearly wishful thinking.

As Bridge caresses her, she's staring off into the vast, shining abyss of the grand sea. She's getting more aroused as she takes in the abundant sunshine. It dances across the water like so many strands of visible air tiptoeing their way across the surface.

"Mmm, that feels incredible," she slurs.

Bridge wastes no time and squeezes her ass cheeks. She's sinking back into him, feeling drunk with desire, as he molests her right buttock while his other hand fondles her left breast.

"Again?" she murmurs, curling into his touch.

"Again," he slurs back. He snakes his other hand into her skirt, lifting it before squeezing an ass cheek in each hand. "Mmmm, you feel so good by the ocean, baby."

She squirms as he tickles her asshole with his index finger. "We're giving Max so many stories to tell his colleagues."

"For sure we are. And hey, maybe we can make a baby here on our first day visit, like right now. You in?" Bridge bares her ass.

"You know I am."

She loves the brisk ocean breeze on her bare pussy. It's an aphrodisiac, burgeoning her libido to flare even more swollen, effectively wetting and thickening her clit. Bridge's fingers pressing her are helping her reveal her desire, every inhibition dissipating. She wants his cock in her now. "Please, I need you."

He swivels her to face him. "Twice in one day might make it happen, right?"

She nods and then gives him a small smile as she fingers his hair. "Kiss me in front of this gorgeous ocean. Please kiss me." She bites her lip and dips her chin, giving him a coy look. "Then fuck me in front of it. My precum is begging to soak yours." She unleashes a sexy grin, which he returns, saucy and primal.

"Now, that I can do," he says with strong conviction. He pulls her close and touches her face softly, swiping at her cheek with his thumb. "Either way, we're sure as fuck going to have fun trying." He runs his thumb across her lips, then pushes it in past her slightly parted lips.

She sucks on his thumb, wetting her urges to consume his tongue. She holds his eye contact as she sucks the entire length inside her hot mouth, rippling her tongue along it like she does the frenulum of his cock, which always drives him wild. The sound of the waves behind them is not shushing the brightness of their passion but instead swelling it. He pulls his thumb out of her mouth and replaces it with his tongue in a deep kiss. He moans and pulls his tongue back out, then grins. "Didn't think we'd get such a fuck fest today seeing houses."

Juniper grins, then presses her lips shut so Bridge can force his tongue in. A flirty foreplay penetration thing she likes to do to help him feel like he's conquering her, but she gives it to him eagerly every day, though, no conquering needed, but for role play, it's hot. He wiggles his tongue, working his way into her mouth, coaxing it wide with the force of his bold claiming tongue thrust.

She grins through a moan as his tongue barges fully into her mouth. He jabs his tongue along hers, slowly at first, then with faster speed, caressing hers. She reciprocates, and they kiss, their start into a sure promise of a fuck. She sucks his lower lip with strong suction. He returns with a taste of her upper lip. It's a battle of who is sucking harder.

Juniper breaks their kiss, then moans into his mouth. "You better fuck me before I go insane."

His gaze turns ardent as he leans back. He removes her shirt with urgency. She never did put her bra back on, so she's deliciously bare-titted just like that. She chuckles in her head, imagining the owner finding her bra in his bedroom. Her nipples are hard, wrinkles cradling the tips. He traces the edge of her oval areola on her right breast with his index finger, meandering it slowly to ride over her pink nipples, feeling up her bumps as he works his way to savor the gathered, puckered tip of her tit.

He opens his mouth wide to dominate and devour her nipple, sucking it all the way to the back of his throat, causing her to moan, arch, and roll her head back, her hands threaded into his lush, thick hair. After a minute of orally pleasuring her nipple, he comes off and slips one arm under her knees and the other behind her back. He carries her to the little rug closest to the edge of the game room. He lays her naked body down gently, taking a moment to breathe in the scent of her pussy.

She spreads her legs, giving him access. He takes the hint and kneels between them. He gathers her thighs up, one in each arm, and pulls her to his mouth, breathing a flow of hot breath on her labia and clit before completely absorbing her right lip into his hot mouth. She moans and arches her back, engrossing herself in his sucking as he next migrates his tongue, wiggling across her slit to eat up her left labia lip. He takes it all into his mouth and sucks. His loud mouth smacking, paired with how amazing it feels, riles her up even more.

He lets her flesh slip out of his mouth before he murmurs into her pussy, "Mmmm. Your scent drives me wild."

He flattens his tongue and rides her pussy, starting from the edge of her ass cheeks, then along her slit and up to her clit. He takes over her most sensitive spot with a wide-open mouth, sucking, sending her into a full clit erection. Her fingers fly to her hard nipples, and she plays with them. He watches her manipulate her mini pinecone shapes as he sucks her. He grins, but this makes him lose suction across her, so he readjusts, sucking hard, before shoving two fingers in.

Her moans fill the air, commanding the room as she yells out. She's writhing incessantly as she rides her orgasm up that sweet hill. The trigger hits. Her body clenches, her arms and legs draw up, and her body falls into a succession of jerks. Her lips purse, releasing her mewling whimper as she comes.

He pulls his fingers out and consumes her creamy white cum on his fingers. He laps up her essence slathered across her hole, hoovering up all her wetness into his mouth.

He releases her and kneels back, glancing at the ocean, then back at his wife's satisfied face. He sighs. He looks so happy, and so horny.

"Please, fuck me now, please. It's your turn to cum." She moans, arching her back while grabbing fistfuls of the shaggy carpet. Her arousal hasn't waned one bit. "I want more. I want that hairless demon to ravage me. To rule me. Oh, just fuck me, Bridge. Take me as yours in our new home."

He situates himself on his knees before her and grabs his hard cock. He slowly approaches her pussy in a knee crawl. He then tickles his cockhead lightly against her wet pussy.

She revels in it, that picture-perfect state of euphoria. She wants more of it, so much more.

"Yes, please, now, please." She touches her lips as she again murmurs, "Please, Bridge. I want you inside me to the sound of those waves. Right now. Hurry. Please."

He pushes her bent legs, so her knees end up near her armpits, and then he penetrates her.

It feels incredible, and she cries out in pleasure as he fully enters her with a deep thrust. Rubbing his arms, she savors how he's utilizing his muscles as he props himself up to fuck her. They bulge and harden beneath her fingertips as he rides himself into her; she craves that. She can't resist feeling him up, loving how strong he is and how he can pound away into her until she comes. She rotates her head back and forth as he heartily thrusts into her. The fast slamming always brings her to the height of an orgasm fast, making her likely to cum again, especially if her clit gets hit right. Blissfully, he knows the spot. Being a woman and able to enjoy multiple orgasms rapidly is truly a gift of being female. She grins as he keeps working with fervor.

As if he's reading her mind—no, he just knows her—he reaches down and presses his thumb hard against her clit between the cleft of her lips. She cries out and digs her nails into his shoulders as her whole body reacts. She is so happy because his erection will last longer since they just fucked less than an hour ago.

Juniper moans, exclusively thinking of Bridge's dick riding her clit into a deluge of pleasure, his cock so deep in her with each thrust it's practically a part of her internal organs. She feels at one with him, and he always gives her a gift; his rule is that she comes first, and he wants to give it to her. Her body curls into her full climax as her body jerks and twitches. The wave of pleasure takes her soaring.

His control is slipping as she grabs at the base of his thighs and squeezes while moaning. He's going to come. He pumps her until his spunk seems all drained out of his balls, successfully breeding her. She prays it works this time.

He leans down and kisses her lips, which causes her to slowly open her eyes and smile.

"Damn, that was yummy. You spoil me." She grins, a big, satisfied one that hugs her heart.

"You deserve it and more every day, baby," he says as he lies next to her, his breathing still labored.

He takes her in his arms on the shaggy rug that isn't quite theirs yet, but might as well be, as his ejaculate seeps out of her pussy onto it. The very same rug that they will soon own and fuck on anytime they want.

She sighs as her easy smile grows bigger. Her voice comes out sultry, soft, sweet, bedroom-ready. "I will never get tired of the sound of those waves. And just think, we can basically have sex on the beach every day of our lives now."

He pulls her closer and snuggles her into his body, her softness swallowing to cradle his hard muscles. "That's the plan."

"We really should go so Max can lock up." She starts to get up. "We've had sex twice in his near proximity." She giggles. "That's naughty."

"Oh yeah, totally naughty. But let's just lie here together for four whole minutes, then go. I'm loving cuddling you."

She cozies back into his arm and rests her head on his chest. "Okay, I'm in. But why four minutes?"

"Because five seems too long and three is too short to hold you."

She makes a cooing sound and plays with his nipple, making it hard.

He clears his throat. "Don't mess with me too much, I might fuck you again and make Max wait longer."

"I wouldn't mind. I'd love it."

They both smile, staring up at the ceiling of the game room. She knows this will be a good lovemaking spot for years to come, as will every room of this house, until a baby comes along and makes that a challenge.

A challenge they'd both welcome, surely, as they can always find time to fuck, babies have to sleep, right? Ah, what does she know about babies, but she knows she wants to understand every challenge, every joy, and every blessing of having one.

Bridge kisses her forehead, and they both make moves to stand up, as the four minutes must be up by now.

# Chapter Three

"John Penn, best-selling gift to humans, author extraordinaire, hits number one again with his new thriller novel, *Winning the Game*. It's a complex, twisty novel that will have you on the edge of your seat, biting your fingernails, and gushing with the monumental wins. The MMC is a king, and his moves will not only jar you but also make you wish he had your back because no one loses with that guy. John has done it again with this one, and I see movie reels in the future.

No one can out-pen John Penn. He's the master, the ruler, and the creator of the modern-day dark suspense novel for adults. This is a don't-miss book; run to your nearest bookstore and buy the book. An eBook won't do, you need to hold John's words in your hands and experience the heat, the magic, the spellbound stirrings his words will gift you with. This man is a genius of untold talents and surprises." Art Hanswell, book critic, podcaster, and master interviewer, reviews John Penn's new book.

John Penn smiles as he sets down his tablet. Nice review, Art. Very nice indeed. He'd have to remember to send him a copy of each new book, pre-release, and also, maybe a bottle of scotch, and some steaks. He knows how to take care of his supporters, and he's achieving a reputation for such. It's paying off very well. He makes a note on the little notepad on his desk to ask Millie to set that up. Maybe Art also deserves a box of chocolates. He adds that to the note.

He turns his attention back to his laptop screen. He gazes at it with longing as he rakes his clean hand through his wavy dark hair with a sigh.

"Wow, Juniper. What I wouldn't give to fuck you on my rug." He shakes his head as his expression turns sour. He glances down at his deflated cock, which now rests in his wet hand. Images of Juniper in the throes of ecstasy flood his brain. "Beautiful. Just erotically gorgeous. Cunt and tit heaven. The kindest, sweetest, sexiest, most wonderful woman in the entire world. Juniper, you're an absolute fucking goddess." He sighs again as he watches Bridge and Juniper on his computer screen as they head up the spiral stairs of his house, fully dressed. "I'd give anything in the world to do all that you, Juniper. Literally anything." He sighs. "Instead, I have to give you my house."

He rewinds the video and watches the part again where she's grabbing her own tits, her torso twisting, her mouth wide open as she moans; she's writhing with pleasure, as if out of her mind.

"I knew it from the very first time I saw you at that coffee shop that those tits and cunt were going to be spectacular. And now I see I was so right. What a fucking treat to see you naked. Finally." He can still see her in his mind's eye at that first sighting in the coffee shop. Her blond hair was swept up into a ponytail. She had scrubs on, having just finished her shift at the hospital. He knew instantly that she was the one, the only woman he needed in his life. Every other one would pale in comparison. It was her, only her.

He grabs the water bottle from off his desk and takes a big swig, his cock hardening again as he watches her molesting her own nipples, moaning deliciously, thrashing her head back and forth in her passion. He pauses the video again and stares at her image. Her beautiful lips are pursed. They are supple, plump, and curved. Perfect. He can almost taste them. His excitement explodes. This must be the part where she whimper-moans when she's about to come. He grins with lewdness as he hits play.

"Oh. Fuck. I want you, Juniper. Fuck. Fuck. Fuck." He grabs his raging hard-on and strokes for a few pumps before he pushes pause to savor her, and then he pushes play again. "Mmmm...damn it, baby girl, I want to fuck you so bad. I need to."

He chugs his hand up and down the shaft of his meaty cock as her body scrunches in fervent ardor, then jerks with the culmination of her coming. Her moans drive him to come again, though only a little ejaculate comes out this time. As his cock relaxes, he glances at his phone. A text is coming in. He grabs some tissues from the tissue box next to his computer and cleans himself up. The text is from his agent.

Agent Steve: How're you?

John: Fine.

Steve: Book progress?

John: Always.

Steve: The publisher now has the book. Reading.

John: Nice.

Steve: Godspeed with this next book. Make a whammy slam dunk deal, bro.

John: Working on it, fucker.

Steve: Good fucker. Do it. Bye.

John: Go fuck yourself.

John snorts, smirks into the phone. "Fucker."

Steve: Already did. Wife ain't opening her legs, so I've got no choice but to.

John: Ha! Sorry.

Steve: Mmmm, no u aren't.

Steve: Fucker. You like it.

John: You're right. I'm not sorry. And you don't deserve pussy, if I had a cunt you wouldn't be in mine either, you slimy SOB.

Steve: Fuck you. I'm contemplating a mistress.

John: No, fuck yourself, go for it.

John laughs and tosses his phone onto his desk. Enough of that fucker. He takes one last look at Juniper's butt walking away on the screen as she heads to his kitchen. He should be there with her, not Bridge. He shakes his head, wishing she were still nude.

He saunters into his new kitchen. His old one is now for Juniper, so he can watch her in it. He pours himself a gin and tonic over ice and grabs a lime wedge from the fridge. He squeezes it into the drink, the tangy scent hitting his nostrils. He glances at his mail. His catalog for ocean fishing has arrived. He'd save that morsel of delight for perusing later.

He glances out of the large window facing the ocean. The sea is scattering the falling sun's rays into a million glimmers on the rolling waves. The surface looks like glitter. He meanders out to the deck so he can hear the sounds, too, of the awesome view. He inhales the salty scent as the rush of the waves crashing to the shore soothes him. The wind pulls at his hair and grazes his flesh. His shirt is still unbuttoned. He stands at the rail, his drink in his hand. He nods as a couple strolls along the shore in front of his new beach house. He gives them a wave back. Everyone is so wealthy here; he can see it in their clothes, their demeanors. They have no worries. And so far, everyone seems really friendly, but there's no attempt at small talk, just nods and waves are the acknowledgment. The social distancing is perfect. Fine by him. He doesn't need any useless chitchat from couples looking to spew about the nothingness of their lives. He's got enough of that on his own.

The waves rage and caress the sand, one crash and spill of water after another. A golden retriever dog bounds along the shore, his fur flapping as he bounds along, his owner jogging behind him. He needs a dog. Or a cat. Juniper would like a cat; she has one, but he needs to give her one. He sips the gin and tonic and saunters over to his Adirondack chair, slides back into it. He left his other chairs at the house for her, but since he loves the style, he bought more for himself for the new house, too. He pulls the remote from his pocket and starts his music up. Instantly, it blares from the speaker above his head. He leans back with a deep sigh, tapping his fingers to the music on the wide slat of wood that makes the generous armrests of the majestic chair. His balls are empty, to the tune of Juniper, which makes him happy. He closes his eyes and pictures her again. Her hair falling to her shoulders in gentle sheets of golden strands, framing her lovely face. He imagines her smile and giggle—both of which are exquisitely intoxicating. Even her fingers are beautiful. And don't get him started on those toes. He grins and licks his lips. Somehow, his cock begins to thicken again.

"If only," he says to the breeze, which takes his wish and carries it off across the shore to die a soundless death above the sea. Having her is the only wish of his heart that matters. Juniper. He even loves the sound of her name. Love could happen instantly. She had proven that. No slow-burning desire there; it was an instant eruption. Her body and features, that soft voice, wow!

Her guiles had seeped into his heart from the moment she ordered her latte. Standing behind her in line, he was taken at the first whiff of her floral shampoo, and his cock hardened into a rod almost immediately. He wanted to bend her over right there. Love at first sight doesn't exist, huh? Fuck you, cynics, they don't know what the fuck they're talking about. They don't know Juniper. It does exist, and he'd found it with her.

He smirks. Well, at the very least, it was extreme lust at first sight. Being a writer, he knows reality is a façade. His cock can attest to that. It's never lied to him. He chuckles. Now, just to get her to see all this and live in his beach house. All he needs is to have her fall in line to be fully his, then his life will be complete. A successful author's career needs a sexy trophy wife to go along with it. That's surely going to take some doing. But he isn't taking a 'no' for an answer. It will be a trick, but he knows he'll win because he also knows he can do it. He will have her one day, and she'll be his forever to hold, caress, suck, and fuck. Eat chocolate éclairs with on New Year's Eve, and drink mimosas with every sunny summer morning right here on this deck.

"Sorry, Bridge. Your time is about up."

He will make it happen if it's the last thing he does. He'll have her body, and all her amazing orgasms will be his to enjoy. She'll be his to use, come all over, his sexual muse to guide into orgasm after orgasm. She'll be his star, sun, moon, and air, and he'll be hers. He'll give her the world, and she'll take it, gladly, like the sweetheart she is. They will be the magic couple everyone envies.

He downs his drink and throws each ice cube out to the hot sand one at a time, where he watches them die into a wet spot. The backdrop of the strong beat belting out of his stereo pumps up his energy.

He's on the road to greater success. It's just a matter of time, and she'll be right next to him on this deck, dressed in a very skimpy, barely-there bikini, a smile on her face, and a twinkle in her eyes. A twinkle meant just for him.

He sighs. Time for another drink and another view of Juniper getting fucked by Bridge. He despises Bridge, but he sure loves watching her take his cock. He'd love seeing her take any cock, even a plastic one. Bridge fucks her like a raging bull and she comes every time. He knows he'll watch that scene again and again until they move in, which he is hoping will happen very soon. Then he'll get new homemade porn videos daily to jerk off to. His own little private porn star. They are certainly exciting to watch. His heart flutters. He can't wait to find out all their kinks. And his imagining fucking her himself is the best part of it all, getting all his kinks satiated, and hers. Someday that will be him shoving his fat cock up her quaking cunt, and that will be a very damn good day indeed.

# Chapter Four

Bridge appears in the doorway of the bedroom as Juniper opens her eyes. He has a jar of coconut oil in his hand. He toggles it back and forth as she stirs in their new bed. Bridge sighs. Finally, his love is awake. She looks scrumptious. His manhood roars.

"Morning, my sunshine," he says as he shakes the jar again to tease her.

She lets out a grunt, sounding groggily still half asleep as she stretches her arms straight up into the air, then lays them on the pillow above her head. She arches and twists further so she can stretch out her lower back.

"Watching you wake and stretch like that is driving me wild," he says.

The sheet falls away from her body. Her pale pink, rosy flesh begs for his fingers.

She stretches again, moving her shapely legs, her movement ending with her rotating her ankles and pointing her painted toenails. She kicks the sheet fully off herself.

Bridge holds his position steady, though every cell in his body is urging him to rush her. Only his carefully laid plans prevent him from jumping over to ride her.

"Well, if I didn't already have one before, that display of erotic stretching would have given me one." He chuckles as he takes a step into the room. He holds the jar up again like a torch. She's a vision, a tasteful image of feminine energy that ever blesses his life. He's a very lucky man, and he knows it because his wife's body is a pure decadent work of art. He shakes the jar again and grunts.

"Aww, hon, you know I can't see a thing. Quit teasing me. What're you holding?" she asks groggily.

She fumbles around on her nightstand for her glasses, on a bedside table that used to belong to a famous writer, no less. One that now holds her books, thongs, shea butter massage oil, lingerie, and an assortment of toys. He's really due to buy her a new one.

"Babe, you don't need to see what I'm going to do to you." He hides what he has in his hands behind his back; she doesn't really need to know. "In fact, you aren't going to be seeing at all, so no glasses needed." He pulls something long out of his pocket as she cranes her neck, trying to see it.

She squints. "What is it? And what are you up to?" she asks as she begins to rise. She glances down at herself. "Hey, and why am I naked? I didn't go to bed naked." She laughs. "Did I have a swiper in the middle of the night who came and stole my clothes?"

He clears his throat as he walks closer to the bed. He gives her a teasing look. "Like a horny ghost?"

"Yeah, I hope he was a sexy one because I don't remember anything about any ghost hook-up." She giggles as she yawns and stretches again, then she settles back down flat on the mattress. "I still feel tired." She stares at her tummy. "Okay. And what is this?" she asks as she fingers the shiny circular sticker next to her belly button. She runs her finger over the sticker again and again. "A sticker?"

"Leave it there. I put it there." He chuckles again. "It has a purpose."

She laughs. "Okay. Do tell. Crap, I know I'm a heavy sleeper, but how did you undress me and put a sticker on my belly without me even waking up?" She gives him a skeptical look. "You didn't roofie me, did you?" she asks with a tease in her voice.

"No, I watched you until it looked like you were in your deepest sleep, and then I undressed you. I love watching you sleep, you know that." He laughs, his face full of humility. "You aren't that light of a sleeper, babe," he teases, to which she gives an eye roll. "Plus, you had quite a bit of wine last night, which makes you sleep even more deeply." He grins at her. "Thanks for cooperating with my plan."

Juniper scoffs with a grin, then shudders as she tries to process him doing all this to her without her waking up. "I guess I'm not that light of a sleeper. Clearly." A bursting laugh escapes her lips. "Good thing I trust you, geez."

"You have nothing to worry about," he says sweetly.

She pouts. "Yeah, and it's totally not fair that you only need like five hours of sleep and I need like ten." She runs her finger over the smooth metallic sticker on her belly. "What's this for, anyway? You brand me like a cow?"

He chuckles heartily. "Don't give me a new kink. No. It's a heat-sensing sticker. When you can see it, you'll see it's a picture of a lotus, the sign of fertility. Before I put it on you, it was just silver, and I watched it as it warmed against your skin, and the flower appeared. I did this after I undressed you." He snorts. "Rubbing that in. But you know you didn't have much on to begin with, so it wasn't hard to undress you." He points to her skimpy PJs on the floor.

"True. That's very true." She remembers dressing for bed in the skimpy tank top and even skimpier shorts. She pulls the sheet back up over her chest and hugs it. "You still haven't told me what you have behind your back, and what's the long thing?" With her glasses on, she thoroughly scans him with extreme interest in her gaze. "I'm super curious. And are you gonna fuck me already or what?"

"Oh, I'm gonna fuck you, alright. What I have...it's only for women with sexy hot bods who look a certain way that beg for fucking. Like you." He rounds the bed toward her side, giving her his best predatory, hungry glare. "And they must be prepped before said fucking." He points at her. "Like you."

She scoffs, touches her lips, and says, "Oh really, now, and bare nakedness with a shimmery sticker on one's belly isn't a good enough state to be fucked in?" She raises an eyebrow as she laughs. Her laugh is light and fluttery, singing like a flute playing in the distance.

"Well, that's good too, but this particular treatment is quite sensual and strict, and requires precision with extreme attention to detail. And thorough skin inspection."

He slowly creeps along and stops once he's parallel with her face. He remains still as he stares into her eyes.

"Close your eyes, babe. I'm going to need to concentrate hard so I can't have you watching me." His tone is commanding, and that's on purpose. He wants her to just comply without question. She usually does when he's using this tone.

"Okay, Sir. Your wish is my command." She giggles and closes her eyes. "I'm game."

Bridge removes Juniper's glasses and presses the piece of her clothing he snatched from the hamper to her eyes, a black lacy bodysuit she wore during last night's fuck. He secures it as a blindfold around her head. "Get a whiff of yourself?"

She cackles. "And you! Wow, what is this?" She reaches up to touch it, but he playfully slaps her hand away.

"Oh, saucy." She smiles as she rests her arm on the bed. "And I must say, I love all this baby-making sex."

"Oh, I'm just getting started. And no touching it. I don't want it to shift," he demands, trying to remain serious. "Obey me."

Her full, beautiful lips flatten, stretching out as she grins deeper. She licks her lips and says, "If I didn't know better, I'd say it smells like sex. Like your come, like my pussy juices and my come."

"Not for you to worry about. Just breathe, baby. Breathe in the scents." He pats her taut belly over the sticker. "Relax and get ready to orgasm so much you become such a floppy mess that you might fall back asleep."

She sighs and writhes her body against the soft bottom sheet. "You have me very intrigued, Mr. Bridge," she coos. "Sir." She writhes and moans, his actions seeming to be arousing her.

"Good. Now lie back and be quiet while I do it all to you." His voice is very stern and serious, yet if she could see him, she'd see his eyes are alight with playfulness. He's having fun as he drags his fingers along the flesh of her torso. He smiles as he watches her react to his touch.

She laughs and wiggles, causing her blond hair to shift and glide about in the sunlight. It looks like gold. "Do what? So serious, Mr. Bridge, Sir."

"Shhhh…" Bridge removes the pillow from under her head while savoring her curvy hips, her bared, peaked nipples, and her bald pussy that looks wet at the edges already. "Ummmm. Yummmm. You look luscious. Hot as fuck, babe. Beyond fuckable," he hums. "We're going to make a baby, so this is serious business."

"Oh, really? But I don't even get to brush my teeth first?" she asks with apprehension laced throughout her words.

He pulls open her drawer and rummages for something. "No more talking, Juniper. Just feel my touch."

She jumps as he opens the mint tin. He holds the container under her nose, then pries her lips open with his fingers. He places two round mint disks on her tongue.

"Ooooh." She grins as she sucks on the mints. She smiles her thank you to Bridge. "Much better. Thank you."

He crawls around the bed like a dog looking for a good place to lie down. He's not satisfied with his position, so he keeps moving, making so many movements that her body shifts about. He's a big man.

"Might as well be jumping on the bed," she jokes.

Bridge fidgets on the bed some more as he spreads out a large, white, fluffy terry cloth towel fully flat. "Patience, baby."

Juniper flinches when he removes the metal lid of the glass jar of coconut oil. "What the heck do you have?"

The spinning sound of the metal lid on the glass grooves is the only sound in the room.

She stays mostly mute but stifles a giggle.

"This is pure torture to your morning lust, I know, but it's making your pussy wet in anticipation. I can smell you."

A shiver runs through her body. She writhes in smooth little undulations as her nipples constrict further.

"You can't sit still, and I love it." He blows a hot breath over her tits, which causes her to flinch and her peaks to thicken further.

She shudders as he blows breaths all over her chest, abdomen, and belly, ending with several breaths of hot air over her pussy. He hovers as if he's going to lick her pussy, breathing just centimeters from her labia lips.

She squirms and moans as he seduces her; his breath on her bare skin is the promise of pleasure he will provide.

"Fuck, I want you. I'm going to suck and lick you until you beg for my cock."

He grins but backs away from her pussy. He laughs when she sticks out her lower lip in a pout. Crawling up the bed, he stares at her lips and leans in, his hot breath bathes her mouth beneath his. He slowly descends closer and closer until there's no room left between them, and the next movement will have to be their lips touching. He attacks that sticking-out pouty lower lip of hers by sucking it into his mouth. Her eyes are inviting as he sucks her, then he opens his mouth to her open mouth, their moist, hot breaths colliding. The strong mint flavor floods his taste buds as his tongue meanders its way into her mouth, devouring her kiss. He caresses her tongue with his, forward and back, then sucks.

He leans away from her mouth as she hungrily and blindly tries to locate his with hers, gaping up, open like a hungry little one. He grins at her; she looks like a baby bird in a nest, swaying back and forth, blindly trying to find his mother again. He gives her his mouth, and her response kiss is hungrier than the last. He peels his mouth from hers as he reaches for the jar of coconut oil. It's time to start the next stage of his seduction.

He tugs on her body. "Slide over, baby. Lie on this towel."

She wiggles herself over, feeling up the towel with her hands to make sure she's landing on it properly. "Hmmm. Something messy is about to happen."

"No talking. Don't make me spank you for not obeying."

She looks as if she thinks he's kidding, but he's not. He scoops out a hunk of coconut oil and lays the jar on her upper abdomen, just beneath her large breasts. She flinches against the weight of it. Bridge grins. He loves making her feel things and watching her reactions. Her expressions are always even more priceless when blindfolded. He's a kid in a candy store.

"Mmmmm," she moans. "I smell coconut."

He savors the look of pleasure on her face. "You must really want that spanking, huh?"

She snickers but stays quiet.

He watches as the lump of coconut oil begins to melt against the warm skin of her stomach. As the white wad becomes liquid, he takes two fingers and begins to spread it across her skin in ever-widening circles, avoiding the sticker. He scoops out another dollop once he's fully spread that first batch across her belly and plants a small lump of oil on each breast. He delivers a kiss on each of her nipples as the coconut oil melts and streams down like clear rivers.

She responds with a small arch, pushing her nipple to his mouth, and grins.

He sucks each nipple, sucking hard, pulling her tit to the back of his throat, elongating it to the max each time, which takes a good amount of suction. He watches as the warmed oil continues to melt on her skin as it slides past his lips, dribbling down his chin and neck as he sucks her, some melted oil leaking to his lips. She moans and shoves her hands into his hair as she works her titties over in his warm, hot mouth. He nibbles at her areolas, making her groan louder.

He loves the tease of seduction, ramping up her arousal and desire. It's the dance he loves almost as much as the satiating climax. He wants to take her on that journey and be the driver of it.

He lets her nipple slip out of his mouth before he leans back and spreads the oil across her breasts with his fingers, thoroughly coating her nipples in firm strokes. He lets her hard nipples pop out as his hands pass over them. His cock is growing harder as he finishes off by spreading the luscious oil across the round bottoms. The curve of her breasts is unmatched, giving her the most amazing side and underboob. A place he loves to cup and lick. He can't get enough of her. He sincerely hopes she gets pregnant this time, if nothing else, but for her. Of course, he wants kids, but she wants them more urgently, and he hopes to give her exactly what she wants, always.

He next coats her curvy, toned legs, then her arms, and strokes along her long, elegant neck. He spreads the oil across the tops of her hands and fingers, skating carefully around her wedding ring, then he lavishes more oil on her palms before visiting her rounded hips to spread oil across them. Seeing her wedding ring brings him back to memories of their wedding day, and how lucky he felt securing his future with her. Images of her in her wedding dress, then later in the hotel room fill his brain.

"I'm a lucky man, babe."

She coos a soft agreement.

He keeps caressing her hips; he can't wait to dig his fingers into her as he pounds her from behind, maybe make a handprint from a hard spank. He likes to exert his dominance here and there, nothing severe, but she likes the confirmation as well, so he indulges. He has no desire for extreme stuff, though. He massages every inch of her front, each stroke eliciting a squirm, moan, or writhe, then he flips her over on the towel, with a naughty, eager grin.

"Now we're getting there."

She wiggles against the soft terry cloth and moans gently. He starts on her backside by plopping a coconut oil scoop between her shoulder blades. She moans her intense pleasure as he works it into the skin of her back. She's getting so shiny all over, and he hopes he can still get a grip on her flesh. He deeply massages her muscles, straddling her hips as his balls rest on her ass cheeks. As he moves, working on her back, he lightly drags his cock along her skin, leaving slashes of precum on her lower back and ass like a drip trail.

The slow dance of his hard cock being dragged along her skin is driving her wild as she purrs and coos, grunting her want for more, playing along with his game by not speaking. He needs her desire, and he loves it when she begs for his dick inside her.

Once he has fully coated her full back and arms in coconut oil, he crawls to straddle her shoulders, facing her backside, then bends over, bringing his head down to her bottom so he can lick at her pussy from over the hump of her ass. He grinds his hard-on into her back as she sighs and shimmies her shoulders beneath him. He slips a hand under her pussy as he licks, slightly pressing at her clit. She responds by raising up her ass, pressing it up into his neck, the curve of his chin slightly parting her ass cheeks as he dive-bombs his tongue to eat her out. He loves this angle and slurps greedily at her.

He leans up, propping himself on his arms, and shoves a rolled towel under her pussy to get her ass slightly raised to his mouth. He releases a big breath, but the angle's still not quite right. He repositions himself on his elbows above her crotch and breathes his hot breath over her labia lips. He can feel her chest heaving beneath him as she begins to pant with want. She moans as he licks her slit. She writhes beneath him as he slicks from her anus to her clit in several successions, like he's licking a large, flat lollipop. He purses his lips hard and drags them along her slit, which causes her to cry out a big groan.

He assesses her reactions and adjusts his plan accordingly. He's a smart man. He learned long ago that his pleasure was second to hers because her pleasure is his kink. He's assured to come almost every time, that's a no-brainer. He needs to get her there, and her getting there will lead to him getting there fast. It's a self-perpetuating positive loop. It's worked like a charm, and has made both her and him very happy with their sex life. Now they just need a baby!

He sticks out his tongue for a lick. He so enjoys the muskiness of her scent, the strong taste of her, slightly tangy like a lemon, full and powerful like musk. He dangles his tongue over her clit, touching it down and then pulling it back, causing her body to squirm, jerk, and dance beneath him. He grins wickedly, loving the tease. His focused attention makes her wiggle her ass around as she writhes, soaking up all the friction of his aggressive licks and sucking. He rides his mouth over her, pleasuring her relentlessly. She will come first before he moves on.

Fuck. He loves this.

"Damn, I could do this all day."

He climbs off her. He smirks at the sight of her hands gripping handfuls of the towel. She's getting desperate for him. Perfect. He grins, then scoops out more oil. He loads her ass cheeks with it. He settles between her thighs and takes a few minutes to rub his cock along the orbs of her ass cheeks, smearing the melting oil in her crevice and along her asshole with his hard-on. He loves to watch his cock ride against her deep ass crack, spreading her ass cheeks as his cock drives up, making her cheeks jiggle. He never presses his cock in; she's not into that, but he loves his manhood nestled there.

He slathers a dollop across her pussy, making her moan and thrust against his hand, lurching her body as he plays with her beautiful, plush, feminine folds. Another hunk of coconut oil he smears along her inner left thigh, the thick, solid oil melting rapidly as he rubs it in.

"Nice and easy, there, babe," he assures in a soft voice, praising her.

Then he massages the creamy white oil fully into her other firm thigh, making it shine in the morning sunlight just like the rest of her oiled body. Her muscles are becoming putty in his hands; she's so lubed up and floppy, yet tense with desire, ready to spring into action. He enjoys watching her libido raging as she writhes and moans in response to his touch.

It's almost time.

He roams his touch all over her, rubbing, caressing, fondling. He slithers his body against hers. He rises up slightly, the full length of him nearly touching her as he partially hovers over to tantalize with his cock in as many spots as possible. He glances down, and the oil is making his own skin shine. He slithers his hand along her pussy as he rides her skin with his own.

"Mmmm…yes. Oh, yes, you feel amazing," she murmurs, her head tips to the side so he can see the profile of her lush lips.

Oiled skin on oiled skin. The feeling is luxurious.

Next, he drags his hard cock along her right thigh, her moans and whimpering peaking. All he wants to do is drive his cock into her wet, hot pussy, but he will wait. He knows her whimpering moan sound well. She often does it when she's about to come, too. He rubs coconut oil into her thigh and mixes his precum drops with it, spreading it down her leg as far as the slick oil will go.

"Need you," she whispers.

"No cock yet, baby girl. Want you to come for me first." He's the leader, and he loves stating the mantra, and he adores her submission to it.

She complains in a grumpy groan, likely feeling unfairly edged, her clit swollen and thick, ready to burst into convulsions. The aroma of her own essences wafting off her blindfold is likely driving her crazy.

He can't wait to watch her lose full control at his hands.

He massages the oil into her shins, heels, and the bottoms of her feet, keeping his touch sensual and constant.

She groans her pleasure at the massage of her soles and grins into the softness of the towel, the lower edge of her smile grazing the soft loops of the terry cloth.

He's horny as fuck, a downright beast of a bear, a ram with the gumption to take what he wants, but when he fucks, he can also be sweet as pie, too. A perfect combo for a lover in her mind is what she always tells him. This is fantastic, and that's why they are such a perfect match.

She bites her lip, telling him she's wondering what his next move will be. Her lust is raging as she can't sit still or be quiet. She thrashes against his touch, mounting a climax closer and closer from the simple intentional rub of his hands. He knows these signs well. It's yin and yang, pure lust wrapping their auras together, love smoothing it all out, neither existing without the other.

He pauses his touching of her as he kneels on the bed and savors the gorgeous, oiled body of his wife lying so helplessly delicious and open for him. She's fiercely gripping the sheets, waiting in the agony of no action. From previous debriefings about sex, he knows she's also likely loving, relishing, and almost hating his slow seduction, but in an impatient yearning kind of way. He adores that. He can also tell she's lustfully anticipating all of what's yet to come.

He enjoys the slow tease further as he then drags his index finger in a snaking, continuous S shape all down her back, riding up over the humps of her buttocks. He looks up with delight to see her not only still clenching the sheets with her hands, but now also biting the towel, as well.

Stellar.

He chuckles in a low appreciative rumble.

He desires her backward in a flat doggy position, so he repositions her for optimal penetration from behind. She gasps when he presses himself against her inner thighs. He dances his cock along her ass cheeks and her fleshy vulva, triggering gushes of anticipatory moans. She vigorously grips the pillow lying above her head with both fists and squeezes hard. She seems desperate for him inside her. Her body tenses, seeming cocked, ready to respond with a rapid orgasm.

She's in the ideal state.

He pushes his cock head into her.

She groans in delight.

He pulls his cock away from her pussy and lets it fall on her ass as he leans down over her and whispers into her left ear, "You want it in you now? You want me, baby?"

She nods heartily under his hot breath. She shivers.

He can sense her pleading silently, her desire for more raging in her brain. His cock twitches in anticipation of fucking her wet and ready pussy, sliding effortlessly through her oiled lush labia lips.

He hasn't let her cum yet; she's waiting like a good girl, though she's been close. He's thoroughly enjoyed edging her along the heights of her orgasms, role-playing the Pleasure Dom, and teasing her desire along the way just as he's enticing his own lust for her. He enjoys prolonging the foreplay for as long as he can stand it, while pushing both of their boundaries of patience to the max.

He rubs her clit as her body rolls in pleasure. He keeps going until she seems right at the edge, then he presses even more firmly as he rubs. She shrieks at her peak and her body convulses, her sounds following in the rise and fall of the course of her big O.

"Good girl, very good girl."

He's ready.

He places his dick at her pussy and slowly enters. He glides in so easily as she moans her approval of his entrance into her body. She lifts her ass up slightly, presenting her hole for a good angle for the fuck. He stops and repositions the towel to the best spot, and he rides himself back into her, moving in and out slowly, then increasing his pumping speed. She moans loudly, and he can tell she's very near her apex again.

"Wait for it, baby, so it can be huge for you," he whispers. "Hang on."

Her response is to whimper-moan. Her movements and sounds indicate she's losing her grip on control and is about to plunge into that unstoppable explosion of her climax.

He wants to give it to her.

He pounds hard until he feels her vaginal walls clamp down on him, her body convulses against the bed. He knows her toes are likely curling, even though he can't see them. Once her body relaxes again, he pulls his hard-on out of her and flips her over. She's a floppy rag doll and allows him to reposition her body on the towel. He pushes her knees close to her armpits.

He kisses her on the lips, then enters her again, fucks her in missionary because he knows he can get her to come hard this way. Fast pussy slaps also get her going, but not now; he's riding her hard enough and fast enough to fuck her into coming again. Her moans increase in loudness and rapidity as he slams her down into the bed. He thrusts aggressively, causing her round tits to bounce and gyrate hard with each pump, her hair dancing against the towel beneath her. Her mouth is gaping open as she makes her pleasure sounds. She groans and grabs the bed sheets again, tightening her grip. Then her hands migrate to feel up the muscles flexing in his arms as he rides her. She squeezes up and down the length of his arms. The benefit of missionary is he can see her face and she can touch him.

She moans out a "Yes." Her voice coming out as a soft coo, softly like a small cat. "Please, fuck me. Please, fuck me, yes, more," she murmurs. "Yes. Yes. Yes," she chants.

She's close. And within seconds, she launches into another climax.

He watches her body clench up and then jerk repeatedly as her pussy convulses, scrumptiously squeezing his cock. He lets out a low, long groan as he, too, almost loses it and comes, but he clamps down on the urge and charges on. Watching her come is so very hot, though, so he has to pull out of her to prevent himself from coming. He wants more of her before he's done.

He flips her over, easing her shiny, oily, spent body back into position, squarely on the towel. He doesn't want them to have to wash the comforter. Next time, he will need more than one towel laid out for this. He pushes her thighs flush together and then coats her in oil all over so he can easily glide his balls along her skin. Then he presses his oiled fingers between her thighs so he can coat her for an easy slide through. Her flesh will be so slick and slippery for his cock to ride her thigh tunnel right into her pussy. He has a clear double-intentioned method to his message, by design.

He reaches beneath her and tickles her pussy lips. Then, he straddles her and slips his cock into the tight cave of her flushed thighs, making an entrance to her vagina. He thrusts into her pussy with all of his strength, riding her slicked thighs, using her body to get off, rubbing his balls, and deliciously driving himself to near coming.

It won't be long.

He releases a guttural gasp at the deluge of pleasure, then loses grip on preventing his ejaculation. His cum floods her pussy, painting her white inside in hot spurts with his seed. Even though his load is spent inside her, he keeps thrusting into her to give her a bit more pleasure until her moans die down again. He wants her fully satisfied before he's done, plus, maybe the sperm will get pushed further inside her and increase the chances of baby-making. He knows nothing about all that, but it makes sense.

"Ladies first," he whispers huskily.

"You spoil me," she coos.

"You deserve every second."

He stops thrusting and falls limp on her back. He's rough and tough, but that was overwhelming. He's not too macho to mask his stupor of euphoria. Hell, no. He cherishes that shit. He lies frozen, not moving a muscle, their panting almost in unison, but not quite, as his breathing is more ragged. He turns his face toward her back and gives her a closed-mouth peck on her left shoulder blade.

"It's pure bliss being inside you," he whispers.

"Wow," she says with a sigh. "Yeah. Agree. That was utterly amazing. And now my skin feels awesome, like I bathed in a tub of oil. Mmmm. It was so hot and sexy, just lovely. I loved your idea."

"Yeah, it was really sensual. Hope you think so, too. You're amazing, babe." He kisses her shoulder blade again and reaches up to untie the lingerie from her head, then flings the makeshift blindfold to the bed. "And you're welcome. Next time do me. I need moisturizer, too." He chuckles.

"Gladly," she whispers. "It was very sensual. Incredibly so." She grabs for the lingerie and pulls it close to her eyes. "I knew I smelled cum. I wore this last night when we fucked." She twirls it in the air, trying to whip him with it, but, being face down, she's totally unsuccessful. "Your body is like a sauna."

"Worked up a sweat fucking you." He grins, his face still pressed against her back.

"Yes, I dug it out of the hamper to heighten your arousal. It worked, didn't it?"

She scoffs. "Yeah, it really did. You're sort of a sexual genius sometimes, you know that, right?" She starts to shift her body.

"Oh, you love me all the more for my perverted-ness, don't you?" He laughs. "Porn is good for something; it gives me ideas."

"True. And hell, yes, I do love it. Now get off me, you brute. I really need to pee." She starts to roll to the edge of the bed. "You're like a dang heater. I'm gonna fall back asleep if I stay under you like that."

He laughs and lies flat on the mattress. "That wouldn't be so bad." He pauses. "Wait, aren't you supposed to be flat after sex for a bit so my sperm can swim upstream?" He's joking, but not. He thinks he read that somewhere.

"Yes, shit, but I'm gonna pee myself if I do that. I can't this time. We'll just have to have sex again later for that."

He chuckles. "Got it. I can do that for sure."

She scrambles quickly off the bed. "Gotta pee, gotta pee, gotta pee now!" she chants as she runs in an awkward half-folded funky hustle, making her way across the room quickly.

Bridge cracks up. "Careful, granny," he jokes. "Need some assistance?"

She gasps loudly in desperation and almost runs for the toilet. "Oh, no!"

He lumbers off the bed slowly and walks to the bathroom.

As he enters, he watches as she slips on the tile but quickly recovers so she doesn't fall. She scuttles to the toilet in a series of clumsy-looking movements. Her face erupts into an expression of panic as she lands on the toilet in a rapid sit-down, which mostly seems like a crash because she slips right off the seat. Her arm smacks the wall as she steadies herself against it.

"Fuck, I'm so slippery!" She scoots herself over the toilet properly while pressing her hands to the walls, then freezes in an awkward pose as her pee streams out, striking the water below with a strong force. She's laughing hysterically. "I can't stop it!"

He's laughing hysterically, too, doubling over. When he calms a little, he manages to ask, "Holy shit. Are you okay?"

"It's going on forever!" She gasps for air before saying, "Finally. That was a lot of pee." She shakes her head. "Geez. That was crazy! Did you see me slide right off?" She laughs again, pointing to the oily smudge mark her arm made on the wall.

Bridge cracks up, laughing along with her. "Yes, it was totally hilarious!"

"Yeah, it really was something. Oh my gosh." She can't stop laughing. "I didn't expect all that! And..." She grimaces. "Let's just say I think I may need to clean the floor, too."

"Ha! Guess I slicked you up too much, huh?"

"No, I loved it. It felt amazing. I will have to move more carefully next time. I seriously almost fell in my scramble to not flat-out piss on the floor. It was like I imagine walking on ice must be like." She scoffs, twisting her head back and forth, making her shiny hair dance. She stands and then moves to wash her hands, now walking slowly and deliberately, taking her time. "I'd be sad if you never did all that to me again."

Bridge admires her curves, which just don't end. "Your wish is always my command," he says as he hugs his wife from behind, snuggling his semi-hard cock against her ass, riding his hands up her belly to cup her generous breasts.

They gaze into each other's eyes in the mirror, his head nestled to the left of hers. "You're my treasure."

"I love you, Bridge. And I love how you fuck me, how you surprise me with fun stuff in sex like that. You thrill me and cause me to shiver in the excitement when I don't know what to expect. Every fuck is awesome. Seriously." She nuzzles the back of her head against his shoulder. "And I love this house. So very much."

"Me too, baby, me too. I love you, and I love fucking you here; it's wonderful. I'm so glad we bought the house." He sighs. "But sex with you anywhere is out of this world, baby."

"Mmmmm," she murmurs, nuzzling her cheek into his chest. "Me too, what a great decision we made to buy it. And we still have a few more rooms to christen."

"Yeah, can't wait." He kisses her hair and caresses it with his face. "Let's go make eggs. I'm starving after that."

She nods as he releases her from the back hug. She slips on her robe, her slippers, and then heads out of the bathroom.

Bridge watches his wife, happiness consuming him. Their indulgent sexual morning became even more complete with the promise of good food.

# Chapter Five

John enters a "u" in the field. The game gives him a "success" message, and he throws his hands in the air with a cheer, a smile migrating across his lips. He loves the little word games. He basically loves words, period. They are his heart and soul. He gazes out at the ocean, his heart nudging him to check the video feed to see if she is awake yet. Surely, they'll be intimate, as they are every morning, and he doesn't want to miss it. It is a strange dichotomy he grapples with. On the one hand, he wants her with every fiber of his being, and despite hating Bridge, he likes that Bridge gives her so much pleasure. Her pleasure is his pleasure, and it feeds his soul to watch her enjoy her body. So, how can he hate Bridge fully? Yet, Bridge has what's his. But John also knows this is temporary, and he can do anything for a short time, knowing what's coming for him to enjoy with her in the future.

His mama had taught him that good things come to those who wait. He misses her terribly. She would have liked Juniper very much. He laments that the two will never meet this side of death. It's a hard fact that only a fantasy novel about the afterlife could change. No matter, he knows exactly how his mother would react to Juniper, and she would one hundred percent approve of John's choice.

He rises from the deck chair and moves toward the sliding door. It's high time to check on his woman. And besides, he needs to get set up to watch. The natural lighting of the sun doesn't work well with watching a video stream. He needs to be inside the house to see everything. He doesn't want to miss out on any details. Juniper's sexuality has been blooming since they moved in. Well, it seems that way to him, anyhow. He can't know for sure because he never watched them before they moved in.

He settles on his living room couch with a snack and coffee, and opens his phone, noting the tissue box is still on the side table. Juniper is waking, and Bridge is in the doorway of the bedroom holding a jar of something. She looks so beautiful sprawled out on the bed, nude, and slowly waking, the most beautiful sight he's seen in his entire life. She has an innocent pureness about her, even with her raging libido that he finds intoxicating. She's this irresistible mix of cuteness, elegance, grace, and horniness, all while being a sweetheart at the same time.

He turns up the volume so he can hear them more clearly.

He makes a sour face as Bridge begins to coat her with the contents of the jar, which apparently is coconut oil. He grunts. Those should be his hands coating it on her. He watches the whole seduction scene, and he's impressed with Bridge. The dude has a fantastic seduction game. No wonder Juniper responds to him. But John could do it even better. Jealousy fills him further as he watches them, but so does satiation. He fucking loves this woman. She's a sex goddess and deserves every orgasm Bridge guides her through. He'd never deny her any of the pleasure.

Twenty minutes later, at the end, John leans his head back. "Whew!" he exclaims.

He grins as he uses a tissue to clean the cum off his spent cock.

"Made me messy as fuck, Juniper. Fuck me, that was hot as fuck. Holy shit. Better than any porn video on the planet." He shakes his head as he rewinds the video to his favorite part when Bridge eats her out from on top of her ass, lying backward. "Juniper, I'm going to do that to you and make you cum harder than Bridge ever could."

He nods with a raised eyebrow, takes a sip of his black coffee, a bite of his croissant, and watches Bridge eat out Juniper all over again. Then he flips to the live view and gazes at her like she's a gazelle in a lion's eye as she walks to the bathroom, looking like she belongs on the cover of a nudie magazine.

"My tongue must be oodles more talented than Bridge's; this I know. I could easily eat you for an hour, make you cum probably ten times, baby. Bridge could only handle it for a short time. Geez. Bridge." He snorts. "She only came twice, you loser. Don't you worry, Junie, I'll pleasure you longer, sweetheart."

He chuckles as he flips to the live-streaming view of the bathroom. He watches her almost slip, and then flat-out belly laughs when she slips right off the toilet. "Beautiful, sweetie, you're beautiful even when your ass is sliding off a toilet like a clown."

He laughs at her expressions as he replays her folly three more times, laughing so hard his stomach hurts. It's like naked bloopers. That should be a show. Or porn bloopers. He'd fucking watch that shit.

Watching her tits bounce as she catches herself on the wall gives him a hard-on again, so he rubs one out while staring at Juniper's tits bouncing. Kind of crass on the shitter, but she's so fucking sexy, she's even hot on a toilet. Once he's cum again, he blows up the image of her tits and saves it to be his screensaver.

"Junie, I'm going to blow up your tits and put them over my fireplace." He chuckles as he stands and tucks his deflated, wet dick back in his pants. Much less mess this time for round two. He shakes his head as he fingers her nipples on the screen.

"Someday I'm going to pinch these for real. Yank them and make you moan and cum on my hand as I finger fuck you." He caresses the image of her nipple. "Mark my word, Junie, you will be mine."

He chugs the rest of his coffee as his phone vibrates. He glances at it; it's his agent. "Hey, Matt."

"Hey, John. How is your day going?" Matt sounds rushed, but still keeps up the small talk for the moment, like a good little agent.

"Good. You?" John walks into the bright light of his kitchen, not nearly as beautiful as his old kitchen, he laments, but it works for now.

"Good. Hey, I reviewed that contract, and we're all good to sign. It's a definite go." He pauses. "You going to be able to deliver the novel on time? That's quite a quick turnaround time."

He scoffs. "Oh, ye of little faith! Don't you remember how I pounded out my second book in two weeks? Come on, bro."

"Yeah, yeah. I know you can handle it, no problem. It's just, this one, it's longer."

"I'll be good. I'm sufficiently motivated by the money they're gonna grease my palms with. I can practically take a bath in that sum."

"Yes, it's quite hefty. You're now one of the legends, my friend."

John smirks. He's not wrong. "Don't hear you complaining yourself."

"Just a sec, John. Be right back."

He shuffles through his mail and pulls out an advertisement for a pool. Junie will need a pool. He cocks his head with a grin. He needs to get started on that. She would love it, and boy, would he love her in a bikini all the time. He might not ever let her get dressed. She could be naked or in a bikini as they fuck on and off all day long, every day. What fun we will have, Juniper! She'll never need to work because he has more than enough money. She can do whatever the fuck she wants and, of course, take care of their kids, because she wants kids and he will give them to her any way, shape, or form that works.

Matt sucks in a breath. "That I'm not complaining about one bit, my friend. You are a gold mine with that amazing writer brain of yours." He scoffs. "You're my best talent, Johnny boy. I really need no other clients than you."

John grins. "My muse is egging me on. I want the money for her." He picks up a stack of photos and flips through them. He grins at one of Juniper playing with her tits in the shower, her head back, her luscious lips parted in a moan. Not even Bridge saw her masturbate that time; only John got that sole pleasure. The next photo is of her bare ass, bent over as she dries her toes. He spanks her ass on the picture with his finger, smirking to himself, then glancing at the flogger on his bookshelf. His grin grows as he ticks his head to the right sharply, that's only for playful fun, though.

"Well, whoever she is, let her egg you on hard so you can get this done in three weeks' time."

"I'll deliver, Matt. You know I will." John stacks up the pictures of Juniper and turns to examine his fridge. Nothing good to eat. He will need to order something.

"Okay. I'm going to eat now, so bye."

"Wait," Matt says. "About the book signing, did you look at those dates?"

"No. But I will. Now let me go so I can eat and write." John pulls out his stack of delivery menus from the drawer and fans them out on his counter.

"Okay. Keep me posted. I want to keep you on track," Matt says. "I'm going to be on you like a dog in heat."

"Yes, Dad." John rolls his eyes, shakes his head. "Bye now."

"Bye." Matt clears his throat. "Mind me now, or your ass is grass."

"Yeah, yeah. Buzz off, fucker." John ends the call without waiting. "Matt, sometimes you're an asshat," he says to his phone.

He pulls out the takeout menu for his favorite Asian fare and peruses it. "What shall we eat, my little Junie pie?" He glances at the framed picture of Juniper on his island. She is dressed in a tight little black dress with a flowing scarlet shawl draped over her elbows. She and Bridge had been dressing up for a party, and she had nicely posed for Bridge to take a photo before they left the house, which was so nice of her because he got a copy, too.

"I'll delight in feeding you whatever you want soon. I'll let you pick everything. I'll worship you as you inhale it into your beautiful body, to give you energy and nourishment to fuck me, suck on my cock, and pleasure me to untold heights, as I will bring you to yours, multiple times each day." He grins and chuckles as he taps open his phone and dials the restaurant. "And fuck your gorgeous mouth."

"Yeah, I'd like to make an order for delivery." He holds the menu up so he can recite his order properly. "And make it as fast as possible. I don't care about the fees."

# Chapter Six

Bridge watches his wife as she rides her hand up and down the shiny gold pole in the corner of the exercise room. She's glowing, her eyes sparkle as a sexy grin develops.

He's feeling smug. It was a bold move, but the look on her face tells him he did the right thing.

She shakes her head with a full smirk living on her lips. "I still can't believe you had this put in. Nostalgic gold, too. Are they even gold in the dance clubs anymore?" She reaches her hand up high and twirls herself in a spin around it, trailing her hand halfway down its length in a spiral. Her pale yellow sundress twirls out as she spins. He almost gets a peek. "This is going to be so much fun." She snickers.

"I don't know what color they are; I haven't been near one in years. Don't need that when I have you, now do I?" He crosses his arms over his muscular chest, and a naughty grin flits across his face. He nods at her. "Mmmm, how about now for some of that dance pole fun?"

She stops her spin and leans the length of her body fully against the shiny pole, her left arm still clinging to it up high, her other arm resting lengthwise. It's a damn sexy pose. A gritty, naughty smile erupts on her porcelain face, a naughtiness that matches the glimmer in her eyes. "Yeah? Now? Oh, but...but...but I'm too innocent for this." She cocks her head away from the pole and puts her right hand on her hip. "But it could be doable, if I have a teacher."

She's so enticing, he's lost to everything but her in an instant.

He scoffs. "Innocent my ass." He grins at her. "Okay, I'm game. I'll tell you what to do. I like this idea for a game." He loves dominating her in roleplay, and it meets her kinks, too. He adores how she voices her love for his leadership in the bedroom. The debriefings after sex sometimes turn into more sex.

"I'm just a sweet little schoolgirl, innocent as could be. I don't even know what I'm supposed to do with a pole like this." She bats her eyelashes and gives him first a blank stare, then a clueless, confused expression.

Bridge scoffs, then chuckles. He's infatuated with how she falls into role-playing without even mentioning it. He always follows her lead when she's in the mood for things like this. Fuck, is he a lucky man...something he totally adores about her sexuality is her spontaneity. The more freedom he has given her, the bolder she's become, and he couldn't be happier. He reaps the benefits as much as she does, maybe more. No. Not true. She gets more, way more, by his design.

His cock is already hard, seeing her grip that pole so tenaciously. It hardens even further as he imagines playing naughty schoolgirl with her. He certainly gets off spanking her when she gets like this. And it makes her come, too, often squirting like a fountain.

"Are you my teacher?" she asks with a little sweet smile. "Because I'm just not sure exactly what I'm supposed to do next." She crosses her ankles and touches her lips with her free hand, her other one still gripping the pole as she twists her body. "Do I put my...boobies...on it?" She presses her cleavage against the pole. "And shake them to slap them on the pole, like this?" She shimmies, her breasts slapping the metal pole with each one on repeat. "Oops. I said 'boobies'. Is that a naughty word, teacher?"

Bridge grins as he pulls the big, blown-up bouncy exercise ball under his ass and sits. "Why, yes, it is, little girl. That's one tally for a spanking." He clears his throat and says in an authoritative voice, "You know I'm keeping track, little girl."

She gasps, totally overdoing her reaction. "Oh dear. You will spank me. On my bottom?" She makes her eyes go wide as she says the word "bottom" and covers both ass cheeks with her palms. "Not my rear." She turns toward the mirror, her back now to Bridge. She leans forward and lifts up her sundress to show Bridge her bare ass. "This bottom?"

He chuckles. "Yes, that bottom. And that's another tally for flashing your bottom to me." He's burning to say "ass," and watch her overreact.

"Oh! Really? That's naughty too?" She hasn't moved a muscle. Her hands are still holding up her sundress to bare her ass for him. "Hmmm, guess I have a lot to learn from you, teacher. But you will see my bottom when you spank me, so what's the difference?"

"You're already assuming you're getting a spanking?"

"Well, I said the bad words, didn't I?"

"Don't sass me. Another tally. And another for not wearing underwear to school. That's naughty, little girl." He holds up four fingers. "That's four lashings so far, young lady." He clears his throat. "And enough clit spankings to match." He gives her a beaming grin. He's itching to grab the handle of the flogger in his back pocket and brandish it wildly.

"Oh, I'd better shape up, then." She leaves her dress folded up on the top of her buttocks, and since she's still leaning forward a bit, it stays.

"Many more, and you will have a red bum from my punishment. This will be a good lesson to teach you to do the right thing. And I have the right tools to do it." He cracks up as she swivels to face him, giving him a very shocked look. She doesn't even laugh or giggle or let on that she's playing. Damn, she would have made a great actress, or with her body, an adult film star. He's had fun imagining that during his private play time, where no real eyes were watching. He snickers.

"Wait, what's a clit?" She places her index finger on the corner of her mouth with her face full of fake contemplation. "Teacher, do I have one?"

"Oh, I will definitely give you a lesson on that. It will be the best lesson. Yes, you most definitely do. It's a girl penis. You will love feeling it." He bounces on the ball, his cock raging, fully erect and full of blood. The strands of the flogger still nestled in his pocket hit the ball with light slaps. He'd love to pin her to the pole and ride her like a beast, but he's holding off. This is too much fun.

"Hmmm. I didn't know I had a penis. What if I rub my bottom on the pole, like this?" She gets in front of the pole and rides her ass crack up and down in a rapid up-and-down motion. Not even a hint of a smile creeps across her serious expression.

Damn, she is good.

"Quit wiping your butt on the pole, little girl. That's unsanitary. Another spanking, I'm afraid." He shakes his head with a chuckle as their naughty eyes meet, conjoining in silent mutual agreement on the continuation of this role play.

She manages a silent giggle without breaking the firm line of her lips, stifling the full eruption of a laugh. "Oh, my butt is dirty?" She puts her hand over her mouth in mock shock. "It's not that dirty. I took a shower today, teacher." She turns her head away. "What's in your pocket?"

"Yes, it's filthy. I can tell from here. Disgustingly filthy. Raunchy. Though I could clean it off for you with my tongue, since it's clean, if you're telling me the truth, that is, girlie. And I just brushed my teeth, so I have a very clean mouth." He clears his throat. "Never you mind about what's in my pocket," he says sternly.

"Oh. You want to touch your clean mouth to my dirty bottom?" Her tone is so innocent; she deserves an award. Though this almost elicits a smile from her, she manages to swipe the hint of it away.

She's definitely winning this game.

Bridge chuckles, thrilled he made her almost break character and smile with that one. He sometimes tries to get her to lose control when she does this role-playing scenario. He rarely gets even this minuscule type of slip out of her, so this is a huge success. Since her resolve has been weakened, he's going for gold now; he's going to make her giggle out of character if it's the last thing he does.

"Yeah, I'm the official butthole cleaner 'round here. Fastest and cleanest tongue in the west, so I can whip your asshole into the cleanest shape in no time." He laughs heartily, fully relishing that he can indulge in it. "I'm the fastest, most efficient, butt licker on the planet."

Juniper bites her lips together, efficiently curbing her laughter, though her eyes are cracking up. "Hmmm." She does a little spin, a full 360 degrees. "Will you tell me, teacher, how I'm supposed to dance on this? I mean, if it were on the floor, it would be much easier to dance on, but, being vertical, I just don't know how to dance on it."

Bridge runs his hand down his hard-on through his jeans. She's good, deftly changing the subject so she can get away from her almost loss of control over her laughter.

"Well, you see, you just wrap a leg around it and kind of hang on it. You can swivel around it, wrap both legs around it, and hump your pretty little pussy lips on it."

"Oh, dear teacher, hump? And did you say 'pussy'?" She wraps a leg around the pole and twirls around it. "I like cats. I have one. Her name is Mags. Short for Maggie. Do you like pussy cats?"

"Oh, yes. Yes, you have a cat and a pussy, and now you said 'pussy', another naughty word. So, another spank will land on your ass." Bridge nods for emphasis. His grin spreads big and wide. His dick hardens with the thought of slapping her round ass, making it red and wet from his precum. "I'll just call you Red-butt Rosie tonight. Get you a nice pillow to sit on." He wiggles his hips to get the rope strands of the flogger to sway behind him.

She gasps, aghast. "Oh, my. But I thought pussy cat was a good word, Sir? And, Mr. Teacher, you said it first, and so doesn't that make it okay for me to say, too, right, teacher? Right?" She grips the pole with her knee, wrapping her shin around it as she slides her leg up, and then back down. She pumps it, bringing her thigh to the pole, almost giving him a peek at her commando pussy, her eyes lit with teasing play.

"You sassing me, girl? Another spanking." Bridge bounces aggressively up and down on the ball, his cock throbbing full and engorged, pressing fiercely against his jeans, the head peeping out of the top of his waistband. It's getting a bit tight and uncomfortable, so he unzips it to relieve some of the pressure. His meat needs some space, for fuck's sake!

"Teacher, are you undressing in front of me? Oh my gosh. Isn't that kind of naughty to undress in front of your student? Doesn't that break some kind of law?" Juniper covers her mouth with her hand, then lifts her dress, presses her bare crotch to the pole, and rides it around. She flinches at the first touchdown, then rubs herself against it. "Oh, it's cold."

"Not for long," he heckles, loving that she's got her bare lips on the pole now. "You want me to undress? Well, that's naughty, little...what is your name again, little girl?"

"Alicia. I'm Alicia." Juniper grips the pole up high and swings around it, smearing the pole with more of her cunt juices. "You can call me Ally if you want." She shoves a finger in her mouth and sucks it like a lollipop. She pulls it out with a pop. "Ally pally, ollie mollie, like a lolli," she says in a sing-song voice.

Bridge chuckles. He wants to go lick that juice-smeared pole. "Stop that little girl, I mean, Alicia, Ally, you're getting your vagina juices all over the pole and making a sticky mess." He gets a naughty gleam in his eye. He whispers, "And a delicious one." He grins at Juniper as he says, "I'll make you clean it off with your tongue, you naughty girl." Or he will, he smirks.

"Delicious? Like candy?" Juniper bites her lips hard. She's trying desperately not to laugh. She takes a deep inhale to stop her laughter from busting out. She leans against the pole and swivels, and as she does, she makes strong eye contact with Bridge. "Do I do this?" She twirls herself around the pole, then stops in front of him. She lifts up her sundress and puts her butt crack on the pole. Leaning over, she jiggles her breasts with her hands, making them shake wildly inside her sundress while riding the pole with her ass. "Maybe I just need to cool down a bit. I'm kinda hot at the moment." Still bent over, she pulls her sundress over her head. Not only does she not have underwear on, but she also doesn't have a bra, so she's fully naked in mere seconds. "That okay, teacher? I'm just kinda hot. Too many clothes on." She flings her dress into the corner of the room, where it lands on the stacked barbells.

"Oh, little Ally, that's naughty, too. One does not strip in front of their teacher. I shall have to teach you a lesson, little lady. I'm sorry, I'm going to have to paddle your buns massively in punishment. Give you a bright red butt." He grins because he doesn't have to hide his smiles like she does; this is her character roleplay gig, he's just the watcher. "A teacher must deliver discipline to the students who don't follow the rules." He reaches back and fingers the flogger while staring directly into her eyes.

"Bright red butt," she agrees plainly. She glides her toned belly over the pole and bends herself around it, catching his eye contact as she does, giving him come fuck me eyes. She gyrates her pussy against the pole, then her ass, leans her right hip against it, and shakes her tits at Bridge. Her big, pink areolas are tipped with thick, hard, pointed nugget-like tips that deliciously shake as she dances. Oh, how he loves to pinch, pull, and suck them. He's yearning to do it something fierce. She rubs her nipples against the pole, then plays with them herself, pinching and twisting, pulling them while staring at Bridge. She's having a love affair with his eyes as she humps her ass against the pole, beating it like she's trying to knock it down.

"That's new, Ally. Don't knock it down." He is practically drooling. He can't wait to get his hands and mouth on her, his cock inside her warm, wet vaginal walls. Precum is seeping out the top of his cock. He swipes his hand across it because he can't resist touching himself.

"Am I doing it right, now, teacher?" She stands up straight and threads her right leg and arm around the pole, slithering against it, sliding and rolling along it in slow, undulating pulsations. Watching her luscious, curvy body move is a seduction he can never resist. She pauses with her ass facing him and catches his eyes in the mirror.

He's twitching; he's so ready to pounce. "I could look at your ass, tits, and pussy all day, Ally baby. I'm going to fuck you hard, you little wench, after I smack your ass like a naughty little schoolgirl like you deserves." He grunts. "You won't be able to sit for days."

She lets a little grin sneak out as she shakes her buttocks at him.

He claps loudly and points at her. Ha! He wins!

She cracks a real smile, then quickly frowns.

He bounces on the ball, the tip of his cock throbbing, still poking out the top of his unzipped jeans, precum dripping out in clear droplets.

"You've been made. Caught you giving a real smile, ya know? You better bring that ass over here now. It's time for your punishment, little Ally." When she doesn't move, he speaks more sternly. "Wiggle that butt over her for your spankings, Alicia. The teacher needs to teach." He nods as he speaks. "Come on now." He motions with his hand for her to come over.

"No can do, teacher." She spirals her body around the pole and licks it while connecting her gaze with his. She sighs, then says in a cooing voice, "I'm busy tasting the candy coating on this pole."

"That's not sanitary, little girl. Stop licking that. Besides, I have a better pole for you to lick."

She smirks as he watches her lick.

"You're asking for a licking. One you won't easily forget."

She stops licking and grins lewdly at him. "I don't care. Spank me then." She sticks her tongue out and then does a long, slow, exaggerated lick of the pole.

"Oh, don't you worry, that's happening. I need you to come lay on my lap now, though, or I'll double your spankings." He clears his throat. "Obey your teacher."

"Make me," Juniper says in a sassy tone as she slams her pussy into the pole. She leans back while hanging on, dipping her head backward, a deliberately defiant grin growing. Her breasts fall toward the floor as she jerks her body back upright.

"I'll spank you on the ball, then make you get on all fours for the doubled half to mark your flesh with my special tool." He clears his throat and yells, "Now get your sassy butt over here right now. Or I'll get the paddle, too."

She releases her hold of the pole. He can tell she's getting more aroused. She's told him his anger sends jolts to her clit when he gets extra stern with her. She seductively meanders across the foam workout mat, taking one step after another in slow motion, deliberately swaying her hips as she walks. Her eyes flash with electricity.

When she's close enough, Bridge grabs her arm and pulls her, forcing her across his lap. She squirms slightly, making them both bounce on the ball as if they were one. He holds her body in place on his lap; she's sandwiched between his thighs and his other arm. He begins to spank his lovely wife.

She moans and swivels her head to watch him spank her in the mirror, pretending with shrieks of surprise, and shaking her head. Sighs and smiles break through her acting charade. He loves that.

He imagines her wet pussy is gushing more and more with the vibrations each spank sends through her clit, but for extra assurance, he makes a finger swipe across her bean every now and then.

"Naughty little schoolgirl," Bridge says as he slaps her butt. The skin-slapping sounds ramp up his lust, and precum oozes out on the waistband of his jeans. So much precum today, fuck. He slips two fingers into her wet pussy between spanks and drags the wetness from her sopping wet hole to her ass.

Juniper hugs the exercise ball with one arm, and she wraps her other around his leg. He's getting a kick out of her holding on. He hits her bum a few more times. Her flesh is getting red already.

"Getting red." He reaches for the flogger and whips it across her buttocks.

"Humpf," she retorts. "Oh!"

"Now, get on your hands and knees, little girl. Time for a switch. The teacher's going to show your pussy a lesson for smearing up that pole with all your wetness. Teacher's gonna show you what your pussy's wetness is really meant for." He spies the leather flogger hanging on the arm of the treadmill, and quickly snatches it.

Juniper lets a laugh slip out as she crawls to her hands and knees. She flips her long blond hair to the side so she has a clear view of herself and Bridge in the mirror. She watches as Bridge moves into position behind her, his curved, turgid cock swinging. He swings both floggers, their strands zing through the air rapidly. She cries out and flinches with each hit. He drops them and they land on the mat with a plop. He pushes two fingers into her pussy for a few pumps, then hauls off and slaps her clit.

"Clit spankings, too, little girl."

She moans with obvious pleasure.

He loves it. Ramping up his game, he slaps her clit hard, and her pussy wets his fingers and palm. He keeps doing it, and she whimper-moans. She's ready.

He pushes and pulls two fingers in and out of her rapidly, increasing his motions, drawing out more of her wetness. He wants her to beg, so he keeps increasing his pumping faster and faster.

She groans, her torso dipping down. "Please," she purrs. "Please, now. I can't wait any longer."

"Good girl." He knew she'd cooperate. He lines his cock up with her pussy and penetrates along her labia lips ever so slightly as she moans against his entrance. He pushes himself all the way into her, and then doggy style fucks her roughly as they both watch in the mirror. He rocks her body from behind, making her tits swing back and forth.

"Oh, fuck. Yes. Yes. Yes. Fuck," she whispers as he pelts himself against her ass cheeks, so they jiggle wildly.

"It's so hot fucking you with a red ass, baby," he grunts as he pounds. He admires his good work.

She moans against his body slams. He imagines the sting of his body banging against her red butt cheeks must be jarring. The line between pleasure and pain can be a fine one, but he feels confident that she has her safe word just in case. The skin-slapping sounds are egging on his orgasm; fuck, he's getting close.

Her orations reach her usual peaking level. Her body curls, her head falls to the ground between her bent arms as she shakes. Her contractions squeeze him inside her, and he starts to lose control, so he slows his thrusting. This also gives him the chance to finish her off right.

He runs a thumb across her clit. She cries out louder, gasping. Her torso jolts in a recoil; her sensitive spot is clearly overstimulated, so he leaves her alone for thirty seconds as she comes down off the high. After she's done jerking, he pulls himself out of her and flips her to her back, then rotates so they can sixty-nine. She takes his cock into her mouth with a moan, and he groans as he slams his mouth onto her pussy, licking her labia, and dragging his tongue along her slit.

He devours her clit with his open mouth, sucking her hard like a suckerfish. Her clit is engorged and hard as he runs his tongue all across it. She lavishes her tongue under the ridge of his swollen cock head, down his shaft, along his prominent vein that travels down the front of his penis while riding his shaft with her hand.

Juniper sucks in rhythm with how Bridge is licking the full length of her pussy. He keeps his tongue wide and flat, ending with a full-on suck on her clit each round. She releases a huge moan every time his mouth visits her clit.

He glances in the mirror to see their sixty-nine dance and his desire to grin happily emanates from his eyes. He loves sex with her, he loves life with her. He is a very blessed man.

He stops because he needs a break, or he will come. Which is what they want, but still, he wants more sex first. He crawls off her and lines up his body with hers setting up for the missionary position. That's the best position for depositing his sperm in her, according to all the men's forums he's read.

"Let's make a baby this time." He's about ready to burst, so he moves slowly.

He spreads her legs, and she bends them up. He pushes them toward her armpits, getting her legs as wide as he can. He glances down at her open pussy, and his cock twitches in anticipation of entering her. Fully consented access to her body, heart, and soul has made him literally addicted. He kisses her, open-mouthed with unchecked passion, sucking and caressing her lips and tongue, savoring her other parts while giving his cock a longer break to lengthen their lovemaking.

Alas, it's in vain. That's it. He can't wait another second. He grabs his dick and lines it up to enter her pussy, he tickles it along her labia lips in a short tease.

"Oh, please, Bridge, fuck me. Please. Please fuck me now." She flops her head back and forth as she pleads with her words, her eyes closed. She seems so overwhelmed by desire and want, still likely sort of lost in the euphoria of her previous climax.

"I need your cum."

He presses his thumb to her clitoris with deep pressure, and she gasps, then screams out her pleasure when he rides it fast with his digit. Clit stimulation is what she needs, and he sure is fuck gonna give it to her. But he's no longer able to wait. He needs her. He penetrates her pussy and can't slow down as he rams into her with all his might. The strength of his pelvic muscles rocks her into the climax of her orgasm.

He lets out his primal growl. She whimpers her end to her apex, her body slowing its convulsing. Bridge feels their wetness join together inside her pussy.

"Ah fuck that was just fucking delicious." His goal is always for her to climax, but also, really, his real goal lately...is hoping she will get pregnant.

"Mmmm, so good, Bridge. So good."

"Lay still, let our cum soak together inside you, and make us a baby. We need that magic sauce," he whispers as they hold each other's gaze. He runs his fingers along her forehead, down her cheek, and over her lips.

She nods with a serious look. "It's best for me not to move for a while, yeah." She points to the rolled-up yoga mat nearby. "Grab that and slide it under my butt for elevation. Let's further trap your swimmies inside me so they can find my egg."

Bridge crawls over and grabs the purple rolled-up yoga mat and slides it under her raised hips. He snuggles into her body, kisses her forehead, and slips his arm under her head to support it.

"Let's let you cook for a bit." He smirks. "I didn't spank you too hard, did I?" he asks with a chuckle in his voice.

She laughs. "Kinda, but it sent jolts to my clit, made me wetter. More aroused. So, it was okay. I didn't drop my safe word." She pauses as she releases a soft scoff. "But yeah, ya fricking iron man smacking hand though. Whew! You don't know your own strength." She smirks.

"Oops. Sorry. I got a little too into it. I love those slap sounds and the sight of your ass jiggling after I smack it. Such a turn on. I love to dominate you." He rubs her hip, carefully avoiding her reddened flesh. "I'll kiss your ass, literally, and rub lotion into it. I'll make it all better, baby." He likes making it red, too, but he's keeping that to himself for the moment.

She guffaws. "Oh, it was jiggling alright." She rubs her face on his flesh. "Hmm...I noticed you got a little too into it. Was kinda hot you correcting me, though." She lets out a light laugh. "Love how it reinforces your dominance. And the double flogger idea was killer, by the way."

"Yeah, I got into that. It was the same for me." He kisses her forehead. "I admit, I kind of love it."

She sighs. "Kind of?" She snorts. "Wow. Well, I'm famished, though. Should we order pizza? I don't feel like cooking after that magnificent fuck. I'm still sorta shaking. Not sure I want to stand and cook."

"I see that." He hugs her closer. "I always want to make you shake like this. It's so sexy, primal, when you do. It drives me crazy to watch you come. Such a turn-on. All of it." He drags a finger from her chin, down the curve of her neck, the flat of her chest above her breasts, and up the mound and over her nipple and back again, tracing her luscious curves. He has memorized her body in his brain, but he can't ever get enough of touching her. "Yes, pizza sounds good to me."

"I used to hate sex in the bright lights, but somehow in here, it's okay. Must be watching us in the mirror turns me on so much that I don't mind the bright lights in my eyes." She blinks.

"Well, I love the lights, I can see every speck of you. Every dip and protrusion. Every freckle and crease. Every inch of my cock that is going into you." He kisses her forehead again. "And I love all that so much. And I love you."

She looks at him dreamily as she says, "I love you, too."

He runs the back of his right hand down her soft cheek.

"Happy baby-making fuck, maybe, eh?" He softens his face as he takes her satisfied look in.

"Maybe, love, just maybe we did it this time." She traces his nipple with her finger, riding it along the rise of his flesh. "I wish you didn't have to go."

He sighs. Ah, this again. He gets it. He doesn't want to leave her either. But he must. "Yeah, me too. It isn't for a few weeks yet, though. But I knew I'd need to go to Europe at some point. Just going to get it over with. Besides, the other manager from Texas is going, too, and we need to go at the same time. They've made arrangements in their schedule for us to come. The timing just works out across the board." He squeezes her. "I'm sorry, I have to go. I'd rather stay here and keep up our marathon baby-making spree."

She blinks back a tear. "Why didn't we plan for me to come along again?"

He stares at the ceiling, then glances at his wife. The light showing off the glow of her skin, the delicate, pale pink blush of her nipples. "I wish that could have worked, but remember, I have a very grueling schedule while I'm there. I think we will only get a few evenings to sightsee. So, you would have been alone every day, and some evenings."

"Oh yeah. But I think I would have still liked that. I could have gone sightseeing alone."

"Oh, I don't like that idea, baby. Too dangerous to go out alone. Let's plan a trip to Europe sometime, okay?" He peers into her eyes, lifts her chin. "Hey...oh no, baby, ...you're really sad about this. Aren't you?" He pulls her close in a big bear hug. "Aww. I'm sorry, baby. Don't be sad. Maybe you can still come." He strokes her hair, plays with it as he knows she loves that.

She nods against his warm chest. "I'm being dumb. I'm sorry. I couldn't get off work with such short notice anyhow. Plus, we'd have to find someone to take care of Mags, too." She sniffles, trying to snuff out her tears, then snuggles her cheek hard into his chest as if the strength of him will seep into her from sheer friction. "I'll be fine. Maybe I'll have a friend sleepover, like I did when I was a kid." She giggles, thankfully switching to a joyous mood. "We can eat junk food and cheese, drink wine, and watch movies. Sounds kind of fun, actually. A girl's night." Her smile brightens her eyes as she sits up. "I'll ask around and see if any of my friends are free. Then I won't be alone the whole time you're gone."

"Good plan. Now, let's get that pizza." He hops up. "You stay put, lie back down, and try to manifest that baby. I'll go order the pizza." As he leaves the exercise room, he calls back, "I'll bring you some strawberry iced tea."

"Thank you. I love how you take care of me."

"My pleasure. Always." He craves it. It's not just for her, it's for him, too.

# Chapter Seven

Juniper sets out two stemless wine glasses. Of the three friends she asked to come to the sleepover, with Bridge gone, only one could come. Busy lives, babies, work, and all the legit excuses, but still she wanted them all to come. No blame, but it's a bummer. She shrugs, it's midlife, and it's what she wants, too, if only she could get pregnant. She hadn't hung out with her little group of friends for several years. She missed their college days, their days of incessant togetherness, and all the adventures they'd gone on as a group effort. But babies and husbands and kids all come first now, as it should be; it's the stage of life they're all in.

She looks wistfully at her stomach, a weak smile trying to erupt, but failing, wondering when it will happen for her and Bridge. She scoops up a wine glass in her cupped palm and cradles it, placing her other hand on her belly. She knows it's a long shot now; the pregnancy test today was negative, so it's not going to be this month, at least. So, she's partaking in wine again. She had such high hopes of calling Bridge in Europe and telling him it was positive. No such luck. She smirks. They'll just have to keep on fucking. Her smile finally fully erupts. There's an upside to this after all.

She swirls the empty wine glass in the air like it's a magic wand. Glaring hard at the shiny glass, she says, "I'd gladly give you up for a baby." She sighs, sets it down, and picks up the bottle of wine. "Just will consume you tonight while I still can, I guess. A sad consolation."

Her phone buzzes in her pocket. It's a text from Bridge.

Bridge: I'm in the Netherlands. Will be getting on the plane soon. Just wanted to say I love you, and I miss you already.

Juniper: I love u too. Only Sara can come over, so it will just be the two of us. Miss you too.

Bridge texts a heart emoji and a hug. Juniper texts the same back.

Juniper: Have a good, safe flight.

Bridge: I will. Thank u. Have fun with Sara.

Juniper: Thanks. I know we will. Girls' night here we come...

Juniper: BTW test was negative.

Bridge: Next time, babe. We'll get it done next time. Love you.

Juniper: Love you too.

She sincerely hopes he's right. It's a damn good thing the trying is so fun.

Having the day off is great, but not so much when alone. She plays with the buttons on her shirt. She should have picked up a shift at work and at least made some extra money, oh well. Her alone time is almost over now as Sara will be arriving soon, anyhow.

She pops a mug of water in the microwave and hits two minutes. She opens the cupboard and takes out her box of tea bags. Vanilla chai sounds about right to her on this lonely day, so she plucks out the little cream-colored packet. She sets the little teabag box back in the cupboard. She spies that strange box in the cupboard, which she spotted that first day she and Bridge were at the house for the tour. She never heard back from the agent on it. She narrows her eyes as she gazes at it, her suspicions flaring once again.

What the fuck is the little key for, anyway? She wants to take it to John Penn and ask him, demand an explanation. But that seems like a silly thing to do. And would he even agree to talk to her? He sounds kind of like a recluse.

"Hmmmm," she says aloud while considering calling John herself.

The realtor never got the scoop on the unexplained space in the corner of the house, either. She can't find a possible way to explore it. She smiles, remembering the one day recently when Bridge almost sledgehammered the wall open to find out, but she stopped him because that could mean serious repairs they don't have money to pay for. Maybe she'd have to seriously take matters into her own hands, though, and just contact the author herself and ask him. She'd love to talk to a real author anyway, and since they bought his house from him when he wanted a quick sale, she bets he would be willing to talk to her. She makes a note to ask the realtor for his contact information.

She lifts her chin and says, "Well, John Penn. I may be contacting you myself to find out about this secret room of yours that is now ours." She taps the note with her finger and nods. It's a definite plan. She shouldn't be talking to herself out loud; that's weird.

The microwave beeps and she pulls out the hot mug of water. The deep blue, azure mug was her mom's favorite. She had inherited it when her mother passed on. Thinking of her mom makes her smile. Her mom would be so supportive in her baby-making quest, but alas, she no longer gets such support. She misses her mom every day. This isn't helping her sad mood one bit.

She slips her teabag in the hot water and meanders the house with plans to sit on the deck, grabbing her book as she saunters through the living room. Mags comes out on the deck with her and plops down in the full veil of sunshine descending through a cloudless blue sky. The happy cat rolls her back against the rough deck boards to massage herself, which incites lots of purring.

Juniper smiles at her sweet pet. She stares off over the flat abyss of the ocean for a few minutes, contemplating a hopeful conception happening in her womb soon. She's trying like crazy to manifest a baby. If she thinks about it enough, it will happen. With a tear forming in her eyes, she lowers her gaze to her book.

She needs a distraction, so she opens it and reads while listening to the repeating rush and lull of the ocean waves. After sipping tea for a full fifteen minutes while reading, she hears the doorbell ring in the distance. That's odd. She isn't expecting any deliveries. Standing up and stretching, she picks up Mags, who flops herself like a rag doll against her hip. She carries her relaxed kitty inside with a smirk. She never likes to leave her out alone on the deck, just in case she were to run off or get snagged by a hawk or something horrendous like that.

Juniper adjusts her shirt to be more presentable, as it had fallen low and now showed too much of her boobs for the general public to see. No need to give whoever is at the door an unwanted peekaboo boob shot. She grins; she always loved to do that to Bridge, though. At times, she'd slip her shirt to the side and bra off a nipple and take a pic to send to him. It always made him so horny, and he'd come raging at her like a bull in heat. She needs to do that again later today and torture him with it. She doesn't quite get her naughty grin wiped off her face before she opens the door. Oh well, who cares anyway?

The man standing on her front step looks vaguely familiar, but she can't quite place him. He returns her naughty grin, which causes her to flinch and clear her face of the lewd expression.

Oops, crap. He saw it. Too late now. He probably thinks she's a freak, but he returned her smile with a rather sly one of his own. She shrugs off the weird feeling it gives her and shows him a sweet smile instead.

She crosses her arms under her full breasts and says, "Hello. How can I help you?" Bridge would be so pissed at her for opening the door for a stranger like this. But she's no child.

The man stares back at her. He runs his fingers over his supple red lips and down the slight brownish stubble of his chin, effectively wiping his naughty grin from his mouth and replacing it with a pleasant one, too.

"Um. Yeah. Hi. I'm John Penn. I used to live here; you bought this house from me, and I seem to be missing some important files. Do you mind if I take a quick peek for them in the office? Just to make sure I didn't leave them in the file cabinet. I kind of think I did." He looks apologetic, and harmless.

Her heart thuds in her chest, and she tries not to squeal with excitement. John Penn is on her front step! Bridge will be so jealous that she got to meet him. She smiles back, her eyes twinkling with excitement. She had just been thinking about him, and he appeared on her front porch like magic. What luck!

"Oh, wow, hi," she stammers, feeling starstruck. She hadn't seen any unusual files in the office, but she hadn't gotten to the point of putting their files in the filing cabinet quite yet, so who knows, they could be there. The files still sat in a box in the corner of the office because the task seemed too unimportant to actually do.

She nods, making her blond hair flop. "Sorry, I'm a bit awestruck meeting you," she gushes.

The man grins deeply, moving a hand down his front. She tries not to pay too much attention to his movements, but she would swear on it that he ran his fingers down near his cock. "I'm flattered."

She almost scoffs at herself. She's imagining things. That's ridiculous.

But, seriously, meeting him is a dream come true. She could let him in; he's famous after all, right? He's very well-known and in the public eye, not some weird, strange man. Plus, the house was just his house, and he gave them an amazing deal on it. She grins at him. Who was she to say 'no' to such a man?

She says, "Sure. Come on in. It's truly amazing to meet you." Her heart races being in the presence of such a talented man.

She steps backward and motions with her arm to welcome him inside. "I really love your books. I've read three of them. My husband has read even more. We're huge fans!" Maybe she could even bother him for an autograph, if she could quickly find one of his books. Bridge was reading one recently, so it must be around somewhere. Her tummy is giddy at getting to have a famous author in her home. "My husband was reading one just recently, in fact."

At the mention of Bridge, John seems to startle a little, and he looks around quickly.

"Oh, he's not here now, he's traveling," she says in a flash comeback. Maybe she shouldn't have told him that, but who cares? It doesn't really matter.

He nods, then appears calm. "Thank you. I love to meet fans. I'd be more than happy to sign a book for you." He looks very pleased.

This soothes and excites her at once. "Okay. Great! I'll look for it, but first, let's look for your files."

He follows her, perhaps a bit too close, to the office. He wishes he could reach out and cup her firm ass cheeks in his palms. He watches her delicious rump jiggle-jumping under the hem of her sheer blouse as she walks. His dick hardens further in his jeans as he thinks about fucking her the way Bridge did in the exercise room again last night. He loved the flogging action, too. They almost use that more as a sex room than a workout room, and he couldn't be happier about it. He had added extra cameras to the workout room a while back, and he is loving that he did. Last night, he had watched them fuck over and over again for hours, replaying and relishing the sight of her bouncing tits and her glorious golden hair bobbing wildly as Bridge had fucked her. He'd been fixated on her jiggling, generous bubble butt as Bridge had pounded into her like a wild bull in heat. He'd savored the video especially as he deliciously spanked her ass, suckled her titties, and made her come over and over again until she couldn't move. She had practically been in an orgasm coma. He wonders if her ass is still red under those capris. He wishes he could pull down her pants and check. Imagining doing this hardens his dick further.

He watches her face as she turns to face him as they approach the file cabinet. He's in hog heaven, being in her aura in person is stunning, and he's already addicted to it. He needs more of this. Her smiles are so welcoming and lovely. Being this near to her is exquisitely divine. She's a glorious flower right there for his hungry inhale. He feels almost drunk in her presence.

"Have at it," she says as she moves her arm in a sweeping motion over the filing cabinet. Even this simple movement is somehow incredibly sexy to him. Every move she makes sends his lust into an ever-enlarging fireball. "You were amazingly generous to include all of your furniture and the exercise equipment with the house. Thank you for your deep generosity. I'm in love with the gym."

As is he, with her and Bridge in it incessantly, naked and copulating like rabbits. He grins back at her. "It's all my pleasure. I'm so happy you like it all."

She sits on the corner of the desk and crosses her arms under her perfect, full breasts, cradling them. He imagines what they must look like cupped by her arms. And truthfully, he has a true inkling of how they look for how many times he's seen her naked. It's not hard to imagine at all.

"We are totally in love with all of this house," she coos.

"Well, it suits you because you look very happy."

She nods, a shy expression overcoming her.

She's too sweet. He stares at her. Then he realizes he's openly ogling her tits, so he snatches his gaze from her and directs it toward the file cabinet. His mind drifts to her alone in the workout room. He loves watching her work out, too, so he understands her being in love with that room. He's congratulating himself on his plan. He had left several things in the house on purpose, so he could come look for them, including some files. He knew they'd be in the office. He's been waiting for this day for too long. It seemed Bridge would never be gone.

He sighs as he pulls the drawer open to find his files nestled alone in the drawer. He catches her staring at him, watching his movements, so he returns her direct gaze unashamed.

"You're more than welcome to all the furniture, too. It all fits this house, so I just wanted to start over and find stuff to fit perfectly in my new house. You know, Feng Shui and all." He scoffs lightly. "Well, to have my interior designer do that, I mean, I'm too clumsy at it. It's not my skillset," he smirks, hoping she likes that he hires that out. "It's expensive, but oh so worth it." He winks at her with a sexy grin to hammer it home. Juniper, baby, there's lots of money. "Women dig it when a house looks nice, right?" He can give her the house of her dreams, and the sky and all the stars in it with his stash, and a pool and a hot tub, plus trips to Europe. She'll be a spoiled little trophy wife by his side.

Juniper giggles, pushes a lock of golden hair behind her ear.

John watches every microsecond of her movements, memorizing them, tracing her earlobe with his eyes. She licks her lips. "Yes, very true. I bet with your profession, you get your pick of women."

Not yet. But soon he will.

He straightens up his back and arches slightly so the thin, dry-woven fabric can hug his hard-earned ab muscles a bit. It works as her eyes scan his abdomen, filling his fantasy cup damn full, having her eye him up. After finishing his exaggerated stretch, he says, "Not really. No. But I have one I'm very interested in. And I'm working on her." His eyes drop from her lovely face, to eye-cupping her breasts, and then his gaze falls, visually fingering her belly and on down toward her pussy. He knows what she looks like under those clothes, and it's making his boner poke its head against his jeans, making a quite obvious mound at his groin, no doubt. He relishes that she might notice. He shifts, pushing his pelvis out. He'd give it to her right now if he could.

He almost grins as he follows her gaze, traveling down to his crotch, then lingering there. She's checking him out. Aw, hot damn. Just scrumptious as fuck. Having her look makes his cock twitch.

Her eyes go wide as she blushes. She hops off the edge of the desk, looks wildly back and forth, then holds in a giggle. She looks awkward as she fumbles with her phone. She bites her lower lip and is clearly trying to hide a smile as she stares at the screen.

He grins, watching her, savoring catching her staring at his engorged cock pushing out his pants, is the best development he could have hoped for. He savors her demureness with sheer delight as her cheeks stain even darker in a pretty red blush. He's beyond thrilled that she seems to get how aroused he is. Fuck, he could almost cum right fucking now. What he wouldn't give to shove his packed meat into her beautiful pussy. Push her, then bend her over the desk and take her from behind like a rabid beast. He gasps as his pants rub his cock as he moves. That's a bit too much. Shit, it's real; he almost comes as he tries to distract himself by thinking about his files. Climaxing in her presence would be epic, though.

He glances at the documents hanging in the drawer. The drawers...look at the drawers, fucker. He forces his eyes to remain on the files, which are basically empty but for a few pictures of his mom and brother, and a few random car receipts he doesn't really need. Really, who the fuck cares about these things? He grins at her, even though her eyes are glued to her phone.

"Well, I found them. So, I'm glad you and your husband didn't throw them out. I'd be screwed if I lost these." He smooths his hand through his hair while giving her an expression of relief.

Juniper dares a flicker of a gaze at his eyes. Her cheeks are no longer blazing red.

He wishes they were still beet red, however. He likes her looking like that.

John grins about the plans he has made for the night. He had not seen anyone come to the house to change the locks, so his key should still work. But even if they had changed the locks, he'd still get to watch Juniper and her friend in the lower outdoor entertainment area, and then he'd sneak in while they were busy, as surely, they would hang out there for a bit, even just to use the hot tub or swim.

He blesses Bridge for leaving town. Tonight will be a dream come true. He can hardly wait to be in bed with her, to feel the warmth of her naked body next to his. If only he could stay the whole night and rouse her to fuck in the deep of the night as Bridge often does. His cock twitches at the thought as he follows her out of the office. He suppresses his desire to reach out and finger her hair, to caress her cheek, and unpeel her shirt to see more. He desperately wants to bare her ass, to slip her boobs out of her bra and suck her titties to sharp pointy nuggets, making her moan like Bridge does every day. The fucking lucky bastard.

She stops in front of the island and pushes her hands into her pockets. She raises up on her tippy toes, then drops down to place her heels flat on the ground. "Funny thing. I was going to call you and ask if you know about this space at the corner of the house. There seems to be perhaps enough space for a room, but there's no door." She turns and points toward the corner of the house beyond the kitchen and exercise room. "Do you know? Is there some sort of secret room there?" Her eyes twinkle. "It's kind of exciting to think there might be. Very mysterious."

John raises his eyebrows and nods toward the corner. Well, shit. His hand is getting forced. "There? Ah, yes, I have the keys at home. I accidentally took them. I totally forgot about that. I'm so sorry. I'll drop them off sometime. Would that be okay?"

Juniper's face lights up. "Sure. That would be great. The realtor didn't seem to know much about it. But I know the sale happened so fast." Her face erupts further into an expression of intrigue. "So, I'm dying to know. What's in the room? If this hadn't been your house, I don't think we would have bought it without having seen that room first." She laughs like she's absolutely sure of it.

Someone as famous and good as him couldn't have nasty secrets.

He chuckles. "No problem. I'll drop them off soon. It's just a small storage room. Nothing that exciting. Sort of like the size of a walk-in closet that I kept my safe in. I'll show you how to open it, too. As you've said, the door isn't visible." He nods at the wine glasses. "You a wine lover?" The last word hangs on like a delicious treat.

She smiles. Her eyes smile too, melting his heart.

He's happy to be putting her at ease. Clearly, asking her a personal question about her likes is thoroughly relaxing her.

Her shoulders slump and she sighs, then runs a hand through her hair. "Yes, very much so. I have a friend coming over soon, and we will dive into that. We're doing a sleepover." She giggles. "Like teenagers." Her eyes fill with mischievous joy, and it warms John's heart to see her so giddy and giggly. "We're going to do facials, eat junk food, watch movies, and drink lots of wine, something we couldn't so easily do as teens. In fact, I bought three bottles special for tonight, but hopefully, we won't drain them all, or we will be dead to the world and enjoy none of that!"

John is counting on all that happening. "Well, when you're safe at home, that's the time to indulge in lots of wine." He winks at her with a wide, generous grin, hoping she's getting the impression of his permission to do it.

"True, you're absolutely right, and good point. At home is the time to live it up and go a little crazy. I'm looking forward to a fun girls' night in. I haven't spent much time with this friend lately as she is always busy with her husband and young kids."

He cocks his head at her and taps his nose. "For sure. You will have fun, no doubt." He takes a step toward the front door. "Well, I should be going. I've taken up enough of your time." He takes a few more steps and gets an idea. "Wait, would you guys hate me terribly if I took one set of weights from the exercise room? I know I have like three sets in there."

She freezes in place and looks horrified. Her cheeks heat as she struggles for what to say. "Um. Oh, sure. There are so many. I can get them for you. Which weights did you want?"

He hides his delight at her blush, biting his smile from the inside of his mouth. "Ya know, forget it. You keep them, I can buy a new set." He had gotten the reaction he wanted concerning the new dance pole, so he can now leave. Seeing her display shyness about her sexual secrets is a delight to him.

Mission accomplished.

She has visibly relaxed her shoulders after his declaration. Her slight embarrassment makes her even more beautiful. "Ah, ok. But you certainly can have them, you've given us so much here."

"No, it's okay. I shouldn't have asked. I want you to have it all." He continues walking toward the door. "Are you both enjoying the game area too? That was always one of my favorite parts of this house."

"Oh, yes, very much so. It's about the best setup one could ever want. It's just perfect. Totally love it." She tilts her head. "I'm sure my friend and I will enjoy it tonight, too."

John can't wait to see them relaxing. He will delight in watching the girls do their things. It will be a very enjoyable night indeed. His anticipation of off the charts. He takes a step out of the front door and turns back with a wave. "Well, you enjoy. See you soon."

"Oh," she gasps. "Hey, I almost forgot. I found a key in the little drawer in the kitchen cabinet. Is it for something in the house? Or the hidden room?" she asks with hope.

"Oh, that. I actually need that." He laughs. "It goes to my safe. Do you still have it?"

"Oh, yes. Okay. That makes sense. I had wondered if it was for the room. I'll go get it for you."

He waits at the front door, peeking at her butt as she stretches to reach for the key high up in the cupboard. He grins, smirking. What a nice little parting gift this is.

In her hot little hand, she holds the key to the room, but he's sure as fuck not telling her that. He will have a new one made that looks different, so when he comes back, she won't notice. He had left the key there on purpose as a backup so he could use it sometime, like tonight when he sneaks in, but now it will already be in his pocket. This will make it all even easier. He almost wants to thank her for that.

"Ah, thank you. I have a code for the safe, too; this is just the backup key to get into it. You have a nice day, sweetheart." He turns back to her. "So nice to officially meet you."

"Yep, same. And have a good day. Bye," she says as he descends the stairs.

# Chapter Eight

Oh shoot! She had been a bit taken aback by the obvious chub in his pants and then him calling her sweetheart, so much so that she had completely forgotten to ask for his autograph! Dang it! She'd have to ask for one when he dropped off the hidden room key. And he'd need to show her how to get into the room, too, so he'd be here for a few minutes. She'd get her chance yet.

Geez, clueless much? She smiles sheepishly; she had really been a bit starstruck being that close to him and temporarily lost her mind. She smirks to herself, watching him go as she shuts the door. He seemed like such a nice man.

She chuckles as she saunters over to the kitchen, shaking her head, remembering his raging arousal. That time of day, apparently. Sometimes it seems easier to be a woman, as no one can tell the horniness factor at any given moment. Poor men are helpless to their thoughts because everyone can see if they get turned on.

She scoffs, then outright laughs as she pours a glass of wine. "And God bless them for it," she says to herself with a haughty grin.

She starts some light cleaning to get the house ready for her friend to come over. She's so excited she can barely contain herself. She vacuums and throws in a load of laundry, noting that she'll need more fabric stain remover soon. Bridge can be a messy eater at times, and she flies through that stuff way faster than she expects most weeks. She shakes her head as she sprays the spaghetti sauce spot on his beige T-shirt. Sometimes he's like a little boy when he eats. Her mood turns bittersweet as she realizes she'll likely go through even more stain remover when they have a baby.

"Hmmm...Bridge, Bridge, Bridge. I'm not sure this one is going to come out. It's been sitting for a few days." She glances at her phone because looking at his soiled shirt makes her wish he'd text her. "You're like a little kid hiding your dirtiest laundry at the bottom of the hamper. You naughty boy." She smirks. Oh, how she misses him desperately already. They'd probably be getting it on right now if he were here. This makes her want to go grab a toy and fuck herself, imagining it's him instead.

Mags saunters into the laundry room. Sometimes she likes to see what Juniper is doing, and she comes to find her wherever she is in the house. Mags jumps up on the counter and prances toward Juniper on top of the washer, purring as she moves, her signal for begging to be petted.

"Hi, Mags. I'll pet you in a moment." She tosses the sprayed tan shirt in the washer basin and turns to get the laundry soap.

Mags rubs up against the big jug of detergent, causing it to shift and then tip. She moves quickly to catch the large plastic container.

"Whoa!"

She hates it when it gets half full because, as a side dispenser model with a spout, it tends to become unstable on the edge of the counter when it reaches a certain level of emptiness. Then it can easily fall to the ground. She shakes her head; she needs to stop buying this design because it is annoying to walk through the bathroom and see it lying on the floor all the time. At times, there's been leakage to clean up, too, which has sucked. She secures the jug in place and picks up Mags.

Scrubbing the cat's neck as she purrs, Juniper says, "We don't need you nudging this off the counter by rubbing up against it, again, there, little missy."

She gives Mags a kiss and releases her. She sprints off with a hyper-spurt of energy. Juniper fills up the detergent cup to the top and pours it into the little drawer, pushes the buttons, and turns the shiny dial to start the washer up. "Now, to work out for a bit before Sara arrives."

Juniper slips into her yoga pants and a tank top and walks into the exercise room. She scrolls through to her favorite channel on her phone. She wants to hear certain songs during her workout. She slips her tennis shoes on, then does some stretches, various yoga poses, and leg lifts. As she turns to grab her water bottle, the new gold stripper pole catches her eye with its high sheen. Talk about being distracted by a shiny object!

She still can't believe Bridge bought it. What must the installers have thought of her? Of Bridge? She likes thinking about that, though. That's pretty hot. They likely thought he was a lucky dude. Shaking her head, a naughty grin spreads across her face as she imagines their conversation as they installed it.

She's pretty ripe with want from missing Bridge, even though he just left. And all these thoughts were raging in her, inciting her to want something more carnal. Sex had been incredible last night. Images of Bridge watching her dance at the pole pound her brain, and she begins to feel her pussy getting wet. She bends her body into the downward dog pose. Doing yoga almost always makes her horny, too, as she imagines Bridge fucking her in those positions.

She's getting way too turned on to ignore it. Plus, leg lifts are next, and doing leg lifts commando skyrockets her inner wanton slut mode to engage. Her lower lips slide against each other, which seriously makes post-workout sessions the best fuck sessions. She grins and chuckles to herself.

She whispers, "I need you here, Bridge."

She sits on the exercise mat cross-legged, struggling to fight her horniness. She glances in the mirror at herself as her libido rages further.

"Fuck it," she says. "I'm horny as fuck, so why not?" She stands up and strips all her clothes off, then dashes off to the bedroom.

She digs in her bathroom cupboard and pulls out her vibrator and sucker, plus a bottle of lube. She notes the washer sound indicates it's on the last spin, so she'll have to remember to put the clothes into the dryer after her alone time fun. But orgasms trump laundry every time.

With a lecherous grin, she sprints back to the exercise room, her hair flying behind her as she dashes. Dancing is exercise, right? She nods, cranks up the music, and begins to dance in front of the mirror, naked. She twists, wiggles, giggles, gyrates, and spins around, making her boobs and her ass cheeks jiggle freely.

What's the fun of being alone if she's not also naked?

Then she makes her way to the blessed pole and leans against it with her back along the long, hard, cool shaft of it. She plucks at her nipples, making them big and hard, just the way that always drives Bridge crazy.

She grabs her phone and snaps a few saucy pics of her fully erect peaks to text him later. This gets her even hotter. Sending Bridge pictures of her to masturbate to sounds ideal. Then he can have some sexy fun later as well.

She dances-crawls back to the pole in rhythm to the beats of the song, wiggling her hips, giving herself a sexy look in the mirror, and shaking her firm ass. She's getting so wet, her desire for an orgasm mounting as she presses her breasts to the metal, then flings her arms up to grab it above her head. She swings herself around it in a swirling pivot. She rubs her buttocks on it and gives her own ass a slap. She relishes the cool hardness of the rod against her hot, sensitive skin. Then she turns around and rubs her pussy against the pole, masturbating on it, grinding her throbbing wet lips and clit against the firmness.

Its roundness fills the slight curve of her open pussy lips as she smears her juices across its shiny surface. She gives herself a naughty grin in the mirror, daring herself as she spins once more. She imagines Bridge egging her on, and she grinds her butt crack into it...Bridge would have loved seeing all of this. The cold, unyielding metal works as well as any sex toy.

Bridge totally loves watching her masturbate, especially with the vibrator and the sucker. He likes to sit on the chair in their room in the corner and watch her show. He's always rubbing himself, edging along, playing with his engorged cock for as long as he can stand it before he rushes to the bed in uncontrolled passion and rams himself into her. She loves it when he loses all control. It's such a hot moment as she is always so ready, swollen, and wet by that point, yearning for his hot penis thrusts to rub her engorged clit into wet mountains of orgasms. Oh, yes, please! This always means bliss is hers to enjoy. He always puts her first. The memory of that thickens her clit further. He's such an amazing lover.

She feels big and swollen, and, without having to touch it to confirm, her clit is peaking in erectness. She fully intends to fuck herself with the vibrator until her pussy lips are nice and swollen, and after the vibrator has gifted her several orgasms, rendering it covered in her own personal spunk. She'll go at her sweet nub until the toy runs out of power. She giggles at the thought of it just suddenly dying...damn...that would suck, especially without Bridge here to finish her off. But luckily, she has other toys.

She doesn't bother to dim the lights in the gym. It's only her home anyway, so who cares? She shrugs, crawls away from the pole toward the vibrator, her ass pointed upward and bared. She nudges the lube bottle on the ground with her knee, dragging her freshly painted red toes along as she moves. She glances back at her own ass in the mirror and watches her butt as she crawls, shaking her buns to the beat of the song. Damn, she does still have a nice, round, curvy ass. No wonder Bridge is so obsessed with it.

Assimilating the urges of what she imagines an onlooker would feel while watching her is such a turn-on. She reaches back and feels the cheeks of her butt. It's so firm, hard to the touch, but big enough to still have a hefty amount of jiggle to it. It always feels delicious to her when she walks around because her ass cheeks are taut, yet they still move.

She gives herself a tiny spank and giggles, dropping her head toward the mat, which makes her hair sweep along as she inches forward on all fours. Her mood is growing lewder as she enjoys her impending alone play time. She can be the most reckless when she plays alone, where she can safely delve into dark fantasies, ones she holds secret from everyone else. In her head, she's always safe, and she's the director of all the debauchery.

Once she reaches for the vibrator, she sits with her legs open wide, facing the mirror. Her pussy skin is a bit darker than the rest of her surrounding flesh, with her entrance being quite pink, and she becomes even darker, almost purplish, toward her anus. She squirts some lube on the head of the purple rabbit vibrator, not forgetting the little bullet-shaped nub that will rub her clit.

Looking at the vibrator makes her pussy salivate down her slit. She fingers her pussy to wet it further, so ready to score a big O or two.

She pours some more lube on her fingers, then rubs some on her erect nipples, too. The delicious hibiscus smell fills her nostrils with the familiar erotic aroma. Closing her eyes, she imagines Bridge rubbing it on her pussy mound and down her slit, slickening it further. She rubs the lube down her belly and keeps going, lingering a bit to rub her clit, then she smooths her hand down to her soaking wet labia.

Wet as fuck.

She falls into a fantasy of a stranger appearing at the door. He's attractive with brilliant blue eyes and a fit body encased in black leather, like a biker, and he seems charming, but faceless. He forces his way inside with some excuse of needing to fix something that her husband had ordered, and she'd better let him do it, or her hubby will be mad. The man informs her that her husband might even spank her when he gets home for disobeying another man.

Shivers shudder down her body as she imagines the mystery man rushing her, his intense, dominant gaze indicating he's not intending to take any sort of refusal from the likes of her. She's helpless to his need to ravish, and he bends her over the couch like he plans to do bad things to her. He grabs her pants and roughly pulls them down to bare her butt. His hands maul her naked ass, press into her hips, then he gropes her tits under her shirt like his hands are hungry for more. He must have her; his passion is out of control. As he crushes himself against her, his erection presses firmly, announcing his devious plans. She glances back at him and, for a split second, his face is featureless, then he's John Penn. She gasps. She wipes his face clear from her mind. No, not him. He's not right. Then he's Bridge, role-playing with her as an intruder instead.

She rubs fast up and down her slit while watching herself in the mirror. Her eyelids are heavy, closing with her own self-lust. She's going to come. Her risen clit is fully erect to match her hard tits as she savors her heightening urges. She throws back her head as she feels herself up all over her body, her hands the man's hands. The slickness of her pussy is soft as melty, but not yet liquid, butter, bleeding itself on its waxy paper wrapper. Her juices will leave their marks. Her fingers rapidly stroke along the rippled soft tissue of her pussy lips, over her bald fleshy mound, then she dives to unhood and pleasure her clit.

Relentless.

She gasps, pressing it, making herself moan out in whimpering whispers, and then primal groans that surprise even her. She narrows her eyes at herself in the mirror.

"I'm a bold little fucker with a clit to press. And I'm not giving up 'til you sing, sweets."

Picturing his hard-engorged cock bouncing before her, the faceless man switching from Bridge and back to faceless again, his manhood in his hand, blood-tinted and almost purplish-red, his skin stretched to its max, there's no doubt, it's going inside her. He's going to get his, no matter the fight she puts up. She feels small, but she's taking up every bit of his ginormously intense focus, so really, she's as big as his galaxy. He erupts in his groping of her, his primal grunts turning animalistic. Then he's her sixty-year-old neighbor with the kind eyes and dirty hands because he won't stop gardening, but his ardor is wild, and he must have her. He intends to ravish her. He mutters it as he presses his turgid cock into her quaking hole. He rides her, grunting as he gets off.

"Yes," she slurs. "Fuck my hungry slut hole. Use it."

He is silent because he's working so hard, his white hair flopping as she glances back at him. He's pounding himself into her like a horn dog. His mouth is open in a crooked snarl.

She lies back on the mat and switches the vibrator to high. She knows exactly how to drive herself to an orgasm with this blissful thing in a matter of mere seconds. The neighbor man switches again to Bridge, but she wants someone more selfish. She wants to be used like a sex doll. Imagining the man is faceless again, drilling himself into her, she mutters incoherent words. Firmly gripping the vibrating unit over her labia, she twitches, then presses it her clit.

"Fuck," she mutters as her body jerks aggressively.

Her moans escalate so quickly, her low whimpers turning into full-fledged awkward squawks like a slow, steady river current suddenly turns into rapids without warning and without any border to acknowledge, it just roars on. She slips out of her fantasy for a split second, then crashes right back into it as the man comes inside her with a beastly growl. She swirls the vibrator round and round her clit, slamming the toy into it, her moans getting so loud the neighbors might hear. This is usually the point where Bridge storms her and fucks her mercilessly, just before she's about to come. But he's not here, so she points the vibrator tip at the entrance of her vagina. With her other hand, she plays with each nipple, pulling and pinching them the way Bridge always does. She pumps the vibrator fast in and out, then pulls it back out of herself and traces her pussy lips with it up to her pussy mound. She presses the vibrator head right at the slotted dip of her mound so she can push the toy firmly and unhindered down onto her clit. Her pussy oozes.

She hums a soft moan as she runs the vibrator down to her anus and back up to her delicious, thickened organ. As she climbs the vibrator with her rocking hips, her moans grow louder, insistent, speckled with short whimpers and kitten-like mews, then she penetrates herself with the vibrator again—the man is still fucking her. He's not done. The toy vibrates the area inside her asshole too from inside her pussy, its motor is ridiculously strong, shaking her whole pelvis to jump itself into the upper levels of ecstasy. Getting so deliriously high, rising to swallow that orgasm, she moans out so crazily she fears she may scare Mags.

She pumps the vibrator into her hot pussy while riling up her G-spot. Her clit lurches, readying to launch, shattering any remnants of calm. She mounts the vast expanse of her desire, joining it to a brilliant, blinding white orgasm nudge that brings her a hint of the impending wave of delicious yum. She allows herself near the hump of the impending release. It erupts. She comes over it hard, she can't stop it, her arms drawing to her sides, legs bending, toes curling, her lips pursing as she whimpers, her body jerking along to the vaginal contractions. After she counts four contractions, she's too overwhelmed to keep counting. She slowly rides the smooth vibrator on herself, getting louder as she momentarily lets the toy toggle her too-sensitive clit, which, after climaxing, is way too sensitive for her to handle anything touching it, so she swiftly moves the toy.

Her post-cum gland is so sharp with sensitivity, it almost hurts as she dabs the vibrator on it, making her recoil and grunt out. This is where Bridge likes to torture her into the next climax. Instead, she selects her vaginal slit for post coming play to allow her clitoris a short lull in stimulation. It needs a tiny break in its tender state. She closes her eyes and hums, savoring the aftercare she's giving herself. She drops the toy back down to the lower part of her hole, nudging it just barely to enter the mouth of her vagina. Just a nuzzle. Nothing more. It hums nurturing comfort for her, and she smiles.

Her arousal is a sneaky one, though, and it noodles around in her head.

She can't resist. She pulls and tugs at her nipples almost to the level of exquisite, pinched stinging, like when she swats Bridge's hands away. She hesitates for just a moment, then the man is back partaking of her, and she dips the toy head into herself.

"Ah, fuck."

She quivers as aftershocks erupt inside her in a series of scrumptious pings. After several more pumps, she returns the vibrator to her clit again, dabs at it lightly to not overwhelm it with pain, with only a bit of pressure, a small amount is all she needs. She smirks, not unlike how it only takes a tiny bit of aged cheddar to flood the mouth with intensity. She dares a bit more pressure and lets it vibrate her womanhood. It takes on a mind of its own as it hurls her into another orgasm. Her mind hurdles toward coming as she pictures how Bridge fucked her in this very spot last night. The release of her cum flows like that familiar opening up feeling she adores.

She never gets to actually see her magic, however, but she always relishes it, nonetheless. She ought to video her pussy during coming sometime to see what it looks like. She smiles. Bridge has shared what he's seen, though.

She drops both arms to the exercise mat with a groan, the vibrator still dancing in her hand. Her face spreads into a sheepish grin. The orgasms are enough for now. She decides she's got to move on with her day as she rolls to her side. She doesn't get this far with the vibrator because Bridge is usually around, so it was exciting to do it all alone for once.

It's not the same without Bridge, though, but at least he was present in her thoughts, and the play was yummy, with a happy ending for her. Safe inside her head, she can go as dark as she wants. Something inside her runs with it, and though she's not exactly sure where all the urges came from, it always gets her off. Easily. Indulging in such things every now and then is never a bad idea.

Feeling euphoric, she sighs out the rest of the intensity of that last orgasm. She freezes. Hmmm...nah...how about one more? She grins and pushes the vibrator between her legs along her vaginal slit, riding its firmness like she rides a bicycle seat. She rolls her hips, grinds into it with a ferocious pelvic swivel, before she pushes the vibrating unit into herself once more. She moves onto her belly and pushes her ass in the air.

Not being very visual, she doesn't usually look at herself, but this time she peeks in the mirror again and groans as she watches as she fucks herself, watching the thick purple rod ride in and out of her pussy. She relishes the sloshing sounds of her wetness and cum combined with the lube. She wishes she had recorded this to send to Bridge so he could have joined in on her fun, but she's not stopping this train. Imagining him beating off to such a video helps her rise into a fat orgasm once more, which leads her to another luxurious release, causing her to shudder and her feet to curve, her toes to bend. As the orgasm tampers down, her feet come together, her legs remain flat on the mat in the shape of a diamond.

She sighs. "Wow. That was utterly fucking outstandingly downright flat-out fucking amazing," she says aloud. "The man of many faces who fucked me and got me there. And Bridge, thanks for the memories to push me to the edge."

Now she's talking to herself again. Fucking herself and talking to herself. Laughing out loud, she grins, her little secret that no one needs to ever know. She doesn't mind if Bridge knows it all, but for now, it's her own gift to herself. She feels sleepy and spent; she cuddles her body in a self-hug.

She lets out a slow, satisfied sigh. "Shower time," she whispers, feeling odd for talking to herself once more, but who cares? She sits up, notices wet spots on the mat that will need cleaning up. Dang. She giggles, smirks at her satisfied image in the mirror. "Damn. I feel invincible now." She giggles and stands up. "And crazy because I keep talking to myself." She shakes her head as she almost skips off to the shower, feeling light and airy, free, and yet wonderfully spoiled after her orgasms. It's heaven-sent, aww, dang, she feels beyond fantastic, fabulous, flippant...like a fuck-pampered goddess.

In the shower, she soaps herself up in lavender soap and lets the hot water stream down her body and drip along the full, beautiful width of her smile.

Satisfied.

# Chapter Nine

John Penn smiles as he watches her beautiful, beaming, wet face in the water stream as the steam piles up in billowy chunks of fog all about the shower stall. He had stroked off the whole time during Juniper's self fuck, edging himself along, until he had let himself come on her final climax. He had imagined his cum coating her flesh in thick strands as she squirmed in delight beneath him.

It. Was. Epic.

His filthy, wanton slut pleasuring herself makes him feel right with the world. Her sluttiness matches his own libido. They belong together. They match up so well.

Her finale is her shower, though, the fantastically satisfying epilogue to the most gorgeous display of self-eroticism he had ever seen in his entire life. She deserved every second. And it couldn't have been more perfect as they came at almost the same time. It had been a thing of beauty. He can't wait for later when re-watching his favorite parts will give him orgasmic delights. He'll come over and over again. And he'll have the video forever. But better yet, he'll have her.

He loves her so very much. She's perfect.

He can't wait to be near her again tonight. Being in her presence earlier today had been so intoxicating, he had let his heart take her scent into itself, and he knew it was never going to leave his heart. Ever.

He loves her like the river licks its bottom, hugs its curvy bends, snakes around big rocks, caresses tree trunks, suffocates the weed stems while lapping its tops in the air, the way it holds even the wisps of seaweed, massages its fish, and bubbles into rapids of passion only to rest again at the next bend. The river and its bed are one, cradling each other, just as he and Juniper fit. The river ever-caressing every speck of the sandy rocky bottom, just as he'll never stop caressing her. A few tears dare to litter his eyes.

It is a beautiful thing.

He had most certainly fallen in love with her the first time they met, and it had only grown stronger since. He never imagined himself falling in love at first sight until he had held her in his sights, Juniper, the most infinitesimally stellar person of his entire life.

She is like no other human he has ever seen before. It wasn't just the beauty of her hair pulled back in a ponytail that danced along the neckline of her shirt that day, nor just the wisps of fallen hair nuzzling her neck. It was the sparkle in her eyes, her zest for life, and her caring heart. He couldn't have written her better if she were one of his characters in his books. He had wanted her instantly, too, the joy in her laugh, the sweet pea kindness she exuded, evident in every word she spoke.

She is beyond any angel he's ever seen, and more deserving of that word than any other human he has ever met. Every day that he has watched her in his own beach house on his screens, he is blessed, and it confirms firmer in his soul, lacing up his belief that he needs her in his life because she is his very blood, his breath rolling round the deep pockets of his lungs, the very synapse that makes his brain function. He must have her. And he will. He will. He just knows it in his heart and in his brain—fuck that, he knows it in his soul. Tears spill down out of his eyes, and he wipes them away with shame.

"Men don't cry, John." His dad beaned him on the top of the head and swatted his bottom. "Now get out there and be the star of your team." Then he'd always mumble stuff John wasn't allowed to repeat.

Those sentences haunted John as far back as kindergarten, Little League, when his dad was the coach. That's what he always told him, even when he was whipping his ass, he wasn't allowed to cry. Tears were for losers, and he wasn't raising a loser. He had the God given right to beat him into a good boy.

John snorted, angry with himself. Not thinking about that fucker, he sniffled, shoving the thoughts of his dad to the back of his mind where he could control them.

He sighs. He just needs her at his side, in his life, rolling around with him in his bed so he can be fucking the shit out of her every day. He knows he cannot live without her; he's adequately, and thoroughly, absolutely, unequivocally addicted to his Juniper. This he is sure of. No adequately is the wrong word, and as a writer, he knows the importance of the right word, every time, every word, every scene.

His heart is monopolized by her, choked off like a fat hard-on in his hand ready to launch, his heart is but a dribble of dead blood without her, he's an insignificant pebble not worth a ride in anyone's shoe. She finishes him in a way he can never achieve himself. She is the integral sheath lining of his heart, the only reason allowing it to beat on. She is his reason for existing.

He just needs to woo her into seeing all this.

He watches as she folds her beautiful body into the shape of a bent-over flamingo in the shower, shaving her right leg while balancing on her left. He'd give anything to shave her legs for her, to run that sharp, dangerous edge of the razor over the delicate, fragile parts of her pussy mound and lips. He'd never cut her. Fuck no. Blood is not his kink. He'd watched Bridge shave her in a bath one night, and he had been beside himself with harsh, tender jealousy. He almost lost control. He had been so close to driving to the house with the intent to storm in, but he had stopped himself as he realized he was not very rational at that moment, and that last vodka sour had not helped his mind think clearly.

But that night, swerving when he had simply walked toward the key ring rack had fully convinced him he couldn't drive worth a shit with how drunk he had gotten. He had lain on his bed and passed out, dreaming of shaving her in his tub, occasionally weeping like a baby.

He needs to be smart, not be some dumbfuck loser.

He snaps out of those thoughts as he watches Juniper pick out clothes in her closet. She picks a sheer magenta top with a beige bra for underneath, no underwear, as she's almost always commando, except when she wears panties for Bridge to take off, and a beige pair of capris. All nicely hugging her generous, seductive curves.

She wanders to the laundry area and throws the clothes into the dryer, except for the shirt Bridge had spilled something on. She sprays the clothing again with the stain remover and lays it flat on the counter. She takes such good care of Bridge, not that he deserves it.

John stands and stretches, shoves his phone into his pocket, and walks to the kitchen to get a refill on his coffee. He puts his phone on the counter and takes a deep breath. He rakes his hand through his hair, then rubs his temples, shakes the threat of tears from his eyes. He needs to get her out of his head so he can write; his deadline is looming. He takes a sip of coffee, hoping it will clear his mouth from wanting to taste her, but no such luck. He sighs again and walks over to turn his laptop on. He has a few hours to work, but his anticipation for tonight's plan clouds his brain, and he becomes a victim of something that never happens to him...he's got writer's block.

"Juniper...I just need you."

# Chapter Ten

The doorbell rings, and Juniper sets the corkscrew on the counter. She'd been about to open a bottle of dark red Cab. She dances her way to the doorbell, jiving and gyrating to the song on her way, shaking her booty.

She flings the door open and grins at Sara, one of her very besties from college. "EEEEEEE!" she screams as her arms shoot straight up in the air.

Sara's arms fly up just as Juniper's do, ready for a hug, as she copies, "EEEEEEEEE!"

They throw their arms around each other and dance back and forth as one, Juniper's long blond hair swinging, almost mirroring Sara's long brown hair as they sway.

"Come in! Come in! Omigosh," Juniper says as she releases her friend from the hug. "You're really here! I'm so happy you could come tonight. I've been looking forward to this so very much." She clasps her hands together in front of her face and shakes them.

Sara steps into the house, does a slow whistle as she sets down her black suitcase just inside the door. "Wow! Juniper, this house is beyond amazing! I can't believe you and Bridge snagged this. And a famous author's house at that. Hol-y crap! And," she asks with a sly smile, "Have you met the amazing, famous John Penn? Is he sexy? Would you fuck him?"

Juniper bursts into a laugh, then nods exaggeratedly, still giggling with her eyes wide as she says, "Yes, well, he was actually just here, believe it or not. He really is a nice guy, but he was sporting a major chub. I. Mean. Major. Plus, he gave us all his furniture with the house. Can you believe that? Can you imagine such wealth that you don't even care about your furniture?" Juniper shuts the front door and locks it, as they don't plan to be going out anyway. She leads her friend to the kitchen and points to the bottle of wine. "Red alright?"

"Really? Wow. No, I can't imagine. And. Famous cock in your own home. You lucky bitch. See here now, I bet you could have had him if Bridge let you. And yes, any wine and all wine. I really need a glass. It's been a long day. So, back to famous dick, he's hot, and you'd fuck him?" She stares intently into Juniper's eyes with great interest and clearly on bated breath.

Juniper flickers her eyes at her friend and nods. "Yes, and yes. He's quite sexy."

"Nice," Sara says with a slow nod and a growing naughty grin. "He's creative, bet he's adventurous with sex." She raises and drops her eyebrows repeatedly. "Juniper, I'm so looking forward to a break from hearing kids scream at me. They're relentlessly needy sometimes. And I'm so looking forward to catching up with you. Adult conversation, woman to woman. I miss it." She cocks her head, widens her mocha-brown eyes. "And I need lots and lots of wine." She grins deeply, her eyes matching her words in need.

"Heck yes, and good food too. I've been cooking today to make us some yummy stuff. Stuffed mushrooms, bacon pepper poppers, a pumpkin seed cheese ball, focaccia ham and cheese finger sandwiches, and cheesecake bites. Oh, and I have some brownie bites left from the other night, too. We had food sex." Juniper raises both eyebrows twice. "Was fucking hot as fuck."

"Chocolate and sex. Hell yes." Sara sits on the stool at the island and shakes her head. "Enjoy your sex frenzies now, because once you have a baby, your time to fuck shrinks way down, even more so as they grow and stay up longer, and the times you do have, you're often too tired to do it. I know you want one, but be prepared, it will change your sex life forever." She combs a hand through her long brown hair. "I mean, we still do it, don't get me wrong, but it's not every day anymore, and we have shorter time frames to do it in, so quickies are more common, less adventure, less kink, so sometimes I masturbate with a toy for extra if I can get away alone for a few." She shakes her head. "But, damn, do I miss all that freedom of fucking whenever and wherever we want." She smirks. "Life with kids. Damn good thing they're cute."

Juniper grabs the bottle of wine, a wistful look on her face, the wedge of a tear pushing behind her eyes. She hadn't thought of all that, but she still wants a baby, regardless. "Yeah, but worth it to have a baby though, right?" She must be exaggerating. And even if not, a baby must definitely be worth a few less sex sessions. Or just try harder. Get creative. She imagines that she and Bridge would just get more creative for sure.

Sara stands and throws her arms around Juniper. "It'll happen, baby, it will. Just don't lose hope, and in the meantime, have fun fucking Bridge's brains out." She does a single heavy nod. "Mark my word, that belly will be sporting a baby soon with all the fucking you two are doing."

This makes Juniper smile wryly as she releases her friend. She's not wrong. They are constantly doing the tango. She looks down at her as she says, "Yeah, Bridge bought me a pole."

Sara's jaw drops, as do her hands, straight down her sides, her fingers outstretched like she's being electrified.

"What? No way! Shut the fuck up. Like as in a stripper pole?" She brings her fingers up to her temples and presses. "Show me. I'm so jealous, oh my gawd!" She giggles. "Your kid will use it to play fireman, then it will be too hard to fuck against anyhow, so do it now, a lot!"

Juniper chuckles as she gives the timer on the oven a quick glance before saying, "Yes, and I love it. I mean, I think he bought it for himself more than me, but I'm loving the shit out of it. Even used it myself last night." She smirks. "It's actually great for a workout, too."

Sara giggles as she follows Juniper toward the exercise room, adjusting her flowing pink top as she walks. "No, you didn't..."

Juniper nods quickly, making her hair bounce against her shoulders. "Oh, yes, I did. And it was beyond amazing. A total turn-on." She enters the exercise room and points to the stripper pole in the corner, a sigh escaping her lips as she remembers her erotic self-love session.

Sara's mouth drops open again, and her hands go to her cheeks. "You fucking lucky ass bitch! I want this, but I can't have it." She walks over to touch it, and Juniper gasps with relief, suppressing a guffaw. She's so relieved she cleaned it off this morning as her friend runs her hand down it. "Maybe we should dance for each other tonight, huh?" She giggles as she grips the pole with both hands and shakes her hips, then shimmies her boobies at Juniper with a saucy look.

Juniper chuckles. "Yeah. Well, you're hot." She puts her hands on her smooth, curvy hips and says, "Wanna get drunk and fuck?"

Both women giggle with giant, naughty smiles.

"I thought you'd never ask," Sara says in a cooing voice.

"Wish we could; those were good times, weren't they?" Sara asks with a cocked head. "I miss those carefree friends with benefits days. We should revisit that for old times' sake." She narrows her eyes as she gives Juniper her bedroom face. "Huh? Would Bridge care?"

Juniper considers her proposition. Would Bridge care? "Delicious. Yeah. Remember the time we drank two bottles of Sauvignon Blanc and shared the pizza, then sixty-nined each other until we each squirted? I didn't even know I could do that until you got a hold of me."

Sara grinds her butt crack against the pole. "Yeah, you did me damn good, too, that time. It was unforgettable. Just took lots of oral to get you there. Wine wets the tongue just right to suck a cunt, just sayin'." Sara cocks her head quickly to the right, then gyrates her pelvis at the pole. "Matt would love this, but now with kids, we can't have such a thing in the house. Kids calling it a fire station pole and playing on it would pretty much take all the sex appeal right out of it." She smirks. "Too bad we're married; we coulda had fun on this pole tonight."

Juniper laughs. "We still could and just dance...with clothes on."

"Kiss, then play, masturbate on the bed beside each other with toys?" Sara spins herself around the pole and wraps her toned, thin shin around it. She throws her head back while still holding the bar securely above her head with one hand. "We must behave, darling," she says in a syrupy, exaggerated British accent. "Randy, I say. Behaving is subjective, anyway."

Juniper nods through a giggle, holding her hand over her mouth. "We could record each other's naughty dancing and stripping and text the videos to our husbands. They might just give us the green light for more."

Sara stops spinning as a serious expression takes over. "I fucking love your brain, girlfriend. You're a genius. This will work." She stands up. "Hell, Matt would love to watch you and me fool around too, for real, but I know Bridge would freak, wouldn't he?"

Juniper turns serious. "Yes, he gets very, very jealous, which is dumb, it's not like anyone could ever replace his dick in my life; you would just be supplemental fun."

Sara stands up and puts her hands on her hips. "Don't ever say that again, or I'll bitch-slap you. I'm not anyone's supplemental;

I'm the main attraction." She points her nose in the air in indignation.

Juniper chuckles, then turns toward the kitchen as the oven timer goes off. "I know. You're right, and I love you, but nothing replaces cock in my opinion."

Sara does one more spin around the pole and then follows Juniper to the kitchen. "You have a point there; nothing better than a man slamming into your clit. But you need to try a few new toys, I'm thinking." She sighs heavily. "Fuck. I'm getting really horny with all this talk. Dang! Whew! Let's eat and drink. I need to do something with my mouth." She clears her throat. "Something satisfying." She plops her little butt on the barstool at the island. "Sorry, I'm a bit overly horny. Matt and I haven't fucked in like five days. He was a little pissed I was going to be gone tonight because he wanted to tie me to the bed and have his way with me."

Juniper pulls the pan of stuffed mushrooms from the oven, places it on the stovetop, then replaces the hot pad back on its hook next to the stove. She has no idea Sara has become so kinky. "Aw, well, shit. I'm so sorry. I hate to interfere with your sex life, especially when it's difficult with the kids."

Sara twirls her hair between her manicured fingers, admiring her red, shiny nails. She says, "Ah, it's okay. We haven't hung out in a long while, and I knew you were lonely without Bridge. Matt can fuck me tomorrow night after the kids go to bed. And he'd better do it fucking hard, I need to cum from cock." She pulls out her phone and checks it. "Those mushrooms smell amazing, by the way."

Juniper grabs the bottle of red and stabs the sharp corkscrew tip into the cork before twisting it down. "I love these mushrooms. They're going to taste amazing with this Cabernet, too." She finishes twisting the corkscrew in and pushes down the levers to pop out the cork. "Don't you masturbate, though?"

"Haven't even had time for that lately. But yeah, if it's too long between times, we both do if we can't match up free time. But I really like to wait to make it explosive when we do. Like edging, ya know?"

Juniper pours the whole wine bottle into a decanter. "Yeah, I get that. But I also like getting off daily, so, you know, I guess I always pull out my toys if Bridge is gone." She widens her pure blue eyes. "Or even if he's here. He loves to watch me fuck myself."

Sara fingers the stem of the wine glass, tossing the pink seashell charm at the bottom back and forth as she rolls her eyes. "What man doesn't? Or woman, for that matter. Maybe a dickless man wouldn't." She drops her forehead to her palm dramatically, "And. Please, please, please don't tell me you two still fuck multiple times every day, I might have to strangle you." Her freckled cheeks rise to her squinted eyes as she grins widely.

Juniper purses her lips, giving her friend fuck-me eyes. "Yeah, we do. Sometimes twice or three times. Sorry," she says with a wave of her hand. "We're both horny as fuck, I guess. We're legit rabbits. Plus, we want a baby, so, hey, it works out for many reasons."

Sara holds up her wine glass toward Juniper. "Hit me, I can't wait anymore, don't care if it's still breathing, I'm ready to get drunk as a fucking skunk and eat my way to an additional workout this weekend." She rests her free fist on the countertop, then pounds it down. Her voice comes out in a thick drawl as she says, "It smells amazing in here, darling."

Juniper pours her friend a generous glass of wine, almost to the rim, and then fills her own.

"Now that's a glass of wine. You know you're damn lucky, right? Woman, I'm telling you the truth, and I'm gonna harp on it. Take advantage because when you have that baby...fucking every day ain't gonna happen, I'm sorry to say. And twice a day? Three times? Forget it. Not happening."

Juniper tosses off her comment and takes the seat next to her friend, pulling the cheeseball plate toward them. "Oh, I will enjoy it now. We've been doing it on the beach a lot since we moved in, too. I love that. Hearing the waves during sex is awesome. Or we swim or use the hot tub and crawl out to fuck wet in the warm breeze. I can't ever get tired of listening to those waves." Juniper scoops a round water cracker through the soft cheeseball. "You brought your suit, right?"

Sara nods. "Yes, still working on my mom belly reduction, but I brought it. Don't laugh or I'll stab you with this...what the fuck is this anyway?" She holds up the long, black, shiny, tapered, curved bar by its square base. She turns it around while examining it closely. "Do we really need suits, though?"

"No." Juniper pops the cracker in her mouth and chews, shaking her head vehemently. "I don't know what that thing is. Some kind of sculpture, I guess. It came with the house. It's some kind of polished long rock, I think. Odd art. Sorta elegant, but looks like a skinny boner to me, with a nice G-spot curve."

Sara smirks as she fingers it along its length, rubbing her fingers up to and over the pointed tip. "Or a healthy log of shit. Maybe a fucking dagger!" She smirks as Juniper cracks up.

"Shit or a weapon." Juniper's eyes light up with the joy of her laughter. "I will never look at it the same again, thanks a lot. Now I've got a petrified shit statue on my kitchen counter. Great." She rolls her eyes as another wave of laughter takes over her beautiful face. "You always could make me laugh, you know that? I miss the shit out of you."

"You know where the garbage can is," she says, rolling her eyes, then snorts. She sets it down and then takes a sip of wine. "Yeah, me too, missing the shit out of you. Remember that's how I got your pants off the first time we fucked, you remember that night?"

Juniper almost spits out her mouthful of wine. "Do I? Oh, my gawd, how could I forget? You were on point that night with your humor. I practically laughed them off."

Sara scoops cheese from the cheeseball onto a cracker. "Easy peasy. Yeah, I totally planned it ahead of time, you know. Have I ever told you that? Like I typed out my routine, what I was going to say. I played you hard, seduced the fuck out of you, and it paid off."

Juniper looks at her wine glass as she traces the top edge of it with her finger before glancing at her friend, the full realization shocking her. "Um. No. You didn't...ever tell me that. No," she says with a surprised grin.

Sara chuckles, drawing her legs up to sit cross-legged on the stool. "I so did. You were hot as all fuck, still are, and I wanted you, even though we were friends."

Juniper takes a sip of her wine. She gives a single nod with a pleasant expression. "Friends with benefits." She raises her eyebrows several times as her grin becomes salacious. "You taught me all about that, my friend. It taught me about my own body, to be honest."

Sara touches Juniper's arm and rubs it. "Yeah, it was wonderful, wasn't it? Until a couple of dicks broke us up, literally." She crawls her fingers up Juniper's arm. "Damn, bitch you have some soft skin. What do you use?"

Juniper shakes the hair off her face. "Coconut oil. I use it all the time. Stuff is amazing. I slather it all over myself, put it in my hair, and even cook with it. Plus, it's great for foreplay and a sex tool."

Sara clears her throat. "Yeah, and anal."

Juniper chokes down her gulp of wine. "You didn't?"

Sara lets out a big sigh. "Did. Now I love it." Sara tucks her hair behind her ear. "And so does Matt. Coconut oil is like a miracle product. I got into it after Jackson was born. We were both horny and nothing was fulfilling us, and I was still healing after the birth, so vaginal sex wasn't gonna happen for weeks, so one day I told him we could try it. He'd been wanting to for years, and I was terrified of it. But I got used to it, had to build up to it gradually, though, with plugs, and then I even began to crave it. Enjoy it." She pops a cracker into her mouth. "Believe it. It makes me cum hard. And now he eats my ass too." She grins. "Literally, my pussy drips. Not kidding."

Juniper's eyes are wide. She plays with her wedding ring, twisting it, her eyes shifting back and forth. Her nerves light up. "Yeah, we haven't gone there, except a little bit of ass play, ya know, fingers, licking, but no anal sex. Honestly, I think Bridge would like it. Fucking terrifies me too much, though. We tried it once when we first started dating, and it hurt so bad, I said never again."

Sara touches her lips, squints one eye at Juniper. "Need lube and go slow. Like over a long, long, long time, like weeks. Coconut oil is your friend." She chomps a cracker. "You could start with a small toy or anal beads to condition you. Some like it right away, others over time, others hate it and never get into it." She grins with a wink. "I read a lot of sex stuff." She rubs her hands together to get the cracker crumbs off. "You may be one who never likes it, babe. And that's okay."

Juniper shudders. "I don't know. I'm not convinced it could ever feel good." She pours more wine into her glass, then refills Sara's. The whole idea kind of disgusts her, but a tiny part is curious, too. But she's not curious enough to try it.

"Thanks," she says, picking up her glass and tipping it toward Juniper. She uncrosses her legs and puts her foot on the footrest on the island. "You're missing out, though. I love it now. You should at least try it. You might like it."

Juniper visibly cringes, and a ripple of a shiver travels through her whole body. "The mere thought of it gives me the willies. I hate it. Maybe it's because I'm a nurse and I feel like it would mess up taking a shit. I mean, part of what I do is make sure my patients aren't constipated. Anal sex is completely counterintuitive to healthy bowel movements and the sphincter."

Sara cracks up. "Okay, Ms. nurse prude and nerdy." She's laughing so hard her body tips, and she almost falls off the stool. "Seriously! But hey, we don't do it that often to make it a serious problem. I wouldn't do that." She grimaces. "No diapers, no thanks."

Juniper shudders. "Well, it's true. No way. No, thank you. Ever." She laughs as she shudders again.

"Wine messes with your health, too, and that doesn't stop you from downing bottles like you breathe." Sara stabs her finger at Juniper's bicep in a teasing poke. "I'm right, and you know it."

Juniper shakes her head. "Maybe, yeah. But the difference is, I enjoy wine." She rapidly shakes her head, waving both hands back and forth in front of her face. "Okay. New topic. I can't take this anymore. No more ass talk. I might start legit gagging. So, tell me about your new toy."

"Well, it doesn't mess me up at all. I can take cock in the ass the same way as in my pussy. Both different, but both good."

Juniper allows her annoyance to bloom on her face as she does an exaggerated shudder, complete with a look of horror.

"Hmmm," she says. "Ass ain't pussy, and it don't have a clit, friend. It's not the same thing." She shakes her head vigorously. "Not the same thing even remotely."

Sara struggles to swallow the wine in her mouth due to her raucous laughter.

Juniper is at the ready with a napkin in hand in case the wine flies back out.

Sara manages to swallow the gulp, hard, then coughs. "Shit. You're killing me. That was touch and go. I almost didn't get that down. You're too funny." She laughs again. "Don't turn into a prude on me, now we're in the prime of our midlife, Juniper."

Juniper drops her jaw. "I'm in no way a prude just because anal makes me want to wretch. Come on! That's not fair," she protests. "We each get to like what we like and avoid what we want to." She gives her friend a joking, shocked look, only she's not kidding. "Now tell me your review of that toy."

"Oh, yeah. I was going to tell you about that, wasn't I?" Sara wipes saliva and wine from the corner of her mouth with her thumb and index finger, squeezing them from the corners of her mouth and meeting them up in the middle of her lips as a final swipe. "It's amazing. Fucking incredible."

"Ok, so spill it already. I can't wait." Juniper walks over to the pan of stuffed mushrooms and scoops them all onto a plate. "These are cooled off now. We can eat while you tell me all about it." She carries the plate over to the island and sets it between them, noting they look picture-perfect, also telling herself to stop trying to be perfect. She grabs one and pops it in her mouth, following it with wine to savor the flavors together.

"These look amazing, right out of a damn culinary magazine. I've always been jealous of your ability to cook. Bet Bridge loves it." Sara daintily picks up a mushroom and places it in her mouth, and groans as she chews. "Babe, these are beyond amazing. Stellar," she says in a muffled voice over the mushrooms still filling her mouth. "I mean, wow. This is restaurant quality. You should have been a chef."

"Thanks. Yeah, Bridge loves my cooking. I love to do it, really. It's fun." Juniper pops another one in her mouth and chews. "Yep.

So yummy." She points her painted toenails to express her enjoyment, rolling her eyes as she savors it.

Sara claps her hands. "Okay. Toy. It's got a clit rubbing part that's shaped like a pitchfork, clit finger way shorter and smaller, and it...well it's a classic rabbit vibrator but with an app that can control it from a phone, laptop, or even with the buttons on the unit so it's great for foreplay, solo play, or post intercourse play, if he happens to cum before me, which happens to him more and more lately." She rolls her eyes. "Premature ejaculation is becoming a thing."

"Wow. Yeah. I need that with Bridge gone. We could play long-distance. I've thought about one of those, too, but I didn't know they made rabbit vibrators equipped with it."

"Exactly. It's versatile. It's killer because it hits your G-spot and clit at once. It's the best toy ever."

"I might need to do some online shopping tomorrow," Juniper says with a grin. "You've convinced me."

JOHN SIPS HIS WHISKEY as he once again replays the video where the women talk about fucking him and him being sexy. His cock is packed turgid with blood, watching Juniper nod.

Oh, fuck, Junie. Whew. He can't ask for a better piece of delicious video, other than her talking about him like that. Holy shit. That's priceless. Fucking gold.

Hell yes, he's adventurous with sex; he'll do anything and everything she wants. Anything. He's probably more of a sex freak than she is, but whatever she is, it's perfect, and he'll do it. He'd pleasure her first, make sure she came first every time before him, every damn time they fucked. She'd be so satisfied she would never want to leave him, never want for more sexually, ever. Every wish of hers, every fantasy, all would be fulfilled, every desire met whenever she wanted it. It would be his mission in life to make her moan and cum in his arms. He'd want anal, but he'd never force her into it. He wouldn't need it. He needs her, not her butthole. He'd let her call the shots on when, where, and how they fucked, not that he wouldn't ask, but it would always be her decision. He'd just be happy to be able to really fuck her for real.

"Tonight, Junie, tonight. I'm going to lie next to you in bed, while you sleep, and imagine fucking you while I jerk off. You'll be out cold again from too much wine, and I'll be having fun for the both of us." He smirks. "For now, that is."

He pours himself some more whiskey and takes a sip, contemplating a shot of something stronger, anything, vodka or tequila. Something to build his buzz to a solid front. He's considering whether he should drive and park far away or take a lift, but he doesn't want any eyes on him, though, so maybe driving and bringing a disguise as he walks up to the house would be the best idea. He's no fool. He can't take any chances at all. He strokes his cock as he watches the two lovely women chatting, planning their naughty fun in the exercise room. Now that's going to be a show, and he's planning to actually be in the house watching from the room for all of that juicy hoopla. It will be delicious and a true sexual odyssey of their two female minds, and with Sara, it seems there may be new ground for Juniper sexually, being that she's now married as they play, and he can't wait to be a witness to it.

# Chapter Eleven

After their feast of delicious homemade appetizers, cheesecake, and a brownie bite apiece, Juniper checks her text messages, online feed, and email while sitting on the deck listening to the waves, while Sara takes her shower. She hadn't had one for the day yet and begged Juniper for some time to indulge. That is totally fine with Juniper; it gives her some time alone to unwind on a full belly, at the seaside.

At times, she relishes moments like this—just her, the waves, and the salty air. The rush and roar of the wind across the ever-rolling ocean is so soothing and one of the best parts of living on the ocean. She needs to pinch herself to make sure this is real. Being one with her thoughts of the moment is a state of being that she seeks for mental recharge.

She smirks, thinking about her last self-pleasuring session and how much fun it had been. All by herself, and it had been so beautifully satisfying. Her thoughts had gone immediately to Bridge, as usual, watching Juniper dance on the pole. It had been so erotic; she had wanted to repeat it, and without him there, thinking about him during it had been the next best thing for her self-fun. She could feel her urge to use her vibrator later spinning to high mode in her gut. She knew one thing for sure, that toy was going to live on her until she came like that mighty wave smashing against the sand out on the shore, frothy and fussed into foaming white bubbles, churned up with the turbulence of delicious enjoyment, her curled lust unfurling in liberation ushering every pore of her being into euphoria, and blasting her pussy into convulsing wetness. And doing it next to Sara while she plays gives an added layer of excitement. So, there's that to look forward to. She's never been one to buy into the shame society forces on women about sexual pleasure; as far as she is concerned, it's her birthright.

Mags stretches her furry legs in the evening sun, rolling to her side and remaining there, barely opening her eyes. Juniper smiles at her little kitty. She is just such a joy to have, and having her company helps when she is missing Bridge something fierce.

"Boo," Sara says, coming out onto the deck in a plush beige bath towel, a full, generous glass of wine in her hand.

Juniper grins at her friend. "Enjoy your shower?"

Sara bows partially while trying to keep her wine glass from spilling, her brown eyes warm and smothered in mischief. "Nice showerhead. A fabulous, happy ending came from all those streams of hot, steamy spray." She flashes Juniper her eyes. "I know you want to know."

Juniper purses her lips and then laughs as Sara walks to the edge of the deck and drops her towel, giving Juniper a nice view of her cute little full moon and a full visual of the rose tattoo on her upper right ass cheek. Where Juniper is soft and curvy, Sara is slender, petite, and doll-like. Juniper has the birthing hips, despite no actual birthing, but holy fuck does Bridge love to grab them and fuck her from behind. Whereas Sara's hips are sleek and slim, she's still solidly feminine and sexy.

"Tattoo still looks good," Juniper says through a grin.

"I show you my nicely toned, perfect ass, and all you talk about is my old as fuck damn tattoo? Some friend you are." Sara snorts playfully, then turns and gives Juniper a full view of her perky tits and perfectly smooth pussy, too. She pinches her breast tips with both hands. "Miss them?"

Juniper nods. "Yeah, I do." She has missed them, actually. She isn't sure if she's truly bisexual or not; maybe she's just bi-curious for the acts, more like a demisexual, but she sure loved fucking Sara in college. The change was a welcome one, even if it was just for the sake of adventure. "Just for fun, do you want to do the videos now?"

Sara crosses her arms under her breasts and tips her hip to one side. "Yeah, why do you think I'm naked? And it will definitely be fun." She gives Juniper a sexy grin, then wiggles her body seductively. "I'm still turned on from my playing in the shower."

"Well, I thought we'd strip for the video, seeing it's a stripper pole," Juniper smirks at her naked friend. "Maybe you need to get dressed."

"Pfft. Well, we could just be pole dancers." She shrugs, then puts her hands on her hips in a huff. "You strip, I'm already naked, so I'm dancing sans clothes." She pulls a chunk of hair over her right nipple to tease it. "Though I could put my thong on. That's hot to wear with no bra, and be totally nude otherwise."

Juniper stands up and stretches. "Yes, something extra naughty about having bottoms and no top, even just a thong. Ever fantasized about being a topless waitress?" She slides the screen door open and ushers Mags back in the house with her foot.

"Yes, and role-played it, too."

"Same. I did it once, serving Bridge dinner. It was a hot, sexy blast. And you obviously know how it ended." She scoffs. "We ate cold food. Hey. Let's get more wine. The food has killed our buzz." Juniper glides over to the kitchen and selects a fresh bottle of wine from the wooden rack. "You going to sit that naked ass on my bar stools?" Juniper raises an eyebrow as Sara rises to sit.

"I just took a shower, my dear clean freak of a friend...so this ass is crystal clean." She grins as she pops a cracker into her mouth. "You could eat off it, and I'd let you do that." She smiles her naughtiest smile. "Matt won't mind. He'll think it's hot if you do that to me. He'll want to hear all about it."

"I'm not eating your ass, Sara, so don't ask." Juniper rolls her eyes over a grin. "No thanks."

"Just saying you could. I scrubbed this booty good." She laughs. "You could slurp your wine off it. I'd let you. And I'd reciprocate." She maneuvers to wave her naked booty in Juniper's view.

Juniper cracks up and doubles over. "No." She straightens up and brings the corkscrew to her lips to hide her laugh. "Stop. I'm not doing it, you dork."

"Just saying it's hot and right here. Ready for the licking. Pretty sure Bridge wouldn't mind. We could video that and send it to the men, too. They'd love it."

Juniper giggles. "You are terrible. And no way." She opens the bottle of wine and pours them each a generous glassful. "I have to say, your tits still look amazing, even after having your babies. You breastfed, right?"

"Yeah. But I wore a bra twenty-four seven. My youngest wouldn't get off my tit until he was almost two and a half." She rolls her eyes.

"Well, it clearly didn't hurt your boobs any; you still look amazing." She lets a saucy grin take over her face. "Your husband drank from you? I don't know why, but that's kind of hot."

Sara sips her wine. "Oh, hell yeah, he did. He loved it too. Suckled my tits just like my babes. It actually helped me make more milk, so I let him. It was nice having bigger tits for a while." She winks. "Can't wait to see yours again, baby. You always had such hot handfuls, teardrop-shaped breasts, and your big crinkly nipples always made my clit hard sucking on them. I haven't had a good female nip licking in a while now." She cracks up as Juniper shrugs, suppressing a grin. "I'm due. Women just know how to eat pussy naturally; some men learn to be kickass at it, but women are just naturals."

"Not happening, sweet pea," Juniper says, ending with a cough, though if Bridge didn't mind, she'd really enjoy it. Maybe...

Juniper tops off Sara's glass of red wine.

"You're trying to get me drunk so you can lick this ass, aren't ya?" Sara plays with her left nipple. "It's yours. I don't need to be drunk." She winks.

Juniper walks around the island with the bulb of the wine glass nestled in her right palm. She takes a seat next to Sara. "Give you some wine and a shower and you turn into a horndog anal whore, huh?" Juniper takes a sip of wine; the flavor is bold with a rogue punch packaged in a shade of deep red. "Besides, if I did anything, it's gonna be chowing down on those tits and devouring your pussy, not probing your butthole with my tongue." Juniper rolls her eyes, then shudders. "I'm not into anything ass play."

"I'm always into it all. I think I must have extra hormone producers in me, or something." Sara's smile simmers as she flicks her long brown hair over her shoulders so her locks cover her entire back in a lush veil. "And you know it." She taps her finger in the air. "And you aren't being realistic, by the way. You are into ass play, you and Bridge do spanking stuff."

"True, we do. And true, you always have been." Juniper takes another sip of wine. "This wine is really robust and rich. I like it. You?"

Sara finishes swallowing her generous sip and nods. "It really is. I'd buy this one again."

Sara slides off the cushioned seat, making Juniper cringe as her bare ass swipes the seat. She hides her repulsion as best she can.

She smiles at her friend. "Damn, you are bold, aren't you? Wiping your naked butt on my chair like that." She's getting significantly buzzed now after chugging her wine.

Sara dances, shaking her hips, shimmying her little titties. "Yes. Now let's dance. You need to get over this ass phobia thing of yours." She shakes her finger at Juniper as she starts sauntering her naked body toward the exercise room. "My cunt wants that pole. Now."

Juniper giggles. "You talk so sweet. Just like a porno title." She hops off her seat. "And, so, you have an ass fetish. I have an ass aversion. So be it."

Sara shrugs and grins. She snickers as she crushes her breasts closer together with her biceps. "That probably is a porn title, too, I'm guessing. No doubt. Sometimes I want to make a porno. Ever considered?" She watches her own breasts as she moves.

"Which one is the title?"

"Oh, both would be good titles." She smirks. "Hey. My cunt wants that pole. Two meanings of pole, and so, you have an ass fetish. All fabulous porn titles."

Sara dances her way to the pole, shaking her booty for the mirror and watching herself. She skips like a kindergartener the rest of the way to the pole, making her pert nips jump. "I'm a porn star first. I kinda want both of those titles for my porno." She grabs the pole high above her head with two hands and pivots her body around it, making a complete circle, her tits facing in, her ass out, her feet scurrying along to keep up with her swinging body. She slaps her tits against the brass, making sexy, hot skin-slapping sounds.

"You'd better hurry and get that phone ready. I'm gonna dance my pussy to all-out wetness and then some before you even start the video, my friend." Her words at the end come out slurred.

Juniper sets down both wine glasses on the little table next to the treadmill and selects some music for Sara to dance to. "How about this one? Kiss?"

"Yeah, hurry. I can't wait to show the video to Matt."

"Patience, patience, my little horny one. Is this song gonna work?" Juniper flips her phone around so it's the right way and taps in her code to open it. She aims it at Sara and says, "Action." Juniper walks closer to her, stalking her dancing body like a true adult film star actress.

Sara nods to the music, her perky tits bouncing along, her dark brown nipples in solid, stiff, pointed peaks. "Good choice of song, babe. Next one, give me that getting-off song." She gyrates her naked body at the pole and then leans in and touches her pussy to it, opening her labia with her fingers before fully pressing her pussy slit flush, then she jerks back like the metal is hot. "Not yet, pussy baby, not yet. Whew! I need to edge." She pats her mound and lets a laugh rip. "Damn, I'm getting too close to coming already, having you watch me like this, baby Junes." She twirls her body around the pole while holding onto it above her head, her arms fully straight up, making her breasts taut and stretched. She pivots and gyrates her pelvis at the rod as she spins around it, then shakes her hips, throws her head back. She flips her back in an arching lean, then springs upright with a snap, licks her lips, and bites it, letting it slowly pop back out of her mouth.

"I'm wet as fuck. Saucy, Juniper, Matt, oh, really wet, I'm positively soupy right now." She releases her grip and plays with her nipples, pulling them straight out from her body, making the areolas stretch out far as she tugs. "Might need you to suck these for me now, baby."

Juniper giggles at her friend. She won't lie; she's very tempted to wrap her lips around her friends' titties and just suckle, make her moan and writhe like she used to. The thought gives Juniper's pussy a jolt, and as she walks, her labia slide against each other quite easily, arousing her further.

Sara reaches down and rubs her pussy mound, then snakes her finger between the slit and on down to her clit, which she rubs vigorously while letting out moans. "Oh, fuck. For you, all this for you, Matt." She makes direct eye contact with the camera, then with Juniper as she mashes, pulls, and rubs her lower lips. "And for Juniper. Want some tasty precum? Matt wants to see that." Then, she turns back toward the pole, leans forward with her thighs spread, knees slightly bent, grabs it, and smashes her pussy to it, sufficiently smacking it to the tune of her luscious oral sounds, as if she's fucking it. She rides her wet little hummer on the pole, sliding up and down, grinding fast as she moans and whimpers. She's making an erotic spectacle of herself.

Juniper's heart is pounding as her pussy wets itself. She does a silent laugh as Sara's pussy actually makes a sloshing sound on the pole. "Oh my gosh, you sound so wet, Sara." Sara is turning her on so heavily, Juniper wishes she could fuck her tonight.

Sara moans as she continues, apparently unable to converse. She grunts, then stands up, groping her tits with her hands, yanking at her nipples repeatedly, making her lips pucker like she's giving a kiss. She licks her lips, grunting. She flips around to spread her butt cheeks wide. She points her ass at Juniper, then jiggles her cheeks, one in each hand. "Get a close-up, Junie...come on. For Matt." She smacks her ass cheeks, one at a time. "Get it, get my ass, get a close-up deep in my ass crack. Get video of my hole. It's throbbing and gaping. Matt, it needs you." She barely gets the words out as she pants, her chest heaving in a way that's driving Juniper even crazier with want, the solid desire to rub her own pussy growing almost unbearable.

She might flip a switch and beg Bridge to allow this to happen.

Juniper gasps and cracks up. "Oh my gosh, Sara. I'm seriously videoing your asshole." And strangely not minding it, must be the wine. She sighs. She really is too clinically anal about buttholes, but being a nurse, that seems to come with the job. Juniper cracks up nervously, trying to deny her fear of all things entering the anus, while Sara is glorifying it right in front of her eyes, poking at her own hole. She's shaking the phone up and down. "I'm getting some shitty video here." She laughs, but how can she not? "Oh. That's just wrong." She cracks up like a maniac as Sara sticks two fingers up her butt and pumps them. "Sara, oh, my, you're hysterical. You're killing me."

Sara stops finger-butt-fucking herself and saunters over to Juniper, swaying her hips to the new song. As she looks right into the phone, she says, "Matt, tell Juniper to fuck me, like the old days." She puts her tit right up to the phone, and pinches it, moaning, offering up an extreme close-up. "We'll video our fuck session and send it to you and Bridge."

Juniper's laugh bubbles up from her wine-soaked gut and out of her puckered lips. She looks at Sara through her fingers over her left eye as she giggles. "Sara, behave," she warns her friend, shaking her head. She's craving rubbing Sara's crinkled-up brown areola with her tongue. But. No. She's not fucking Sara. Not now. Too weird. It's been too long for such things. She did that in the past, but now it's over. She's all about Bridge now, and that's how it will stay. But she's certainly loving indulging in all the raunchiness!

Sara turns her backside to Juniper and spreads her ass cheeks again and taps her finger on her butthole, then whispers into the phone, "Matt. Fuck me now, you big hoebag slut of a man. Make me your ass slave. Use my hole." She dips her finger into her butthole for a few more pumps, then turns toward Juniper. She nods toward the corner and points.

Juniper bobs her head in agreement, following Sara closely, zooming the video to get the best possible close-up shot of her ass. "Let me ass play with you, Junie. I'll be very gentle."

Juniper freezes and stops walking, stalled by the thought of that actually happening; she's petrified. Nope.

She glances back at Juniper, frozen in place. "Come on, sweetheart, keep following me. Don't worry, I won't do anything you don't want, love. But I have the perfect skinny butt plug for you. Or I can use my pinky. If you want; if not, hey, no biggie, babe."

Juniper's heart is slamming against her chest. She sort of wants to fuck Sara, but she fears Bridge will be pissed. Unless she asks him for permission, and if he's okay with it, maybe, just maybe. But ass stuff is out of the question.

After a few more minutes of Sara gyrating to the music, not touching herself to continue edging, she dances all the way over to the corner. Once there, she unabashedly mounts her bean with her hand in an intense rubdown quickie, working herself like a madwoman while moaning and groaning.

Electric jolts zing across Juniper's clit as her breathing rate increases.

Sara's legs shake as her body clenches, curling, she buckles. Her chin drops closer to her chest, and her body convulses, and yep, she's coming. She lands on the floor in a heap, panting heavily and gasping. "Fuck," she mutters.

Juniper's mouth drops open, a bead of drool slips out the corner, and she swipes it away, embarrassed, but so turned on she's ready to charge her friend and suck every bit of her skin to make her come again. Her clit is literally throbbing, begging to be touched. She gasps, trying to get the feeling to go away, but it persists, nagging her with a growing want to give in and fuck her friend. She contemplates calling an intermission and texting Bridge. If she gets his okay, she could give in and suckle Sara's pussy.

The realization hits her. Time to get real. Fuck. She wants that to happen so badly.

Sara falls into a pile on the floor. Her eyes are half-closed. She's a sight to behold, looking like she's undergone a big ordeal. Her grin tries to emerge while sucking her own fingers. She grins at the phone Juniper's holding at her waist, and then up at Juniper as she threads her tongue through her open middle and index finger, bouncing on her bent legs above the exercise mat.

"Yummy. Want a taste?" Sara continues to lick her fingers seductively, slipping her tongue all over her digits, down the crevice between each one, and generously sucking the length.

Juniper wants her like she craves meat when starved, like she wants to sink into the hot shower and let the water touch every speck of her mound, every crevice, each inch of her sweet intimate lips, every ripple and dip in her flesh. She wants her clit on Sara's like they did in college, scissoring each other, fingers constantly moving and slicked, their sensuous, supple, hardened buttons knocking on each other until they both come.

Then the calmness afterward.

The lovely, sensual snuggling, breasts cuddling, their heartbeats slowing as their arms encircle each other, breathing returning to normal as the linger of their orgasms soaks the air around them thick like a lingering gasp.

Sara was the one who actually taught her to come, and she's been forever grateful. She had enlightened her so much about the importance of letting go and accepting pleasure. Juniper credits Sara with the birth of her understanding of the joy of sex, and the magnificent abilities of her female anatomy. Bridge helped too, of course, but Sara was the launching pad of it in her youth.

Sara returns to the center stage of her video, the pole, as Juniper backs up, still videoing at a good distance, trying to get the best video shots. Sara laughs and does a twirl and pinches her nips, takes a slap of her own right ass cheek, her face full of a naughty grin. She's having the time of her life.

"Good for you, my Matt, as it was for me?" She kisses the air between herself and Juniper's phone. "Stop the video," she commands. She does a sideways flat-hand motion in front of her neck, then stands with both hands on her hips. "Now send that to both our husbands, and get ready to strip, my Junie. Bridge will be begging for it."

"Both?" Juniper asks with a look of shock. Bridge too? No, not both. Shit.

"Yes, both. They will like it. It's safe; it's just us four, so don't worry." Sara saunters over to her wine and chugs the entire glass. "I need more now." She stumble-walks out of the exercise room and makes a direct line drive to the wine rack.

Juniper downs her whole glass of wine, then mumbles, "If we are sending this to both, I need more damn wine." Juniper strolls to the kitchen after Sara, swinging her empty wine glass in her right hand.

Sara pulls out a bottle from the wine rack and then stretches up on her tippy toes looking for the bottle opener in the cupboard above the sink, her little booty cheeks bunching up taut as she tries to make herself as tall as possible. "Juniper, where's the corkscrew?" she asks in a whiny, desperate voice.

"It's already out on the counter, there by the sink." Juniper sucks the last drip of her wine off the rim. "I'm going to need to chug a glass to relax me if we're sending this to both of our men." She shakes her shoulders in a shudder, trying to wrap her brain around getting ready for her turn in front of the camera. "And you should grab a snack, or you are going to crash."

Sara screws the corkscrew in and pushes down the lever to pop the cork out. Juniper admires Sara's breasts; they are so perky, being smaller. It's like she can't look away. I guess that's the long-term benefit of smaller boobs; they stay perky. She smirks as she glances at her own jugs.

She pulls the cork off the skewer with a jerk, making her tits jiggle. She catches Juniper watching them. She pops a brownie bite into her mouth and chews sensuously.

"See. A snack. Legit food." She points at her tits. "And these are yours if you want them, you know that, right?" She shimmies her chest at Juniper as she puts the cork between her teeth and bites it, leaving it there and shaking her head. "Grrrr," she says. She pulls out the cork and places it on the counter. "You and Bridge ever talk about swinging? Matt and I would totally do you both."

Juniper lets out a fast snort-laugh with widened eyes. "Oh. My. Gosh. We've never talked about that."

Sara pours her wine glass full to the rim and then dances over to Juniper to fill hers.

"Drink up, sexy buttercup," she says, then follows it with an air kiss at Juniper. "Maybe you should. We could all help in making you two a baby."

Juniper normally would feel bad about that comment, but the thought of conceiving while doing a foursome is too hilarious to have any bad feelings about. Matt would clearly need to wear a condom, though. Or not fuck her. She's not having any question about who her baby's daddy will be. No way.

"Wow. When you put it that way, maybe I should talk to Bridge about that. Sounds rather fucking hot as fuck." She takes a very large swallow of wine into her mouth and works hard to get it all down, then hacks as it turns rough.

"You should. We would. And these videos could be the start of it." Sara plops her naked butt down on the stool and slips a cracker into her mouth. "See. I'm eating. Again. You gonna be ready soon? I can't wait to video your naked bod."

"That sounds insane, but fun. Matt could wear a condom, or not enter me, I guess." Juniper sits on the stool next to her friend. "And. Yes. I need more spiked grape juice if I'm dancing for three sets of eyes." She grins at her friend. "Man, you've got me thinking of a foursome baby-making session. I can't believe this. Only you, Sara. That's really rather fucking hot. But honestly, Bridge kinda gets jealous, so I don't know how that would work." She smirks. "But a breeding foursome romp, fuck, that's hot as fuck."

"Well, we can accommodate that. We could have Matt not touch you, only me and you go at it. Or rules, like Matt doesn't stick his cock in you, but can do other things. Bridge wouldn't be too jealous for that, would he?"

"Fuck, I have no idea, Sara; we've literally never talked about that kind of stuff, like ever. But I've really been craving a threesome or something." Juniper takes another sip of her wine while darting her eyes from Sara to her wine glass. "Not that Bridge isn't enough. He's actually an amazing lover. But a threesome would be hot. And Matt not penetrating me, that would probably be smart to prevent Matt from being my baby's daddy by accident. Oh my gosh, can you imagine what a disaster that would be?"

Sara nods with a big chuckle. "Yeah, that would not be cool. But seriously. I think it's time we consider this, then. Who knows, maybe Bridge would be up for it. I'd sure as fuck let his hot bod fuck me. Matt would allow it. If we all talked about it extensively." She eyes up Juniper. "The question is, would you though?"

Juniper swallows her wine, then raises her eyebrows. "I mean, I think I wouldn't mind it. I've never done anything like that before. But that would be weird if Matt can't touch me. Would he and I just watch when you and Bridge went at it?" She can't believe her brain is going where it's going.

Sara nods. "Or, you and I both on Bridge, and Matt just watches. He wouldn't mind. He'd just edge himself, I'm sure. Besides, he likes watching people fuck, he wouldn't be put out if that's the way Bridge would want to play." Sara plays with the little pink pearl charm on her wine glass stem. Juniper smirks as she realizes Sara changed it. "Would you let Matt fuck you if Bridge said it was okay, though?"

Juniper takes in a big breath and lets it out slowly. "I think so. Wow. This is a lot to consider. A lot to think about." Her heart rate isn't slowing down one bit; in fact, it's raging.

"Well, don't stress about it. Just let it roll around in your head for a bit and let your lust suck on it." She grins and points to her right erect nipple. With a giggle, she says, "To think about tit." She cracks up. "I mean it." She pauses. "I do think the snacks have helped me. Right?"

Juniper cracks up. "Oh no, you didn't, you meant tit. I know you." She stands up, feeling juiced up enough to be the star of the next round of entertainment.

Sara smirks and hops off her stool. "Guilty. I'm guilty as fuck. You know me too well, Junie. Now, let's go and get your video on."

"Should we wait and send them both videos at the same time?" Juniper asks in an unsure voice. She needs to follow Sara's lead on this stuff.

"Yes," Sara says. "Hang on. I gotta pee first."

As she walks by, she swats Juniper on the ass. "Spank you, my pretty." She makes a clicking sound with her tongue. "More on that later."

Juniper grins, shaking her head.

# Chapter Twelve

Juniper scrolls on her phone while she waits for Sara. She's taking a long time in the bathroom, so she's wondering if she fell asleep in there. Juniper pops a brownie bite in her mouth, chews, and swallows it with a chaser of the luscious berry-loaded red wine. After a few more minutes, Sara finally saunters into the room, a gleeful grin on her face.

"You fall asleep in the bathroom or what?" Juniper grins with a teasing look.

"Nope. I was taking naughty pictures and sending them to Matt. I told him it's a preview of something hotter to come." She spins and throws her arms into the air and almost falls down.

"Careful," Juniper steadies her friend. "Or our fun will be done."

"I'm good. Ms. Worrywart." She steadies herself with her arms out. "And Matt is in for the foursome. Just need to convince Bridge now." She grins saucily. "Get your best lingerie on, suck him off, and beg for it. Make him so happy he'll have to agree."

Juniper shrugs, then follows Sara back into the exercise room. She's a bit reluctant to be daring with Sara, but a lot horny, and now also plagued with a giant load of apprehension about asking Bridge for a foursome.

Sara is sashaying her slim hips and rubbing them with her hands. Being hugely aroused will help Juniper with the dancing act for three sets of eyes, no doubt. Juniper watches Sara's seductive, sexy dancing. It comes so easily for her, like it's her second nature.

Juniper is impressed with how open Sara is. She's even more adventurous now than she was in college, which makes Juniper seem stuck. What new things has she tried lately? She's turning into a frump.

Juniper sets her wine glass next to Sara's on the little table and turns around, but then abruptly turns back to take one last large gulp. Her desire for Sara is mounting, winning against her resistance to give in to her. It might just win the battle. The wine is helping her relax.

"Good wine is not meant to be gulped. I should be spanked for chugging this expensive stuff." She shakes her butt at Sara, stripping and dropping her clothing pieces to the floor one by one as she walks. She's not really enticing Sara to spank her, but she wouldn't likely refuse such a thing either.

"Oh, I could do that and video at the same time if you want it." Sara smirks and waves her open hand at Juniper, slapping the air on repeat. "I'm ready to slap that curvy butt, just order me when to do it. I'll be your sub turned dominatrix anytime, you little slut. I'm pretty much a switch, anyway. Skin-slap sounds would be hot on the video. Men love that shit."

Juniper laughs at her friend. She's not wrong. Hell, she loves that sound, too. Wow. This is insane. She dances away from Sara, still shaking her booty, daring her friend to dominate her butt. That's a new erotic feeling. Being dominated by a woman. She sways her body to and fro on her way to the pole and says, "Action." She grips the pole with both hands, pushes her ass out, and presses her forehead to the metal.

"Oh, I already started the video, baby love. That little butt wiggle was too hot not to start." Sara clears her throat. "You're live. Dang, you are so hot. Matt's gonna blow his load right away just from looking at you."

Juniper giggles freely, loving the compliments. If she were sober, her cheeks would be red right now; instead, her face is glowing with sheepish delight. Thanks to the wine, she's adequately masking how that comment embarrasses her. It'll be her secret, though, as she glimpses Sara's expression, she gasps. Clearly, she can't hide her true feelings as well as she thought she could from her friend. Sara is grinning appreciatively back, like she's won something.

"Well, aren't you the sweetest thing?" Sara says with a cock of her head. "You're a natural star at this, hon. You'd make lots and lots of money doing this. And I'm not kidding. With that body of yours, and that classic beauty of a face. Whew! You are killing it, Junie!"

"Oh, well, shit," Juniper says with a hand over her mouth, suppressing her giggle. She turns her head away from Sara. She startles as she sees a flash of something going by outside the window, a something that looks like a person. She freezes in place as she expresses a loud gasp. "Whoa, Sara, I think my eyes are playing tricks on me." She shakes her head and returns her gaze to Sara, who is starting up another song. "I thought I just saw a person out there, laugh out loud. I'm getting drunk as a fucking skunk. Now I'm seeing things!"

"As they say, just dance, baby. Just dance." Sara shakes her hips to the song, bobbing her head, bouncing her body up and down. "Damn, I'd better not dance, or our men will be seasick watching this wavy video." She cracks up. "Sorry, boys. I'll behave. At least in that way, but I'm not promising in others."

Juniper lets the music fill her body and her mind, the pounding beat seeping into the layers of her brain. She closes her eyes to immerse herself in her sexual feelings, letting the passion of her aura leak out of her body to satiate the dry air. She's feeling juicy. The song playing is about fucking. She can't remember the name of it or who sings it, but it's hot and erotic as all fuck. With her eyes still closed, she grips the shaft of the pole with both hands above her head and sways around it, making a full 360 circle, swinging her ass out away from it. When she returns to her starting point, she wraps her right leg around and leans back, dipping her head toward the mirror in a back arch, making her full breasts spread across her chest. She lets out a luscious moan.

Sara groans. "Aww, fuck me, Junie. Holy shit, you are gorgeous. Those boobies of yours are still killer as fuck. You haven't changed a bit. I bet Bridge loves to titty fuck you."

Juniper slides her right leg up and down the pole. "Ummmm, yeah." The fluidity of dancing freely in front of her friend is skyrocketing her arousal. "Oh, I feel so yummy right now."

"You're making my pussy leak, baby. Wanna touch myself watching you." Sara lets out a thick, grunting moan. "Aw, fuck. My pussy is just gooey right now. You're driving me wild."

Juniper's sigh fills the air as she presses each of her breasts with her free hand, swiping her fingers over both nipples, each getting a turn, causing them to harden. She caresses the wrinkles nestling up to the tip of her tit, her little bumps emerging to the air. Bridge loves to slowly arouse her nips and watch them transform.

"Fuck, I've missed your huge pink nipples and those nugget tips. Damn. Love how you wrinkle up. I want those in my mouth." She sighs deeply. "Boys, you two care if Juniper and I fuck? We'll record it and send it to you for your own masturbation pleasure."

Juniper ignores Sara's comment as she falls into a reverie of her own sexuality, gracefully undulating her body to the beat of the music. But deep inside her, she's aware on some level because she's also kind of relieved that Sara is taking over the asking for her. She abandons the worry of what Bridge will think and sinks into her own eroticism. She's floating, almost asleep, dreamy, drifting seamlessly along the flow of her lust just as a breeze swallows a moment as it passes by on the beach, ever-flowing, not stopping, existing without boundaries or fear, but yet touching everything in its path with its soundless breath. A place where her sexual energy is spiritual, matriarchal, sacred.

A plane of existence where nothingness is everything, and everything is yet so full of energy, alive and vibrant. Electric. Her nipples are hard, her areolas tightly wound up and fully wrinkled like intricate maps. She runs her fingertips over her puckered flesh, savoring her own skin gathering up to form the most pointedly hard tit. As she leans back, supporting herself on the pole with her shin and bent knee, her hand wrapped around the metal shaft, she slides into a feeling of freedom and empowerment. She's herself just as she desires to be, no hindrance, just full on flourishing in her own sensuality. She pulls at her nipples, tugging them away from her body, pinching, coaxing them out to ultimate hardness. She moans as she works her breasts over. She sinks into a mental realm as if she's alone; she's so carefree.

Making eye contact with Sara, she reorients herself to the fact that she's not alone. She stands and presses her cleavage to the pole, relishing the hard coldness against her hot skin as she presses her body fully to the metal, the unforgiving metal, hard like the shaft of a packed hard-on. A sexy, confident grin slides across her face. She mashes her breasts against the pole, rubbing them against the metal. She's a goddess putting on a show, yet she's doing it for herself. It's erotic bliss. Orgasms seem to be looming nearer; she relishes the promise as something births inside her. Her breasts pop as they become freed from the pole when she pushes them across back and forth, as if she's riding it with her tits. Her pussy is wetting further as Sara coos from across the room watching her, moaning her pleasure as Juniper erotically plays on the pole with her body. She's using the pole as she would a sex toy, her breathing rate ramping up.

Sara is moving closer and closer to Juniper, as if she's stalking her. This turns Juniper on.

Wrapping her lower leg around the pole, she mounts and rides it, spreading her juices all over it. She grinds herself, moaning and grunting as she rubs, gyrates, salivating her pussy juices on the metal, savoring how her wetness is mingling with Sara's. That's hot.

Overcome with want, she murmurs, "Oh, fuck, Sara. I do want you to fuck me. Oh, help me, I want it so bad I can taste it." She runs her tongue over her upper lip and shoves her index finger into her mouth and sucks on it, just for something to suck, her oral lust brutally and demonically biting into her sanity. She's rolling in a flurry of passion.

"Please. Please," she mumbles in a garbled way over her finger in her mouth.

"Boys, we're moving to the bedroom to fuck. Sending you this now. If you object, text us; otherwise, we're fucking the shit out of each other. Respond now. We are horny as fuck." She taps her phone, then raises her eyes to meet Juniper's.

Juniper wraps her upper half around the pole, her firm belly pressed to it. She's alternating between gliding on it with her abdomen and grinding her pussy against it, then she places her butt crack on it, her free hand ever traveling her body before dipping in her hot mouth. She drags her fingers from her mouth, down her neck, through the valley of her cleavage, slithering down her belly, slicking along her special spot before diving two fingers into her wet, hot pussy. She's in an all-out frenzy of ardor as she works her pussy lips between finger-fucking thrusts.

Sara grabs her hand and pulls her. "Let's fuck."

Juniper is woozy, horny, and wants to be ridden by cock. Her clit is throbbing, and her wet labia lips are slipping against each other as she walks. She obeys Sara, pulling her out of the exercise room. Her thoughts are dreamy, lucid, like liquid arousal as she practically floats behind Sara, feeling like she's watching herself in a movie rather than doing it.

"I'll come back for our wine. You're in a euphoric state, and I'm gonna take you further by eating you out. I'm going to make you come hard, baby. And then do it again and again."

In the back of Juniper's mind, she's got this inkling of fear that Bridge will be angry with her for fucking Sara, but then at the same time, she'd never leave Bridge for Sara, anyway. Sara's married too, and has kids. That's not what this is about. It's about sexual satisfaction, gratification, and pleasure. And, besides, they are going to do a foursome anyway, right? So, no harm done if they fall into an appetizer of the act with just her and Sara. Right?

What will Bridge think? Her worries sober her up a bit. She had never told Bridge about her and Sara's sexual escapades in college. Would he think she was wrong for doing this? She almost collapses to the floor as Sara drags her along, stumbling toward the bedroom. Once in the room, she looks around, not sure what to do next. She giggles all the naysaying thoughts away as she watches Sara lick her pretty lips from the doorway.

"Stay here. I'll be right back, lover."

Juniper adores the warm, drunk, ripe feelings, her urges flourishing, readying to be fucked by her friend, just like old times. She's moving only with clumsy giddiness, almost drifting down to the floor. Wherever Sara leads, she's ready to follow.

Sara is still lingering at the door. "Don't fall asleep, baby. Try to stay standing until I return."

Once Sara leaves, Juniper falls immediately to the bed and writhes on the soft, cushy comforter, her want consuming her entirely as she runs her hands all over herself. Fall asleep? Hell no, she wants to fuck. She doesn't know what time it is, but her dancing felt really short, hot, but rather cryptic and unfinished. That's okay; she'll finish her dance here on the bed. She wiggles under the glow of her own grin as her hand migrates to her pussy and she pushes two fingers in and pumps, pressing her thumb to her clit every so often, moaning into the silence of the bedroom.

Sara appears out of nowhere. "Here's your wine, Juniper. Do you want a sip?" Sara's voice is buttery smooth and seductively sweet as syrup as it seeps into her ears to massage her panting inner animal lust. She wants Sara so fucking bad. "I brought a few brownie bites, too."

Juniper sighs, which ends in a sultry moan. "Yeah, I'll take a sip," she whispers.

Juniper sits up, using the pull of Sara's hand on her arm for help. Sara helps her take a sip. Its deep, rich flavor floods Juniper's mouth lusciously. "Yummm," Juniper slurs. "Did the men respond?"

Sara shoves a brownie bite into Juniper's mouth. "Yes. They said, 'Go for it' now have some chocolate for erotic energy." She pops one in her own mouth and takes a sip of the red wine.

She tries to process Bridge saying 'yes', and it's a bit of a hurdle. But maybe this turns him on, which turns her on even more. Immediately after Sara sets down her wine glass, her mouth lands on Juniper's. Juniper tastes the wine and chocolate on Sara's tongue, adding to the same flavors in her own mouth.

Sara slides fully in place as she straddles Juniper's upper thighs and threads her hands through Juniper's hair. Sara's kissing is hungry, but gentler than Bridge's as she takes Juniper's upper lip between her two lips, sucking it and letting it slip out several times. She'd forgotten what kissing a woman was like.

Juniper responds to Sara's kissing with a primal-sounding grunt. She indicates her own growing hunger for Sara as her hands briskly ride up Sara's back in groping grabs. Their breasts fondle each other as their bodies move against each other with the tight embrace of their kissing, their nipples sliding against each other's breasts, and then pop back into shape as they slide free. The kiss sucking sounds pepper the air in between their soft moans of pleasure as they continue to kiss and reacquaint each other with their bodies. Being with Sara is easy, like a passionate muscle memory fleshing out.

The familiarity of the kiss surprises Juniper. It's as if they just kissed yesterday— loving, delicate yet deliciously devouring with sheer wanton intent. Kissing her is so different from kissing Bridge. Not bad. Just different. And she's missed it. The difference is jarring, but in such a delicious and good way.

Sara mounts Juniper's pussy mound with her own slit, grinding her pelvis in gyrating undulations, slipping around, riding her pussy down, slathering Juniper's thighs with her pussy juices, then back up to her mound and lower belly.

She wants a part of Sara in her mouth, so she turns her head and suckles her arm. "Mmm, I'm your jungle gym. Ride me, Sara." She licks her arm. "You taste like all my memories. Sara, you're so amazing," Juniper murmurs. The act of being with Sara like this again is even more wonderful than she'd anticipated. "I'm so happy," she coos.

"Yes," Sara says confidently. "Me too." She's breathless as she pants into Juniper's mouth. "Kiss me," she commands. She slides her tongue along Juniper's, joining their slick tongues along their full lengths.

Sara's hands migrate to Juniper's breasts. She presses her hands into them, cupping, squeezing, then plucking at her nipples, causing Juniper to moan and whimper into their deep kiss. Sara breaks the lip lock and moves down Juniper's body. She opens her mouth wide and fully consumes Juniper's right nipple. She sucks hard, bringing the tip inside her mouth, massaging her areola with her tongue, causing Juniper to moan. Juniper cradles the back of Sara's head as she suckles.

"Aw, fuck, that feels amazing," Juniper murmurs.

"Just wait." Sara climbs off Juniper's middle and crawls to sit behind her, pulling her head back to rest against her pointed, perky breasts. She sucks on the tops of Juniper's ears, licking as she plays with her nipples from behind. Juniper's hands reach behind to play with Sara's hair, then they migrate to Sara's thighs, which are cradling her between them. There's so much safety in the position and trust. It's so amazing to soak in their connection again. It hasn't waned one bit.

"Play with yourself, Juniper," Sara commands in a whisper into Juniper's ear. "I want to watch you."

Juniper obeys, and her hands both land on her pussy instantly. She rides two fingers in a rapid plunge into her wet hole. Sara's leadership is a welcome return to the full revisiting of their college days. It's like slipping into warm bathwater as she presses her index and middle fingers firmly against her clit. Sara had been the first person she'd ever masturbated in front of. She moans as she undulates between her own hands at her vagina and Sara's body around her. She's free, yet safely held as she presses herself against Sara's caressing of her breasts.

"Go on, that's it," Sara urges as she squeezes her thighs together, hugging Juniper between them. "Come on, baby."

Both of them are moaning, writhing, nestled in a moving, sensual dance together.

"I'm gonna fuck you, Juniper. But I want you to ride my face first, just like we did in college. Remember that? Make you come for me, sweet baby, my little cum-slut. I want your cum on my tongue."

Juniper coos softly as she nuzzles her cheek against Sara's shoulder. Feeling Sara's skin all along hers is both luxurious and erotic. Her senses are so heightened that she's climbing quickly to a climax, whimpering-moaning her feelings out. She will give Bridge anything he wants for allowing this, well, almost anything.

Sara kisses the top of Juniper's head and then whispers, "Yes, baby girl, come for me. I want you to come. Come on. Let yourself go there while I hold you. I want to watch you climax. Do it."

Juniper feels that familiar pressure near her belly button that she often gets when she's about to come. She teeters at the top of the orgasm as she rubs herself aggressively, still pumping her fingers inside, then, losing the control to stop it, she freely crashes down into the peak. She twitches, her arms and legs drawing tighter to her body as her toes curl, and she yells out through pursed lips as her body shudders. Her vagina spasms in several successive contractions. The giant overwhelm of it is scrumptious. She moves her fingers off her sensitive clitoris with a gasp. Giving it the break it needs always after she comes. She leaves her other fingers still inside her hot, wet vagina. She doesn't want to move.

"Give me your fingers, Juniper. I want to taste you."

Juniper pulls her fingers out of her and raises her hand over her head. Sara grabs it and shoves her fingers into her mouth and sucks.

She pops off Juniper's fingers with a loud mouth smack. "Mmmm, you taste amazing, baby," Sara murmurs.

"Sara, I want you to come, too." Juniper starts to rise out of Sara's legs, turning around and backing up to line her mouth up with Sara's pussy.

"No, baby, you first."

Juniper giggles. "Silly, you just felt me shake. I did come already."

"No, I need you to do it again, then you can eat me out. Or at least ride my face for a few minutes, I want your pussy rubbing my face, my chin, my mouth. Come on now. Bring it here. I want more of you." Sara lies down and scoots back a little, tapping at the corner of her mouth with her index finger. "Hold on to the headboard and fucking ride me like the bitch in heat that you are." She stares into Juniper's eyes with an intense gaze, daring her to disobey.

Juniper chuckles at her friend's words. She feels exactly like a 'bitch in heat'. The wine is bringing out the dominant in Sara tonight, and Juniper is loving that. Being with Sara had always been a wild ride back then, and that clearly has not changed.

Juniper gives Sara a saucy, excited look as she crawls up and positions herself in a squatting position over her face. It's been so long since she did this with Sara, it's a good thing she's a bit inebriated because she doesn't think she could ride Sara's face sober anymore. Bridge likes for her to do it. Hell, she loves it too, but it's been years since she was this way with Sara.

"Don't be shy," Sara slurs with seduction thick in her voice. "Ride me, hard. Drown me in you."

Juniper gathers her gumption but remains still.

She gasps as Sara aggressively grabs her hips and attacks her pussy lips with her mouth. Juniper falls forward and grips the headboard, white-knuckling it. Another gasp catches in her throat that rings out almost as a scream in fruition when Sara open-mouth suctions her clit. She's like a damn leech! Sara was always so good at oral. Being a woman herself, perhaps, she just gets what feels good. Juniper throws her head back, instantly thrust into a torrent of moans as Sara's mouth consumes her with full-on mouth-sealed sucking. Then she eases off, flicking her with the tip of her tongue before running the full flat of it along her flesh, then rippling her tongue in waves.

Juniper is gasping, moaning, and panting so hard, moans coming out soft, then whimpering, then to the point of almost screaming as Sara varies her oral stimulation.

"Aw, fuck," Juniper grunts as she begins to gyrate her hips across Sara's face, riding up to her nose then back to her mouth, slipping down her chin then back once more.

Sara's hands grip Juniper's ass cheeks even harder, like vises, as she pulls her down flush onto her mouth, not allowing Juniper to move anymore. Sara's claiming her, and the power she asserts makes Juniper melt. Staying upright is getting difficult; she's so weakened by pleasure.

Sara sticks her tongue in Juniper's pussy and rapidly tongue-fucks her. Juniper squeals, allowing her body to twitch and curl toward the bed. She's most certainly going to fall. She whimpers as she loses control, her body jerking as she comes in Sara's mouth. She makes slurping sounds as she laps Juniper's pussy as her body quakes.

Juniper crumples against the bed frame in a mutter of anguish, full on, sitting on Sara's face. Weakened by the ordeal of climaxing so strongly, she rolls off like something sloughed off and lies on the bed recovering from her massive climax. She can't even speak.

Sara strokes Juniper's hair and cheek. "Good, huh?"

Juniper's mouth is still ajar; she nods. After a minute of coming off the high, she can finally speak. "Oh, my, fucking fuck fuck. Holy shit. That was unbelievable. You must be watching lots of lesbian porn to know how to do all of that. You've upped your game, which I didn't think was possible. You demolished me." She guffaws as her grin grows.

"I love watching women fuck, that's true. It's much more interesting than men and women, which is about the same every damn time, so way more fun to do than watch, in my opinion. But now women fucking, that's sensual and different. That's the cat's meow right there." She traces her index finger along Juniper's round breast and then spends time on her nipple, making it harder. She takes it into her mouth and sucks it, stroking the areola around her closed lips, and then licking the nipple tip with her tongue. Letting it slip out, it pops from her lips all shiny and wet. "Ready to sixty-nine, baby love?"

"Yes, or I just eat you out. You need to come now." She makes eye contact with Sara. "I think you rode me more than I rode you."

"You were taking too long, so I took charge. And fat chance. I want your cunt in my mouth again, bitch. Now flip it and get on all fours; you're on top. I like your ass in the air." Sara grins her devious, naughty grin at Juniper, the moonlight lighting her face from the skylight above. "Hop to it," she says when Juniper doesn't move. "Or delicious punishments will happen, again."

"All right, but I think I owe you."

"You do, yes, and this is what I want. Now put your pussy on my mouth, be my bitch. I want to suck another ounce, or five, of come out of you."

Juniper giggles. "I'm not sure I can make that much." The euphoria from coming twice has intensified her drunkenness, and she's floaty and light. "I fear I might suck at it right now; I'm so woozy."

Sara laughs. "Yes, suck at it is the point!"

Juniper cracks up. "Oh, so true. I'll do my best."

As Juniper positions herself over Sara, she has a flash of a thought of Bridge again. She almost cringes physically as she realizes she never checked her phone herself for his objection or agreement to her fucking Sara, but she trusts Sara.

She bites her lip as guilt edges on the front of her drunk state, but she quickly brushes it off as Sara's mouth once more devours her pussy. Her hands are all over her, mauling her ass cheeks, pushing Juniper down to smash into her face. Juniper sighs as she gets lost in Sara's pleasuring, and moans as she opens her mouth wide and takes her friend's right labia lip into her mouth, sucking it, then she moves to her other one. She licks Sara's slit multiple times, then tongues her way to Sara's clit where she first licks, then fully consumes Sara's clit into her mouth. Sara's is larger than Juniper's, like a little appendage, or tiny dick. It always made Juniper laugh that her own was so little in comparison, and she's more shaped like a V there, but Sara's is a little like a man's cock, a mini one.

Admittedly, Juniper imagines Sara's clit is easier to suck than her own flat one. She sucks and rolls Sara's clit on her tongue as Sara's mouth falls off Juniper due to her moans, which turn into screams. Sara's clutching at Juniper's hips, bucking beneath her as her nails dig into her flesh. She's driving headfirst into a giant orgasm.

Juniper doesn't stop but leans to one side a bit so she can press her thumb into Sara's slit. She thumb-fucks her, then adds two fingers, and Sara goes wild beneath her, writhing, moaning, thrashing. She grunts heartily as Juniper eats her out and rubs her G-spot. Juniper's heart pounds with excitement as Sara's body starts to twitch, shaking as she ejaculates, then she squirts. Juniper's upper lip and nose get most of the fluid. Juniper grins as she shakes her head, so thrilled she has brought Sara to this point. She always used to love to make Sara come, and squirt. She has always climaxed with such animation.

"Oh, fuck," Sara groans out. "Yes, Juniper. Oh, fuck yes. I needed that. Holy fuck."

Juniper rolls over to lie next to Sara. "You squirted."

"Um, yep," Sara says breathlessly, her hand reaching for Juniper's thigh. "That was fucking fabulous. You haven't lost your mouth skills, my dear love."

"Neither have you. Like I said, you're even better," Juniper puts her hand over Sara's that is resting on her thigh. "How about another brownie bite and more wine? I'll run to the kitchen for more."

"Bless you," Sara says, still seeming to be floating in post-coming euphoria. "I need a cooldown period."

Juniper slips off the bed and walks toward the kitchen, thinking about the intensity of what just happened in her bed with Sara. She can't help but smile. It was so damn delicious. Not better than with Bridge, just different. Very sensual, luxurious, somehow more careful and sweet in the throes of passion, but no less intense.

She stops cold as she notices a granola bar wrapper on the counter that wasn't there before. Odd. She picks it up to examine it, cocking her head at it. She doesn't have this kind in the house right now. Her eyes twitch back and forth across the kitchen as a creepy feeling invades her. How strange, and almost...wait. She scoffs and laughs at herself.

"Duh, Juniper. Sara is here. She probably brought this granola bar into the house and ate it. Boy, am I paranoid." She chuckles to herself, shaking her head as she grabs four brownie bites and the already open wine bottle. "Relax, Juniper. Geez. Freak out much?"

She swings the wine bottle as she saunters along, humming to herself, balancing the four brownie morsels in her other hand. Oops. She forgot napkins. Aw, screw it. She'll need to wash the sheets anyway after Sara's big squirt. Let the chocolatey crumbs fall where they may.

Sara has rolled to her side on the bed, giving a nice, graceful, slender side view silhouette of her body.

"Is that kind of granola bar good? I haven't tried it."

"Mmmm?" Sara mumbles in response to her question. "Granola bar?"

She waves her hand, dismissing her twinge of worry over a random granola bar wrapper. She's sure Sara is just drunk and forgot it. "You seem sleepy; maybe we should call it quits and go to bed."

"Fuck you, madam. I haven't gotten your pussy in years. I'm sure as hell not done. I paused the videoing though. I already sent it to our men. They're probably spraying bed sheets with their cum by now."

Sara sits up in bed and opens her hand as Juniper places two brownie bites in the center of her palm. "These brownies are like crack. I could eat the whole container for a meal."

"I know, right? They are to die for." Juniper grabs their two glasses of wine. She hands one to Sara. "And amazing with this wine."

Juniper sits on the bed, and the two friends nosh on brownies, sip on wine, and make flirty eyes at each other.

"You ready to ride our pussies together?" Sara smirks, then opens her eyes wide before popping the last bit of brownie into her mouth.

"Yup, let's fuck." Juniper takes a long draw of wine, savoring the blast of rich berries on her tongue yet still savoring the lushness of the chocolate. She downs another sip and takes Sara's glass from her outstretched hand.

"Hey, wait. I've got an idea." Sara reaches to take the wine glass back.

# Chapter Thirteen

John grits his teeth, still fuming, pissed at himself for leaving that granola bar wrapper on the counter. He almost spoiled his entire brilliant plan like a total idiot. His mom had always teased him as a teen that he'd make a terrible criminal because he always left a sign he was there—a crumb of food, a sliver of a wrapper, or a water bottle cap. He rolls his eyes. Apparently, she's still right, even from the grave. That had been such a dumb move, but thankfully, Juniper had brushed it off. Both women should have been asleep by now. Surely with the amount of wine they've had, they'd be out, but they're still at it. He watches them. They are still entangled together on the floor of the master bedroom, with a giant plastic sheet on the ground beneath them. They are pouring wine on each other's bodies and taking turns licking and sucking it off, the luscious little minxes. They are moving on to rubbing coconut oil all over each other and getting each other off with different vibrators—a whole basket of multicolored and shaped ones.

He's had a very amusing night watching them. He chuckles to himself. How long could two women go at it? They are both clearly horny as all hell, and he'd surely give his right kidney, left nut, and a pinky toe to be in there with them, making it a threesome, but only because Juniper would be one of the three. Sara's hot, but she's not Juniper. He had seriously loved watching them drink wine all night, hearing their chatter when they were in the entertainment area. Their talk about sex and erogenous zones had been delicious, especially. He had stroked himself on and off the whole time, edging himself along as they danced in the exercise room, and fucked from every possible angle. But he was proud of himself for never coming. That was one of the hardest things he's ever done because all of it has been seriously the hottest, most sensual, erotic display he'd ever seen in his entire life. No porn could ever touch that, not even close. They were real. That was pure, real, thick, wet, grunting, slip-sliding, sensuous, delicious erotica, practically alive in its bold unfolding before his eyes. It had been legit mind-blowing to watch. He'd surely savor the video for the rest of his life, and watch it with Juniper, no doubt. She'd want to relive it, he guessed.

But he's so happy with himself for being able to hold off because he's saving the explosion for when he's lying in bed with Juniper later. The thought of it makes his cock throb against his jeans, tightening them around his ass. He had to stop touching himself and dip his dick in his water to cool off when the two women were sixty-nining in the bed. Their moans alone drove him wild. They had been like a drug to him, making the passage of time seem like nothing more than a single breath as he watched them in their insatiable hungry tryst on the monitor.

The little hidden room had been the perfect hideout all evening. It had been so satisfying that Bridge hadn't broken into this room and seen all the security and camera equipment set up. He'd been worried many times since they'd moved in that Bridge would hammer into the space. That would have ruined his plans if all his equipment had been found and removed, though he did have his app to watch the hidden cameras remotely, unless they shut all the cameras down. They'd have to find them all, though.

A pit of dread forms in his gut with that thought. He shakes it away because he has no control over that dreadful outcome. He's not going to dwell on that. He rubs his hands together with an evil grin. He seriously can't believe they haven't ripped the wall down yet to see inside. Only Juniper stood in the way of Bridge with a sledgehammer that day, and he was immensely grateful she'd pulled through for him. He had been on pins and needles watching, fearing Bridge would smash walls to expose his little secret watching hideout. Bridge could be a brute. Juniper was his angel, as usual.

The other brilliant part of his plan was that he had purchased the security package that allowed him to watch his house from outside of the home, like how people watch their dogs at home alone when they're at work or nanny cams for babysitters. He had the whole house equipped that way, with so many cameras everywhere, so he could see every stinking lovely room. Even the fucking bathrooms.

He sighs as Juniper comes again. She's pure bliss to see climaxing. Watching women come is just the absolute best; it really doesn't get much better than that on any level. He loved their exaggerated movements, their bodies crunching up, the twitching, the eye rolling, their shaking bodies are just exquisite works of art. And their sounds, good lord, he'd never get enough of hearing that.

"Oh, Juniper. Sweetheart. You are the very beat of my heart," he whispers, touching her nipples on the screen. "And the marrow of my dreams." She is certainly the only thing he really wants in this world, and someday, he will have her. That's a given.

He touches the keys in his pocket, recalling his fear of being spotted by Juniper or Sara when he first snuck in. Apparently, it had him so brainless that he set his granola bar wrapper on the counter to fill a water bottle from the fridge, and then he stupidly left the potentially incriminating wrapper on the kitchen counter. He had meant to toss it in the garbage, but his nerves clearly had other plans for him. Haste makes waste, as his grandma always used to chide him.

Earlier, when he had first arrived at the house, he had pulled the house key from his pocket with shaking hands and slid it into the keyhole. Satisfaction and relief lit up inside him because it still worked. He had grinned, feeling so lucky they hadn't changed the locks, and as of yet, they had not turned on the alarm system either. Well, he laughed, they can't turn on something they don't know exists. It was a top-notch system that he'd bought and was virtually invisible to the naked eye.

Their trust in the world is his gain. He'd realized his good fortune when he hit it big. For some odd reason, being a famous author brought with it the gift of everyone he came in contact with seamlessly trusting him like he was a saint. Not sure why, but he isn't complaining. Being a sort of celebrity had its perks; he always got the best tables at restaurants, special treatment from chefs who were fans, and financial discounts he didn't need, but was given just because people wanted to do something for the amazing, incredible John Penn. Definite benefits abounded in being a world-famous author. He had his social media managers keeping his nose clean for the worldview, and it worked like a charm.

His heart still hadn't fully recovered, though. It had been racing as he had crept deeper into the house, yet somehow still shoving more blood into his cock, as he had snuck along the front wall of the kitchen. The women had just moved to the bedroom a few minutes earlier when he inserted the little key into the lock on the far kitchen wall and pushed the hidden door open. He slipped inside the secret room unnoticed. He had bided his time right and gotten lucky.

He had been smart in his plan of building this room, but it didn't fully serve his purposes now, of course. The room was inescapable to the outside, with no windows; the only exit from inside the room was to the house. This was a huge problem. To get into the room, he had to be inside the house. That block had plagued him as he had tried to devise his sneaking-in plan. The design had been great when he had lived in the house. He honestly had never expected he'd want an emergency exit to the outside, but he had never counted on meeting Juniper, either. Hindsight was clear; he should have made a trap door for an easy exit. Having the money to do whatever the fuck he wanted was awesome. He was wracking his brain trying to figure out another way to make it so he could get in and out without causing suspicion with Bridge and Juniper. There was no possible way. The reality is that his time in the room is limited because they might indeed sledgehammer it open at any moment out of pure curiosity. At some point, Bridge's desire would override Juniper's objections, and he'd whack right into the room. But for now, he had it, and he is sure as fuck going to use it.

A loud scream rips across the house. It's Sara screaming Juniper's name. John smiles at the screen.

Ah, such a good girl, Junie, making Sara come.

He'd love to have the talents of her mouth on him. From the sounds of it, she knows precisely how to bring a partner, any partner, to ecstasy. She's got mad skills. But, honestly, he already knew that; he'd watched Bridge and Juniper countless times. Her giving him head so often, and how they'd fuck every day, sometimes two or three times in a single day, even. What he wouldn't give to have such a beautiful, horny wife who loved sex. He'd just have to take her someday as planned; well, he'd been coming up with a plan to make that happen since he met her. In the meantime, he dreamed of fucking her, making her food, bathing her, and taking the best care of her ever. Better than Bridge, for sure.

The trick would be to get her to love him back. But he could do it. However, he hadn't always been lucky in love, never staying with a woman for more than a few months at a pop. His longest union had been for two years, but it had been dicey those last six months of the relationship, when she had acted like an insane bitch on an overdose of induced paranoia. He cringes as he recalls her belligerent accusations. She had thought he was fucking the next-door neighbor when that was the furthest thing from the truth. He had merely shared a smoke with her on occasion on the beach as they both commiserated about their miserably inadequate partners. Not that he wouldn't have fucked his neighbor, it just never came up as a potential. Whatever. That bitch was done and gone for a long time now. Thank God.

Yearning for the touch of Juniper often brought him almost to tears. It wasn't just that she was beautiful and sexy, but she was kind, sweet-hearted, generous, sacrificial, and intellectual as all fuck. She was gentle, caring, giving, with a heart that made him ache for her. He had not intentionally fallen in love with her; it was a true accident. He had fallen hard and fast. In his defense, he hadn't sought her out; he had merely bumped into her one day and been instantly smitten. Not instantly in love, no, but certainly popping a boner and a giant desire to spend time with her. But once he knew her daily patterns, he had watched her. He had gotten to know her, and then he was a true goner. His heart had taken a leap of faith and fallen hard for her. He'd do anything in this world for her, and he'd never ever hurt her.

The worst he'd do is some BDSM acts, but that'd be only if they turned her on, too. It certainly turned him on to imagine it, but he didn't need it if she hated it. He just needed her.

He'd seen Bridge and her do some kink, spanking, flogger usage, handcuffs, so he knew the interest for it was in her. He also knew he could probably nudge her further into it a bit, but he'd never force her to do it. Ever. He wants her to look at him the way she looks at Bridge, the way she looks at Mags, and at the ocean, with love in her eyes, and the utmost trust. She has this way about her, a full circular appreciation for the uniqueness, beauty, and quirkiness of each of the loves in her life.

John would be no different. In fact, he might be even more of an obsession for her.

Juniper's an appreciator. She loves things and people in her life deeply, all throughout her cells, into the very swirling, churning dance of her soul, every speed-up and slow-down of her heartbeat. She's just beyond special. A gem. Something extra special about her that is wordless, priceless, something that can't be replicated. Her magnificent aura can only be felt and spied on in those deep, contemplative, curious, loving eyes of hers when she thinks she's alone. She's an angel. She's the perfect woman, a dream, a mirage that is actually living, breathing, fucking, cooking, sleeping, dreaming, swimming in the ocean, taking care of others, a nurse who most likely is the best on her floor. She's a genius in her personality, a model in her looks, and a porn star in her fucking. Yeah. Perfect. Fucking ideal. And fucking Bridge got all of her. It isn't fair. At. All.

Finally, twenty minutes after the women went to bed, he felt safe and snuck out. He helped himself to some of Bridge's cognac, which he sipped on, considering when he should make his move, and he accidentally consumed the full remaining amount. No matter. Bridge would just think Sara did it, so he would slip it back into the cupboard, empty. No harm done.

And, so, it's time.

He opens the door of the hidden room slowly and makes his way to the kitchen liquor cabinet. After sliding the empty cognac bottle in, he creeps to Juniper and Bridge's room, his breath coming in hot puffs as if he's fucking. He'd give away everything he owned to actually fuck Juniper right now. His hand shakes as he very slowly turns the doorknob to the master bedroom. His heart is beating so hard it's throbbing in his groin, from the base to the tip of his hard-on. And fuck, he is still hard, totally fuck ready. He's been hard for hours now, just edging for this very moment. He'd fuck her so good right now, and she'd be in euphoric heaven.

He pauses and stares at her, lightly gasping at the sheer ethereal beauty of her beneath the moonlight streaming down from the skylight. The white glow skates across her pale skin, delicate, complete, and full as a sundried breeze. She's like a piece of irreplaceable art lying on the bed with only the sheet covering her curves and her arm. Her amazing breasts are out of the sheet, completely bare for his visual pleasure. He chuckles, bless her heart, she was so fuck-tuckered out that she hadn't even bothered to put pajamas on. So sweet and innocent, she's a dream.

He cautiously enters the room, going super slow. Once at the bed, he stands above her, admiring her beauty. He restrains himself from touching her bare shoulder. Fuck, it's so tempting to just reach out and stroke her skin. Her hair lies in a graceful curve to the side, like an invitation to touch her.

She sighs and shifts slightly, but her eyes remain closed. He freezes in place. She remains asleep and still. Her entire upper torso rises and falls as she breathes. He wants to lick that hollow spot at the base of her neck, kiss it, nuzzle his tongue into the dip of it. Then he'd bury his face between her tits, move next to arrange his dick to titty fuck her.

The fantasy enrages him as he hovers his fingers over her breasts. He can almost feel their heat wafting up to warm him. He brings his other hand up, so his hands are parallel to hers, and he moves to just above her lovely, flawless skin along her chest. Then he caresses the air above her form, and on down the sheet lying over her stomach, hips, thighs, shins, feet, feeling up the air above her, imagining how incredible she would feel, groaning inside with the almost uncontrollable urge to lay his hands upon her. He's more than tempted. The urge is deftly consuming him to the point that his logic is nearly losing the battle. He's on the very sharpest edge of becoming irrational and actually touching her. He twitches internally, fighting himself to caress her.

Maybe she wouldn't wake up?

She stirs in her sleep again and rolls onto her back. Her beautiful lips part, and her breasts spread across her chest to lie flat and relaxed against her body. She's in a deep wine stupor of sleep. Sweat beads off his temples as he lowers his hands to within a half inch of her neck. He draws in a deep breath as he holds off. Her body heat is rising to meet his hand, and it's erotically delicious.

Damn it, this is hard.

He suppresses a groan as he imagines choking her during sex, forcing her airway closed as his dick is riding her pussy like an oiled piston. He'd help her reach the heights of her orgasm with both his hands and his cock. He shudders, almost touching her. He freezes in place but is so overcome with yearning that a shiver causes his right hand to graze the skin of her neck ever so lightly, so slight that it's as if it's simply the featherlight ease of an exhale. He holds his breath as he waits to see if his touch has woken her. She doesn't move a single muscle, nor do her eyelids flutter open.

He's safe.

His heart is thudding against his chest as he moves around the bed to Bridge's side. He pushes on the bed ever so carefully with his hands to see if that makes her stir, preparing himself to drop to the floor if she flinches at all. She doesn't move. Her lips look full and sensual, moving with all of her as she breathes. The deep valley of her spread cleavage is slowly rising and falling, keeping her lovely body obediently asleep. He sits on the bed and, slowly, as gently as he can, maneuvers himself to lie fully on the bed next to her.

This is it. He's doing it.

His heart is beating so hard and fast. A rush of excitement hurtles from his chest down his abdomen, zinging through his pelvis straight to his cock, causing it to twitch. The intimacy of this act with her cuts deep into him as he unzips his pants. He leans toward her as she slumbers on and sniffs at her delicate, wine-soaked breath. She had so much to drink. John knows she is just out cold in a wine coma; she shouldn't wake, not after all the drinks and the orgasms.

This is outrageously perfect. Having Sara in the spare bedroom escalates the naughty factor, too. He feels like a devious teen sneaking into his girlfriend's house to fuck her while her parents are asleep. He grins. He's shaking as he's pulling down his zipper fully enough so he can pull his engorged cock out.

Juniper swivels to her side. Her hip seems to be holding up the moon-brightened night air, giving his eyes the joy of seeing her true curvaceous form under the thin white sheet, her hourglass hips and waist lusciously highlighted. It's beyond incredible to see her in real life this close and not flat on a screen. Her hair has fallen from her shoulders onto her pillow. He longs to run his fingers through her locks.

While cradling his cock with his right hand, he reaches up for her hair with his left. He ever so delicately pets it down the pillow. He suppresses a giant groan as his hand rides her silky hair lightly down the strands. It's even softer than he imagined it would be. Tears spring to his eyes; he's actually touching her.

His own breathing is rapid, hot, steamy, waging a war against the cool air in the room. Her aroma floods his nostrils and head like orgasmic steam, keeping his lust chugging along. He gently rubs his cock. He's slightly dizzy, euphoric, shaky, his nipples erect, feeling how he feels after he comes or when writing an intense scene. He often falls into a reverie when writing, a stream of consciousness giving him the sensation of waking when he stops writing, so vulnerable, like coming out of a stupor or dream. He attempts to control his shiver so he can pet the strands of her hair again.

He spies the bulge of the little bottle in his pocket, reminding him he needs to deposit it in the bathroom cupboard before he leaves. He had masturbated into a condom that afternoon and poured his cum into a bottle of plain lube, the same kind she buys. His plan was to place it in the front of the cupboard, so she would grab it the next time she masturbates, artfully depositing his sperm deep into her vagina as she toy-fucks herself in Bridge's absence. Perhaps, with any luck, it will result in impregnating her with his seed. She wants a baby so badly, and he wants to give her one. The thought almost makes him shoot his load. With Bridge gone, he knows she will surely be using her vibrator again, most likely this morning when she wakes, or perhaps later today, as she is used to daily orgasms from Bridge.

His beautiful, horny woman. He loves that she wants to come every day. That is something he fully understands, too. And to find that same desire in a woman makes her the ultimate mate for him. He groans inside, imagining how wonderful it will be to watch her masturbating with lube laced with his cum. It will surely effectively deposit his seed in her. Fuck, that's a delicious thought, and his mind fixates on it. He wants desperately to be her baby's papa, not Bridge. Though they'd never know until the baby was born whose it was, and without a DNA test, it would be nearly impossible to know, since Bridge fucked her yesterday. But he was sure as fuck going to try this plan. Not giving up this chance to be her baby's father. He had carefully chosen a lube that was not spermicidal, but the kind she keeps in stock in the cupboard. He didn't know if the sperm would live in the lube, but he hoped she'd wake up and use it in the morning, increasing the chances that his sperm would be live and could impregnate her. He wants to pump it into her with his dick, but he knows that can't happen...at least not yet.

He rubs his cock harder, making the bed shake slightly. He watches Juniper's eyes closely to ensure she stays asleep as he jostles the bed. She appears to be dreaming, her eyeballs twitching in their sockets, her body moving slightly in response to her dream.

Perfect.

He strokes his precum all down his cock, moistening the whole shaft, driving his hand over his enlarged tip and back down again. He's breathing fast as he watches her sleep while jerking off. Loving the feeling, he pumps himself harder, and the movements are getting bigger. The jiggling of the bed raises the eroticism of this as he imagines her waking and putting her luscious mouth on his. Her succulent breasts smash against his body as she presses her wet pussy against his thigh. Her wet hole would surely align quickly, giving her a chance to grind on him. He lets out a silent groan, barely keeping himself inaudible. This is ecstasy to have her a few feet away while he's masturbating. He imagines sucking her nipples, actually licking the air near them. Fuck. He wishes he could touch them and make them hard. He suppresses a gasp as he's so near losing his grip on stopping his ejaculation.

Fuck. Fuck fuck. He's losing his grip. He's going to come. He can't control it anymore.

A perfectly beautiful idea hits him.

He could cum on the sheets too, thereby increasing the possibility of his little guys swimming up Juniper's pussy if she sat on the right spot. Why not?

He gently rolls to his side, lifts the sheet, and sneaks himself under. Ah, the sheer joy of being next to her without any barrier is almost climax-inducing without him even touching his hard-on. He's wanted to feel the inside of his sheets with her in this bed for months now. He's dreamed of his balls slapping her ass cheeks as he fucks her flat doggy-style, pounding her pussy from the front in missionary, then his scrotum slapping the bitty tops of her ass cheeks near her vaginal opening. He's wanted his breath meandering over her tits before devouring them in an open-mouthed kiss, satiating his oral desire for her, then her tongue frisking his abdomen on her way down to suck his cock. He had fantasized about crawling his finger up the side of her breast, cupping its thickness in his hand, before suckling her nipple to a hard little pointed raspberry.

He's practically drooling as he thinks of her nipple in his mouth. His tongue explores the bumps of her areolas, tickling along the base of her nipple tip where the skin gathers in lush wrinkly folds, creating an erotic terrain for his tongue to traverse, and then the joy of caressing her to create her erect nipple. The mere thought of sucking her nipple to hardness to the back of his throat, almost making him cum all by itself.

Hang on, John, just wait.

He's breathing fast as he imagines she must taste like a lemon or a bitter berry when she comes. He has yearned to kiss that neck of hers, her cheeks and nose, nibbling her luscious, creamy earlobe, giving her soft, svelte skin a love bite that will leave his mark on her. The thought of shoving his cock in her while slapping her clit is driving him hard toward climaxing. He's not going to last much longer now.

Ah, fuck.

The thrilling potential of spanking her lovely ass pushes him right over the edge, and his cum spurts out in hot, projectile streams along the bottom sheet of the bed next to Juniper's sleeping body, some even gracefully and satisfyingly falling near her pussy.

Ideal aiming, John.

She is a heavy sleeper anyway, and with the wine, and likely only because of the wine, this stunt he's pulling is made possible. He shivers, trembling out the last drops of his ejaculate. He stifles his panting as best he can.

He needs to increase the chances of breeding her. He holds his breath as he very, very carefully dips his fingers in the cum still residing at the top of his cock and ever so gently dares the ultimate risk and touches his wet cum-soaked fingers to the fleshy edge of the cleft of her pussy. She stirs slightly, his touch likely arousing her a bit in her dreamland. He smiles as this is the utmost in deliciousness. If he could, he'd make her come while she slept. Sex would be questionable. He imagines she must be sore after her escapades with Sara tonight. He grins at her...what a sweetheart.

He lays his cock down on the sheet, in the spot where Bridge sleeps, and pulls out his phone. He turns it on, points it at Juniper's nose, and pushes record. He may not be able to fully touch her now, but he can smell her, eye-fuck her, and most certainly record her for later masturbation fodder. He smiles the whole time he records her breathing. He's a fucking genius.

He knows if he were Bridge, he'd kill him for sure. Hands down. No doubt at all, screw the risk of jail. If Juniper were his, when she is his, no man will get near her like this because he will never leave her side. Bridge is an idiot for leaving her, even if it's for work, and John is taking that absence as his win.

He lays his phone on her pillow and reaches up to her, dares to press a finger to the warm top of her hand. He wants to feel her lips, but that might wake her, so he goes for a less sensitive patch of skin, one that's used to touching a sheet during sleep. She feels warm and alive to his delicate caress. He releases a sigh as his eyes soften, watching her body twitch again. He'd love to hear about her dream as they woke in bed together.

He wants to crawl inside her; he loves her so much. He loves her more than he fears being hurt. He wants her beyond the edge of agony, to the very core of his wet, fat lust, in the very slivers of blood slithering through this thumping heart. His heart needs her to exist on its own. Without her, his heart is just a bag of meat. He leans in and inhales the scent of her skin, which smells faintly like coconut and shea butter, the lotion he knows sits on her bathroom counter.

He studies the delicate curl of her eyelashes and the curve of her cheek, the dip of her skin that creates the middle of her top lip. He follows her curves with his eyes, staining the image to the curvy coils of his mind, but he also videos her again, liquefying the essences of her presence into visual memories for his brain and his phone. He wants to fatten up his masturbation ammunition storage bucket with more videos so he can relish her over and over again later at home.

She changes position in her sleep. His heart races so fast that he might have a heart attack.

Seriously. Fuck. She can't wake up and find him beside her. He'd end up in jail, most likely ruining all his plans for their future together. It's not the time yet for her to know. No one would understand.

He glances down at his dick, which is hardening up again with being so near to her and touching her skin. Shivering against the thrill of being close enough to hear her breathe, he taps the stop on his phone to end the video. He lifts the sheet off himself, the air rushing in to shock his naked, wet penis, just how cold air robs skin of warmth when getting out of a warm pool. He doesn't want to leave her, but he knows he must.

He carefully rises from the bed so as not to jiggle it too much. As he zips up his pants, he watches her stir in her sleep again. All beauty would die before her. She's so gorgeous right now, beyond anything he's ever laid his eyes on in his life. He takes a picture of her; it will probably turn out crappy in the dark, but he doesn't care. He will know it is her in the blackness of it and cherish it forever. He walks slowly and with great care to be as silent as possible as he creeps to the bathroom, his eyes on her the whole time, ensuring she isn't waking. Making his way swiftly to the cupboard, he pulls out the bottle of lube loaded with his cum from his pocket and places it on the edge of the shelf. He pushes the other lube behind other things, so she goes for his first. He contemplates taking it so she has only his to use, but then decides that would be too suspicious and leaves it there, just hidden.

He walks through the laundry area and sees Juniper's lingerie laid out on the counter. He contemplates stealing it, shoving it in his pocket, but he doesn't want to raise too many suspicions with leaving the unfamiliar lube in the cupboard, having left the damn granola bar wrapper on the counter, so he will just touch it, run his hands over it imagining her sumptuous body in it, easy to do since he's actually seen her in it. He runs his fingers over the black lace, and the silky black bodice slides beneath his hands. He wishes it weren't washed so he could smell her scent on it, the crotch of it saturated with her pussy juices. He needs to sneak in and steal her used lingerie sometime.

A sound to his left makes him turn quickly, which causes his hand to bump the laundry detergent on the counter. It falls like a rocket before he can catch it. He watches in full horror, as if in slow motion, as the cat runs off, and the jug falls, then smacking on the ground with a loud thud. He cringes as he anticipates what dreadful thing will happen next. He needs to get away fast. Now!

He's fucked. He will be discovered; the police will be called.

He comes to his senses as he watches the laundry detergent dispenser spitting out the thick liquid soap like an open faucet all over the floor. He runs, making his way rapidly toward the front door, fast as a banshee. He bursts out the front door and breathes a sigh of relief that the dark night will hide him as he hurries down the driveway, scurrying along the street to his car.

Juniper sits up in bed after the loud thud.

"What the...?" she says with a fear that crushes her confidence. She's suddenly glad Sara is here and wonders immediately why there isn't an alarm system in this house yet. Bridge needs to get on that, especially when he travels, for fuck's sake.

Her heart is beating way too fast, and her inhaled breath catches in her lungs. It lingers there momentarily as she remains still, before she lets it out. Each waking breath breeds stark vulnerability throughout her whole body, and once she releases it, she knows she can't put it back in; it will be alive, her breathy fear existing in the world. She'd much rather go back to bed and pretend nothing happened. She slowly exhales as her heart pounds ever harder. Juniper has never been good at vulnerability. One had to be good at it for it to work to the benefit of something. Sara was good at it. Bridge was, too. And these two people were really the only two people she'd let herself be vulnerable to in her entire life, at least as far as she could remember, or let herself remember. It had taken her a long time to become comfortable with being vulnerable with Bridge during sex, and when she finally did, she had learned true sexual bliss; she was able to come, and she let him see her full sexuality because she trusted him.

She glances around the room, her fear keeping her frozen in place. The sound had come from the direction of the bathroom or laundry area. She suffers skyrocketing fear as she imagines it's a rapist in her house, or a murderer. Her desire to recoil and hide under her blankets is overwhelming as she contemplates doing just that rather than putting a foot on the floor.

Will she need to run? Fight for her life? Knee someone in the balls? Stab someone in the eyes?

She forces a scoff. Relax, Juniper. Maybe it was Mags, but she doesn't want to take chances, so she slips out of bed as fast as she can and jogs to the spare bedroom to get Sara. She is still naked because, in her own words, "Who the fuck cares?" They will check it out together, just in case it's someone who broke in. There's a better chance of avoiding an attack if they go in together.

She feels bad for waking Sara, but that thud was loud and real and definitely scary.

She shakes Sara's shoulder. "Sara...Sara...did you hear that sound?"

"What? Juniper...wait, what sound?" Sara sits up in the bed, her long hair swinging as she rises.

"That really loud sound. Did you hear it?" Juniper shivers slightly again at the thought of a malicious intruder. Damn, she misses Bridge being home.

"No, I didn't hear anything." She swings her legs off the bed, readying to stand. "Let's go check it out. Grab a knife as we go through the kitchen."

Is she serious?

Juniper shudders thinking of having to plunge a knife into an intruder. "Well, thanks, Sara, now I'm terrified."

"We'll be fine. Maybe it was just Mags knocking something over." Sara yawns, then grabs Juniper's hand to pull her along. "But, still, get a knife." She nods at Juniper. "Or something heavy."

Juniper nods back in agreement. Once in the kitchen, Juniper pulls Sara toward the knife block, not wanting to let go of her friend's hand for a second. Her hand shakes as she fumbles for the biggest knife, pulling out the smaller one first by accident.

"Oops, not that one."

She raises the largest knife from the wooden block in the air like a damn serial killer as the two women creep toward the laundry room. Juniper's heart is beating so fast that every breath is almost upon the other. What if there is a masked man in there? Or a serial killer who has lined the walls in plastic, like on the show? What if it's a robber who just wants to steal things? Or a rapist who will tie both her and Sara up and rape them?

She can't think clearly...maybe they should be calling the cops rather than trying to confront this intruder on their own. Why didn't she open the safe and get Bridge's gun out? Why is she so stupid?

Juniper leads with the knife raised as they enter the laundry room. With a shaking hand, she flicks on the light.

Relief floods her, and she laughs. "Oh, my gosh!" She drops the knife to her side. "Aw, fuck! I hate it when this happens!" Her hand flies to her temple. "Oh my gosh. I was terrified!"

The laundry detergent dispenser is flat on its side in a giant puddle of liquid. The entire floor is covered in rivers of blue goo.

Sara starts cracking up, too. "Whoa!"

"Seriously, I'm not buying this kind of detergent anymore. This happens all the time. It just falls randomly on its own when it gets less full. Or I guess Mags could have knocked it over, too. She's done it before." The lid is cracked in half and lies in the spilled soap. She picks it up to examine it. "That nearly gave me a damn heart attack! Geez!"

Sara slaps her thighs with her hands as she laughs. "Wow. This sucks. How did you clean it up last time? What a nightmare." She yawns and stretches through her smile. "It's like waking to an exploded poopy diaper in the middle of the night, and it's all over the crib, too."

Juniper sighs as she rapidly blinks at her friend. "I was really freaking out, wondering what kind of creep was in here." She stares at the knife and puts her other hand on her heart. "Slow down, heart. Oh, my good lordy forty." She lets out a nervous laugh. "Last time I threw dirty clothes all over it to soak it all up since they needed to be washed anyhow. I have a basket of dirty towels over there we could throw on it."

She carefully places the knife on the counter and sets the basket of towels near the edge of the spill. Both women grab towels and begin laying them all over the blue lake of detergent covering the floor.

"This should work great," Sara says as she stands to grab another towel.

"Yeah, it will totally work." Juniper lets out an exhale. "I just couldn't shake the fear that there was a person in here. What a creepy feeling."

"I know, right?" Sara stands and puts her hands on her hips. "Okay, now I need a snack, and then we both need to get back to sleep. We had quite the fucking night, literally." She grins.

Juniper mirrors her smile. "Yes, that sounds perfect. My heart is so worked up right now, I need a snack too, and maybe another glass of wine to calm me down so I can sleep." She laughs as she picks up the now-empty laundry detergent bottle and shakes it. "Let's do it."

# Chapter Fourteen

Juniper paces the kitchen, her gut still churning. Being home alone was nerve-racking enough, but add in the weird stuff like the mysterious wrapper, which Sara never claimed, and the detergent falling, and she is a mess. Clearly, the potential was there for it all being easily explained away; she just couldn't shake that feeling that saturated her brain with fear last night when she was scared an intruder was actually in her house. She sat on the barstool at the island and scrolled on her phone. After a minute, she set it down. Feeling unsafe in her own home was more than just unsettling; it was terrifying.

"Not helping," she says with a quick wave of her hand. She glances around quickly as her heart starts to ramp up. "I need to calm down. No one is here."

She needs tasks to occupy her mind. She fills her watering can and strolls out to the deck to water her flowers. The morning sun glistens off the ocean waves like a sheet of a million tiny drops of sun all confluent, as everywhere. She smiles. It's brilliantly jarring to be in the blazing sun, and it calms her. She sighs as the moist, salty air bathes her skin, and the sunshine licks along her face, bringing a bigger smile. This will certainly relax her; being near the ocean always does. This is exactly what she needs.

She grips the railing of the deck after she has watered all the pots, and grabs for her phone vibrating in her pocket. She pulls it out to find Sara has texted her.

Sara: Fabulous night of fucking, my friend. We need to do that again. I'm already hungry for you. Talk to Bridge about a foursome. Matt is soooooo in. He's been drooling over our videos all morning.

She giggles, a hand flying up to cover her right eye.

Oh, the things they had done together. Wow. Just simply wow. Sara always had gotten her to be adventurous. It's comforting to know that it hadn't changed one bit.

Certainly, many of her actions were induced by inebriation and most likely will never be repeated. She had fun, nonetheless. And luckily, Bridge had surprised her with all his gushing about loving their videos, too. She had feared he'd be pissed at her, but no, he had texted her and left a message that it was so hot and that he had loved it and masturbated hard, shooting his load across the shower stall in the hotel room, hitting the opposite wall in a creamy blast. She had grinned as she had imagined him doing that. She can never get enough of being a part of him being turned on. It's like her drug. Sara had opened up a new kink for her and Bridge. Bless her for that!

She sighs as she stretches in the bright morning, not a cloud in the sky. She had woken up to Sara already gone and messages from Bridge. She had slept in so long, not a usual thing for her. But she couldn't shake the feeling of doom.

But thoughts of all of the sexual stuff are helping distract her, and are making her horny as fuck. So she makes her way back into the house with sudden plans to fuck herself with her toys. And why not? Bridge is gone. Sara's now gone, and she wants some. It will surely make her feel better, too.

Mags dutifully follows her into the house, and she closes and locks the sliding door, then makes her way toward the kitchen. She has to work later today, so now is the time for self-fucking indeed. She's scheduled for the evening shift at the hospital and is actually looking forward to it for just being around others. She likes alone time, but this is too much for her; she misses Bridge terribly. Plus, being home alone has become something to endure.

Walking into her laundry room, she finds the pile of detergent-soaked towels on the floor. She scoops them all up, tossing the goo-infested towels into the washer and hits start before walking over to her bathroom cupboard to get her lube out.

Huh, that's odd. There's a new one? She could have sworn the other bottle still had some left. She smirks. Her man. She hadn't realized Bridge bought a new lube. Sometimes they would each buy new toys or lube or something sexy and surprise each other for fun. It was a sexy, hot game they played with each other. She bites her lip through a grin as she picks up the lube and turns it around in her hands. It was a pretty sparkly purple bottle. He must have bought it for her to find as a fun surprise for when he was gone. She would try it and report back to Bridge.

She strips her clothes off and saunters fully naked to her side table to choose a sex toy from her special drawer.

JOHN HOLDS HIS BREATH as Juniper digs around in her nightstand. His cock had been hard for the last hour as he watched her move about her house, water her flowers, soak in the sun, strip naked, and best of all, he saw her choose the lube laced with his sperm. He had yelled out with joy as she held it in her hand with a look of utter excitement on her face. He knew his angel would follow through.

His heart pounds as he imagines his sperm swimming inside Juniper's vagina on its way to her uterus to find its egg. The thought alone almost makes him shoot his load. This is the day their future together starts.

He's legit drooling. He can't keep his mouth closed as he watches in amazement as Juniper pulls out a purple rabbit vibrator and lays it on the bed beside her. That same bed he had been in with her last night while she slept. John's whole insides are afloat with butterflies. This is the moment he's been waiting for.

She squirts the lube on the vibrator and then smears it around the head of the larger arm of the sex toy with her fingers, then gives a swipe over the clit portion. Watching her touch his cum is so arousing; his cock is just about to burst. This, the most epic moment of his life, is about to become even more epic as his sperm will swim inside her body. His heart aches for her, his want almost its own universe for how vast and filled with everything it is, for how alive he feels when getting even a tiny contact with her. She sniffs the coated toy, and John holds his breath.

"Huh, kind of a realistic scent," she says with a chuckle, then lies back in the bed, readying herself to insert the toy into her pussy.

First, she plucks at her nipples with one hand, making them form hard tips, while holding the toy in the air above like a torch. She rubs her hand all over herself, from her breasts to her tummy, dipping down to her labia and clit, to her inner thighs, and back up to her breasts again. Her supple, ample breasts turn her on. She knows that's silly, but it's a thing.

John sighs as she touches herself, imagining it's his hands upon her breasts. She still has the toy raised near her lovely face, her lips pursing as she fondles herself. She presses the little buttons to turn on the toy, and a hum floods out of John's laptop speaker. As she lowers it to press against her pussy, John strokes his cock furiously. It's more realistic as a fantasy imagining he's with her now, with his sperm on the toy, and after having recently been in bed with her, his scent must still be there. His heart is thudding so hard in his chest, forcing more blood into his cock as it shoves blood around his body in the pounding of his racing heart. He squeezes the head of his cock as Juniper moans and pushes the head of the toy into her vagina.

Fuck yes.

It's in her. Part of him is inside Juniper. Oh, happy and perfect day. The ecstasy of it is overwhelmingly delicious and the utmost in its fullness of eroticism. He's done it. His seed is inside his woman.

He holds his breath as she pumps it into herself, feeding his swimmies deeper inside her with each thrust.

He lets a tear out of his eyes as he murmurs, "Thank you, Junie. Thank you. You, perfect, amazing angel."

He strokes his cock as she rides the toy in and out of herself furiously. She's enjoying herself, pressing the little arm of the rabbit vibrator to her clit with her free hand—she cries out in a series of moans, each intense, loud, alternating from soft moans, deep groans, and whimper-moans. She's enjoying herself, and that's so important to him.

John's cock explodes, and his cum blasts his coffee table, sending thick streams of spunk across it, glorious white spurts of cum, drops, speckles, all chocked full of sperm to mess up his table. It's a beautiful sight to behold his cum inspired by her. He continues to stroke his semi-hard cock as it begins to fall soft in his hand. He grins in full satisfaction. It's done.

Juniper's hands are working fast, pressing the toy against her G-spot and her clitoris. John watches as more tears stream down his face. If he were her baby's father, she could never hate him. She'd love him, and they could be a family. A real, true family. He knows that will happen; he just hopes it's his sperm that finds Juniper's ripe egg first, not Bridge's. It really helps that he's gone, so his seed has likely died off by now. He'd been tracking her cycle, and he's almost positive she's now likely ovulating. The timing is ideal. He wipes his eyes with the hand that isn't cum-soaked.

"Get a grip, John." He shakes his head, not normally a crier. "You will love me, Junie. And I will love you and our child. We will live a blessed life, and I will provide generously for both of you. I can take care of you both. Forever."

His heart blossoms as Juniper's arms and legs draw to her body, and her head crunches toward her chest, as it always does when she reaches the top climax of her orgasm. Her lips purse, her tongue slightly protrudes out of her mouth, as her body convulses with her internal contractions. She undulates her body three times in a row, her body reacting to the vaginal spasms as she comes.

Success.

She touches the toy to her clit and her body recoils...she always does that after she comes with a toy, testing the hyper-sensitivity of her clit, which always makes John grin. He loves her habit so much. Her body slumps, and she remains still for a period of twenty seconds. John watches her as his panting subsides.

"Wow," she says. "That was really powerful."

He savors the euphoria so clearly displayed across her face. This makes the act even more satisfying. She got off, too.

She pulls the toy out and sets it on her sheet beside her hip.

He's overjoyed once again to be a part of her climaxing and coming. The only thing better would be to have his cock inside her, enjoying her pussy hugs during those contractions.

He snarls. Soon, baby, soon.

John calms again as he gleefully watches her snuggle herself with an arm wrapped around her breasts. She grins. He grins. His cum is in Juniper for the first time ever. What an outstanding day this is! What an exquisite thing to happen! Euphoric joy floods him. He's done a good thing, and whether she gets pregnant or not, something alive of him is now swimming in her, touching the insides of her vaginal walls, lingering in perfect deposits along her G-spot, her cervix. His sperm could be anywhere and everywhere inside her, and it gives him immense pleasure. It feels like a claiming of her.

"Someday I will deposit myself right into your pussy, my love."

He strokes the screen lovingly along her cheek, then runs his thumb over her lips, down her neck, to the rise of each breast and the hard bulb of each nipple. Her nipples are relaxing, flattening, slowly returning to their rounded, unaroused state. Even when not aroused, her large, pale pink nipples are beautiful. Everything about her is beautiful, including her heart.

How he longs to hold her in his arms, to feel her heartbeat beneath his fingers, to feel her breathing press against his embrace that would be wrapped tightly around her. He'd never let go of how he would love it if she were to gaze up at him from where her head rested on his shoulder, a tiny, satisfied grin on her face, along with a feeling of appreciation at being fully loved by him, shining out of her eyes. He would give anything for that to happen, and he knew in his heart he would make it happen someday, not in a number-one-fan-freaky-style kind of way, but real—a true, honest, and genuine union of their mutual love. If he had to steal her that way, fine, but he would quickly convince her his intentions were good, loving, caretaking, not evil or cruel-intentioned. He'd never hurt her or their child.

He scoffs, then shakes his head. There's not even a child yet. Yet, being the keyword. He smirks, then grabs for some tissues to clean off his coffee table. Then he opens the document for his latest book and begins typing, a giant smile lingering on his face as he works. Climaxing had cleared his head. He's ready to write.

# Chapter Fifteen

Juniper squeals as she reads the text, her heart leaping with excitement as if it's their first date all over again.

Bridge: I just landed and will be home soon.

She bites the grin spreading across her lips and looks at the timer on the stove. The lasagna will be done in twenty minutes. Time to throw the garlic bread knots into the oven. She places the little tied bread pieces on the cookie sheet and tilts her head to the right, examining the intricate and intimate way the bread snuggles into itself. It's almost erotic. Searching for a lighter in the cupboard, she spies that the little mystery drawer inside is slightly open. She fingers it and then crawls onto the counter to peer into it. This is strange.

As she maneuvers herself to peer inside the tiny drawer. It's empty.

"Oh, how odd. I wonder if Bridge opened this." That nagging pit in her stomach enlarges as she ponders all the weird occurrences since Bridge has been gone. Not that it's that unusual for a drawer to be open, but it is for this drawer to be. And again, she needs to stop inventing nefarious issues where there could be simple explanations. Sara was just in the house; it could have been her looking for something, or simply curious.

She pushes the little drawer shut and scrunches up one cheek in frustration. Oh, how ridiculous. She's being paranoid as hell, worrying for nothing. Or could it be...something. That drawer has always been closed.

"Shit," she mutters.

She jumps at a sound in the living room, almost losing her balance from her perch on the counter. She laughs at herself when she sees it's Mags playing as she's trying to catch a fly. She sits on the counter and slips her feet down to the floor, landing in a semi-graceful plop. She glares up at the little drawer. Could Bridge have opened it before he left? Curiosity is killing her inner cat. She would feel embarrassed even asking him such a trivial question.

She checks her phone. No new texts. She peers into the oven at the lasagna. It's getting close to being done. She grins as she watches Mags swat at the fly.

"Mags, get it, Mags. You get that fly."

"Boo!" comes a voice.

She screams; her heart fluttering like it might beat itself right out of her chest as she swings around fast, her arms up in fists, ready to fight this real intruder. She gasps with relief. It's Bridge with his arms outstretched, a giant grin on his face. Instant relief sags her body, and then she perks up to run to him. She's fighting off a burst of tears.

"You're home!" she shrieks.

He takes her in his arms; her head goes straight to nestle into his shoulder.

"Hey, baby, are you okay? I didn't mean to scare you so badly." He strokes the back of her head.

Tears push out of her eyes as she nuzzles into his chest. She bites hard into her fear and sighs. She's got to get a fucking grip on herself. Bridge will think she's gone insane.

"Oh, I'm okay. You're just earlier than I expected, so I thought you were an intruder."

"Ah, yes. There was almost no traffic, so I flew down the interstate. I'm guessing you missed me." He strokes her as she shivers. "Oh, baby. I'm sorry you're so freaked. I should have texted." He sighs. "We should really get an alarm system put in this house. I'm honestly surprised John never put one in."

Juniper nods against his chest as she bites her lip. That would certainly help her if they had an alarm system, especially when Bridge goes out of town. She is already dreading the next trip.

"Yeah," she whispers, trying to calm her quivers.

"Wow. You're really spooked. You aren't ever this jumpy." A look of concern floods his face. He strokes her back, dipping his hand down to the tops of her ass cheeks and back up again. "I'm here. No worries, baby. All is good."

She suppresses any further explosion of her tears. "It's just that I missed you so very much."

He chuckles. "Except clearly not when Sara was here."

She laughs, which she really needed, and swats Bridge's chest. "Well, you were on my mind a lot during it, that's for sure."

"I'm not wrong, though, am I? You two looked like you had quite a fun time. I was jealous. I would have loved to have been here to see all that live."

She leans back off his chest to gaze into his eyes. "You would have? I thought you were always too jealous for such a thing."

"Oh, well, I don't know. It just seems very different with a woman for you, and that you two are friends. Kinda harmless, like friends with benefits without any threat, especially since you two are both married and committed to your spouses. Right?" He winks and squeezes her shoulders.

Juniper giggles. "Well, I'm certainly not leaving this cock for any pussy, though pussy is hot, too." She grabs his engorged cock through his clothes. "Mmmm, I see you are happy to see me."

"Damn straight I am." He kisses her forehead. "Oh, yes indeedy I am. Let's take our time, though. I want to romance you into bed tonight."

"Here's a tip. I'm a sure thing." She cocks her head with a smile.

"Oh, and don't I know it. But. Still, I want to spend time with you first. Hear about what you did while I was gone. What you did with Sara that I didn't get to see. And then later I'll fuck your brains out. Deal?"

She squeals and claps. "Yes, please."

The timer goes off on the oven, and Bridge releases her.

"I made lasagna." Juniper slips the hot pad mitts onto her hands.

"So, I smell. And it smells incredible. I'm going to quickly unpack and take a two-minute shower. Be right back." He smirks. "Don't go anywhere."

"Okay. I won't. And that's perfect. This is supposed to rest for like ten minutes before I cut it, anyway."

She pours two glasses of red wine as she watches her sexy-as-fuck man's butt disappear into the bedroom. She's seriously tempted to follow him and jump him, shove him on the bed, and ride that already existing boner of his until they both come. However, the idea of savoring a romantic evening first will most likely heighten their fucking. Plus, they can edge each other on throughout a romantic evening and make the end fuck even more delicious. She's so happy she can't stop smiling.

She wanders into the bathroom to catch a peek of his nakedness. She can't resist. Dang, she's horny for him. The steam is piling out, clouding up the air as she saunters near the shower. She plays with the stuff in his overnight bag, then hops up on the counter to sit.

"I liked the new lube. Maybe I should have waited for you to use it, but I was too curious." She smirks. She likes him knowing she played with herself while he was gone, since that turns him on.

"What's that, babe?"

"The new lube. The one you bought and stuck in the cupboard before you left. Was it supposed to be something fun for me while you were gone?" She grins like a little schoolgirl.

"I didn't buy any new lube, honey." The last word comes out all warbled as he's clearly washing his face.

Juniper screws up her face as confusion fills her. "You didn't?"

"Nope. That's a fun idea, though. I'll have to do it next time for you when I go out of town."

"Geez. I must have bought it and forgotten about it or something." But a thick something, a something that's breeding ominous vibes, shoves the pit in her stomach open further, yet another weird and off thing, and it's leaving her feeling even more uneasy.

She shakes her head as doubt fills her. She's totally overreacting like a freak. Once again, Sara could have been searching for lube, lotion, soap, or something, and left the lube behind. She's definitely one to help herself.

"Oh, I'm sure. It was probably just hidden for a while and got shifted. Probably was Sara." She shrugs even though he is still behind the curtain.

Bridge slides the shower curtain aside and steps out. His toned, muscular body is glistening all over with the water. He looks sexy as fuck.

He scrubs his hair with the towel, then rubs it all over his torso. "Maybe I moved it looking for something. I don't remember doing that, but maybe I did. I always leave in a rush and forget."

If he's dismissing it, so is she.

Juniper chews on her lip and wiggles her feet below her crossed ankles. "Yeah. Maybe." Dang. Following his lead of disregarding it is failing her. Or maybe not; trying to ignore the worry is making it worse. It's inching about in her gut like a worm and totally not working worth shit. It's all too weird.

She hops off the counter and throws her arms around Bridge to distract herself. "Sure, you don't want a little pre-dinner fuck session?" She presses her belly to him, arching her back, sandwiching his boner between both of their abdomens.

"Normally, I'd say yes. But I want to build it up, so our fun is explosive, max out the horniness we've built." He grins, clearly teasing her, enjoying the full threshold of his taunt. "I want you. Make no mistake."

She bites her lip and sways back further against his arms, which are encircling her snugly. "I want you."

"I want you to be nice and saturated with wine and lasagna when I fuck your cum out of you." His eyes twinkle with mischief.

She mirrors her fuck-me eyes back to him.

"Okay, get him dressed and covered up, then so we can eat. I can't look at you hard if we're going to wait." She releases her husband, but he keeps hold of her.

"I ought to eat naked just to tease you," he taunts with a suggestive expression.

She smirks back at him, then falls into a silly look.

"You're mine," he says in a growly tone.

He pulls her close and puts his open mouth on hers, snatching her upper lip between his. He sucks on it, then slowly caresses it as he allows it to slip out. There is only a slight hesitation before he's back at her, sliding his tongue in along the full length of hers, as far as he can.

She clamps her mouth down on his tongue and sucks it. They French kiss for several minutes, hands roaming each other's backs, asses, and hair, before he pulls back abruptly.

He leans into her ear and says, "Let's take our time tonight, babe. Make it special. Maybe we'll make a baby."

She smiles deeply, so deeply that it fills up her whole soul. She nods as tears of hope threaten to blast her face. "Yes. Let's do that. Not sure if the timing is right, but I do think I'm possibly ovulating." Glee fills her. "Regardless, it's definitely time for a good, hearty fuck. I've missed you so very much." She nods as she backs away from him, a sexy little grin on her face. "Passion makes babies."

"Indeed, it does."

She wants to tell him all the weird stuff that happened while he was gone, but she feels foolish bringing it all up. She's making a big deal out of little things that just don't matter. She's being silly. She's not going to ruin his homecoming with such ridiculousness.

JOHN BITES HIS FINGERNAILS as he watches Bridge and Juniper separate as she dreamily drifts off to the kitchen. He grins despite his worry. His seed is surely deep in her. Sure, Bridge's will join, but his is already loaded. If he didn't love her so much, he'd feel a bit guilty for stealing this daddy-potential moment from Bridge. But since his heart aches for her, and every waking moment his mind dwells on her, he knows in his soul that they belong together. They deserve each other. Bridge was fine for her up until now. He was kind to her. He fucked her frequently. Made her cum multiple times a fuck session, all good things a good lover does; however, Bridge doesn't feel what he feels for Juniper. There's no chance. His love is deeper, wider, taller, so gargantuan. He is consumed daily by her soul, body, heart, mind, her beauty...her essence. He can feel her in this world, which means there is a deep connection between them, something surreal, and they are supposed to be together. Bridge would get over it. He's a sexy man. He'd find a new woman easily. He knows deep in his bones that he and Juniper were meant to be.

He nods. "We belong together, Juniper. We should have met first, but we didn't, so I have to make it happen now."

He sighs and shakes his head as he watches her in the kitchen. "Talking to a screen, you again, Junie. I can't wait until I get to talk to you all the time in person. Hold your gaze with mine, your body in my hands, my fingertips grazing your lush skin. My cock bringing your clit to monstrous stellar orgasms as you, in turn, deliver them for me with your amazingly gorgeous pussy and mouth." He strokes his cock as he watches her dance around the kitchen. She busies herself cutting squares of lasagna, putting garlic bread knots on plates, and sipping her wine. What a fresh delight she is! There is no one like her on the planet.

He'd been building a wine collection for her. He loves wine too, not as much as Scotch whiskey, but he'd just had a wine cellar built for her in his basement and stocked it with five thousand dollars' worth of wine. He couldn't wait to see her go down and pick out a bottle, bring it back up with a giant, excited smile on her face. He'd buy her anything, and with his money, he literally could. Lately, his writing had ceased to be about his wants, but about her wants, so he could give her anything that she asked for. He wanted to give her the world, just because she asked.

Now that's love. Real love.

He wasn't looking forward to watching her and Bridge's fuck session later. Normally not true, but also, he would never be able to top watching her enjoy herself with only his come inside her. But on the other hand, he loved seeing her body and face when she came. So, there's always that. He's a bit bitter about the competition of his sperm with Bridge's, though. If only he'd stayed gone for a few more days.

He usually tried to block out Bridge's face when they fucked, but sometimes, when he took her from behind, John couldn't see her face, so that made it suck. All he saw was Bridge's lecherous looks as he rammed himself inside her. The man could be a brute. But still, seeing her curvy form in any way, especially ass up being fucked, was a delectable sight all on its own; however, seeing her face and her eyes during her throes of pleasure, those couldn't be beat. She has this amazing sparkle in her eyes that is almost so tangible, it literally fills up a room. She just outshines the sun and stars combined. She certainly outshines everyone in a room. She is her own stellar galaxy, bigger than any other, and way more distinct. There's no end to her magic.

John stretches out on his couch for a nap. Since they are going to romance each other before fucking, he'd sneak in a nap first. He didn't need the agony of watching Bridge enjoying her company.

"THIS IS SO GOOD. YOU are such a good cook, baby. How did I get so lucky to get a hot wife who can cook like a chef?" Bridge takes the last bite of his lasagna, then washes it down with the last of his wine. "We have any of that cognac left? I'd love an after-dinner drink of it if we do."

"Oh, yes, we do. It's in the cupboard above the fridge." She hops up and scoots to the fridge. She wants to pamper him to no end.

"Oh, baby, I'll get it. You sit. You made dinner." He rises, grabs both their plates, and delivers them to the sink. "I'll clean up. You pour a glass of whatever you want and go sit on the deck so you can hear the ocean." He smiles sweetly at her. "I know how much you love that."

Juniper opens the cupboard above the fridge. "I want to get it for you." She peers into the cupboard, but then her face falls. "Well. I know there was some left. I saw it here the other day." The hairs on the back of her neck rise as she spies the empty bottle of cognac. Another odd thing. She chastises herself. *Quit being paranoid, Juniper. Maybe Sara drank it. She might need to get herself on anti-anxiety meds.*

Bridge, on the same wavelength, says, "Maybe Sara imbibed. That's okay. I can have something else. Do we have that whiskey I bought?"

Juniper reaches for the whiskey. The unease is swelling in her gut despite her justifying the strange things away. She's getting uncomfortably consumed by full paranoia. Maybe she is going crazy? I mean. Her grandpa had Alzheimer's, and, according to her grandma, he had started to lose his brain in his early forties with early onset. Maybe she's just going to have an earlier onset. She shakes her head, her fears ballooning, about to bubble out of her mouth.

"Bridge, there's been some weird things. Like...things that were off while you were gone." She laments the rash confession right as it leaves her mouth.

He pauses in doing the dishes and gives his wife full attention. "Oh? Like what?" He doesn't sound worried at all.

She wrings her hands, shifts her weight back and forth between her feet as her panic rises. "I mean. Geez. The thing is, they can all be explained away, like maybe Sara drank the cognac. Sara ate the granola bar. Sara left the lube. Maybe I was just feeling creeped out with you not here." She gives a tiny laugh and runs her hand through her hair. "Yeah, that's it." She scoffs. "Or maybe I'm just going crazy."

"Granola bar?" He gives her an amused look. "Hey, babe. Whatever you want to tell me? I'm here to listen." He wipes his hands, then walks toward her. He wraps his arms around her.

He grabs her hands as he stares into her eyes with love in his. He presses her hands to his pecs and rubs the backs of them. "I'm here for you. Always, Juniper."

She tries to smile the worry away. "It's okay. I think I'm just letting my imagination get the best of me."

His face doesn't waver with a single flick of doubt. "I think you just missed me and were on edge. Ask Sara. I bet she drank it. And that's totally okay. We can buy more."

"Sara is a lush." She grins, feeling a little better.

Something arousing rages in her at the mention of Sara. The bit of wine she's had already gives her the confidence to consider asking Bridge about the foursome, but still, her heart pounds like she's asking him to marry her. This is scary new territory. "Would you ever be into something sexual with Sara and Matt? Like anything? On any level, like some kind of foursome? Sara was asking, and I wasn't sure if you'd be into that or not." She hates it that she sounded almost apologetic.

"You mean like be swingers? Swap partners?" Bridge's eyes go wide, and he stops swaying her. A serious look overtakes his face.

"Well, yeah. Or in any way. I mean, you guys both liked the videos we did, right?" She smirks. "You said you loved it and thought it was really hot to watch us."

"Oh yes, it was. But I don't know about me being sexual with Matt around. And you'd want me to fuck Sara?" He looked incredulous.

She giggles. "Well, I'm open to whatever you'd want. Or if you and Matt just want to watch Sara and me live messing around, then each couple goes to their own rooms, that works, too. Sara said she and Matt would be up for any level of hooking up. Literally anything. Whatever you and I are comfortable with." She relaxes as he seems to. "We just need to decide."

Bridge widens, then blinks his eyes very fast. "I've never really thought about this. I'd be up for watching you two, yeah, that's hot. Let me think on it a bit, okay? I'm honestly not sure how I feel about it. But I'd say at the minimum, I'd be into watching you two lez out while Matt and I watch. Not sure I want to show him this," he says, grabbing his hard cock through his pants. "That's quite a bit different from being in the locker room, not that boners don't happen there, but in an intimate setting, it's somehow different." He frowns. "And I don't like any ideas of his putting his cock in you. That's a flat-out no."

She nods her head. "And I totally get that. You think about it. After all, we've been through, I was nervous as heck to ask you."

"Hey, never be afraid to ask me about a fantasy of yours. We're committed to each other. I want you fully sexually satisfied. Always. That's my top priority. And, babe, it doesn't hurt to ask. I'm not mad. If I don't like it, I'll just say no. We can find a compromise. Can we respect that of each other?"

She nods, feeling like a little girl. "Yes, Daddy." She suppresses a giggle.

"That's my girl. And there's that kind of play, too," he says with a chuckle. "I think I could get into more of that, but I wasn't sure if you would be into it."

"Well, we've clearly tapped into that realm a little bit with some of our play, especially naughty schoolgirl; we just have never really called it that. That takes on a different feel." She takes in a big sigh, frustrated with herself for being nervous. This is the love of her life, and he's not going to judge her.

Bridge grabs her face, holding her cheeks in his big hands the way he would hold a delicate vase, and gazes deep into her eyes. He says, "I think we should go downstairs and play some games, dance to some music in the sand, kiss by the ocean, maybe skinny dip, then we can fuck and make that baby. What do you say?"

She nods but can't seem to form words. He's so perfect it makes her ache for more of him.

"How about we do that? And you can tell me all about what you and Sara did, and what you learned about your own body during it, because I want to know. I want to know it all."

"Well, one thing I'll confess. Sara and I used to do that kind of stuff all the time in college," she blurts it out plainly. It's high time he knows. "Though we were never a couple, we just hooked up and made each other come." She giggles as Bridge gives her mock appalled shock. "You know, friends with benefits. Lesbian-style."

"No, not sweet little you?" He grabs her butt cheeks with both of his hands and squeezes. "Not my angel Juniper playing sex games with her friend. What would your mom say?"

"Shut up," Juniper says with a haughty chuckle. "She'll never know because neither of us will ever tell her. Sara's a bit more adventurous with sex than I am, but she gets me to try new things."

"I love anything that gets you more sexually adventurous. And I think you and Sara making each other come is very hot. Let me finish the dishes so we can enjoy each other."

Bridge turns back to finish the cleanup, but leans his head toward her and says, "Now go downstairs and relax as I ordered. And baby, don't forget your wine. I'll meet you downstairs, after I pour myself a drink, too."

She nods and walks over to grab her wine glass, then saunters to the sliding glass door. Mags follows her. As she exits the sliding door, the blast of warm, salty sea air bathes her face. She walks out onto the deck feeling alive and fresh. It tugs at her loose, thin shirt, reminding her that the breeze of the ocean is as intoxicating as listening to those bubbly waves crash continually on the sand. It and the sunshine combined help to calm her taut nerves that were just pretty much ready to snap into a cascade of tears. Bridge had expertly blended them away with his caresses. She giggles, recalling his raunchy, aggressive butt cheek grab. He's her magic potion to feel good.

She leans against the rail to let the breeze coast along her properly until she feels sufficiently massaged by it. She settles into the chair and sips her wine. A crisp, citrusy white wine, she could easily drink the entire bottle in just a few hours; it's so pleasant. Mags rolls out her body in a proper cat stretch on the deck boards, soaking up the evening sun that is still streaming solidly onto the beachfront. Tonight marks a new heralding of a sex life for her and Bridge, post Sara, that is.

She stretches her legs out and crosses her ankles, noting her need to touch up her nail polish. She considers texting Sara the good news about Bridge potentially being open to some type of foursome play, of some shape or form, anyway, clearly not much with her and Matt, but no matter. She understands male ego and all.

Bridge appears on the deck, so she decides to wait with the text. The best way is just to tell her once he's fully decided what he's up for.

"This isn't downstairs," he says with humor.

Juniper's mood dwells on her erotic thoughts of a foursome. Her clit shakes with an electric jolt as she imagines both Bridge and Matt watching her and Sara go at each other live, then each couple fucking separately. It sounds like the best of fantasy of all, as close to a threesome or foursome she will have ever gotten. Life isn't always as easy as what her fantasy life wants; there're rules and boundaries of Bridge to consider, and her own, too, for him. And if Bridge is ready to break a rule, she's all in, and if he couldn't handle more sharing, she'd be perfectly happy with her and Sara only. Her pussy wets as she imagines how it will be.

"What are you thinking about?" Bridge asks as she settles into the chair next to her, a nice, healthy shot of whiskey in his clear, low-ball glass tumbler.

She laughs and looks him in the eye. "You really want to know?"

"Of course, I do." He takes a sip of his drink as he gazes out at the ocean.

A couple is walking by with a young toddler girl and a very bouncy golden retriever.

"Always, baby."

She lets out a loud breath of air, her expression excessively sheepish. "I'm getting rather wet thinking about you and Matt watching me and Sara pleasure each other."

He chuckles. "And I'll be taking advantage of that wetness in a little bit, so keep thinking of that. But I'm beyond positive I can make that happen without it, anyway."

"Yeah, you've only done it several thousand times." She flares her twinkly eyes up at him.

"Or more." He cups her chin into his palm and raises her face up so their lips are closer. "I'm going to shoot my seed way up in you, but first I'm going to lick you slick, make you come, then pound you until you twitch and shake as you come again. I'm hard as a rock right now. Let's go make a baby, shall we?"

Juniper nods. "I don't think I can wait anymore either."

He downs his drink and flashes her a brilliant grin.

She hops up and moves without effort across the deck, making it to the spiral staircase in the short time of a wave crashing on the shore. Bridge is following close behind, both of them almost flat-out running. She giggles as the free feeling of glee takes her. She stops on purpose, and he slams into her. She leans her body against his and seductively undulates her body along the full length of his. To steady herself, she grabs the metal rail of the spiral staircase, leans forward, and gyrates her pelvis to rub her butt cheeks up and down, riding Bridge's hard-on along her ass crack. Her breathing flares as her pussy gushes when Bridge grabs both of her hips firmly between his hands and lets out a deep, low, lusty growl. The growl sends a shock of tingling anticipation through her body, ending in her deep, hungry gasp.

"Aww, that feels amazing, Juniper. Mmmmm, your ass is just perfect." He gives the side of her right ass cheek a swift slap, sending it into a hefty jiggle.

"Umm, yes, Bridge. Fuck yes," she says in a breathy soft voice.

He spanks her again and again as she rides him along her crack.

He pulls back and scoops her into his arms, then straightens up, readying to carry her down the stairs. She places her mouth on his neck, where she open-mouth kisses his warm flesh as he descends the stairs. Juniper would be afraid they would fall if she didn't know how strong Bridge really is. He's still built like a college football player even after all these years because he keeps lifting weights every other day, and jogging along the beach on the alternate days. He's just as sexy as the day they met.

She suckles his earlobe then returns her attention to his neck, kissing her way up and down, nuzzling her face into him.

She catches sight of Mags. The cat follows them downstairs as Bridge glides off the last step and carries her over to the fluffy white rug just at the edge of the covered space. He carefully nestles her body into the fluffy strands of the large carpet, then runs his hands down her curves, from her neck, along her chest to just before her cleavage starts, then down over the large mounds of her breasts. He continues his body exploration of her, hand riding her down her abdomen, dipping into the side indents of her abs, then handling the curves of her waist, landing on her full, round hips, and giving them a hearty squeeze on both sides.

"I missed this," he whispers.

He hooks his fingers under the elastic of her pants and slips them off, dragging his fingers tantalizingly along her skin. He smiles before he drops his mouth to kiss the skin around her belly button.

She squirms as he mouths her skin, smashing his tongue against it to taste her, his tongue flattening and licking her belly, and then pulling some skin into his mouth, sucking it. He continues his meander of her body, traveling his way down over her mound and snaking the tip of his tongue into her cleft.

She gasps and grasps for his head as he open-mouth suctions himself over her clitoris. He sucks her clit hard as she bucks.

She moans out louder than the surf as he eats her out, then moves down to her labia lips, flapping the lips up and down with his tongue before sucking each one into his mouth in turn. The lingering of his fingers in her pussy as his mouth travels down to meet them causes her to lurch her body and arch into his face. He licks her pussy lips up and down, dipping his tongue in while slowly pressing his finger into her slick wetness. He kisses his way back up to her clit and opens his mouth wide, placing the warmth of it over her. Again, he sucks her, pulling on the loose skin with his lips, causing her to moan out and grab fistfuls of his hair, holding his head flush with her pussy.

She whimper-moans to notify him that he's pushing her close to a climax.

He begins to pump two fingers into her very wet vagina, and responds by increasing his pumping speed to match the loudness of her pleasure sounds. He leaves her clit and rides his tongue down her pussy lips, lapping his tongue against his fingers to lick her juices off them as he makes his way down to lick her ass. He rolls the tip of his tongue around her anus as she flinches. He returns to her clit and fully engulfs it into his open mouth, pumping away with his fingers as she writhes herself against his face. Her mouth gapes open, then, pursing his lips, he increases his tongue action and finger fucks her fast. She's so close to coming. She groans out and touches her belly button, yep, she's close. Fuck.

He continues his stimulation until her body convulses above him. Her pussy clenches, spasming against his fingers four times as she comes, and more of her juices wet his fingers. He pulls his fingers out and shoves them into his mouth and sucks the insides of her off himself.

She moans, grabbing at her own breasts as she glides off the high of her climax.

"How's that, baby?"

"Mmmm. Good. Throbbing."

He lowers his body over her, and they kiss for several minutes, groping each other, hungrier yet for each other than they were ten minutes ago. He rubs his cockhead along her pussy, and she moans.

"Please, oh please, fuck me, Bridge. Just fuck me. I'm your whore. Slam into me. Use me to paint my insides with your come." She grunts as he pushes just the tip of his engorged cock into her vagina. "Make me pregnant. I'm your bitch to breed."

He groans out his lust and pushes his cock fully into her pussy, her vagina sucking him right in with how wet it is. He rides her slowly at first, her hands migrating him all over, her head rolling side to side as he pumps.

He stops her head roll and looks right into her eyes, holding her in direct eye contact as he pounds his cock into her, slapping her skin so fast she is either gasping or moaning, but nowhere near silent.

She opens her soul to let him in, giving him deep access through her eyes, fully accepting him as her mate, her partner in life, her man. He's fully there for her, making her feel good, helping her come. His leadership only grows.

Their sexual energy and intensity are maxed, making their baby together in the eye connection of their mutual passion and love. She believes it will happen this time.

"Yes," she murmurs. "Fuck me, Daddy."

She calls him that with great satisfaction.

It stirs something in him because he fucks her harder. She is his, and never will she willingly submit to another. He looks at her with loads of love and lust in his eyes. Feel-good emotions flood her, and her arousal is peaking.

He pulls his cock out of her and presses his hand on her right hip. "Over," he commands.

She obeys and gets on all fours in front of him. He pushes her head down to the rug and straightens himself to line up with her hips, readying to fuck her from behind.

He plays along with the scenario she geared up earlier. "Ass up, little one."

"Yes, Daddy Sir, yes, Sir," she murmurs as her desire to submit to him flourishes.

He enters her pussy from behind and instantly ramps up to slamming into her, causing her to moan out quick, deep throaty chirps and chant, "Yes, yes, yes, yes."

She smiles. That always edges him on to fuck her harder. His abdomen slaps the skin of her bottom, and he's moving so fast and so primal that her yearning to get dominated is getting well met.

He grunts as he pounds his body against her ass, making it bobble with each round. He's not going to last long now, but she's close to coming again, too.

He keeps going until she launches into her apex. Her arms and legs draw in, her body undulates with her pussy clenching, squeezing his cock repeatedly.

He loses it with a deep guttural groan. Feeling all sloshy wet inside, he slows his thrusting. It feels like a big amount in her. He pulls out and pushes her hips over so she can lie down. He grabs a pillow from the nearby couch and shoves it under her pelvis.

"Keep it in longer," he says soothingly.

Hopefully, he impregnated her.

She's sweaty and spent. He's sweaty and spent. They lie next to each other and breathe to the sound of the waves. He turns sideways to snuggle against her side. She swivels her head to look directly into his eyes.

"That was fucking amazing." She touches his cheek. "I needed you in me so bad, Daddy. We didn't exactly last long enough to play other games, though." She chuckles.

His face falls into a full, satisfied grin. "No, we didn't. But...but the night is young. We can still do that."

# Chapter Sixteen

John pours the last of his drink down his throat. Stroking himself to Juniper and Bridge fucking has been delicious, but he edged. He'd rather come later; saving it up meant a big, explosive load he'd get to enjoy. He grins, imagining his sperm and Bridge's fighting it out inside Juniper's uterus, searching heartily for her ripe egg. He's got the leg up, being his cum went in her first. His DNA is probably already loaded as the fertilizer. He wins the daddy status. He'd think he was a sick bastard if he were a character in his book, but he's not that. He's in love with the love of his life. Sick bastards don't love. They can't. But he wonders if he should write a story similar to his own life, only not call it a memoir. It's an intriguing thought. He could share his wonderful love for Juniper with the world that way. Both of them would know the truth, but keep it from the world.

He smiles as he pours himself another cognac. Bridge has good taste. He got desperate for a drink that night, when he was at the beach house, and he had drained the cognac bottle. He had meant to have only one drink, but that's like taking one French fry; it never works. But he loved it so much, he went out and bought himself a bottle of it. Damn good stuff. Idiot has good taste. He smirks and takes a sip. Well, he picked Juniper, so of course, the fucker has good taste. Good taste in liquor and women. A smart guy. He sort of felt sorry for Bridge because he was going to lose more than his cognac to John.

He opens his fridge looking for anything easy to eat. He hates cooking while drunk. Usually, it just ends up ordering something to be delivered. He'd had quite a bit of cognac while watching Juniper and Bridge delve into romance, then fuck. He's getting sloshed.

He leaned against the counter as their interaction replayed in his head. He'd particularly loved watching Juniper when Bridge ate her out. When he dipped to her asshole was his favorite part. She had flinched, then relaxed, and then, when he went ballistic on her clit, she came hard. Her gorgeous body had twitched and jerked, writhed, and her moans had gotten to John as usual, and he almost lost it just listening to her. She is so sensual, so sexual, such a massive turn-on as a woman. He had cheered out loud when Bridge had said he'd consider the foursome. John so wanted to see Sara and Juniper fuck again. That had been the best thing he'd ever seen in his entire life. Two goddesses making each other climax, over and over again. He'd watched it several times, their saunter into all things female/female, luscious clit-on-clit scissoring, their fleshy wet mouths on each other's pussies. It was enough to drive a man wild watching that juicy display of female lust. Watching one female expertly pleasure another was like watching chocolate eat chocolate, consuming itself in its own rich, thick, lush flavor. Thoroughly, and undoubtedly, the most delicious views of his entire life, topping the sunset just beyond the Eiffel Tower and the sunrise over the ocean in the Caribbean. Nothing compared to watching Juniper orgasm with Sara.

He'd written earlier in the day, and not obsessed too much about Juniper, making it three-fourths of the way through the manuscript. His agent would be happy. He loathed taking time away from Juniper worship, but writing was the best and only acceptable reason for doing that—except sleeping, eating, and showering. Everything else sucked.

He snuggled against a pillow on his couch, his dick now a bit softer. He lamented never having married, but now he was grateful to be single because he could pursue and win Juniper. Bridge was too hot to stay alone for long, so he'd find a devoted pussy to pound quickly, no doubt. He didn't need to keep Juniper for himself; he'd find another woman. Juniper belongs to John. She's a goddess. She deserves the daily sexual worship John will give her, way better than the job Bridge does. John will not make her work at the hospital anymore, either, unless she really wants to, for something to do. He'll do everything for her. Hiring whatever home services she wants and treating her like the queen she really is, as being on top of his sexual dream list. He's amazed by the erotic aura she oozes, the solid, loud sex drive she embodies. She is unmatched in the female gender; no one even comes close to her caliber.

John touches his cock as he thinks of their impending foursome and how he'd get to watch their erotic display as the four played. He was sure he could sell the video for thousands online, but he'd never do that because he didn't want the world to see Juniper. She is his and his alone. Sara and Bridge could have pieces of her, make her come. But the whole of her would be his for the rest of his life.

He has a plan.

He is going to swipe her, gently, or drugged, if need be, and drive her to his newly purchased yacht. It will be all gassed up, stocked, and ready to zoom off across the ocean. She will wake up at the right time, if he has to drug her. Gently drug her. This is something he needs to research. He must do it right so as not to harm her, or the baby, should there be one in her. Her every desire, need, and want will already be on the yacht for her pleasure. Food. Drink. Clothing. Even a woman to use if she wants one. He could easily find one at a harbor. He had to think on that idea a bit more, though, bringing in a stranger. Would such a woman be able to be brought aboard if Juniper protested being taken? Maybe he'd have to wait until he won her over. He can't have the world knowing he'd kidnapped her. He'd just kidnap her—he hated calling it that—and she'd want him in no time, so it would no longer be kidnapping. She'll see his love and want him.

He hangs his head. He really doesn't want to kidnap her. He wants her to come of her own volition. He can't stand the thought of having to kidnap her, because she might get scared.

He'd woo her. Cherish her. Love her. Pleasure her. Give her the whole damn world to win her mind, body, heart, and soul. He knew he could do it if given enough time alone with her. Juniper is not stupid. She could not be bribed, though. She is too genuine for that. But. His love for her is real, and she'd see that and fall in love with him, too. And if it took a lot of time, so be it. If it took lots of money, so be it. John had loads of money. It will happen. She will be his. She will love him back. He is one hundred percent sure of it. He just needs to do it; he needs to take action.

But when?

He can't get over his fears that he might have to force her at first. But that's why the thought of drugs occurred to him, so as not to traumatize her if she resists things. He doesn't want to be too physically aggressive with her. Ever. Not that. It's too hard to overcome such trauma. He understood that from his own upbringing, and he'd never do that to her. Plus, he doesn't want to suffer under a hurt look on her face or in her eyes at his hands...ever. He'd die before he did that. So, drugs just made sense. Then he could just pick her up and whisk her away as if she were no more than a little doll. No harm done.

He carries his drink out to his deck and looks out at the glistening ocean. The waves are doing their endless up and down thing, sounding awesome as usual. He has the urge to get sand between his toes and wade in the water up his shins, so he descends his deck stairs. He dons his slip-ons, which he leaves at the end of the stairs in case the sand is hot, and walks out onto his beach. The sun blasts his skin, and the sand bleeds into his slip-ons, annoying him, so he removes them and walks barefoot. The sand is a bit hot, but he's heading for the wet sand and the water anyhow, so no worries about burned soles. He gazes off across the vast, beautiful sea and imagines Juniper and their children jumping the waves. He smiles and takes a sip of his drink, wondering how many boys and how many girls they will have before they're done.

A woman and her toddler come running toward him from his right, chasing a wild lab who is all-out running like he's after a steak. They are both calling his name, which John can't make out, but they both sound full of fear. The dog is coming closer to him, and they are falling further behind because the toddler is slow. John sets his drink in the sand, risking sand spray spoiling his beverage, and goes for the dog as he goes by. He misses him, the dog dodges again, but John charges after and manages to step on the dog's leash. He gets choked and jerks back as John reaches down and grabs it. The dog looks happy, though, panting away with a grin on his face and not a care in the world. He's having fun. His eyes are bright and excited. He seems not to care at all that he's been caught.

John pats his head and pets his back. "Ah, good dog. You shouldn't be running from your mama and sister like that, mister." He continues to pet the dog until the woman and the toddler finally reach him, both gasping desperately for air, their hands going up and down as they try to settle down.

"Oh," the woman says. She gasps for more air. "Thank you so much. We just couldn't get him," she says, barely getting it out before taking another deep breath. "George, you stink butt."

John hands her the leash, noting her beautiful breasts burgeoning out of her bikini top, her slender thighs showing off their muscles beneath the hem of her white lace cover-up. Her smile is poignant, unforgettable, and her voice soft and arousing.

John smiles at her, then turns his eyes to the toddler, who is clapping her hands and then throws her little arms around George's neck to give him a big hug.

"Georgsh, you can't run from Mama and me." She lays her cheek on George as he sits, still panting like a piston. "Sanks, mista." She looks up at John with baby doll, round blue eyes, shiny blond hair like her mom's. It looks so silky, it's as if someone sanded it to slick perfection.

John's heart melts. Aw. What a sweetie. "Ah. You are very welcome, sweet girl. I didn't want you to lose your doggie."

"Mama. He nice. Can he have our pie?" She releases George's neck and stands up, her curved toddler belly sticking out, making her middle look more like a half-moon before it bulges out for her little tush.

She's the sweetest thing, and it tickles John's urge to have a little girl of his own. He's always wanted a daughter, someone so sweet and loving, innocent and devoted. A person to cherish and love, who would surely love him back forever. He'd get that dream with Juniper. And, honestly, he'd be fine with a boy, too. Just to be a dad would be such a treasure and blessing. He often envied those who were able to have children so easily and naturally. "Ah, that's okay, sweetness. You should share it with your mom. But thank you."

The mother smiles at John, grateful for not having to say no to her little girl.

"And Daddy," she says with an emphatic nod that she repeats. "And we haves the cream. Wight Mama?" She shoves her hands between her knees, then hops.

John's smile widens at her slight lisp, which is beyond adorable. She throws her hands straight up in the air like she's just gotten the best idea ever.

"Mama. Can Georgsh eats pie too?"

"No. He shouldn't have pie. Pie isn't good for doggies. But you can give him a dog treat." She smiles down at her daughter and pats her back over the ties of her tankini top.

"Oh. Okays. Georgsh wikes dat." Again, she shoves her hands between her knees, ending her speech with excessive nodding.

"Thanks for helping us snag George. He was on an all-out mad dash. He's a sweet dog, but he gets out of control at times."

"That's a puppy for ya. He's a puppy, right? He looks young."

"Yes, just seven months old, but full of energy and bursting with excitement twenty-four seven, or asleep." Her eyes twinkle like the sea.

"Oh, I believe that. You sure have your hands full with these two." John picks up his glass and inspects it, brushing off the outside, then swirling it to see if grains dance in the amber liquid.

"Yes, do I. Holy Hannah, do I." She shakes her head, but her smile tells John she loves every second. "Bella, we should get home. Daddy will be home soon." She turns back to John. "Thank you again. You look familiar. Have we met before?"

John smiles. Ah, the recognition. It happens more and more all the time.

"Well, you may have seen my face. I'm an author. John Penn."

Her hand flies to her mouth, and she squeals. "Oh. My. God. My husband just read your latest book, and he loved it. I get to read it next." She squats down a bit, hand still over her mouth.

"Mama. Can I swim? In da osean right here?"

"Oh, no, baby, let's head home and do that, okay? We don't want to bother Mr. Penn anymore. It's an extreme pleasure to meet you. Maybe if we see you on the beach sometime, we can bring our book, and you give us an autograph?"

John's grin widens. "Of course, anytime. I'd love to." She warmed his heart.

"My husband is going to flip when he finds out we live on the same beach shoreline as you."

She starts to walk, first grabbing Bella's chubby little hand, then dragging her along like she weighs no more than a string.

"Bye bye." Bella waves at John as the wind tosses her hair in her face, and she smooths it out of the way, but it flies back in a mere second. She lets go of her mom's hand and runs at a seagull standing on the wet shore. She screams and giggles as the bird takes off into the air. "I git it. I git it." She chases after fruitlessly, but her squeals portray her glee.

He watches the trio get smaller and smaller as they continue down the shoreline. Juniper will make a beautiful baby girl, just like she is. So beautiful. Just like little Bella. Juniper will make the best mama. John can't wait. He wets his feet in the waves, then heads back toward the house, picking up his slip-ons on the way. He doesn't want to miss anything good with Juniper and Bridge, and he certainly doesn't want to miss any fucking or sucking. His cock starts to fill with blood as he thinks about their last fuck session once more. No one can make his cock swell like Juniper. She has some sort of magic over him. She's just that hot. That good. That's damn perfectly special. Gushing about her even in his thoughts engorges his cock to full, the head of it stretching taut, readying for precum to bulge out the tip.

His stomach growls as he takes another sip of his drink. He was getting pretty toasted before the foray onto the beach, so slowing down a bit for the walk wasn't a bad idea at all. He types his favorite Asian takeout into his phone and orders orange chicken with white rice and pork egg rolls, then settles in his office to watch more of the Juniper and Bridge show.

BRIDGE MASSAGES JUNIPER'S feet on the couch. Her head rolls back on the pillow behind her. A glass of red wine is waiting next to her on the table. She lifts her head and picks up her drink, readying to take a sip.

"This better be my last night of drinking until I get my period, just in case." She brings the glass to her lips as hope fills her. She takes some wine into her mouth, holds it there to savor it, and rolls her eyes. "Damn, this is a really good one. Very berry infused."

"Good. Perfect one to end on, then."

"Oh, now don't get cocky. I won't get pregnant that way," she chides.

"No, but I know how you will get pregnant. And soon I'm gonna ram this cock into you again to increase our chances even higher."

Juniper raises her right eyebrow at Bridge, allowing a saucy gleam to shine. "Oh, is that so?" She giggles. "Well, you are nothing but thorough on that front, that's for sure."

"Damn straight, I am." He massages up her shins, placing her feet against his cock. He tilts his head. "Foot job foreplay?"

"Umm. You got it, lover." She situates herself better on the couch for the foot action.

She rubs her feet along his hard-on that is bulging out of his pants. He leans back on the couch, a groan wafting out of his mouth at the first strokes of her feet over his cock. Even though his cock is still under his clothes, he appears to be in ecstasy.

She likes to see him this way.

"Oh, damn. Baby, that feels so good. I love your feet." He strokes her shins as her feet rub and press his cock.

Juniper leans forward and slips his pants down to bare his engorged cock to the air. She massages his hard-on with her feet, up and down the shaft, over the bulging veins that bubble out in announcement of his lust. He moans as she feels up his cockhead with her toes. She wraps both feet around the shaft and rides it up and down as Bridge moans, throwing his head back.

"Mmmmm, fuck," he murmurs as he watches her feet handle his dick. "Fighting it, so you'd better stop, or our fun will be over for a while."

She giggles as she pulls her feet from his hard-on. "Well, we can't have that yet, now, can we?"

He bends down and sucks on each of her toes in turn, causing her to release moans.

"A bit of precum on that last one," he chuckles. "Foot job hazards."

She rolls her head to the side on the pillow to watch him finish off her toes. Having her toes sucked is quite erotic. She had been very resistant to this when she had first met Bridge. To her, it seemed kind of gross, but he made it sexy for her real quick, and now she loves his attention to her feet. Oh, the things she thought she'd never do, yet she ended up doing with Bridge. And there was more to come, no doubt. The impending foursome bubbles up in her mind. She can't stop her smile from growing.

"I see that look. Maybe Sara and Matt could come over tomorrow," Bridge says before devouring her pinky toe, rubbing it up and down inside his mouth with his tongue.

Juniper's head pops up. "You really can read my mind, can't you?" She snickers, then eyes him intently. "Seriously? Are you sure about this?" Her heart pounds harder as she ponders what will happen tomorrow if they do come. Somehow, he knew how to send shivers up to her clit just by sucking her toes, pressing and sucking in the right places. Who knew feet could be so erotic? Or maybe Bridge is just that magical.

"I'm positive. I'm open to trying new things. I want us to have fun sexually, get hot together, and get pregnant. Not sure what it all will mean for me yet. But I'm open to trying something. I really want to see you eat pussy live, to be honest. After all the times I've eaten you out, I can't wait to watch you do it." He chuckles, and his eyes get that naughty, sheer sheen she loves when he's about to get hardcore down and dirty, and nasty, and fuck her something fierce.

She giggles with hearty delight. "Oh, you do, do you?" She sits up, grabs his shirt, and pulls him to her until their mouths meet. "I intend to show you then. Just to satisfy your curiosity. And your lust."

"Oh, don't give me that bullshit; you love it." He pulls her onto his lap and threads his hands through her hair, cradling her head as he open-mouth massages her tongue.

She pulls back and whispers into his mouth. "You bet your ass I fucking do."

They kiss through grins, which quickly shift to sealed mouths on each other, leading to pulling on lips, then sucking on tongues. The kiss gets more intense as they slide their tongues along, feeling every speck of each other's. Their hands roam, traveling each other's bodies, prepping, ramping each other's lust up for their lovemaking. Their want for each other becomes passionate as they suck each other's flesh. They writhe, melting together like butter left on a hot stove, slickening upon itself due to the heat.

"Fuck me, Bridge. Just shove your cock in me and fuck me like your whore."

He presses her back against the couch and hovers over her as he pulls off her shirt, his cock dancing free in the air with his movements. His hand dives for her pussy, sliding into her pants before he pushes three fingers in and pumps. She's so wet his fingers slip right in.

"Oh, yeah. Fuck. That's it. Pound me with your hairless demon," she whispers into his mouth, readying to devour.

Bridge finger fucks her while kissing her mouth, his other hand reaching for her nipples. He's skirting the edge of edging her like a damn pro. They moan against each other's mouths. She reaches for his cock to give it a squeeze. He pinches her right nipple and gives it a tug. As she moans, he brings his pussy-frosted fingers up to her other nipple and pulls both of them away from her body. She writhes beneath him, moaning and kissing whatever part of him comes near her mouth. He takes her nipple and sucks it, lapping at it with his tongue, rolling her hard nugget, then full on sucking it hard so it stretches toward the back of his throat. She groans and threads her hands through his hair. He slips off her nipple and teases her pussy lips with the hard head of his cock.

"Paint me inside, Bridge. Coat me with your hot cum," she moans as he enters her pussy in an ardent rush. He pulls out and sits back to gaze at his amazing wife. She whispers, "Taste my core, baby. Lick me inside with that hard cock of yours."

He gives her clit a few slaps and she groans out with each strike, clawing the air to reach him, but missing. He lowers down over her again. She squeezes his shoulders as she murmurs, "Yes. Yes. Yes."

Bridge begins with a slow thrust into her that rapidly escalates to fast pounds that cause her to moan loudly. She doesn't dampen the sounds coming out of her mouth. She desires to massage his lust to a bursting point, her desire for him further raging after each slam of his body against hers.

She's riding that climax high, about to drip herself over that edge, and fall. Unable to collect herself, she dives into release. Clenching up, her body tells Bridge she's mounted her own orgasm and is now sliding blissfully down it.

"Yes, babe," he mutters softly.

As she shudders, her pussy milks his cock, spasming and tightening around him multiple times.

He grunts, then releases his load into her pussy. As her moans are dying down, his grunts thicken the air.

She sighs happily.

Bridge smiles back. He swivels to spoon her on the couch, his cock ever softening, pressed into the curve of her buttocks. They stay, snuggling, both wonderfully spent, curved together as sleep takes them.

# Chapter Seventeen

Juniper brews a cup of coffee for herself, then for Bridge. He's making omelets, and she's in charge of coffee and nothing else. She loves to cook, but it's awesome when Bridge does it. He's so sexy in the kitchen, especially at the stove, or when chopping vegetables. She watches him sway his hips to the music as he slices an onion.

"I love watching you cook." She sets the electric blue pottery mug down on the counter next to the chopping board that Bridge is cutting on.

"I love watching you cook." He glances up and meets her gaze, a giant sexy grin overcoming his face. "And do everything." He grins salaciously.

"You are hotter."

"You're hotter," he retorts quickly. "Everything you do is sexy."

She giggles and takes a sip of her coffee. "Well, not everything. But I do love your omelets. You make them better than I do."

"Not true. But it is my culinary specialty. One of my few, that is." He pushes all the onions into a little ramekin bowl with pink flowers all over it. "Next up, the peppers."

"So, I just texted Sara, and they're in for tonight." Juniper puts her finger in her coffee to stir it—it's hot—then shoves it in her mouth to lick it off. "They found a sitter on short notice. Let's just say she was quite motivated when I told her what you said." She scoffs with a smirk, tossing her hair off her shoulder with her hand. The sun catches her locks as she moves, and they glow. "We just need to figure out what to have for dinner. They're bringing drinks. Lots of drinks, apparently." Juniper feels a little sick to her stomach as she recalls the cognac bottle. She had asked Sara if she had indeed finished off the cognac, and she said she hadn't. But at the same time, she could have been too drunk to remember. Someone drank it, and Juniper knew it wasn't her. And, clearly, it hadn't been Bridge, unless he forgot. Whether she remembered it or not, it had to be Sara. No one else had been in the house. She shakes her head, trying to throw off her apprehension, giving Bridge a return smile. The worry of being unable to reconcile it bothers her.

"You, okay? That look on your face just now was a little off." He scrambles the eggs and milk by spinning the handle on the handheld eggbeater. "Something worrying you?"

She scoffs and waves her hand in the air. "No. I'm fine. It's nothing." She stands and stretches. "I'm going to pay homage to the ocean for a little bit."

He nods and begins to dice the tomato. "Go for it. Enjoy. You know where I'll be."

After giving him a calm, reassuring glance, which doesn't mirror how she feels, she strolls toward the sliding glass doors to do her ritual step outside to sip coffee in front of the ocean. She leans on her forearms on the deck rail, cradling the mug between both hands as she peers off into the vast beauty of the sea. The endless motion of it is intoxicating and calming; even when it rages, she's still calmed by it.

She's jittery; her heartbeat is elevated. Damnit! She can't smooth out the jaggedness of all those odd occurrences. It's all just too weird. But is she overreacting? She can't shake the willies about something being off. But her proof is flimsy. She can't prove it, but she's got the creepy crawlies, that unexplainable feeling people get, like déjà vu or like the odd sensation people who claim ghosts are real often talk about. She's not crazy. She had seen this show once, in which a woman claimed she felt cold whenever a ghost came near her in her house. It got so disturbing that the woman had moved, but she swore the ghost was real; even her face showed she believed, unless she was a good actor, of course. But the point being, people have a sixth sense that is undefinable, and hers is irritated as fuck. Something is wrong.

Juniper squints off into the bright sun as the uneasiness consumes her. A pelican is flying low along the water, gliding gracefully, giving itself just a small area above the sea to edge along, its wings teetering occasionally to keep itself in a straight line. Finally feeling a bit soothed, the sea is working its magic because she feels calmer already. Just being out on the deck and watching nature is exactly what she needs. The wind washes up the side of her, lifting her hair, taking a bit more of her worry and confusion with it as it blows on. She takes a deep breath of it into her lungs. The end of her inhale brings a smile to her face. That's better.

Her smile widens as she sees a little girl, a toddler running across the shore, her hair shining like rays of the sun itself. She's giggling and running full blast, her little chubby arms flailing up and down wildly as she runs from a wave trying to snag her, her mouth open in a big O. Her mother jogs behind her holding the leash of a very energetic lab. A morning run with her little daughter and pup. How sweet. Juniper longs to do this herself and lets one hand migrate to her belly.

"Please grow, little bud of a baby," she whispers as she watches the mom, daughter, and dog trio continue on down the beach. "We want you. Please grow."

She watches them get smaller and smaller, a wistful look of longing dominating her face. Bridge taps on the sliding glass door with his foot, and she wipes her expression clean. She turns and opens it for him, and he carries two plates that beam an appetizing yellow, full of omelets brimming with veggies under the shining sun. Both the plates and Bridge look lovely. She smiles. Mags follows him out, hoping for scraps of egg or cheese, no doubt. Like a dog, she follows the food. Her little family is about to enjoy a meal in the sun, ocean-side. Perfection.

"Thank you," he says as he places them on the table. "Thought you looked beautiful out here, so it'd be nice to eat on the deck, so I can take in the view of you and the ocean at the same time." His grin is big, bright, and genuine.

"Aww," she says, touching his arm. He always is such a romantic, never failing to tell her how beautiful she is, how sexy, and how much he loves her. He makes her feel so good all the time, and she knows she's very lucky to have him.

"Need a coffee refill? I'm going back in to get mine." He extends his hand, ready to take her mug.

She nods and gives him her cup.

She takes a seat at the table and watches the waves while she waits for him to return, her stomach growling as she inhales the delicious aroma of the freshly made omelet.

Bridge arrives with a tray carrying two mugs and two glasses of orange juice, and the salt and pepper shakers.

"This looks so delicious. Thank you for making it. My sexy personal chef."

"You're very welcome, my baby. I love to take care of and feed you." He settles into his chair and places her mug and juice near her plate. "I'm going to run to the store later today to get those supplies to put up those garage shelves. Did you need anything else while I'm out?"

She nods. "Yeah. Sure. That'd be great. Then I won't have to go out. Will you get some French bread and a couple of bottles of red wine, and a gallon of milk? We have wine, but I'd like some extra in case we run out. I'm trying to decide whether I should do one more night of drinking, or if that's too risky. I think the window is long gone for this month, but it's a mystery sometimes, so who knows."

"I'd say maybe just have a little so you can enjoy tonight, just don't get sloshed." He grins and winks at her.

"True. I could do that. Too bad I don't know for sure at this point, but I think I already ovulated, so it's most likely safe and out of the window of possibility." She loves wine, but she'd never do anything to compromise a baby's health.

"Well, you're the nurse, you know about these things more than I do. I trust you." He pats her arm. "You're the smart one, babe."

Ignoring his compliment, she says, "Well, if I'm counting days, I think I'm good. Maybe I'll just have some tonight, a little, but I should get used to having less right now anyhow. I don't want to screw anything up for them." She glances at her belly with hope in her eyes. "Because, you know, just maybe."

Bridge rubs her arm. "You won't. And you'll be an awesome mom."

She smiles and takes a bite of her omelet. The flavor bursts inside her mouth, the scrumptious cheese adding to the texture and flavor, the tomatoes adding juice. "Yum," she says. "This is delicious. As usual. Thank you."

"You're very welcome, baby."

A DELIVERY MAN DROPS a package on her doorstep as she's out watering flowers on the front of the house; he nods, and she waves. Strange. She doesn't remember ordering anything. Must have been Bridge who ordered something. Hopefully, it's a new sex toy. He often surprises her this way. She grins. What a wonderful man she has.

She picks up the small package and brings it inside. Her heart is pounding with excitement. Ah, Bridge. He knows how to get her going in all the most important ways. She carefully cuts into the package. As she pulls the box open along the tape, she grins broadly. Yup. Sex toy it is. It's a set of Ben Wa balls. Something she has not tried yet, which is perfect. She adores trying new sex paraphernalia. She reads the package and then shrugs. Sounds easy enough. She just needs to wash, lube up, and insert them, then walk around or exercise. It's supposed to feel good, be arousing, be great for before foreplay starts, and help improve the pelvic floor, too, thereby improving sex. It's a win-win all around.

She rips into the package with a naughty grin; she can't wait to try these out. Sara uses them, but she calls them 'cunt balls,' in direct opposition to men's balls. She had laughed heartily as Sara had explained one day over coffee at a coffee shop. She could hardly wait to pull her pants down and shove them in, and later share with Bridge and Sara how she liked them, or if she didn't. But she was guessing she would, unless they hurt, but how could they be bad? Even if they aren't all that pleasurable, she's all for anything that improves sex, not that she and Bridge need it, but improvements are always fun and luscious.

She slathers them with soap and scrubs them, rinses them, smiling at herself in the mirror as she rotates the little silver balls in her hands. Spreading her legs and then her vulva lips, she lubes herself and the balls up heavily with the new mystery lube, and then she pushes in the first ball. It slides in easily. She pushes the second one in and ensures the little loop of string to pull them out is sticking out of her pussy lips. There. It's a done deal.

As she walks, she can feel them in her vagina. It's like a sensation of fullness, pressure, and it actually is pleasurable as she walks, sort of massaging her inside as she moves. It's subtle, but definitely enjoyable, and it keeps her thinking about her pussy as she puts away the basket of laundry. The balls are very intriguing, kind of a passive way to ramp up the lust, not that she needs that, horny as she always is, but new enhancements are always a bonus, and fun. This is a winning plan.

She grins her way through folding the whole load in the laundry basket, enjoying the movements of the balls inside her. She could imagine getting into wearing these out to dinner with Bridge. They still need to try out that remote-controlled vibrator at dinner since they'd only used it at home so far. So many fun things to do yet, and re-do, and Bridge is delightfully up for all the new adventures, too.

She heads over to the kitchen, thinking about food prep for their evening fuckfest with Sara and Matt. It will certainly be a delicious evening. She had settled on making stuffed shells and Caesar salad, hence why she had asked Bridge to get the fresh bread. A little Italian meal to go with their foreplay foray into couples swinging. She isn't sure what's going to happen, but her heart is already racing, her clit gets a zing when she thinks about Sara messing with it, and Bridge and Matt watching. And the balls inside her are ramping her up quite nicely.

She fans herself and says, "Woo."

"You having fun without me again?" Bridge enters the kitchen, two loaves of fresh French bread wrapped in paper in his hands, and a giant grin on his face.

"Oh, you should know. You sent it to me." She walks over to him and swats his butt with the kitchen towel in her hand. She takes the bread from him. "I like them, by the way. Thanks. Something new."

He cocks his head and grabs her right butt cheek. "Them? The bread? I'd love to take credit for something else, too. What did I do this time?"

She giggles. "You forget so quickly? The balls."

He cracks up. "My balls? You're thinking about my balls?" He grabs his crotch and makes a silly face. "I like that!"

She laughs harder. "No, you goof. The Ben Wa balls you ordered. They arrived. I was so excited, I put them in right away. I love the subtle internal massage they give. The constant movement of them as I move, and the feeling of something in my pussy is keeping my mind on my pussy as I do housework and cook. I've got to try exercising with these in me next."

"Ben Wa balls? I don't even know what that is, but if it's in your pussy, I want to know about it." He grabs her and wraps his arms around her waist, spreading both palms down the round cheeks of her ass, then he squeezes both cheeks.

"What do you mean? You didn't order these? Well, I didn't do it." Her jaw drops as she tries to pry herself from Bridge's arms. "I need to find that box. Maybe it was a screwup and was meant for the neighbor. Oops." She bursts out laughing. "Problem is, they've already been riding around in my pussy for over an hour. Major oops." She shrugs as Bridge lets go of her.

"Well. Maybe we can replace them. But then they will know we know they ordered sex toys. Talk about prying into your neighbor's business." Bridge opens the fridge and takes out a bottle of water, downs it in thirty seconds, replaces the cap, and tosses it in the recycle before Juniper digs through the garbage to find the box.

She flips the ripped-open box over to look at the address label. It's ripped in half, but it clearly says her name and their address. "Wow. It lists me as the recipient with our address. I must have been looking at them online and accidentally hit send to order, or something. Maybe when I had too many glasses of wine and I just forgot." She laughs with a shrug. "Hazards of drinking, I guess. At least I like it, so it wasn't a wasted purchase. It's getting me hornier." She gives Bridge a seductive look.

"Well, I'm all for that. Well worth the money then." He leans back against the granite counter, hands gripping the edge. "You're giving me a boner, but I want to wait until tonight. So, are there rules with this? Or we figure it out first?"

"Yeah, I think each person figures out their own rules, or each couple, and then we chat, then we play, but don't cross any lines." Juniper shoves the box back into the garbage can. "Just think about what you want, not that you can't change it, but I think we should have clear boundaries before we start, so there are no bad feelings or mistakes. I don't want to do something that will end up hurting you. I just want us both to enjoy whatever we do with Sara and Matt." She gives Bridge glowing eyes with a little sexy grin. "And I can't wait. I'm really excited we're trying this. You're amazing for agreeing. And really, they are the perfect couple to do this with, too. However, they might be a bit more adventurous than we are, which could be a good thing. We'll need to talk about all that before we start."

Bridge crosses his arms over his large chest. "I'm still not sure how far I can go with this. I'm trying to wrap my brain around it still. I'm not real keen on Matt putting his dick in you." He looks skeptical.

"Oh, Bridge, that's totally fine. We don't have to go there." She nods and walks over to him, pressing her pelvis to his, her lower abdomen cradling his full, hard cock as she runs her hands up his chest, over his pecs to rest on his shoulders. "I don't need his dick in me. I'm good with just Sara's pussy."

He grins deeply. "Well, I might be okay with him eating you out or sucking your tits, but the thought of another sperm shooter near your pussy when we're trying to get you pregnant also makes me nervous, to be perfectly honest. What if his sperm beat mine in the race to impregnate you? We'd have a giant dilemma." He looks sad. "I'd be devastated."

She sighs. "Yeah, me too. So very true. So, first rule, no Matt sperm near my pussy. Okay. Makes sense. Rule two. You already said you're fine with whatever Sara and I do, as long as the part she plays with me doesn't have Matt's sperm on it yet." She smirks.

"Right. We have to pay attention to that, too. And toys also. Toys that have been in Sara, if they've fucked recently, even."

"Okay, rule three: any toys that go in her do not go back in me. That's fair." She furrows her brow. "Gee. This makes me kind of nervous, considering what Sara and I just did. She could have had sperm on her pussy, but she did shower, though, so I bet all traces of sperm were off her, plus she had peed umpteen times, so I don't think that is an issue there. Plus, I think she said they did anal last time, so sperm wasn't even in her pussy most likely."

Bridge raises an eyebrow. "Oh, she and Matt do anal?"

Juniper sighs. "Yes. I know. I know. I'm the only prude stooge with that. You know how I feel about anal."

"I do. And I don't need that. I love your pussy." He kisses her forehead. "But let's just say I won't be upset if a finger or toy finds its way into your ass tonight, any finger." He grins. "I just don't want you to miss out on any potential pleasure."

She puts her hand over her right eye and pinches her nose between her pinky and ring finger, then grimaces. "Ugh. You would have to say that, wouldn't you?"

"Maybe it's a little finger, like one of Sara's, just to start."

"Don't push me, Papa," Juniper says while poking at his chest with her right index finger. She resists the urge to frown and pouts instead. "That shit just scares me. As you know."

He pulls her head to his chest. "I'd never do anything to hurt you. Or scare you. I love you."

She nods. Her hormones must be raging as she's fighting a burst of tears. She swallows and squeezes Bridge to get her mind off her worries. She needs the worry train to stop plaguing her.

"I know," she says as the pit of her fear drags her gut to her toes. Whew. She needs a reset, and fast.

"Hey, you hungry? We could do a light lunch or a snack?" He rubs her back and kisses the top of her head at the part in her hair. "I can make us a sandwich or fruit and cheese plate if you have stuff to do to get ready for the evening." He fingers her hair to secure it behind both her ears. "I just want you to wipe that worry off your face. We will have fun. No sad-face stuff. We don't have to ever do it if you don't want to." He squeezes her between his arms. "Okay?"

She nods. Damn. These hormones are riding her hard. She swallows down the bad feelings and leans back, smiles big. "Yes. Definitely, we will have fun." She takes a step away, pulling herself fully out of his arms. "I'd better remove these balls in case they make me sore. I don't want to mess up tonight."

"Okay. I'll work on a snack. Do we need any cleaning done? I can help. I don't need to do the shelves today."

"I've done most of it. I think it's all good. Will you just check the game room downstairs and see if there's anything that needs to be done down there, please? And check the bathroom down there, too."

"I'm on it, boss." He gives her a nod.

She grins and heads off to the bathroom to de-ball her pussy. Ha! That's now a thing.

# Chapter Eighteen

John watches greedily as Juniper removes the balls he sent. One by one, they pop out of her pussy, and she washes them in the sink, and then places them on a plump pink hand towel on the counter to dry. They glisten wet in the light just as they had when they were just pulled out of her. He grins. His plan was a huge success. He had gotten the brilliant idea and put a rush order on them, hoping she'd use more of the lube with his seed in it to increase his chances of impregnating her. And, honestly, he just wants to be a part of her pleasure, or at least his sperm. He wants to do things to make her feel good, and he noticed she didn't have any balls in her collection. So he placed an order immediately, and she got them quickly, just in time. He knows her so well that she inserted them right away. Such a good girl.

He's so ready to watch the foursome tonight. His cock has been drooling precum all day just thinking about it. His own personal homemade porn, starring his beautiful Juniper. He can't wait to see her cum over and over again and be pleasured to the absolute max. She deserves that, the sex goddess that she is. She should always be made to feel good and cum multiple times every day. He just wishes his cock, his tongue, and his fingers could be the ones doing it for her. He'd love her up, then snuggle with their little girl on the couch while Juniper made them breakfast. Juniper and his baby, he couldn't ask for a happier life. Then they'd all enjoy their food together, every meal. All satisfied. It would be beautiful, and he can't wait to live that fantasy out.

He runs a hand up his hard shaft, then spreads the precum over the head of his cock with his thumb. He would have to wait until later to finish off this hard-on. Plus, he really needs to work on his book. He has a goal of 5,000 words done before the foursome. He knows he can do it. He does it all the time. He sits down at his laptop, setting his coffee cup next to the picture of his mom and dad, now both long gone after a car accident that had stolen them from him. His life had never been the same after losing them, but luckily, his older sister was there. Being twenty, she had stepped up to raise him until he had reached eighteen. His world had died when he lost them, but she had saved him. She was his savior and confidante then, the sun in his life of darkness. She is all that to him after all these years still. He needs to call her soon and catch up on her life. It's been a full week since they last talked, which never happens.

He wiggles his butt into the soft computer chair and sets his mind to flow freely with thoughts, trying desperately to ignore his boner. He gets his hands typing fast, but not as fast as he can dream up the story, something that has always annoyed him. He's been tempted to speak his books out, but that seems almost too fast-paced, and he'd end up with rushed prose and scenes. He pauses and scans the page. After rereading the previous paragraph to reorient his brain to the time and space in the story, he shakes his whole body, closes his eyes, and falls into his current scene. His flow is untouchable magic once again as his fingers play the keyboard in a song of key clicks. Ideas come to him so fast, like lightning fast, which is always a delight, being a writer, and part of why he is such a huge success. He's never out of ideas.

JUNIPER SQUEEZES HER breasts. Damn, she's horny, and she just wants to fuck. The lusty feeling is full in her, widening her sexual interest, mounting it to a peak, and making her pussy really wet. She's in a great place mentally and sexually for this foursome to happen. Her mind is clear and open, and she's convinced that maybe she might try new things tonight, if someone else suggests them. Maybe, just maybe, she'd try something that scared her a little. Suddenly jumpy, her libido is begging for her to touch herself, so she needs a distraction. Food prep should do it. It's close enough on time to start on the salad.

Bridge is in the garage working on the shelves, so she pops open a bottle of red wine and contemplates putting the balls in to let Sara remove them. She'd get a kick out of that for sure. After taking a large sip of wine, she scurries to the bathroom and coats the balls in the lube again, and shoves them back in.

Sara uses them, so it will be her pleasure to remove them. Bridge won't mind; he'll like watching her do it. She's still getting used to it all.

She wonders what it would be like to be spanked with the balls in and the vibrations the slaps would give, making the balls shake inside her. Maybe they'd be spanked right out if she were wet enough. She giggles at the thought and practically skips to the kitchen because she just really wants to feel those balls jiggle, so she does some exaggerated leaps. They do move more and feel yummy inside her.

She texts Sara.

Juniper: I have those balls in, like the ones you have. So you can remove them from my pussy later.

Sara: YES! You got some? I'll pull them out while I'm licking your pussy, baby.

Juniper: Yes. I'm counting on it. I'm horny as fuck right now.

Sara: Same love. Matt too. He's dying to see you naked in person. It won't be long now, and we'll be there.

Juniper's cheeks flush. She really hadn't thought about what it would be like to have Matt staring at her naked body nonstop all evening. It will be hot, but it might be awkward. However, the thought of being watched also slicks her pussy, or maybe it's the balls inside her, but she is so wet.

Juniper: See you soon. Hurry!

Sara: Yep. Just waiting on the sitter to arrive. Be there soon to make you scream.

Juniper laughs as she texts Sara a fire and purple devil emoji. Then she gets a naughty idea and pulls her pants down and takes a pussy pic, then sends it to all three of them with a giggle leaking out from behind her hand.

Bridge comes into the house, catching her with a lewd expression.

She holds up her phone. "You got my text?"

"You trying to edge the fuck out of me or what?" he says with a laugh and a clear boner pushing his pants out. "I know there's going to be a lot of edging going on tonight, and I guess it starts now." He saunters over to Juniper with a swagger. "Nice pic. I saw a string hanging out. You put those balls back in?" He slips his arms around her lower back, pushing his hard-on into her belly.

"Yep. I texted Sara and told her she can pull them out later. She liked that."

"Oh, I bet she did. This is going to be interesting and very hot, seeing you with a woman. I had no idea you had that history with her. Pretty damn hot, babe. Daddy likes."

"I honestly didn't know how you'd feel about it, so I just never mentioned it. Guess I should have."

"Right. Well, we're trying this now. But honestly, I just want to pound this into you. And it's pretty fucking hard to resist." He rubs his hard-on against her belly as she grins and pretends to melt down, sliding her tits down to his cock, which he willingly rubs against.

"Mmmmm, this is a bad idea," she whispers as he presses her back flush against the counter to get away from him.

"The worst," he murmurs, taking a step back. "I just want to rip your clothes off and bend you over this counter and fuck you like a ram."

"Oh, well, shit," she says, zooming back to him and grabbing his ass cheeks, forcing him into her cleavage hard. "I'm so hot, oh my Gawd."

He rubs his cock through the fabric, titty fucking her with his clothes on. "Same. Shit."

She's ready to claw his pants off, but forces herself to move away. She opens the freezer door and stands close, so the coolness wafts over her.

"Fuck. I'm gonna lose control. I need a cool down like now." She laughs as she sticks her hands into the freezer.

"That work? Let me at it." He shoves his hands in the freezer beside her, and they lock eyes as they chuckle.

"We're pathetic." Juniper huffs up her chest with a big, deep inhale.

Sara and Matt walk in through the front door that Bridge had apparently left wide open.

Sara laughs, then asks, "What the hell are you two doing?" Sara laughs harder. "Kinky freezing hand play? Oh, I'm in." She catches Juniper's eyes in hers, then cracks up even further when Juniper laughs. She sets down the bags on the counter. "You two in some kind of torture sex game here, trying to freeze your tits off? New BDSM game? Frigid fingering? I'm more than curious, and absolutely ready to join in."

Juniper turns away from the freezer, shakes her hands. "Well, it is making my nips hard. We were getting a little too hot after I sent that photo, so we were cooling down."

"My brain is stuck on hard nips. May I see?" Matt asks as he sets down the bag.

Wow. Juniper chuckles. He's wasting no time at all.

Juniper glances at Bridge, wondering if this offends him. He smirks and turns fully away from the freezer, shutting the door as he nods at Matt and Sara. Thankfully, he doesn't look mad.

"She's got really hot tits, just remember, whoever has got their mouth on them, I still own them." Bridge gives them a stern look, but he is clearly also joking.

Sara runs a hand through her long brown hair. "Oh, totally, Bridge. And we'll discuss all the rules before we start. And comfort levels, so we are all clear." She removes the bottles of wine, rum, and cognac from the bag. "We brought enough for the whole block to get wasted." Sara clears her throat. "And...um...let's see said promised hard nips, Juniper, baby." She waves her hands up in the air repeatedly. "Come on. Let's see those tits."

Juniper bites her lips and grins. The thought of baring her chest for the three of them is deliciously hot.

She gazes at them all, making direct eye contact with each in turn.

Bridge nods with a grin. "Flash them, my love. Thrill them with your hotness. Best tits ever. No lie."

Juniper tilts her head to the side. She slowly unbuttons and removes her shirt from her shoulders and chest while keeping it gathered at each elbow, so it still covers her up. Her nipples will harden further in the open air, so she's got her mind set on a dramatic reveal. She drops her shirt to the floor in a fast move, her pussy practically dripping as she watches their excited reactions to seeing so much of her flesh. She undoes her bra and slides it off, making her nipples pop as the cups move down her breasts. Yep. They are hard as they can possibly be, from the air and from the act of bearing them to three pairs of hungry, horny eyes.

"Wow. Just wow." Matt's jaw actually drops. "Holy fuck. Stellar tits. Porn star worthy," he mutters with wide eyes.

Juniper can imagine his cock getting harder from across the room, and it makes her want to rush him, throw him on the floor, and ride his cock, even though she knows she can't.

Matt whistles, and it's highly satisfying to her; she never knew she was so into exhibitionism, but the instant slickening of her pussy is telling her it's true. She is an exhibitionist.

"Yeah, see, I told ya," Sara says to Matt. "Her tits are beyond amazing."

"Boy, I'll say. You belong in high places of visibility with those beauties."

"Yep, she's gorgeous." Bridge crosses his arms over his chest. "Stunning. My little personal bunny."

Juniper wiggles, making her boobs jiggle, and she grabs them and presses them, letting her big pink nipples slide out from under her hands as she moves them up her breasts.

"Wow," Matt says again. "I'm hard as a rock."

"Wait until you get your tongue on those wrinkles in her areolas. It's oral bliss," Sara says with a grin. "Am I right, Bridge?"

"Oh, yeah. For sure." He nods, and Juniper watches him for signs of jealousy or anger at Matt verbally loving up her breasts. He's smooth, though, not a hint of discomfort or anger, which surprises Juniper a lot. And pleases her. She really detests jealousy. Jealousy is about him, not her, or her pleasure. There's nothing positive about it.

Maybe this foursome will work.

Juniper grins a naughty grin. "Well, since you all love them so much, maybe I'll just stay topless for dinner, as a constant visual foreplay."

"Balls deep, you rock, Juniper." Matt opens the rum, then a two-liter bottle of soda. "My dick won't be sagging a bit here, I see. Full blast, Bonerville."

"Well, I'm wet as fuck already myself. My balls might fall right out, I'm so wet." Juniper takes a sip of her wine. She's eating up all their glances at her tits like it's feeding her starving lust. Though clearly, she's not starving, just raging like the ocean outside her house, wet, gyrating, mounting itself to crescendos of peaked waves that curl and crash onto the sand like the repeated pounding of a good fuck. She's hot and getting hotter by the second.

"I might be in heaven. Tits out. Two sexy women. Loads of alcohol, and the smell of good food," Matt says as Sara removes her shirt with a lusty leer. "And no kids in sight."

"First rule, women stay topless for the night." Sara throws her shirt behind her, not caring where it lands.

"I fucking love you, baby," Matt says as they join and French kiss for a full minute, as if Juniper and Bridge aren't there.

"Wow. Well, that was a hot kiss. Fuck," Juniper laughs. "I love watching kissing, and I'm hot as fuck right now. So, let's get drunk, eat, and fuck." She holds up her wine glass. "And fuck again."

"Woohoo!" Sara says. "Never has there ever been a better plan, baby."

"Beverage?" Matt asks with a nod to Bridge.

"Sure, thanks. I'd love a rum and soda. You pouring?"

"Yes. And good to see you two again, by the way. Thanks for trying this out with us. We've never done the swinging thing before with friends like this." Matt takes the glasses Juniper is offering and fills each halfway with ice from the fridge's dispenser. "But we've been wanting to for a long time."

"Yeah. We're happy to oblige. This is a first for us, too. I'm usually the jealous type, so this will be interesting." Bridge raises an eyebrow.

"I won't do anything without permission. This is fully consensual and meant to be for fun only." He pours rum into each glass, filling it halfway, then tops it off with soda.

"Right. I'm still feeling this out. But the number one rule is your cock doesn't go in Juniper. She and I are trying to get her pregnant, and we don't need a surprise dad." Bridge smirks. "I might have to kill you if that happens."

"Totally understand that. Wouldn't blame you one bit on that, either. I love being a dad, and I'd never take that from someone. I hope it works out for you two." Matt takes a sip of his drink, then raises his glass to clink cheers with Bridge. "To making babies."

Bridge raises his glass and taps Matt's glass. "To making babies."

"You two are talking babies over there?" Sara asks incredulously with her arms raised. "I thought we were here to fuck?"

"Yep. We are. But, rule number one." Bridge nods. "No, Matt cock inside Juniper. She just ovulated recently, and we've been fucking like rabbits to make a baby. We don't need papa sperm confusion."

Sara laughs. "Um. No. That would be a catastrophe." She shudders. "Whew! Hadn't thought about that. Even condoms can fail."

"You need any more help with food, Juniper?" Bridge asks.

"No, Sara and I can finish. It's almost done." Juniper smiles at her husband kindly. "Thanks for asking, but we've got this. Go get reacquainted with each other."

"Absolutely, and let me know. I'll come right back," he says. "Care to sit with me on the deck?" Bridge asks Matt.

"Sure, sounds great."

The men walk toward the deck, leaving the women and Mags in the kitchen. "All three kitties topless," Bridge jokes loudly before walking through the sliding door.

Sara immediately directs her attention to Juniper. "So, how are the balls treating you? You like them?" She cups Juniper's right boob and gives it a quick kiss on the top.

"I do, yes. It's subtle, but I like it." She adores Sara's affection.

"It really helps strengthen your muscles, too, so it improves sex."

"Always a bonus," Juniper says with a raise of her eyebrows as Sara fondles both her breasts.

"Things can always get better, or just different, as different can be better all by itself." She smirks as she squeezes Juniper. "Though with you two fucking every day, I bet you're in tip-top shape in there." She taps just above Juniper's pussy mound. "Getting all that cock action."

"That's true. But I'll always take a chance at an improvement." Juniper moves, and Sara's hands fall from her chest. She places the bread on the cutting board and chooses a serrated knife from the knife block. "Better get some work done, or we will never eat. But I love all your touches."

"Same," Sara says with emphasis. She picks up the black skinny statue off the counter and strokes it. "This is almost like a dildo, ya know. Would you ever?"

Juniper scoffs. "You're right. It is. I bet it would work well as one. We'll have to try it out tonight, perhaps."

Both women connect and hold each other's gaze for a bit before they crack up.

"Might have to be a part of the plan to try later, seriously. I would," Sara says through her laughter.

"I know, right?" She begins slicing the bread, each movement making her big boobs jiggle. "I'll never look at that thing the same again. I have a stone dildo on my kitchen counter."

"Your boobies are driving me crazy the way they are dancing about. I knew Matt would flip over your tits." Sara grabs a piece of bread off the cutting board. "Watching you do that naked is proof that people need to wear clothes, or we'd never get anything done, we'd all be constantly fucking." She swipes yet another piece of bread, and Juniper narrowly misses cutting her finger.

"Sara! You're like a little kid! Keep your fingers outta here. I almost cut you! I don't want to have to take you in for stitches. Plus, it would ruin our fuck fest if we had to rush off to the emergency room."

"Sorry, I'm just starved. I didn't eat much today. I was cleaning like mad to get ready for my cousin's visit. I had a hard time finding an overnight sitter, but then my cousin Gigi could do it. I had to basically clean the whole house from top to bottom; she's a massive clean freak. If I didn't make it sparkling, she would have cleaned it herself and not paid attention to the kids." She shrugs. "I had to do it."

Juniper adds the cut slices of bread to a cloth-lined basket. "Yeah. Kids need the attention. They deserve it. Who cares about the house, though? I mean, clean is good, but not more important than kids." She shakes her head, wondering how people's priorities get so fucked up.

"Yeah, she's going to be a miserable mom, I fear. She won't let her kids do anything fun, I bet. They'll be terrified of making a mess or getting dirty because she overreacts about it so much."

"Maybe she will loosen up when it actually happens." Juniper uncovers the butter plate and adds a knife.

"Yeah, maybe. Well, that usually happens more with your second. With your first, you're a bit hyper about literally everything. My cousin will be a nightmare, though, with her germophobic ways. She and her husband are trying right now, too." She scrunches up her shoulders. "Could be two babies appearing in my life about the same time if all goes as planned."

"Oh, I wish. We've been trying for a while, so I'm hoping this time it happens. If it doesn't, it's not from lack of trying." She laughs.

"No? I bet not. Bridge seems like he's a horny fucker."

"Oh, you have no idea. But I love it." She bites her lip. "Matt seems so, too."

"Yep. He's a horndog indeed. Man has a perpetual boner."

"Perfect. All four of us are horny as fuck. A great match." Juniper reaches over and caresses Sara's boob. "I rather like you topless in my kitchen."

"I like you topless in your kitchen." She smirks with a lecherous grin.

Sara hops off the stool and pulls Juniper away from the counter. "One kiss," she says, with a clear intent in her eyes.

Juniper nods.

Their mouths collide, and Sara takes Juniper's top lip in hers, then Juniper does the same back. Their tongues lick and swirl around each other's mouths. Their hands gripping each other's backs, migrating to their shoulders, and Sara grabs Juniper's tit as they open-mouth kiss, writhing against each other, their tits rubbing each other's fronts.

"Fuck. Now that is a hot, pretty picture indeed. Shit," Matt says, causing Juniper to step back from Sara. "Oh, don't stop on my account. I love watching this. My dick might spontaneously explode without a touch, watching you two, but it'd be worth it to watch you kiss like that again."

Sara runs a finger down Juniper, from her lips to her hip. "No problem, we can do that lots of times tonight. Right, babe?" She breaks her kiss and moves toward her husband.

"Yes, Bridge will want to see too, no doubt." Matt sets the glasses on the island. "I'm just in for refills. Don't stop that. Keep it up. Watching you two was an added bonus. I'll be drink-boy any and every day if I get to come in to see that." He pours the drinks while Sara hugs him from behind, her cheek flush against his back.

"I'll give you a show like that anytime, lover."

"Ah, you're the best on the planet, though I know you love it as much as I do, or probably more."

"Probably, no doubt about it." Sara strokes his cock through his pants.

"Fuck," he mutters as his body sways with her.

Juniper grins. "This is fun to watch you simply touching him like this. I think I'm going to like this swinging thing. I wasn't so sure how Bridge would handle it. I'm still not sure, but if we follow our rules, I think he might just be okay with it."

"We'll get it right for all of us. And I won't stick my cock in you, even though the thought makes me drip." He laughs as his body jerks. "Just being honest here. You're hot as fuck, Juniper. I've always thought so. But getting my mouth on you will be a whole amazing feast in and of itself."

"When is dinner? We need to get to the fucking." Sara releases Matt and walks over to snag more bread, buttering it before taking a bite. "I'd better eat more. I'm getting drunk off one glass. I need some more bread. Lots more. I'm not usually such a lightweight."

"Fifteen more minutes, then it needs to just cool a few. Let me get out the cheese. I made a small cheese and cracker platter for an appetizer."

"Perfect. I need protein, too." Sara takes a seat on the stool at the island as Matt gives her a boob kiss.

"You can have my protein later," he says with a wink.

"Oh, I have no doubts about that. And you better save me some," she says, giving his ass a swat as he swiftly carries the drinks to the living room. She chases after him, trying to swat him again as he dodges her.

"I'm gonna pay that back," he snickers when he is way out of her reach. "You won't be able to sit."

Sara just raises an eyebrow as her mouth stretches into a smirk. "That's par for the course."

Juniper smiles, loving watching their flirty teasing of each other.

After a topless dinner on the deck, all sufficiently stuffed and liquored up, Sara stands and raises her hands with authority.

"Okay. Rules. Time to review. Number one rule is no Matt cock in Juniper and no Matt sperm near her pussy either. Number two is Juniper, and I can do whatever we want, but no sharing of toys to prevent cross-spermination." She pauses as laughter erupts, "and all things pre-Matt cock there as well. Bridge can do whatever he wants. All okay with all that? Rules can change on the fly if consensual, except rule number one never changes. I'm okay with anal from anyone. Wait, scratch that. I'm happy for anal from everyone." She laughs as everyone's chuckles match hers in intensity. "Does that cover it all?"

"Yep," Juniper nods. If she weren't drunk, she'd be worried someone would see her topless on her deck, but now she gives no fucks, and she even likes the idea. The sun feels amazing on her bare breasts, and she's been feeding her lust off everyone's glances of her bare tits. She had never eaten a whole meal topless before, but it was quite exhilarating and erotic. "And I'm horny as fuck."

"Same," Matt says. "I've been sporting a hard-on this whole time. I'm ready to use the fucker."

Bridge chuckles. "Yeah. I'm at the same point. Raging hard-on." Bridge connects his gaze to Juniper. "More baby-making is on the agenda."

"Breed me, you fucker," Juniper says with a naughty grin.

"Hot," Sara says. "Freaking hot as all fuck, you two."

"Okay, we'll clean up. Then fuck. Keep drinking. Somewhere in there, we will have dessert."

"Perfect," Sara says with a smile that's truly masturbation worthy to Juniper.

# Chapter Nineteen

John practically drained his full cock, leaking out precum, watching those ladies eat topless. It had been beyond sensual to watch their tits as they ate. Simply mesmerizing for a boob man like him. Never before had he seen such a sight, watching those two beautiful women enjoying food, drink, and congenial conversation while bare-chested. It was entirely erotically stunning and had lit up his mood. With each movement, they'd jiggle, nipples hard, sometimes brushing against the table, or the women would grab their tits.

He smirked. Even they couldn't keep their hands off them. He chuckled. The men had taken to pinching, touching, stroking, even suckling and nibbling their nipples a bit with dinner, adding a bit of sauce or wine and licking it off. Matt had ventured to Juniper's nipples, and Bridge had taken a turn sucking Sara's. The whole exchange had left John breathless and with a raging hard cock.

He dares not touch it now, though—he's way too hot, and this had just been dinner. They hadn't even started serious fooling around yet. Lecherous spirit that he is, his lust thickens, rising up from his pelvis, consuming his entire body. He gasps, trembling. This whole situation is delicious, and John will watch this video over and over again like a precious snippet of Juniper's eroticism. His prying eyes are pure, though, as he really just wants to see them all interact with Juniper, touch her, and make her happy, make her moan, savor in her orgasms, and come hard. He yearns to see her body draw up with overwhelming pleasure, quiver, then stagnate as she enjoys her delightful spasms running the course of her epic contractions. It's exquisite to watch when she comes, observing her in a full, unadulterated climax. It's usually enough to make his load charge out of the end of his hard cock, making him moan right along with her. The spiritual union of it jars him every time. It's so hot that they often come at the same time this way. If she only knew. She'd like it, no doubt. He feels it in his heart that somewhere in hers, she must sense his peaking, too.

He sips his martini and shoves a queen olive in his mouth. He watches as all four of them clear the table, bringing the dishes inside. They all work together, teasing each other with butt cheek grabs, grinds of cock against ass, stroking of pussy, and, of course, French kisses, plus nipple attention of all sorts. The men remove their shirts, too, so the women start snacking on their nipples as well. The four seem pretty hot and bothered as they finish the cleanup. Sara and Juniper kiss again as the men cheer them on, then strip fully nude. The show is outstanding and perfect.

The doorbell rings, pulling John from his immersion in the scene. His dinner has arrived. Fantastic. He's famished.

JUNIPER SUCKS ON SARA'S tongue as Sara's hands maul her breasts. Matt slides in to join the women, rubbing his cock against Juniper's ass as he grips her hips firmly from behind. Bridge finishes loading the dishwasher.

John snickers, feeling happy that Bridge has been left out of Juniper's fun for once.

"Oh, wait for me," Bridge jokingly whines. He moves quickly, trying to finish up.

John wishes Bridge looked pissed, though.

No matter. It's so erotic, and his cock could not be any harder watching them love up on Juniper. The whole scene is on sensual overload already. Bodies enjoying each other on a physical level, but with an underlying emotional connection.

Bridge shakes his head and scoffs.

John was hoping Bridge would lose it watching Matt grind his cock on Juniper. Grab him by the neck and shove his face down, smashing his skull to the tile floor for doing this to her naked body. John likes Matt, and honestly, Juniper clearly loves his attention. He can't get mad at that; surprisingly, it's still just serving to egg him on further to watch yet another man get busy with Juniper. Serving nicely to inflame his raging lust to the point he feels like he will lose control and reach a new level of ecstasy watching this orgy.

Bridge runs the backs of his fingers along Juniper's cheek as she is French kissing Sara, their mouths devouring each other, wide open, then closed, taking each other's lips between. He drags his hand to their conjoined mouths and fingers their kiss along where their lips touch. They both turn toward him, tongues tasting his fingers in luscious licks and sucks.

Juniper breaks the kiss, much to a delighted Bridge, who pulls his mouth to hers to instigate a union. She devours him orally. She's so hot her kissing is feverous, and it flares John's lust even further for her.

Sara moves on to sucking her tit, fondling the other while Matt is still grinding against her bottom, with his hands holding the rounded curves of her hips, occasionally reaching under her to massage her pussy. Juniper moves to the center of all three of them. She is getting so out of control sensually, moaning and writhing against all three of them. Her body undulates, rolling against the mouths and hands of all three of them.

She's on fire!

She throws her head back as Matt has his hand down, manipulating her pussy. Sara is flicking her tongue across one nipple while pinching the other. She alternates the licking with full-on sucking of Juniper's nipple, letting it pop out of her lips as she slips off. Matt is fingering her from behind, so Bridge squats down and maneuvers himself to lick at her clit. John loves the teamwork approach.

Juniper's hands massage her husband's scalp as he eats her out. Her moans are those of a helpless being, putty-like, fluid, writhing in between all their wanton lust, rolling and climbing in the swirls of her own. She squeezes her thighs around Bridge's head and screams out.

"Oh, my gawd, oh my gawd, oh, my, oh, my, oh, my," she chants. She's wiggling, panting, her large bosom heaving. "Fuck, fuck, fuck," she murmurs. "Mmmmmm." Her expression skyrockets to helpless panic, swimming in ecstasy.

Sara is tugging on her tits, pulling them, stretching further than they seem they should go. Matt is pumping his fingers into her vagina fiercely, now squatting behind her, his face right at her ass. He spreads her cheeks apart and sneaks a lick of her asshole. She recoils, shoving her pussy into Bridge's face as she lurches forward, but Matt follows her undulation and keeps licking her ass. She tries to shimmy away, but the three of them have her pinned in a trio sex vice. Matt moves from her, but she reaches back and pulls him close again, so he resumes. He tickles her; his tongue traveling the wrinkles of her puckered flesh. Her groans are guttural, strong, intense, ethereal. Sara joins in with the tongue stimulation of Juniper and consumes both tits in turn, alternating with her hand playing with one not being sucked.

John knows her feelings on ass play, and the hairs on the back of his neck rise. He tries to simmer himself down because Juniper has not uttered her safe word. She appears to be in pure mind-blowing ecstasy, so he settles down a bit.

"Lie down, babe," Bridge urges in a tender tone.

Juniper obeys and sprawls out on the floor, relief flooding her face. They all descend upon her.

Her body begins the infamous clench. Her limbs draw up and in to her body, and as if on a trigger, her whimpers mewl out. Sara reaches up while sucking, caressing her nonstop. Juniper purses her lips, and her whole body convulses.

"Oh, fuck, yes," Matt says as he leans back to view her luscious body move in orgasmic gyrations. "Let your pussy squeeze my fingers, sweetheart. Ah, fuck yeah! That's right. So nice. Easy now. Let it take you all the way."

Juniper's moans almost sound like she's fussing, bleating out of pain, her sounds involuntarily blitzing the mostly silent room. The only other sounds are those of mouths sucking flesh, and a moan here and there. John has heard her make these sounds before, usually when she's really either sleepy, drunk, or massively turned on. She sounds animalistic, raw, emotional, bloated in the throes of complete uninhibited sexual bliss. Her body rolls in place, completely taken over by the sensual wave of her coming hard.

"Oh, fuck, this is so hot," Matt says with conviction as he strokes his cock and watches Juniper simmer down. "I'm so hard after that. Fuck."

"I know. She's a fucking goddess," Sara murmurs as she strokes Juniper's sides.

Bridge comes off her pussy and leans back.

Juniper lies still, chest heaving, head rolling to the side, limbs now relaxed, flaccid. Her eyes are closed.

"She just came really hard," Bridge says. "She gushed at me." He chuckles.

"Squirted?" asked Matt.

He nods. "Yep. For sure. Small one. She lost complete control of her body, thanks to us. And that was pure ecstasy for her." Bridge strokes her cheek. "Baby, I'm going to carry you to the bed. We can continue there."

John is a bit irked at how compassionate he sounds. That should be him, not Bridge. Anger flares inside, and then he scolds himself. He must check his emotions to avoid ruining the whole night.

Juniper appears still awestruck and barely nods.

Sara chuckles. "We've put her into a sex coma."

Matt laughs. "I think we did. That was truly unbelievable."

Sara nods. "It really was; it was like our souls were touching hers, her very sexual energy bathing us. As I was telling you, she has this unexplained aura about her that's almost palpable, especially when she's having sex." She sighs, shaking her body. "It's an exhilarating experience to have sexual relations with Juniper." She keeps her smile as she hops up and does a little dance, as if her energy has just been rejuvenated. "I'll get our bags with the toys and other paraphernalia." She turns toward the door to retrieve their bags. She moves in a slow, sensual dance, as if floating across the room.

Matt follows Sara in a hurry. "Wow. I agree. It really was surreal." He wraps his arms around her slight frame and kisses her head. "You're next, my love. You get the bags. I'll help Bridge with Juniper. Then we'll make you come."

Sara gives him an appreciative look, nods, and goes for the luggage.

Bridge gently lifts Juniper, and she curls to him in a near-fetal position with her head against his chest. Her body scrunches up tightly against his broad upper body.

She's hunkering down in her recovery inside Bridge's arms.

Bitterness fills John as he clenches his fist, his brows furrowing.

"Yeah, Matt. Can you strip the bed down to the bottom sheet before I lay her down?"

"Sure thing," Matt says cheerily as he rushes ahead of them into the bedroom.

"Wait, Bridge." Juniper lifts her head. "Can we go to the rug downstairs? I'd love to hear the crashing of the waves as we continue."

"Oh, absolutely, love. Great idea. Maybe we can bring a few extra pillows and blankets from the bed." He nods to Matt.

"Got it," Matt says. "I'll meet you down there."

"I can walk now, Bridge." She grins sheepishly up at him, turning her face toward his. "That was really...powerful."

"You were so beautiful. Happy to experience it with you, as always. I'm so thrilled you enjoyed it." He kisses her forehead. "I want to carry you, though. I want to take care of you."

She releases a light giggle. "I've never felt that way ever before in my life." She sighs and curls her head toward her clasped hands. "That was amazing."

John switches his view so he can follow their movements through the house.

"Yes. It really was," Bridge states. He steps out on the deck; the ocean breeze lifts Juniper's hair. "You reached new heights back there, I'm guessing. Must have been with all three of us on you."

"Yes, that definitely was why. Hey. Can you make sure Mags doesn't come out?" she asks with a warning in her tone.

"She didn't. I saw her on the couch. I think you scared her with all your crazy sounds." He chuckles.

Juniper laughs. "It almost felt like it wasn't me making those sounds. Poor Mags. She probably thought I was dying."

"It was really hot, babe. Really hot." He winds down the staircase, looking back and forth, being extra careful in his footfalls. "You've got everyone on high alert, horny now."

"I think I was in the perfect mental state, too. Full of delicious food and with the perfect buzz. I was like in a different state of consciousness."

"That's ideal." He lays her down on the rug, snuggling a large, square pink fluffy pillow under her head.

She grins up at Bridge. "Matt ate my ass. Oh, my gosh. Never had that done before." Her hand flies to her mouth as her eyes give off the finicky sheen of embarrassment. Her humility is adorable.

Bridge touches her cheek. "You never want much anal stuff, baby. It's okay to try it, though. I'm glad you gave in to trying it this time." He smiles down at her as he settles in next to her, his upper body propped up on his elbow. "That's what tonight is about. Just trying new things, stretching our sexuality. Each of us might do that in our own way."

Juniper nods and looks intrigued.

The wind blows a gust at them, tossing Juniper's hair up and tousling Bridge's.

"Ooh. That breeze feels so good," he murmurs.

"It does. The temperature out here is perfect right now."

Sara appears with a suitcase, a freshly opened bottle of wine, and the stems of two empty wine glasses nestled between her fingers. Her expression is full of delightful anticipation. "Okay, that was round one; many more to go. That was just the appetizer. I brought wine for us, Juniper. Matt is taking care of extra pillows, blankets, and a drink for you, Bridge."

He nods and stands up to help take some items from her. He collects the wine and the glasses and sets them on the bamboo-skirted bar. The lit aqua and yellow lanterns hanging from the top of it give his skin a glowing sheen. Setting the glasses a few inches apart, he fills both almost to the rim. He lights a large white candle before carrying the wineglasses to the women.

He hands one to Sara first. "Mood matters."

"It does," Juniper agrees with a happy look. "Totally."

"Healthy glass of wine there. Thanks, Bridge," Sara says with a tilt of her head.

"My pleasure. And I need to liquor the two of you up so you can give Matt and me a fantastic show next. How's that sound for round two? You two edge the fuck out of us with lesbo fun?"

"Is that really the right word here?" Juniper asks with a playful scolding.

"Oh, I'm always game for that with my lovely, hot, ridiculously sexy friend here, Mrs. Juniper-sexy-as-fuck. I'm excited to be back at getting some of your pussy again, truth be told." She shrugs. "I don't give a fuck what you call it; I call it fucking awesome fun." She smiles, which turns into a playful snarl as she claws the air toward Juniper and growls.

Juniper laughs in delight. "If that was the appetizer, I might be dead by the end of the night. Seriously," Juniper jokes with a curled hand over her luscious lips. "That was out of this world amazing." She drops her hand to her stomach, her eyes alight with post-euphoria pleasure.

This soothes John, and he's feeling right again. Juniper is happy, he is happy.

"Yeah, clearly, laugh out loud," Sara says as she settles against a pillow next to Juniper. "It's amazing what stimulating multiple erogenous zones at once can do to a body. We completely owned you. That was like we sexed you into a damn coma."

Juniper giggles. "No shit, I was helpless. Your sex slave."

"And you will be again multiple times before this night is over." Sara raises her eyebrows and traces Juniper's side closest to her with one finger from her side boob, down her torso and waist, stopping at her hip to change directions to gloss over to her pussy mound, where she swirls her finger in continuous circles. "Get yourself ready."

"Mmm, damn, that's really arousing. Y'all might need to peel by lifeless body from off the floor if I get repeats of what just happened. I'll be fluid as a spill, complete mush."

"My goal. To drain you to a complete, satisfied shell of the former Juniper, changed forever by foursome sex, successful tryer of new things." She nods exaggeratedly. "So much so, you will be begging for a night like this again."

"Sounds like an adult film description," Juniper giggles as Bridge hands her a napkin to dry up the spill on her chest, then walks away. "I realize I'm the only one fully naked here."

"As it should be, my sweets. Wait, I should have licked that," Sara says with a laugh as she raises her glass to Juniper. "Cheers to foursome fucking. And a naked Juniper. Always."

Juniper raises her glass, a sexy, shy smile on her face. "To foursome fucking. And naked me." Her giggle is intoxicating.

Sara visibly sways in a swoon, her free hand on her cleavage for dramatic flair.

They clink glasses, and each takes a sip.

"You rub my lust, baby, into an inferno. I love the ability to show our fun live to Matt. Thank you for that." She laughs. "He watches our video almost daily right now."

"Oh my gosh," her eyes go wide. "Are you serious?"

"Very. We could sell that online and make shitloads of money, you know. I watched it with him yesterday, and we had the best sex. Oh. My. God. We were even hotter than I realized."

"Yeah, Bridge really liked it too. He's still talking about it." She meets Bridge's gaze from across the room, where he's fussing with something at the bar. "I was honestly afraid he'd be very angry with me. But since you're a woman, he didn't care. Interesting, huh?"

"It is. Well. And we're both in committed relationships with cis het men, so that makes sense, par for the course." She rolls her eyes, but smirks. "I know, right? Matt really is an exception, though. But, hey, Bridge was obviously okay with you and me having a history of this and repeating it." She raises one eyebrow. "And if you haven't left Bridge for me by now, you won't. So, he might just feel safe in this situation. It's all just for sexual fun, anyhow. Basically, harmless in our situations."

"Yeah. We've just never talked about all this, and so I just don't know, you get used to a person and don't bring new things up unless you do, ya know?"

"Oh, I do know, yes. That's happened to us, too. No harm done. There's a time and a place for everything."

"Very true."

Matt appears with his arms laden with stuff. He has a big grin on his face. "You ladies ready to show off for us? Tease us with what we can't do to you that you can do to each other, and then make us drool?" Matt winks and rubs his cock. "Out of our mouths and our cocks?"

Juniper blushes.

"Don't you know it, babe. We will show you, right Juniper?" She nudges Juniper before whispering, "He's crass, but that's hot. He's the best at dirty talk. Just wait."

Juniper nods slowly, suddenly looking slightly nervous. She sips her wine.

Sara giggles. "Juniper's ready."

"I beg, one glass of wine first. Please."

"Done." Sara grins widely. "Your wish is always my command." She scoffs. "Unless I tell you what to do, my bitch."

Juniper almost spits out her mouthful of wine as she laughs, a lovely, slight blush staining her cheeks again, and a twinkle in her eyes that rivals the sky of stars.

John settles back in his chair with a sigh. She's such an incredible woman.

# Chapter Twenty

John's cock is packed. His lust is charged beyond the max point. He's so damn emotional, but he doesn't give a fuck. Tears escape him, and he lets them flow. A grown man crying unadulterated. He'll never tell anyone this ever, except her. She can know, but no one else. He just loves her so much. Her enjoyment is his heart and soul. It's what makes him tick; it's his air, his food, his water, his reason for existing, and how he accomplishes sexual satisfaction. He's not ashamed one single bit. His father's shaming shrinks away in a glorious death as he recalls Juniper's bliss-filled face.

He turns on the shower to the coldest setting. He's in serious need of a cooldown, or he won't enjoy the rest of their show as much. The danger of loss is real; he doesn't need his dick to be a wasteland for the night. He steps into the frigid water; no need to wait. He gasps sharply and shudders.

"Fuck, that's cold," he mutters as he smacks the tile with his palm.

He dips his face into the water stream to simmer himself down and cool his burning eyes. He jolts away from the coldness but steadies himself as he rotates his face, so all parts suffer from the frigid blast at once. Scrubbing his flesh, he lets the water settle him. This is a brilliant move, rejuvenating his ability to edge and obliterating all his bad feelings. It's working. His attention is consumed by the cold water as it pelts his naked body in a barrage of mind-numbing frigidity.

With a flaccid cock, he dries off with the fluffy towel. How he yearns to be the cause of that kind of sexual stupor in Juniper, desperately so. He dries his eyes with the plump towel, spending extra time on his forehead and jaw because it feels damn good to scrub his skin with the rough loops of the terry cloth.

His cock starts to ache as he remembers the faces of Juniper and Sara. "Damn," he mutters. "Down, boy." He chuckles, avoiding touching his cock further.

Drying off the rest of his body, he ponders what the four of them are doing now, and he cringes. He's fucking missing key important stuff. No matter. He can rewind or watch it in full later. He needed the blast of the Arctic to cool the inferno of his libido after watching all of that. It was a necessary sacrifice.

On his way out of the bathroom, he passes by the litter box, belonging to the new kitty he just bought for Juniper, as she loves cats. Though he's pretty sure it's his litterbox, not the kitten's, because he has to clean it. He's gone poo in the box. Good deal. He seems to understand the litterbox thing on his own, which is good, as John has no clue about how to train him. He really is cute, and Juniper is going to love him.

The little orange tabby is asleep on his couch, curled into a tiny ball of spiky fur. John has been enjoying the little guy. He's very frisky and loves the feather toy John bought. Mags will certainly love him, too. The pesky little thing is either asleep or running around playing like a maniac with every toy John bought. John has enjoyed spoiling him, an extension of spoiling Juniper. The cat really likes the puffy, sparkly purple ball and catnip pouch. But to John's surprise, he's been given multiple smiles a day. He's never owned a cat, and he never expected himself to bond with it so quickly, but despite his reluctance, he's falling in love with the little furry creature. Who knew? Juniper is already improving his life, and they don't even live together yet.

John smiles at the kitty, who squirms in his sleep, readjusting his position with his paws curled to his body. The kitty looks happy and comfortable. John takes a picture of himself with the intent to share it with his fans online tomorrow. They all get a kick out of him being a cat owner now. It's improving his interactions with fans. That helps with book sales. He scrolls the pics he's taken with a giant grin. They all turned out great.

John returns to the monitor to catch the tail end of the women giving each of the men head. Damnit. He missed a good part. He probably missed a bunch of their chatting, too, which he does want to hear, but that will have to come later. But most of all, he wants to watch the two women's actions live. He toys with the idea of going there to spy in person. Certainly, it would be very risky with the two men there.

His cock is packed with blood, so much so that he feels he will burst as the women come off the cocks, and immediately start kissing. He shakes his head. Fuck. That is hot as fuck. His cock twitches as he watches them kiss, probably exchanging some of the men's precum. Whew, that's getting him going! So much for the cold shower. He leans back in his chair, ready for more of the foursome's show.

JUNIPER RUNS HER HANDS up Sara's cheeks as they kiss, caressing her soft facial skin and thrusting her fingers through Sara's long, lush brown hair, pulling her hands back to hold Sara's head. Her desire for Sara explodes, and she can't get enough of her. Their chests smash together. Sara's hands press Juniper's back firmly, forcing their boobs against each other. Sara pulls away and stares intently into Juniper's eyes. Her passion is mirrored there, as they launch.

She grips her shoulders intently, but then stops and grabs a pillow to kneel on so their nipples line up. She holds Juniper's again, her gaze intense, and begins to rub her hard nipples with her own. Juniper responds by placing her hands on Sara's arms so they both have grounding to rub their nipples together. They slip along each other, slightly smashing their breasts together, flattening them. They pop back into shape when free again. The men groan.

"Aw, fuck," Matt murmurs. "I want my mouth on those. All four."

"Oh yes. You a boob man or ass man?" Bridge asks in his deep husky voice.

He snorts. "Do I really have to pick? Technically, I'm an all-woman-parts kind of man, but ass drives me wild. Boobs second. Or pussy. Aw, fuck, I can't pick." Matt laughs as he strokes his cock. "It's impossible."

Bridge whistles as Sara's mouth mounts Juniper's boob. "Yeah, I hear that, but I gotta pick boobs first. Total boob man, but ask me tomorrow, and I might say ass."

"Understood. And I get it. Man, do I get it." He laughs with a sharp shake of his head.

Juniper aggressively takes Sara's nipple into her mouth, and Bridge lets out a whistle. "I love seeing this, oh fuck. You're hitting my fantasies in the sweet spot, babe." He lets out a low moaning growl, which gives Juniper's clitoris a twitch as it always does when he makes that sound. She's like Pavlov's dog with it.

Juniper flicks her eyes over to Bridge and keeps them locked on his while she suckles Sara's nipple, massaging her other boob with her hand. She smiles, trying not to break suction. It's driving him crazy, and she loves it.

Sara's head lolls about as she pants. The sounds she's making are delicious. She arches her back, leaning on her arms, and Juniper follows her movements, tracking her tightly.

Sara reaches for something in her suitcase, which is open at her side.

"Juniper, put these on me." She pulls up a chain to reveal two clamps at the ends. "I have another pair. You want to try?"

Juniper lets Sara's nipple pop out of her mouth with a smack sound, causing the men to groan again.

She widens her eyes as she can't stop the look of shock from taking over her face. "Wow. Shit. Really?" She scoffs. "That looks painful, Sara."

Sara shrugs. "No different from someone nibbling on my tits." She picks up Juniper's hand and drops the chain in her palm. "Lock up my nipples, baby. Tug on me. It drives me crazy."

Bridge whistles. "Well, this oughta be good."

He sounds like he likes this very much, and Juniper's heart flutters faster.

Matt pipes up, "It does drive her crazy. She will moan and curse and scream." He grins widely. "It will make her come completely undone. She likes the flogger, too."

Juniper gingerly picks up the delicate chain with the little squeezer clamps at the end. "Tell me if I do it wrong."

"Not possible," Sara chimes in.

Juniper gently slips the clamps onto Sara's nipples, causing Sara's body to cringe and lurch as she tightens them. "I might slug someone who put these on me," she says with a nervous-sounding laugh.

Sara's gaze at Juniper is intense and direct. "Do it, Junie. Pull on them. Call me your slut." There is no room for disagreement in her eyes.

Juniper shrinks back but then moves closer before gently pulling the chains. They jointly yank Sara's nipples forward.

Sara's eyes close. "Sweet fuck," she murmurs as her nipples are stretched away from her body. "Harder," she demands.

"Interesting," Bridge says softly, but Juniper can still clearly hear him. "You two into BDSM?"

Juniper pulls them harder, even though it seems like she's pulling too hard.

Sara groans as she twists from the tugging, shifting her hips as she endures. "Yes," she slurs.

"A bit lately, yes. We've been increasing it. Sara loves the paddle, too, and I love to spank her ass. We always just did hands until recently." He clears his throat. "We are really stepping up to the next level."

"We do hands mostly and just playful, light spanks. A bit with a flogger tool, too. But I love it."

Juniper can't stop herself from glancing at the men. Bridge leans back, his cock brazenly pushing his pants out in a generous log shape.

"Perfect, sweetie. This is luscious," Sara says in a breathy, angsty voice. "You pulling on my tits is so orgasmic, Juniper. Aww, yeah." She writhes against the pulls as Juniper doesn't let him. "Harder, love, pull harder."

"I don't want to hurt you," Juniper says sweetly.

"See that man over there? He yanks on me. He's not gentle. The pain shoves me into pleasure. I feel ecstasy. It heightens it all for me. You can't hurt me, baby."

Juniper cocks her head, confusion and disbelief filling her. "Oh, well, fuck. Alright then." She shrugs, then pulls hard on the chains. She gives them a few aggressive yanks.

Sara's body jolts in response. She screams out as Juniper is wrenching relentlessly at her breasts. Her breathing increases, as do her grunts, as Juniper's other hand migrates to massage her pussy.

"Fuck," Sara coos urgently.

Juniper pushes Sara's chest, forcing her to lie back. She settles in, arching backward over the pillow. Her head dips to the ground, so her tits are the highest part of her. It seems that if Juniper lifts the chain now, it will be as if she's trying to lift Sara by her breasts. Juniper readjusts the pillow, so Sara's pussy is the highest point of her body instead.

Sara doesn't balk at the change.

"Damn, I love this. So very much," Bridge says, stroking his cock. "I could watch these two all day."

"I'm mesmerized. Just look at that. How fucking sexy is that?" He grins at Bridge. "And look at your wife's amazing ass in the air." He falls silent for a moment. "You're not gonna kill me for saying that, are you?" Matt asks in a joking tone.

"No, you're spot on." He raises an eyebrow and then turns his gaze back to the two luscious women gyrating in front of him. "You two are blowing our sex life wide open, and I'm loving it."

"Juniper seems to agree," Matt states.

Juniper loves what the men are saying, and inside, she agrees. It's too hard to verbally agree, but she will surely be addressing it later when they debrief. She shakes her butt back and forth as she licks Sara's pussy lips several times before spreading her labia lips. First with her tongue, then her hands, she spreads Sara wide open, also pressing her thighs wide. With flat tongue licks, she slurps Sara in four rapid tongue swipes, pulling the nipple clamp chain on the last lick. She moves her tongue up to concentrate on Sara's clit as she messes with Sara's pussy hole with her other hand. She fingers each labia lip, then slips the tip of her tongue into Sara's pussy. It's wet and pink with ripples of flesh. Exploring Sara's body once again is a treasure trove, and listening to the men's appreciative sounds while she does it is quite enjoyable.

She pulls the nipple clamp chain periodically, making Sara arch her back in sudden jerks. Her tits lusciously rise up in response. Sara's nipples are elongated as her back falls into a full arch. Like she's holding her breath, she squirms her legs, tightening them against Juniper's body, causing Juniper to writhe between them, then Sara releases a loud sound of pleasure.

Sara's chest heaves and falls rapidly as Juniper presses a thumb to her clitoris and then replaces it with her tongue, causing Sara's gasp to pierce the air against the backdrop of the waves crashing onshore just beyond them. She flicks Sara's hard clit around with her tongue, then sucks the little cylindrical appendage into her mouth. She lets Sara's clit slip out, and she continues to eat her out for five full minutes amid Sara's whines, grunts, and whimpers. She screams out when Juniper pulls the clamp chain.

"Oh, fuck me, Juniper, just fuck me. I'm so close." Sara sounds perfectly desperate.

"Shut it, you cunt slave, I'm not done tasting you. You're not going to come yet." Juniper can't hide her amusement at the role play as a smile spreads across her face. She's really getting into dominating Sara, which is honestly a huge shift in their entire relationship.

The men crack up.

She glances at the men with a knowing smile. They know exactly what she's feeling, and now she's getting a taste of what they do. She watches the men as she uses her fingers to keep stimulating Sara.

"I love this," Matt says. "Better than any porn I've ever seen, seeing these two go at it. I have to admit I've been gorging on watching their video."

Bridge nods. "Same. I love it. Makes me hard instantly. It's like the flip of a switch." He takes a sip of his drink and dips his head sharply. "It's fucking hot."

Matt nods with a matching naughty grin.

Sara sits up, disrupting Juniper's reign over her. She pushes Juniper back to the rug and places her pussy above Juniper's face. She smashes herself into Juniper's mouth and begins to ride her face, grinding aggressively onto Juniper's mouth, chin, and nose. Sara is moaning and shrieking. Juniper's hands grip her hips tightly as her muffled mouth sounds fill the air.

Sara clearly wasn't having any more of Juniper being in charge.

"It's a battle," Matt says with a snicker.

"I'm a cowboy, baby," Sara lets out in a sing-song voice, her arms flailing in the air as she takes off an imaginary cowboy hat and twirls it in the air.

Juniper watches her from beneath, amused by her friend's reemerging dominance. Sara just can't help herself.

Matt claps his hands and laughs. "Yes, you are, baby. You ride that face and tame it like a wild stallion. Fuck that face. Fuck it. Fuck it. Fuck it. Baby, milk yourself," Matt chants in delight.

Bridge almost spits out his drink during Matt's comment. "Wow. Seeing your wife's face being ridden by another pussy. There are no words."

"I know, right? Fuck. Fuck. Fuck." He shakes his head. "I just want to run over there and push Sara's face to the ground, shove her mouth down to eat rug, force ass up, and pound into her like a damn fucking beast."

Bridge raises an eyebrow. "I'd like to see that."

"Oh, I will do it, but only after these two have tortured us enough. I can't steal this from them."

Juniper is amazed at Matt's restraint after that last comment. Having never been ridden before, Juniper is overwhelmed. She's trying hard to pleasure Sara, but her constant gyrations over her face make it hard for her to do a good job. She legit feels like she's failing.

Sara's small tits bounce as she bounces on Juniper's face. "Uh, uh, uh," Sara chants and then resumes her moaning.

It hurts a bit, but Juniper is not protesting. She wants Sara to come, and come hard, so she endures.

After a minute, Sara's body starts to jerk. Her torso twitches, and her thighs shake against Juniper's cheeks. Here it comes. She leans forward slightly and grips her abdomen as her chin dips down to her chest. "Mmmmm. Oh, fuck yes," she murmurs softly, almost inaudibly. Sara's body jolts, then slumps as she squirts.

"Ah," Juniper squawks, scrambling to maintain composure. She's got a tight grip on Sara's thighs.

Sara shifts her weight, then slips off Juniper. She crashes to the ground with a thud and a gasp.

Juniper sits up, her face soaked.

The men crack up and hoot cheers.

"Get a pussy face bath, did you?" Matt asks. "Sara gives a good pussy-juice facial."

Sara breathes heavily while lying flat on the rug. She's completely cum drunk, and it's a beautiful thing.

"Guess it's her turn for a sex coma." Juniper grins and wipes her face with the back of her hand while smirking. She chuckles. "Wow, that was a first," she says. "And that was a lot."

There's a loud crash that sounds like it came from a distance, but sort of nearby. The men hop up and quickly move in the direction of the sound.

"Whoa, what the hell was that?" Juniper asks as her heart pounds. With all the weird stuff that she's encountered, her mind immediately launches into a flight of fear. She waits, watching in the direction where the men have disappeared as her anxiety rises. She doesn't want to slip into a panic, but she can't help the climb toward it.

"What's going on?" Sara asks, sounding very sleepy.

"There was a sound, and they went to check it out." She's doing a shit job of masking her fear in her tone.

"Oh, I guess I did hear that," Sara responds dreamily. "It will be okay. Those two could take anyone."

That's what scares Juniper the most. That the sound could be someone—someone who has done all the other recent oddities, too. Bridge would tell her she's being paranoid, but something is unfurling in her that's telling her she's right to be afraid. She's never not trusted her gut, and right now, her gut is in full-power alarm.

Sara reaches for Juniper and pats her arm. "Don't worry, sweets. They've got this. I have zero doubts."

That is not a comfort to Juniper, not one single bit.

# Chapter Twenty-One

John's heart thuds. Fuck. What the hell was he thinking, leaving home and coming here? He had a front-row seat on his monitor at home where he could zoom in and see every detail. And he had traded it for this? Watching live had been exhilarating, but not nearly as satisfying. And now he was running for his life. The risk was not worth it.

He skirts sharply around a big bush, then hops over a small garden. He dares a glance back. They are coming full force on his heels.

"Fuck," he mutters as he puts his jets on and runs faster. The alcohol has him moving too slowly, and he knocks himself for being such a moron. He's had way too much to drink for this shit.

He narrowly misses knocking over a planter as he gets a surge of energy from his rising panic. He barrels down the driveway and zooms across the street. He needs to move in the opposite direction of his car so he can hide and get as far away as possible in the process. This way, they wouldn't be able to associate his car with him. Having the police called on him is the very last thing he needs. He can't nab her if he's in jail. He's almost ruined everything with this stunt.

He pants heavily as he sprints. The mask is getting annoying, and he wants so badly to rip it off, but then he'd risk dropping it and thereby leaving some evidence. He cannot have that; he must power through. He scans the yard as he runs. There's a shed in the back corner. If he's far enough ahead of the two men, he could easily slide in there, and they'd have no idea. Or is that an obvious spot?

He's too nervous about that idea, so he keeps running. He runs nonstop for several minutes, and then finally glances back. There's zero movement. He slides into a bush and tries to peer back into the darkness through the branches. There's no sign of anyone at all. He pants heavily as his heart rages.

Stupid. Stupid. Stupid.

He had let his desires turn him into a fool. He'd risked everything just to feel a part of what the four were doing, and it had almost cost him his health, his safety, and worst of all, his big plans for a life with Juniper. This had been too big a risk to take, yet he'd dumbly charged right into it. Blind passion almost got him ruined. Plus, he'd had way too much to drink for this BS. He's not a fucking superhero, just a dumbass. He can't risk being drunk when he does this kind of stuff; that's suicide.

He waits, motionless, and watches, constantly on edge and scanning religiously for any movement. He still sees nothing. The men must have given up, which is very surprising to him. He can't wait to get back home and watch their discussion with the women on the video. He needs to be much smarter, much, much, much smarter. He silently curses himself as he continues to look around.

After about ten minutes, the coast appears clear. He begins to make his way to his car, constantly glancing over his shoulder. His heart is still raging, and he has to be careful. The desire to flat-out run to his car fills him, but anyone spying him running would be a red flag, especially if Bridge starts asking neighbors if they saw anything. Wearing all black and a black ski mask was a great idea, but anyone seeing him in this outfit would be a huge cause for alarm. He glances around and removes the mask, shoving it in his pocket, before speeding toward his car. This is his old neighborhood, so it wouldn't be too concerning if a neighbor saw him. But they would certainly question why he was walking around in the dark, being that he no longer lived there.

He hurries to his car and slides in. Pulling the car into the street, he scans for any sign of anyone. He sees nothing, so he drives in the opposite direction of the beach house, deciding that taking the long way home is worth it to lower his chances of being spotted.

His heart begins to calm down as he enters the interstate. He's made it.

"Fuck, that was close."

BRIDGE AND MATT RETURN out of breath.

Both women rush them.

Juniper's so panicked her heart is pounding out of control as if she'd been chased by this unknown person herself.

"What happened? Who was it? Did you catch them?" Her questions come out in a frantic jumble, her breathing labored.

"Did you get a good look at them?" Sara asks, seeming as panicked as Juniper.

"No, it seemed like a man. But he was in all black, and had a mask on." Bridge accepts Juniper into his open arms. "It's okay. He's gone."

"I'm betting it was just a horny teenager," Matt says, clearly trying to make light of it.

Juniper isn't having that, not with all the strange things she'd witnessed. She's not legit terrified. "Do you think they meant us harm?"

Bridge shakes his head as she peers up at him. "I don't know, but I don't think so. But we really have no idea."

"We need video cameras installed," Juniper says meekly.

"Yeah, especially down here where it's open." Bridge caresses her hair, then kisses the top of her head. "Don't worry. I'll always keep you safe."

She believes him, but she's still scared. Bridge isn't always home.

"I'm kinky, and that could be hot if he were just an innocent, horny voyeur," Sara jokes. She glances at Juniper. "I'm sure it was, hon. Who would want to hurt you? You're an angel."

That's not comforting, but she's going to try to embrace that thought so as not to ruin their plans for the night. It will be hard to shake this, but she's sure as fuck going to try. Everyone will think she's overreacting if she voices her worries anyhow. And maybe she is, but she can't shake the feeling that she's not.

Bridge rubs her back and gazes into her eyes. "How can I help?"

She snuggles into his chest. "You already are."

He rocks her back and forth as Sara and Matt move over to the couch. Perhaps a slowdown breather is warranted. She draws in a deep breath and slowly releases it. The crash of the waves calms her, as usual.

"So, this person was in all black?" she asks, unable to hide the trepidation in her voice.

"Yes."

"That's highly suspicious." She cringes inside, trying not to let her fear balloon.

"It is, yes." Bridge stops swaying her. "It was clearly intentional."

She glances around but keeps her head tucked into Bridge's chest. "What if he comes back?"

"I doubt it. With both of us hot on his heels, he knows we aren't messing around. Two big dudes like us? He's staying away now."

Juniper flicks her eyes back and forth. True. But that's with Bridge and Matt here; what about when they aren't here? She doesn't bring that up because she doesn't want to dwell on her fears. Not tonight.

"How about a snack and a drink? We could join Matt and Sara and just chat for a bit."

Juniper nods. She is concerned she may be done with sex for the night. She's not feeling a damn bit sexy. The intruder has killed her mood. He must have a story; no one just randomly picks a house to watch like that. He had a reason for being at the house, and she knew in her heart that it was nefarious. All the movies she's watched, the dark romance books she's read, there's no way this was just by chance. That man was at their house for a specific reason. Was it her? Had this person seen her and Bridge fucking and just wanted more? She could handle a simple horny voyeur if all they wanted was to get off.

Bridge leads her to the sitting area and then visits the bar to mix her a drink.

"You okay, baby doll?" Sara asks kindly, tilting her head. "You look very deep in thought." Sara looks unperturbed.

Juniper is the only one on edge after that, and she can't wrap her head around the fact that they are all so calm about this. Some dude was spying on them. In a kinky way, if this were a setup with someone they knew, it would be sort of hot, but not in this way. "Yeah, that just shook me up pretty good." She watches Bridge stroll near her, then takes the drink from him. "Thanks."

Bridge sits next to her and wraps his arm around her shoulder. "It's always my pleasure to take care of my woman."

"I don't think he'll be back," Matt says arrogantly. "I think we scared the shit out of him barreling after him like that."

"I hope so," Juniper says in a meek voice.

"Guarantee it," Bridge says as he boops the tip of her nose.

"I'm sure he was just a horny freak who couldn't help himself," Sara says casually. "And we were going pretty hot."

That's all great, but how did it happen? There's a huge part of the story they are missing. Had he been walking along the beach and spied them fucking, and then decided he needed a closer look? Or has he been watching the house? The idea sends a frigid chill down her spine. She shudders.

"Need a blanket?" Bridge asks. He has no worry in his eyes either. He looks calm and collected.

"No, it was just a slight chill. I'm okay."

They all think this is no big deal. She's frazzled as a lit firecracker. She slows her breathing and attempts to see this event as they all are viewing it. She relaxes into Bridge and tries her best to smile up at him. She's sort of okay with playing this masked man off as simply superficial lust, but she doesn't want to end up the fool by dismissing potential danger. Watching the three of them chat in a relaxed manner helps her slide into that mode as well. Slowly, but surely, after half an hour of chatting, she's feeling like herself again.

"So, who's up for more sex? I'm raging like a horny whore again. I want some cock in me." Sara smiles at both men seductively.

"I'll never tire of hearing that come out of your mouth," Matt says happily with a ginormous grin. "Let's go."

"Junie?" Sara asks. "You good to go for another round?"

Juniper smiles and nods, very pleased with herself that she really is ready to fuck again. She hadn't thought she'd make it to this point, but the alcohol and their company have her yearning to be intimate and climax again. "I'm in."

"Great!" says Bridge. "Then it's unanimous."

"Looking at you two nude has been driving me crazy," Matt says with appreciation.

Sara wastes no time. "Then stand up. I want to climb you, Junie."

Juniper obeys with a laugh as she stands up.

Sara is up in an instant. She forces herself between Juniper and the couch, her small hands claiming Juniper's torso in incessant grabs like hungry little mouths. She hops up on the couch behind her and crouches over, kissing Juniper's neck from behind. Seeming insatiable and legit hyper, she moves to the front of Juniper in a frenzy. She kisses her way all over Juniper's front, then hops into her arms, clinging to her like a baby monkey.

Juniper squeals as she falls back onto the couch from the unexpected weight of Sara on her. She laughs as Sara covers her flesh in more kisses. She moves down Juniper's body and spreads her thighs open.

"Let's get to the good stuff," Sara says as she stares intently at Juniper's nude lower lips.

"Yes," Matt slurs, then releases a lewd snarl. "Keep that shit going."

Sara pulls Juniper to the floor, then lines up her pussy with Juniper's. She mashes her slit against Juniper's, humping her friend. Juniper rubs back and they both let out soft moans that float along the air like clear fog, hanging about, thickening the desire for all. The air feels electric. Their moans increase as they scissor, skin on skin, sloshy sounds subtle but unmistakable as they gyrate their pussies against each other.

"Yes, fuck that pussy, girls. Fuck it. Fuck it. Fuck it. Fuck yes," Matt chants. He doesn't dampen his enthusiasm, which makes Juniper smile.

His chanting causes them to pick up their hip movements. Their heads fall back as they lean on their arms for leverage. Their mouths are both open, and moans are flying out nonstop. Their pleasure sounds increase and match the rapid pace of their pelvic gyrations.

"Oh, fuck me, Sara, fuck me." Juniper leans forward and claws one hand down Sara's belly and shoves two fingers into her pussy and begins to pump.

Sara copies and pushes her fingers into Juniper. Both women are writhing and moaning from each other's finger stimulations. They both groan as they finger fuck each other. They pause and align themselves side by side for easier access, which allows their fronts to face their men. This goes on for a minute before Sara lunges for her suitcase and pulls out two rabbit vibrators. She switches them both on and hands one to Juniper.

"I'm pink. You're purple for the night. These have been washed in hot soapy water." She nods at Juniper as she takes it. "Feel safe in using it." She grins deeply.

They lie on their backs side by side, and each inserts the toys into their vaginas. Juniper guides the small, flexible vibrating head over her clit and holds it in place. They each take over control of the other's toy and ride each other's pussies with it.

Juniper is flung to the edge quickly from the strong vibrations. Her body twitches within mere seconds from the simultaneous massaging of her G-spot and her stiff clit at once. Her arms and legs draw up, and her body does a single undulation wave motion. The bliss peaks with her toes curling as her body clenches on itself and her body convulses four times in defined jolts. Juniper struggles to hold on to Sara's vibrator during her big O.

Once Juniper's coming down off climaxing, she can focus on Sara. But Sara pushes her hand off and rides her own pussy with the toy. Within thirty seconds, Sara is coming, her body twitching as if she's being electrocuted. Both women lay back, sweaty and spent, their chests heaving, both completely immobile.

"Oh, my fucking gawd, that was amazing," Sara muses. "Loved the fuck out of that."

Juniper nods, still in the murky mindset of a post-climax fog. Savoring the euphoria, she gazes at the men.

"Okay, I don't know about you, bro, but I'm going in. I can't take it anymore," Matt says with urgency. He downs the rest of his drink and stands, strips his pants fully off, and his shirt, and walks over to Sara, cock swinging as he makes a direct path for her. "I love a sexually spent woman when I get to urge her into more. It's just fucking the best."

He kisses her on the mouth and feels up her breasts, then grips her hips. "No rest for the wicked, my love. Gimme."

"Ummm, and I'm wicked indeed." Sara gleans a sexy grin. "You gonna punish me, make me cum again, lover?"

"Fuck yes, I am your cum-slut bitch." He devours her neck with open-mouthed kisses, trailing down to her breasts. He takes a turn on both nipples and plays his hand into her wet, sloshy-sounding pussy. "So wet, baby." He sits up and slaps Sara's hip. "Flip it. Ass up, face in the rug. Pose for me, my bitch."

Sara rolls over with a salacious look and points her ass at Matt's middle. Wiggling her butt at him, she nestles her face in the shaggy carpet as Matt spanks her ass hard. He grabs the medium-sized black paddle from the suitcase and hits her butt three times with it. She cries out with each of the smacks but moans with the same ardor. He snatches a flogger.

"More, punish me more," she begs. Her desperation is a turn-on.

"Paddle your naughty ass," Matt says with vehemence. "Paddle it bright red so I can fuck it."

Sara shudders and groans out.

Juniper has not witnessed this side of Sara, and it's super intriguing. She can't stop watching. It's like watching a train wreck.

Bridge has not moved a muscle either. The erotic display of aggression before them shocks her, and Bridge must be equally mesmerized. She doesn't even meet his eyes as they both stare at the couple as they continue to carry on. Matt alternates using the paddle and the flogger to hit Sara's bottom. Juniper realizes her mouth is slightly ajar and shuts it. She and Bridge had fun sessions with spankings before, but never to this level of intensity.

Matt reaches under Sara and fondles her pussy with one hand as he smacks the paddle on her ass two more times, making her body lurch forward. Her ass cheeks are now a pink-red color. He sets down the paddle and puts his mouth squarely on her butthole.

Juniper squirms, bleating out little screeches. "Holy fuck," she whispers.

Matt's head bobs as he tongue fucks Sara's ass, his hands firmly on her hips.

"Wow," Bridge murmurs with shock. He meets Juniper with his own stunned expression.

Matt leans back and says, "Wet you good, my cock sleeve." He dives back in for a few more pumps deep inside. Then he pulls his tongue out, stands, and leaves her. He searches for something in the suitcase. Sara's ass cheeks are blossoming to a bright red as if they're evolving over time, like how a sunburn slowly reveals itself. "I'm gonna fuck that red ass, baby." He pulls out some lube and squirts it all over his hard cock. He chugs the fluid all over his turgid shaft, making squelching sounds. He squeezes more lube into his hand and rubs it along Sara's slit.

Juniper is fighting the urge to run from the room. This is a bit much for her if he's going to fuck her in the ass. She flinches but remains seated. This is her fear, and she's cringing as she watches this anal scene set up unfolding in front of her. She's not so sure she's ready to confront this. Panic rises, and she must do something.

Bridge watches transfixed.

He's no help at all.

She stands and goes to fill her wine glass for a bit of a distraction from the horror of the scene. Her breathing is reaching a panic level. She almost sneaks a glance at Matt and Sara, but keeps her eyes on her wine instead. The fucking sounds of her friends having anal sex are very hot, but she's resisting looking because...ew. She knows very well that Sara wants this and loves it. But watching it is an entirely different thing altogether.

She sneaks a peek. Bridge is fully watching, still not moving one single bit, and with a look of lust living on his face. She laments this and is resisting the legitimate urge to flee with the excuse of going to find a snack upstairs. But she knows they will all see right through that, so she dares another glance at her friends instead. The sight of them is jarring, with Matt aggressively thrusting his cock fully into Sara's asshole, fully balls deep. Sara's face and moans confirm that she loves this, but Juniper's brain can't process how this is possible. How is this possible?

"I want Bridge in my pussy," Sara pleads. "Please. Can I? Please?"

Juniper freezes. She's seen DP in porn before, but still felt traumatized by the anal aspect of it, too much to enjoy watching it. She just always found herself avoiding looking at the screen during that part.

"Please," Sara pleads again. "Can I? We've never done it. I want to try it."

Matt continues to pound into Sara's ass as if she didn't ask.

Bridge stands and turns to face Juniper. She lifts her chin to meet his gaze. He's asking with his eyes, and she nods, realizing she may never get over her fears of anal to give Bridge a taste of this herself. So, being the generous lover that she is, she can't deny him this wish. Besides, he let her do her own thing with Sara, and he gave in to the foursome when he didn't seem keen on it at first, so this is the least she can do for him, short of not doing it herself, which is utterly improbable to say the least.

"Do it," she says softly.

Juniper sits where Bridge once was on the couch, settling into the warmth his body left behind on the soft cushion. She is now the sole watcher herself. She keeps her eyes on the three as they arrange themselves for double penetration, trying not to let her distaste radiate to her body.

They both enter her, and she groans out like it hurts, but that dissipates quickly as she must be relaxing into it. Biting her lip, at least, Juniper hopes. As they fuck, Sara flops like a rag doll between them as they hold her up with their strong arms and both thrust into her. Her body looks awkward as they pound into her. The sounds she makes are so erotic, verging on obscene at times. Juniper's pussy wets despite her disgust at watching Bridge participate in an anal act with her friend. Both men are grunting hard as they work themselves into her. Bridge lets out a deep growl.

Okay, she admits it. She's getting really fucking turned on by watching them. She's shocked that she wants to suddenly jump in somehow. She sips from her wine glass, contemplating what she could contribute to this, her lust ever urging her on to go join the three of them. Her focus is on Sara, though, and how she can help Sara enjoy this even more.

Juniper touches her pussy and rubs it and lets out a little simple soft whine. She bites her lip. Sara is clearly in deep pleasure, so how can it be so bad? Right?

Juniper smooshes her lips to one side as she watches, her brain going over time trying to fathom how it's legitimately possible that Sara actually likes this violation of her ass, but her moans and her face tell Juniper that she's riding a coast of sheer ecstasy. She needs to have a long talk with Sara about this. It makes no sense to her.

Sara begins yelling out guttural sounds, which prompts Juniper to down the rest of her glass. It's time for action. Juniper lowers herself to the ground, getting on all fours. She crawls toward them, her tits swaying under her as she moves along. The sight of the two thrusting into Sara violently tugs at her own lust, her emotions swirling in a mess of confusion and want. She can't quite wrap her brain around it all still, but onward she moves regardless. She just wants to be a part of the scene, somehow.

Juniper wants the thrust of Bridge's cock into her own pussy, yet she loves that they are all enjoying each other. It's an odd sensation to want something and not want it at the same time, but still, she's terrified of anything entering her butt. As she approaches, Matt eyes her up, and he slows his hammering of Sara. A satisfied grin travels his face as he reaches over and pulls Juniper close. He completely stops fucking Sara's ass and turns his body to face Juniper, his hard, wet cock swinging as he moves.

He grins, his lush lips curling into something Juniper wants to put her own mouth on and suck. She feels wanted by his actions. His eyes tell her there's no way in hell he's letting her feel unwelcome after joining on her own volition, without any prompting from any of them. Fuck no. She loves that she's capturing his full attention.

Placing his hand on Sara's hip, he pulls Juniper close with his other arm. She kneels in front of him, and they fall into a kiss. She moans into his mouth, readily melting into his sweaty, slim body. He leaves his touching of Sara and puts both of his hands on Juniper's biceps as they kiss. He grasps her breast, and she sighs into his mouth. He caresses the bulges of her hips, reaching with his hand for a swipe along the curve of her ass, then lies on his side, pulling her down to lie alongside him on the rug. She acquiesces and snuggles into him, then kisses him back.

She fondles his hair, her right hand migrating to his shoulders, pressing into and squeezing his firm pecs.

Matt runs his hand down Juniper's side from boob to hip, takes a swipe, and presses her clit before wrapping his hand around to cup her bottom.

Juniper is enjoying his unfaltering forwardness with touching her body; his lust is deliciously strong, and his sexual appetite satisfyingly commanding. He doesn't hesitate with his touch but takes what he wants. He's strong, intentional, passionate, and forceful in a different way than Bridge. Bridge is always hungry for her, too, but his handling of her is a bit gentler than Matt's.

She gasps as he roughly manhandles her right butt cheek, massaging it hard. He pulls his hand away and then gives her a hard spank. Her eyes pop wide as she recoils slightly from the harsh slap, but remains kissing him as fervently as he's kissing her. The firm spank asserts his dominance over her without question, and she melts. This is her kink as well.

As he migrates his focus to her butthole, she stiffens. She wants to try some butt stuff, but she's still so damned hesitant.

He's unwavering in his intentions as he reaches behind himself. He's searching for something while still clumsily trying to kiss her. He fumbles with a jar of coconut oil.

Juniper breaks the kiss and turns her head to the sounds Bridge and Sara are making. Bridge is still aggressively fucking Sara's pussy. He looks extremely sexy from this angle, an angle she's never gifted to see unless there's a mirror in the room, but this is still different since she's behind him and Sara. She takes the jar from Matt since he's still struggling to open it.

"I'm too slippery," he says quietly with a little smile.

"I've got it," she says smoothly.

Sara murmurs a moan. "Fuck my ass, Bridge, please. Please. Will you fuck my ass?" she asks in a desperate begging.

Juniper's eyes go wide, but she doesn't protest. She opens the lid of the coconut oil jar instead. Again, she doesn't want to do anal, so she's okay with him doing it with Sara. Her nerves settle a bit. It's sort of freeing to know he can get to try it without her having to engage in an act she doesn't want to do. She hands the opened jar back to Matt.

"It's okay, sweetheart," Matt says, caressing her cheek. "I won't hurt you, and I'll stop when you want. Okay? And we go as slow as you want. You say it, and I'll stop. I promise you that."

She nods as she points to the open jar of oil. Sara's words of using coconut oil for anything anal sound in her head.

He takes a generous scoop onto his fingers and twirls his hand in the air.

She spins around and falls onto her hands so she's on all fours.

He begins to spread the oil all over Juniper's buttocks, ending by smothering her anus with it. He's kissing her hips as he ever so slightly presses only the tip of his index finger at her pucker, then he very slowly pushes it into her asshole. She moves away from his press, and he pulls back out.

Massaging her anus, he whispers, "I'll hold my finger still, and you push onto it. That way, you have full control over the entrance of my finger, and you can stop at the slightest desire to do so." He doesn't look one bit angry; he seems calm and controlled, which is funny considering how he was just so full of ardor.

Fear emanates from her aura, but as she processes what he says. It makes sense. She releases some of the fear she's harboring and nods, wondering if she should be doing this with Bridge, but then again, he's about to fuck Sara's ass, so this seems to fit in, too. If she likes this, she might repeat it with Bridge someday. Maybe.

"Or if you prefer, we have a skinny butt plug."

She shakes her head. That's scarier for some reason. "Finger," she insists.

He grins at her. "You can do this. But only if you relax. I'm going to eat you out for a bit to arouse you, and then we can try it as I said, but only if you want to." He presses her to move onto her side.

"Get comfortable," he says with a lewd, wicked smile. "I'm going to make you scream in pleasure." He licks his lips.

Well, that's hot!

She's not had another man eat her out since before she met Bridge. The idea is very exciting. The sounds of Sara and Bridge are driving her lust up several notches. They are indeed butt fucking, and Juniper's brain stalls as she watches for a moment. They both seem to be loving it. She's good with that; she just wants them both to have pleasure.

Matt clamps his mouth onto her. He's quite aggressive right from the first contact. His eating her out is quickly ramping her climax to the sky at light speed. Her want for more travels through her body, leaching her juices out from her hot core.

She startles as Matt places his finger over her butthole, while still stimulating her with his mouth. He does not push it in, just rests it there. Her enjoyment of him eating her out fights her fear of him touching her hole. When he goes at her with his mouth even stronger, she belts out a moan that is lush and full. She presses back ever so slightly, forcing herself onto his finger. She's shocked that it doesn't hurt. She inches her hips back a little further, pressing his finger a bit further inside her. Instead of terror, she feels okay about it. It's an indescribable fullness that neither hurts nor feels good. She smiles with relief as he sucks her clit gently. She's made it this far.

He releases his suction before he says, "Yes, sweetheart, you're doing it. You're doing great." He nudges her labia with his nose. "With practice, very slow and guided by you, your ass can take a cock the same as your pussy does." He grins up at her. "And it can make you come hard. Really hard. Sara can tell you." His voice is soft, his tone is gentle, directing, non-threatening, and not demanding at all. "But you may find you don't like it too, but trying it, giving it a chance, will help you know."

Juniper feels raw, a bit weepy from the experience, and emotional, yet turned on, too. It's a complex set of feelings she can't quite wrap her thoughts around.

"The thing to remember is to go slow, so very, very slow," he instructs.

Sara shrieks like a banshee, clearly climaxing hugely. Her sounds are primal and wild as she flops. Bridge pulls himself from her in a rush.

Juniper is hoping Bridge hasn't come inside her because she wants his cock to ravage her pussy. She's been craving it since seeing him fuck Sara's pussy. All the other stuff has been delicious, but now she wants his dick in her.

Matt slowly pulls his finger out of her back hole. She and Matt separate.

"Well done, Juniper. And thank you. I loved it." Matt's appreciative tone matches his expression.

He rises and walks over to the bar, where he grabs a bottle of vodka to make a beverage. Juniper grins back at him. Hopefully, he finds a sink to wash his finger in. She raises an eyebrow at him as he washes his hands in the bar sink, thank goodness. The nurse in her clearly doesn't take a break from germ watch mode. She silently laughs at herself.

She swings her gaze back to Bridge and Sara. They have separated from each other. Though Juniper can't suppress the perpetual shudder that threatens to rip through her when she thinks about their anal act, what she did with Matt has lessened her fears a tiny bit. She's clearly doomed to never fully comprehend what Sara enjoys about anal, though watching her proves her point that it feels amazing. Her friend looks like Juniper did earlier, in a come-drained state of euphoria, with a face of sheer bliss. She gazes at them both with a slow burn grin taking over.

Bridge leans over and kisses Sara on the forehead, pushing her damp hair off. Awww. This hits Juniper. The tenderness Bridge shows for her friend stirs more love for them both in her. He next kisses Sara on the lips with a peck and hugs her. She nuzzles into him for twenty seconds. He gives her a squeeze, and then he stands up. The whole exchange was very sweet.

As he leaves her, she closes her eyes and her head tips to the side, her hair falling against the white rug like a brown veil. She looks as if she's falling asleep.

He approaches Juniper and asks, "You, okay?"

She gives him a slight smile and nods. "I'm okay, yes."

"I'm going to go wash up." He points to his cock with a smirk. "You sure you were okay with what just happened?"

"Yes, I don't want to do it, and you, and Sara do, so you get your fantasy, as does she. She's wanted DP for a long time. So, you gave her a gift of fulfilling a fantasy, too." A sex act is just a sex act, her marriage to Bridge is sound.

"Okay. Good. We honor our pact then. If something bothers us during all this, we say it right away to halt it, so no bad feelings develop." He holds his direct gaze on her, waiting.

Juniper nods. "Right. Agreed." Relief fills her as a comforting feeling grows.

"Ok, good. I think your pussy needs a baby-making pounding now, though." He snickers.

"Yes. I'm dying to have your cock in me. Matt's got me all riled up, no doubt about it." Good, he hasn't come yet.

"I'm so glad you pushed me into this foursome. We're both doing more of what we had on our sexual bucket lists, but safely. And if we feel threatened in our relationship, we stop. Right?" He pulls her cheeks up close to his face with both hands and looks directly in her eyes. "We come first."

She nods in his grip. "Yes. I completely agree. And I have to confess something." She stops as she fears this might anger him. "I let Matt finger my asshole a little. Only a little. And...it didn't hurt, and I didn't freak out. He had such a way with making me comfortable."

He releases her face without any alarm evident. "Well, good. See, you're growing sexually, too. Whatever he did, you seem calmer about it now." He seems okay with it all as he continues, "I'll have to thank Matt later."

She nods. It's true Matt worked magic. But she's still not sure she wants to progress much further in that area of sex. Who needs that anyway?

She grabs his hands. "But now I need you."

"As I need you, babe. Just give me a sec and I'll be right back."

"Okay. And I can't believe you didn't come with Sara. How did you manage that?" She glances down at his still erect cock.

"Sheer will," he says with a laugh. "But I can say I'm not going to last long being this ripe. I'll be back in a flash. I'm going to visit the bathroom to clean up."

"Okay, I'll be here." She giggles. "You should be a porn star with that kind of control."

"Right?" he asks with a snicker.

Juniper heads over to the rug and snuggles in with Sara. She stirs, and her eyes open into little slits.

"Hi," she whispers. "Are you okay with what we just did?" She sounds worried, and it tugs at Juniper's heart.

Juniper pulls Sara into her chest and presses her head down onto her breast. She gently cradles her there. She whispers back, "Yes. It's okay. It's something you both have wanted to do, and so you both got your wish. I love you both, and my fears hold me back from fulfilling his fantasies of anal, so I've always felt bad about that, and now I don't have to feel bad because he got to experience it, and I didn't have to do something I don't really want to do. It's perfect."

"True. And he was amazing, by the way. He's quite the thruster." She giggles. "He fucked my ass damn good."

"Yes, he has a good pelvic thrust. Drives me wild."

"Mmmm, I must say I have to agree," she says with a laugh as she plays with Juniper's nipple. "It's different, ya know. Anal orgasms. With clit and G-spot, your brain has to be in the right spot, but with anal, it's like your body forces you into it, which makes it so, so, so huge. I'd never go back now that I've had them."

"Hmmmm. Interesting. Well, he's going in my pussy next, and I'm so ready for it. He's just washing your butt germs off." Juniper laughs. "Sorry, that's crude."

Sara chuckles. "Yes. But it's true. You don't need to add germs to your pussy, especially when you're trying to get pregnant. I'm guessing Matt and I are done for the night. He might come back, but I know he's come once already."

"He was hard just now when I was with him, though."

"Oh, nice. Maybe I can get him to shove himself into me again then." She glances around. "He's gone upstairs? I'm guessing for a snack. He always gets hungry when he fucks."

"He'll be back, I'm sure. Maybe he'll bring us all snacks." Juniper starts to rise as Bridge returns.

"Can we watch you two fuck?" Sara asks hopefully.

"I'm game. I think it's hot to be watched." Juniper laughs. "We've kinda been watching each other all evening. You don't need to ask permission." The idea of being watched flips her brain right back to the intruder. She shoves that right out of her head. He's not ruining her time with Bridge.

"True. Very true. It is indeed." Sara sits up and hugs her bent legs to her chest, and rests her chin on her knees. "I'm ready for the Bridge and Juniper show."

Bridge and Juniper chuckle at her and exchange glances before they embrace and begin kissing. Bridge's hands migrate to cupping Juniper's ass. He runs his hand down her leg, bringing her thigh up to his hip with his right hand, easily palming her. Her hands migrate across his shoulders, biceps, pecs, nipples, and up to tangle in his hair as they kiss.

Juniper catches sight of Matt as he travels down the spiral stairs with a tray of snacks and drinks. She smiles her approval at him as Bridge kisses her neck, and he grins back and nods. He sets the tray down in front of Sara. She dives into the charcuterie tray, topping her little stack with a piece of salami.

"I'm ravished. I need this. Thank you, my sexy man." She rests her head on his shoulder. "You're the best, you know that?"

"I know." He chuckles. "And so are you, my sweet cheeks."

Bridge pushes Juniper over the back of the couch, gripping her hips as he prepares to enter her, but first, he tickles her pussy entrance with his swollen cock head. She groans and grabs the pillows within her reach, resting her forearms on them.

"Please, Bridge. Please just fuck me. I need you in me now," Juniper says with a whimper. "Breed me. I don't need anything else but your cock in me."

"Nice, whoop whoop," hollers Sara. "Do it, Bridge, fuck that wanton pussy."

"Ah, yeah, go ahead, bro, and put her out of her misery. She needs cock badly. She's waited all night."

"Oh, I intend to give her all of this cock, all the way, balls deep, baby." He slowly enters her pussy, and he lets out a giant groan. "Not stopping."

He speeds up, pounding her from behind, making her ass cheeks jiggle with each slam. Their union makes a satisfying skin slap sound on repeat. She raises her butt up by going on her tiptoes, and he grunts his approval. Her mouth falls slack as she whimpers soft moans as he obliterates her. She raises her head, and he grabs her hair for a yank, then grabs her arm, pinning it back.

He barrages himself into her so hard that her feet leave the ground. He grunts.

"Oh, fuck yes, fuck me, Bridge, fuck me." She squeals, she's so charged up. Her tits are jiggling violently across her chest as her orgasm takes flight, already promising that delicious, holistic, swollen release. "You insatiable raging fucker, destroy my pussy, make her come, Daddy," she screams, marveling how her voice doesn't even sound like her own. "Gimme some good."

"You got it, my little whore. Take my seed like a wench meant to be used and bred." Bridge slams into her harder in beast mode.

"Yes. Yes. Yes. Yes," she murmurs just before her body begins to twitch and jerk like she has fever chills. Her vagina clenches down on his cock as she comes, tightening around his erect penis in several convulsions, milking his cock.

He hollers and presses his fingers deeper into her flesh as he drives himself in deep and fast. He slows as she senses more moisture inside her pussy. Her man has come. He maneuvers her to lie back on the couch and shoves a few pillows under her pelvis to raise her lower abdomen up.

He pats her pussy mound and then holds his hand over her vaginal opening. "Now be a good little pussy and eat my cum so my little guys can penetrate your egg." He winks. "She's hungry for it."

Juniper chuckles with a hand over her mouth. "That was quick, but I'm not complaining, it was hot as fuck. I love it when you fuck my feet right off the ground." She gasps. "Wow. What a night! I've come so many times, oh my gosh. It's been incredible."

"Totally. And I love it." He strokes her hair. "Now what can I get you, my orgasm spent cum-slut queen? Snacks, a drink?" Bridge does a mock bow in front of her.

"Yes, and yes, please."

"That was so fucking hot to watch," Sara says with clear enjoyment. "And it's even hotter thinking that you could get pregnant from it." She shoves several pieces of popcorn into her mouth. "Fingers are crossed for you two."

"I think the window is over for this month, but I still think it's worth a try just in case." Juniper never gives up hope. There's always a chance.

Sara nods. "Oh, for sure. I've heard stories of people who thought they were safe with timing to not get pregnant, and sure enough, that's the time they get pregnant."

"That's what I'm hoping for," Juniper says as she plays with a strand of her hair.

Bridge returns with a plateful of snacks for Juniper and a bottle of water. "For my lovely soon-to-be pregnant wife. I can't wait to wait on you hand and foot for months on end."

"Don't jinx it," Juniper scolds, but smiles back.

"Oh, take him up on the serving you. Trust me. Every bit and every offer." Sara scoffs, then sighs and raises a hand. "So. A vote. Are we ever doing this again?" she asks, raising her other hand, too.

All four of them raise their hands.

Matt grins and nods. "Fuck, yeah. This is perfect. Sara, we've found our perfect couple to swing with."

"Indeed," Sara says with a sweet smile that quickly turns naughty. "I knew you would be, my sweet, sexy Juniper."

"I was the holdback," Bridge says with a sheepish look. "But I'm very pleased we've tried this. Very pleased." He smiles wryly. "I sure had fun, that's for sure. And I got to fuck an ass." He looks very proud of himself.

They all laugh.

"That you did. And thank you," Sara says with her own grin to match.

They chat, enjoy their snacks, then head up to bed, each couple to their own beds. Sleep is very much needed for all.

# Chapter Twenty-Two

John stands and stretches, having come when Juniper allowed the tiniest of anal play. He's beyond utterly satisfied with the goings-on of the night. His grin is ever-present, maybe permanent, and his lust forever stoked. His favorite parts had been everything Juniper and Sara did together, then, of course, Juniper and Matt kissing, with that bit of ass play. Shit. If Matt could get her to do that, he bets he can push her all the way to full anal sex with coaching, but he'd never ever force her to do something she didn't want. He's not that asshole. But the thought of riding her like that made him spew cum all over his desk. He even sprayed his monitor; it was so explosive. Shaking his head, the images flood his brain. He also loved when Bridge fucked Juniper in the end. It had certainly been an epic night. He's proud of them all.

Being back home and watching again, after the chase scene, made him realize he needs to watch from home. That was way too fucking risky. No more of the going there to watch business. He was an idiot to try that. But he wasn't letting that darken the memories of the night. He smiles as he remembers the naked boob dinnertime. Oh, the whole evening was a lush fantasy come to life. It could only have been better with him actually being there and participating, as a wanted guest, not fleeing like a damn criminal. Juniper was on high arousal. Her full-blown lust for the whole evening was stellar to witness, and he felt lucky to have been a part of it. But the truth was, he had jeopardized that with his visit. It had been so gratifying to see her so pleasured, though, and he was so relieved to see her get back into the mood for sex. She deserves all the sex, the true goddess that she is. And she should be given even more, really, and he'd give her whatever and whomever she wanted, on her personal yacht, in Paris, on a beach in Australia, or a sand dune in Hawaii; whatever her hypersexual self wanted, he'd give it to her in a heartbeat.

He needs to hang it up for the night, though, being tired. He'd save the view of the cock-sucking session for tomorrow's jerking. He knew one thing for sure. If she wanted to be a hotwife, he'd even consider getting her dates. Maybe. He couldn't get enough of watching her get fucked.

He leaves his office and walks past his kitty. Having decided his name is 'Harold,' he pats Harold on the head, then Harold attacks his hand in play.

"Aw, you little sweet hairy monster," John says with a grin as he swats his hand in front of his new companion. "You will please her too and play with her, maybe even race around the house with Mags, huh? I can't wait to see that." He tousles Harold's belly as Harold bites him. "You're a little terror, you know that?"

He straightens up and motions his arm for Harold to follow. "Let's go to bed, little dude." He smirks at the little guy. "You going to sleep on the bed again with me? Huh? You little hairy beast." He smiles down at him as he scampers to and fro. "Let's go."

He heads to the bedroom with Harold bounding behind him, pouncing at his heels as he walks. The bed is calling his name. He strips down and tosses his clothes into the hamper. Harold launches and lands on the bed with ease, then bounces all over it like the blanket surface is hot.

John laughs at him. "Look at you going all crazy like that. I think we might have a problem. You don't look even a single bit tired. But I'm dead tired." He moves his hands on the bed to entice the kitty to pounce on him. He considers the idea of getting a toy basket for Harold's toys to keep in the bedroom so he can have toys at the ready. "Time for more shopping tomorrow, I'm thinking, Harold."

He gives Harold one last rub, then climbs into his bed. His mood is pretty good, considering he was chased by those two goons tonight. Live and learn. He will be smarter going forward. The game plan matters, and he needs to up his.

JOHN WAKES UP TO HAROLD hopping on his face, his little claws stabbing his flesh. "Whoa! Ouch. Hey there, little dude. You're a spitfire right off the bat? Huh?" He laughs as Harold paws his hair.

He reaches for Harold, but he's too fast and zooms about the bed, then flies off it in a giant leap. John chuckles as he stretches. His morning wood is announcing itself, but he wants to wait and enjoy it while the video replays. He tries to ignore it and grabs for his phone. Scrolling through his social media, he scans the usually whacko comments and fights his urges to fire vile comments back. He needs to not look at this shit and leave it to his team. He smiles as he reads a positive comment, then gives his usual 'Thank you for reading and supporting me' message along with a heart emoji and hands clapping. It's a simple thing to do here and there to add a real message from himself. Readers eat it up and beg for more. He tries to be genuine when he actually takes the time to interact. He taps into the commenter's profile and peruses her pics. She's sexy with a curvy body, bigger than Juniper, but he could imagine enjoying time alone with her. His cock that had deflated some refills as he gazes at her on the beach in a bikini. She has pics of her family on her timeline, too, including an overweight guy who must be her husband. He often thought of social media as the best place to start with character development. He always got ideas from looking at people's profiles. It was a starting point for character development that was a no-brainer because it's always easier to start with something rather than nothing.

He rolls out of bed and walks to the bathroom. After a good long pee, which, with his boner, proves to be a challenge, he turns on the shower. The water is frigid, so he waits, humming a song. He has no recollection of where he heard it, but it's catchy and makes him feel good. He steps into the shower once the stream is steaming and lets the hot water soothe him. It will be another good day of watching Juniper. It's never been a bad day. Excitement builds in him, and he's getting aroused.

"Down, it's not time yet." He laughs at himself. "Patience."

He finishes his shower and dresses. When he enters his kitchen, he finds a napkin Harold has shredded. He scoops it up. "Harold, I thought only dogs did stuff like this." He glances around, but Harold is nowhere to be found. "Crazy cat," John says as he tosses the shredded napkin in the garbage.

He makes himself a coffee and settles on the couch. He begins to order some more cat toys, then a basket for them. Next, he scans the lingerie and selects a few pieces to add to his collection for Juniper. He literally can't wait to give her the big box of things. She will be so amazed by the gift that she will probably drop and blow him instantly. He smiles. That fantasy has never gotten old. He adds a white lace piece with sheer fabric over the nipples, and another baby doll nightie. He tosses in another sex toy that looks interesting with dual touchpoints, and hits buy. Another fun package will arrive in the mail soon.

He refills his coffee cup and makes his way to his office. It's time to check in on Juniper and the gang. He's curious how they slept, if they are up having sex already, and if he will get more lovely surprises of sexy times from them. He supports all the potential escapades the four of them could get into. The fact that they all gelled last night was nothing short of a miracle. He's not so sure he'd have shared Juniper, and he's quite surprised Bridge didn't pummel Matt into the floor when he started touching her.

Maybe he could do it. He wasn't sure. However, as long as she stayed devoted to him, he could imagine how hot it would be to see her having hot sex with many others. This is something he'd have to think about, though; he might just not be so generous with sharing Juniper with others in real life. But giving her sexual bliss and satisfaction is a top on his list of must-dos. No matter. That shit is in the future and not now. That's a thing to tackle in the future. First, he needs to get her to go with him.

He starts the live feed and smiles. Juniper is alone in the bed and appears to be just waking. Her hair is tousled, and she looks rested. Waking to that vision of her sexy beauty would be an incredible gift.

He spies an envelope on his desk that has the name of the private investigator on it that he's considering hiring. He is on the fence about this part of his plan, though, because if he hires this man to track Juniper, then when he takes her on the yacht, the investigator might cause problems for him. How much would he have to grease his palms to keep quiet about what he knew? That wouldn't be a problem for a while. But if Juniper took a long time to get on board with being with him, his funds could run out, depending on how greedy the dude would be.

Or, his alternative plan is just to keep scouting himself. He might not even need the guy and could DIY it himself. He's got the cameras after all, and he could visit the house again on the ruse of looking for something else, though that wouldn't last too much longer, he's guessing.

He leans back, ready for it all to unfold.

# Chapter Twenty-Three

The morning sun floods the living room with golden light. Despite it feeling magical, Sara shields her eyes as she meanders out of the guest room past the sliding doors. Outside, it's even more blindingly bright, with the sun glistening off the ocean. She inhales the rich coffee aroma as she saunters about the living room. Bridge is cooking eggs of some sort over in the kitchen, and it smells wonderful. Matt is still asleep, bless his heart, and there's no sign of Juniper; it's just her, Bridge, and Mags. Mags is licking her legs in the sunshine, and Sara smiles at her as she approaches. She pets Mags, who begins to purr. Sara glances over at Bridge, and thankfully, he's got his back to her. Geez. She never feels sheepish, but it's settling in on her to feel that way as she gazes at this man who just had his cock in her ass last night. She's not afraid of her desires, though, and she enjoys the surge of confidence. She shoves that bad feeling off and decides to go for her sexy vixen mode instead.

She grins seductively as she stares at Bridge's backside. She boldly strides into the kitchen with a renewed fearlessness. She's going to grab the mood of the room by the horns and ride it. "Morning stallion in the sunshine," she murmurs as she runs her hand along Bridge's ass.

He glances back at her with a fortitude that stirs her arousal. He's extra sexy in that he's wielding a spatula at the stove. "Hey, yourself, sexy. Good morning. The sun's out."

"Indeed. Whatcha cooking?" She hugs him from behind.

He sighs a happy sigh and sways so they both move. "Omelets. You hungry?" He looks back at her, and she moves so she can make eye contact with him, loving the deliciously sexy grin on his face that basically grips her clit.

"Very," she says as she moves over to the coffee pot and loads a dark roast coffee pod into the slot. "I could really get used to this. The four of us, I mean. Waking up and you cooking eggs."

"Yeah, I think we all could. Maybe we should all move in together," Juniper murmurs in a light tone, only half kidding. She enters the kitchen area while stretching her arms high above her head, looking like a vision of divinity even though she just woke up.

"Damn, woman, is this how you always look when you wake up? You look sexy as fuck! If I woke up in a bed with you looking like that, we'd be getting busy in a heartbeat!" Sara wiggles in a quick dance, swirling her fingers along Juniper's front, then ending in a finger snap near her belly. "Nice morning to see those tits in that tank top, love," Sara says, eyeing up Juniper's chest where her breasts are spilling out. "I love how that fabric barely holds you."

"Thanks, sugar buns," Juniper says with a smile as she makes her way to the coffeepot. "I need coffee."

"You work today?" Bridge asks her.

"Yep, at three. I picked up a four-hour shift for someone who needed to go to a doctor's appointment." She pours water into the coffee pot reservoir and selects a Hawaiian coffee pod. "I was just being nice. And I guess it was stupid, but she was desperate. So I offered." She shrugs.

"Okay, damn. I wish you hadn't, but I get it." Bridge flips the omelet.

"Why?" she asks as he slides her hands across the granite countertop before pushing the button on the coffee maker.

"Just wanted a round two today. Was hoping." Bridge clears his throat. "My cock has been begging me this morning. Ya know.

Morning wood phenomenon, afternoon wood, right now wood, and all." He gives the women a flirty look, gazing intently at each. "And Sara's right."

Both women chuckle.

Sara never imagined Bridge would be so open to all this. "I like the sound of that. Means it was good. But unfortunately, being parents calls us home, too. My cousin needs to leave, so right after we eat, we need to head home." She takes a sip of her coffee and sidles up next to Juniper. Cupping her breast in a quick grab, she says, "But let's plan another night of fun soon. Or a day of fun. We don't need the darkness. We just need the babysitter."

Juniper smirks at her friend. "I'm in. So, speaking of that, will you all still let me play if I get a big pregnant stomach?"

"Oh, hell yes, we will." Sara slaps Juniper's ass. "Shut up with that. The pregnant female form is very beautiful and erotic. Symbolizes fertility. Plus, it'll make you have even bigger boobs. So, that's always a plus." She tilts her head to the side, feeling sassy.

Bridge turns around and raises his eyebrows. "It does?"

"Didn't you have health class, Bridge?" Juniper says with an eye roll. "I swear you never did with your sucky knowledge base of most things related to health."

Bridge chuckles. "Not all of us went to nursing school, baby."

"I suppose," she says with a wiggle of her shoulders. "But some of that is basic common knowledge."

"And the breastfeeding. Wait until you see how big her tits get, Bridge. It will drive you wild! Oh, what fun can be had with that. I can't wait." Sara hugs Juniper from behind and cups both of her breasts, and squeezes. She could really get used to this way of life.

"Oh, and the fun starts already," Matt says with a grin as he approaches the kitchen. "Why didn't anyone wake me?"

"We're not fucking, we're talking about pregnancy, sex, and how the boobs grow gargantuan." Sara nods her cheek against Juniper's back, her hands still full of Juniper's breasts.

"Oh, the fun I had with that, Bridge. You just wait. It's incredible. So incredible. I fucking loved it. Damn. Juicy tits are the best to play with, especially when you can drink from them." Matt rubs Sara's ass. "You wanna try that again?"

She reaches back to smack him, barely reaching his arm. "And have another baby? Are you mad?"

Then he snuggles up to her ass. "Threesome snuggle." His hands reach around to Juniper's belly. "Come on, baby, grow in there."

Juniper giggles.

"Jealous, I'm stuck here." Bridge slides an omelet off the pan onto a plate. "Always in the kitchen, the last to have the fun," he jokes. He places the steaming food onto the last empty plate on the counter. "That's the last omelet. We can now eat." He raises an eyebrow at the three of them. "Unless you three would rather stay stacked like fucking bowls all morning."

"Yes, please," Sara murmurs. "I would like that. This feels heavenly luscious. I'm the meat of the sandwich. Just where I want to be."

Bridge grins at her like she's brilliant, and it boosts her spirits even more.

Matt peels himself off and grabs two plates and forks from the island. "Okay. The stomach calls me to duty. To the deck again?"

"Yes," Bridge says. "Come on, ladies. Grab a plate. Better make a move before you start humping." Bridge grins. "I know I would be."

"Topless breakfast just like topless dinner last night?" Matt asks hopefully.

"Well, if we do that, we won't make it back to relieve my cousin of kid duty. So, I'm afraid chick shirts should stay on for this meal." Sara glares at him wide-eyed. "Though I wish I could see Juniper's."

"Damnit!" Matt says with a grin. "Don't, woman. You're getting me going."

The women separate. Juniper grabs the pitcher of juice, and Sara grabs the fruit and cheese plate.

"Next time," Juniper says. "This is why we shouldn't do restaurants."

"Right?" Matt asks with a massive naughty grin. "Home fucking is more practical, yeah."

Juniper releases a burst of laughter. "Yeah."

"Bridge, this looks amazing." Sara eyes up the plates.

"Oh, the croissants," Juniper says. "I'll just come back for them."

"I got it," Sara says as she grabs the plateful of flaky croissants, which is also splattered with a blob of cream cheese and a pile of strawberry slices. "Damn, you two are gourmet. We need to visit here more often, Matt. Look at this spread."

"Agreed, baby."

On the deck, the sunshine blasts them, warming up their already warm bodies. But the breeze deftly sweeps past at a steady rate to freshen them.

"Hmmm, I love this ocean-side dining, sunshine, and salty breeze stuff," Sara murmurs in a low, sultry voice as she sits down. "There's something mysteriously erotic about the sea."

"That's so true. And I can just sit out here with a cup of coffee or a glass of wine for hours and just listen, watch, let it all soak into me." Juniper holds her coffee cup to her lips and sighs. "The ocean speaks to me."

Sara watches her friend, taking in her contemplative state. She wonders why she ever let her busy life as a mom separate her from spending more time with Juniper. "I need this weekly," she states with assurance.

"You use that exercise room much, Bridge?" Matt asks as he pours himself some juice.

"Yeah, just about every day. Same with Juniper. It was so awesome that John gave all of it to us in the sale of the house."

"What?" Sara asks, astounded. "You've got to be kidding me. No one's that generous."

"It's true, he did," Juniper says with a nod.

"No shit, huh? Wow. Nice." Matt nods. "Yeah, I'd be in there every day too." He cocks his head. "But there's something spatially off about that part of the house. When I was in there, sorry, I used it this am to lift some weights super early and then went back to bed." He cocks his head to the side. "It seems like a part of the house is like dead space or something."

"Oh, use it anytime you want," Bridge says. "Just text us; you can come work out anytime. Seriously, man. Anytime."

Sara watches Bridge closely, feeling awestruck that a man would just give them all the contents of the house. "What's his angle?"

Bridge shrugs, then cuts into his omelet, exposing a slew of cheese, mushrooms, green peppers, onion pieces, and ham chunks. "I don't see one. And. Yeah. It's been driving me crazy since we moved in. It's something weird there, but we don't know what it is. There's no door. I'm thinking it's like a panic room or something with a hidden entrance. Did you ask John when he was here, Juniper? We need him to show us." He shrugs. "Or I might just go apeshit and chop into it with an axe, I wanna know so bad." He chuckles. "I'm honestly surprised I haven't yet."

"Don't you dare wreck our new house," Juniper says waving her finger at him. "Then we'll have to spend money to repair it. Just wait and be patient. I just need to contact John again and ask him to stop by and show us. He said it's like storage or something" She shakes her head. "Honestly, we don't need a war zone in the house."

"Again?" Bridge asks with a cock of his head. "He came by?"

"Wait, I forgot to tell you that? What the heck?" She laughs at herself. "Yeah, he actually stopped by when you were gone. He had forgotten some papers in the file cabinet. I figured no harm in letting him snoop for them as we hadn't put much in the files yet, anyway."

"Ah, okay. Got it. I wish I could have been here to meet him. But, yeah, babe, I'll wait. We don't need to chop into it then. Yet," he whispers to Matt. "Or I just take a sledgehammer to it when you're at work today."

Juniper shoots him a nasty look.

Matt chuckles silently, nodding exaggeratedly. "I'd love to help. Sounds fun." He eyes up Sara, then says, "If you need help, I can come back for an hour or so. After Sara and I get the kids all settled and stuff."

Sara grins at him. Good boy.

"Yeah, that'd be great." Bridge flicks his eyes toward Juniper and then back to Matt. "I'll text you."

Matt says, "Perfect."

"Bridge," Juniper warns. "I'm serious."

"I'll be okay, babe," Bridge assures. "I promise."

The men connect their gazes to solidify their plan. Demolition day is planned without Juniper's approval. Sara pats her hand.

"I'll help you with the mess," she says. "Then we can fuck again."

Juniper smiles, though her eyes show worry.

# Chapter Twenty-Four

"So, Juniper is safely away at work?" Matt asks as he shuts the front door to the beach house with an axe in hand.

"Yep, she left a half hour ago, so we're good to swing hammers." Bridge holds up a sledgehammer. "I've been dying to know what's in this room, and Juniper has all but refused to let me chop into it. I've had it. I want to know."

"She did refuse. You going to be sleeping on the couch after this?" Matt asks with trepidation.

"No, she won't care. Honestly, she's curious, too, but she just doesn't want to see our new house wrecked. But I assured her, we'll take care of it all." He nods. "You heard."

"If you say so. I brought my trusty big-ass axe." Max holds up the shiny tool. "I told Sara. She's keeping the secret, though I'm not sure it's really a secret. But she's on our side."

Bridge laughs. "I didn't exactly get the go-ahead after you two left. Juniper'll be pissed at me. No doubt. But I'll just lick her clit and pussy a lot, make her come, she'll get over it." He shrugs. "She wants to know too, so why not just do it?"

"Indeed. Sexual favors work wonders. Don't I know it." He nods. "I've done that many times." He laughs an evil, exaggerated laugh. "But the thing is, I love it."

Bridge hands Matt a bottle of beer. "Same. Here. Liquid energy."

Both men take a long swig. Mags comes wandering through, talking with her sweet little meows.

"Hi, baby, you're going to want to leave. It's about to get loud in here." Bridge scratches behind her ears, and she nuzzles his hand. "Don't tell Mama. But I also think this area might make a great nursery, so I have solid plans beyond just wanting to know. We'll need another bedroom anyway if we have more than one kid." He shrugs. "She'll love it when I'm done with it."

Matt laughs. "Mama's gonna notice. No need to say a thing."

"True." He sets his beer down on the island. Then takes another swig. Then sets it down again. "Let's do this shit."

"I'm in."

Both men carry the heavy tools to the wall. Bridge has taken down the painting of the beach to give them a spot to chop into. He takes a deep breath. Here goes nothing. Sorry Juniper. Gotta do it.

He raises his sledgehammer and brings it down heavily into the wall, making a giant dent with just the first hit. He swings and lands another pound with a loud crack. He motions for Matt to bring his axe over.

"You try about five to six feet over, one of us has got to get through, eventually."

Both men swing and swing. The walls are thick, seeming doubled with two layers of drywall with insulation in between.

"This is fucking weird. See that?" He touches the broken wall and pulls at the insulation. "I just hope we don't hit brick or concrete behind this." Bridge hauls the sledgehammer up and slams it into the wall again while Matt chops with his axe beside him.

After a very hard hit, Bridge stops. "I think I see something." He brings the sledgehammer up over his shoulder again and drives it hard into the wall. Then he repeats it. "I see a room with...fuck, what is that shit? It looks like electronics of some sort." He moves around as he tries to peer inside. "What the hell? This is odd."

"Wow," Matt blurts. "We've hit buried treasure."

Both men keep hammering away at the wall, slowly creating a bigger hole. Bridge gets his opening big enough to crawl through, and he enters headfirst.

With his head in, he then scrunches his shoulders to squeeze his big body through the hole. "Holy fuck," he says and then lets out a slow whistle. "It's a fortune's worth of monitoring equipment in here. Looks like some kind of surveillance system. They never even told us the house was wired with a security system like this. Juniper and I were just talking about adding one, and I was seriously considering putting one in." He belly laughs. "We already have one!"

Matt crawls into the room to join him.

"Damn. This is a lot of equipment. This must have cost a mint," Matt agrees as he scans the room.

"Question is, why stock your house this full with cameras? Kind of seems like John might have been a bit paranoid. Look at this," he says, pointing at a monitor, "it's monitoring every damn room of the house. Even the bathrooms. And the entertainment area, the beach, the garage, and the driveway. That's kind of sick, isn't it, to video your guest bathroom?" Bridge laughs, aghast. "Juniper will freak out over this."

"Yeah, unless you're a pervert." Matt chuckles. "Well, I'm a pervert, but I'd never video my guests taking a piss or dropping shit." Matt laughs heartily along with Bridge.

"I can't believe this is all still recording, too. Like it's just recording for nothing." Bridge laughs. "We've been watched by an empty room this whole time we've lived here. Juniper is going to lose her shit." He begins messing with all the equipment, shutting off the power to each piece of hardware. "Damn. Maybe this guy had a reason to protect himself. I mean, he's a famous author and all. Maybe he had his own number one fan situation, and he was on the lookout for her with all this." He's joking, but he knows exactly how Juniper will react, and she will be alarmed.

Matt chuckles. "Poor guy. Could be. Just wow. Imagine, all of us fucking, and it was recording us the whole time. Hey, wait. We should try to see if we can download it. That'd be hot to have a video of the whole night. This could be useful in the future. We could record ourselves every time we fuck with all this." He rubs his hands together. "Fuck. I like this. I like this a lot."

Bridge grins. "True. Let's turn lemons into lemonade and find the video from last night and download it. Watch ourselves. We just got a gift! See this was a good idea."

Matt starts messing with the equipment. "For sure. I wonder if this records everything or if it just monitors like a live feed." He keeps pushing buttons, and both men look at the monitor with anticipation on their faces.

Bridge is getting aroused thinking about being able to watch himself fuck Sara and Juniper, and then to watch the women fuck. "Oh, this is a gem to find."

"No doubt," Matt says. "I wanted to record last night, but we went so long that I knew it was too much. But if it recorded here, fuck. That's awesome."

"Do we need to tell the women?" Bridge asks, mostly joking, but kind of wishing they could keep it a secret. "Oh, I know. We can't, and I wouldn't. Besides, she will see the hole in the wall anyhow." His face falls into an evil expression. "But, we could keep the recording a secret. But then again, nah, that feels too devious. We're all being open about everything, so we need to come clean."

"Here. I've figured it out. Look. It does record, and it autosaves." Matt demonstrates by playing some footage from last night.

"Holy fucking shit." Bridge leans on his arm on the desk. "I'll be damned. There we are. Fucking. Like real porn."

"Oh, sweet fuck. Look at that shot of Juniper's ass when she's eating Sara out. Oh, damn. I'm getting the hardest chub." Matt glances up unapologetically. "And I can't believe you aren't killing me right now saying that about your hot wife." He leans back with pride in his eyes. "I'm proud of you, man."

"Well, I fucked your wife's ass last night, and Sara is totally a hot. So, I think we're good." He gives him a fierce look. "But don't hold your breath, motherfucker. And you reach for yourself, so help me." He makes a fist and holds up in front of his grin.

Matt laughs, raising his hands up. "True. I'm good. Never thought I'd be okay with such a brick in a small room with a man with no female present."

"Matt, I had the same shitty thought."

"Great minds think alike," Matt says with a grin.

They watch most of the evening on replay huddled together in the little room. "Have a flash drive? Maybe we can copy this so I can take it home, too. Sara would love to watch this. Great foreplay fodder."

"Yeah, let me look. I'll get us each a fresh beer too. Be right back."

"Juniper is home soon, isn't she? You want to be alone with her when she comes home? In case she gets all pissed?"

"Nah. It's okay. I know she wanted to know what was in here, too, like I said, she just didn't want a hole in the wall." He grins. "She'll like that we found video from last night, too."

"What a fabulous find." Matt swallows the last bit of his beer and hands the empty to Bridge. "Like I said, you and I can fix this wall easily. Or better yet, we could just put in a damn door."

"Oh. Yeah. That's a good call. I like the way you think. It must have some sort of door, though. He had to get in here somehow." Bridge contorts his big shoulders to fit through the small opening. "More sledgehammering is needed. This hole is too tiny." He makes it through the hole and then turns around. "The purpose of installing a door will also soften this for Juniper because a giant hole would be needed to add a door, anyway." He pops his head back in the room. "Rationalization gets me everywhere."

Matt laughs and gives Bridge the courtesy of an agreeing look. "Every time. And might keep you in your bed. It's all in how you spin it, my friend."

"Indeed." Bridge heads to the office to seek out an extra flash drive. Juniper had bought a two-pack last time she was at the store, so he figures at least one must be somewhere in the office. It's nagging him a bit that neither John nor the real estate agent told them about the security system. But no matter. Now he knows. And now he doesn't have to buy one. He's got a state-of-the-art system right at his fingertips for free. He just needs to learn how to use it. Maybe he can twist John's arm to come and show him all the tricks and whistles it has. Get him to autograph a book or two also while he's at the house, because, damn, that man can write.

He pulls open the middle drawer of the dark mahogany desk. Sure enough, lying on the magenta felt-lined drawer, there's a black flash drive nestled perfectly in one of the little rectangular compartments.

He hears his wife scream. "Bridge! What the absolute fuck?" Juniper's shrill voice flies across the house as easily as a knife cuts a ripe peach.

"Shit." Bridge grabs the flash drive and hurries to the sound of his panicked wife.

"Hi, baby. It's good news." Bridge gives her a sheepish look, but then turns his face confident as he says, "Look inside. We have a security system already. We don't need to buy one, we have one."

Her jaw drops, and her eyes widen. "Shut the fuck up. Are you serious?"

He admires his wife. Her curves are still obvious; even in the plain shapeless uniform, she's a damn sexy woman.

She scoffs. "And neither the agent nor John told us about this. Why?" She raises her arms in the air, a look of pure shock and confusion dominating her sweet face.

"I don't know. But this is a good thing, right? Babe. Think about it. Now we don't have to buy one. And," he holds up the flash drive as he says, "it recorded us last night, so we have our own homemade sex video of all of us fucking. Just like a gift." He lifts his head in a shake. "It records every room of the house, nonstop."

She throws her hands up in the air. "Did it record us? For real? Oh my gosh, no." She shakes her head. Her face goes barren white. "Nonstop? Every room? Every? Room? For how long?" Her face fills with further horror. "You mean to tell me we've been recorded the entire time we've lived here? Everything? Every damn thing we've done?" Her face flushes as she remembers herself using toys, taking a shit, peeing, picking at a pimple on her ass, shaving her legs, and being fucked by Bridge. Their entire life has been recorded without their consent. "How is this possible?"

"Well, yeah, but no one was in here, obviously, so it just recorded for no one. Babe. No chance anyone saw. No way. The room was sealed by walls. It had a double wall with insulation in between."

"Hi, Juniper. Sorry. Confession. I helped your man do this." Matt waves from the hole in the wall, his brown eyes soft and sensual. "It's going to be a good thing. We promise. We are going to put in a door here. Bridge and I will fix it."

Bridge waves his hand to get her attention. "Babe, focus on me. We will fix this. Matt and I. We'll make it better."

Juniper closes her mouth, but it drops back open. "Holy fuck me to Thursday."

"Okay," Matt says with a chuckle.

"I'm in too," Bridge mimics, mirroring Matt's grin.

"Shut up. I'm coming in. I need to see this." She easily slithers her body through the hole in the wall and pivots slowly, taking the room in. "Oh, my fucking gawd. This is absolutely insane. We have all this in here and we had no idea."

"I know, right? It's like something out of a stalker movie or some shit. He went balls out in building this room." Matt points to the screen. "But, hey. Now we can enjoy ourselves and use it all to our advantage. We could even watch ourselves fucking as we fuck each other next time by replaying it on the big screen. How hot will that be?"

Juniper cannot close her jaw. The shock is too great. She's been on camera taking a shower, putting in tampons, brushing her teeth, wiping her butt, oh, for fuck's sake, even when she had a booger ball stuck in her nose and had to finger pluck it out.

She. Was. On. Camera. For. All. That. Shit. Even if no one saw it, she's been violated. She thought she had been alone. She shivers. All the comforts of her home have been stripped away.

"We need to delete all of it. All of it. I can't let someone find this. It's so personal, me pooping, wiping my ass, peeing all on video. Someone could put us on the internet, or worse, sell it." Her jaw drops again as her fears balloon. "I can't even...this is fucking insane!" She takes a deep breath and lets out a shaky gasp. "Okay..." she mutters with her hands raised, "I'm seriously freaked out."

"I understand, baby. But no one saw. No one could even get in here, there's no door. We literally had to chop into it to get into it. We will delete it all. I promise But can we download our fucking, baby? That would be so hot. We'd all love to watch it together." Bridge stays still with only his head poking into the little room. "Please?"

"Bridge. There are some things I don't want even you to see, like me taking a shit and wiping my dirty, stinking ass is one of them.

That's not sexy. Or okay." She throws her hands in the air wildly, completely disgusted. "And how is there no door? There must be one."

"Doesn't bother me to see you do that stuff." Bridge laughs.

Matt laughs along. "Wouldn't bother me." He shrugs.

"Oh, stop," Juniper pleads. "Ugh. You men! Well, it bothers me. This is no joke." She scoffs and crosses her arms under her breasts. "I need some fucking dignity and respect here. If you want to record us fucking, I'm fine with that, going forward, but I don't want you streaming through all my personal moments of shitting, peeing, and picking my nose to find our fucking! I don't want you watching me taking out blood splattered tampons for fuck's sake! No! No way. Gross!" She shakes her head with vigor. "Besides, that would take forever." Desperation fills her; this is the worst thing she could imagine. She's been violated in her own home by no one. But she still feels the violation like zillions of daggers in her gut.

"It won't be hard," Matt says. "I can easily do it and delete the rest. I promise. Sweetheart, I said I'd never hurt you, ever, and I meant it. Trust me."

"We would cut the bathroom filming," Bridge suggests. "Keep it going just in the main rooms, and only when we want it to record."

She eyes him up as shock still claims her calm. She really wants to take a sledgehammer to all the equipment. Bridge's eyes are sweet, pleading, but sincere, honest, true, and believable. This is her man. Not some freak. She softens. "Okay. Let's take last night and delete the rest. I'm okay with that."

"Thank you." Bridge kisses her on the forehead and runs his hand over her cheek. "Got it, baby. I understand. We can do that. Right, Matt?"

"Absolutely," he says with a nod. "Easy as pie."

"I'd like to know when I'm being recorded. Always. Just saying." She crosses her arms over her large bosom again. "Fuck. How embarrassing. It fucking recorded me in the bathroom. I can't get over it. I'm mortified." She spies a low-ball glass on the ground near Matt's feet. "What's that?" She points.

"What?" Matt asks.

She reaches down past Matt's legs, brushing his shin with her hand as she reaches. "It's one of our glasses." She picks it up and smells it. "It smells like cognac." She freezes. "How the fuck did this get in here if the walls were sealed?"

Something ugly forms in Juniper's throat, and it sinks fast to her gut like it's weighted with toxic heavy lead. A random glass in a room that has been sealed for months, where no one had access until Bridge pounded down the wall. Somewhere deep in her, her cells start to shiver. Panic begins to rise. All the weird stuff...what if?

Bridge snakes himself through the hole, expertly, like it's an ordinary move. "Oh, I bet that's just from John when he lived here. Clearly, no one has been in here since we moved in. We couldn't get in without sledgehammers. It's probably just a remnant of when he lived here, baby."

"But, so, there must be a way in, then. There must be a secret entry, I mean, clearly, John got in when he lived here and left this glass, yet we've never seen a way in." Her stomach churns, her throat thickens, and a gasp hangs on the edge of her lungs, waiting to fall into the world. Horror grips her. A secret room with a hidden door, concealing a space that watched her live her life without her knowing. She is not okay.

No. It's not possible. She refuses to believe it. No way.

But once the doubt is born, she's doomed. She guards herself from the full thoughts of it because it will bring her something too crazy to be true, and she just doesn't want that to live in this world. Nope.

But all those unexplainable events happened. She can't deny them. She starts to shake as her worry skyrockets. She gasps out loud. The memory of an image from the other night of a body darting past the exercise room window when she and Sara were dancing flashes in her head. She tries to pull in all the strands of her panic, all the memories of the strange occurrences. She can't contain her fears; they flourish, her anxiety brandishing the air like a loose hose with a nozzle set to full blast. Wildness fills her, and she jolts as if she's been poked with a hot poker.

She scrambles out of the room, banging her ankle on the broken drywall as she exits. She just needs to get the fuck out. Her breath hitches, then she begins to hyperventilate.

"Juniper, are you okay, baby?" Bridge asks with a strong edge of concern in his voice. "Babe?"

Her heart pounds as her suspicions start to solidify into something real. "I just want to see something," she hollers back as she hurries away.

She rushes to the front door and runs along the deck to the corner of the house where the security room is. She searches along the wall with her hand, feeling for a crack, an opening, a hidden panel, or a door of some sort.

Confusion stalls her brain. She feels all along the outside wall. Nothing, there's nothing like a hidden door or latch. All she finds is smooth, uninterrupted siding. Her shoulders slump as she rubs her temples.

She's being paranoid. That's got to be it. She's been stressed with trying for the baby. Her mind is going too far into a nutburger state. She shakes her head hard, making her hair flop. That's it. She's making mountains out of molehills. Bridge isn't freaking out.

A sound draws her attention to a nearby bush, and her heart stops as she tiptoes toward it. Her heartbeat is charged, ramping up way too high as she slowly creeps forward, her hands in fists at her sides. Something jumps, and she screams.

Mags comes out of the bush, sauntering slowly, meowing.

"Oh, fuck, Mags, you scared the shit out of me. I guess this is my fault. I left the door open, and naturally, you follow me out like you usually do." She starts walking back toward the front door, where Bridge is standing with a smirk on his face.

"You, okay? I heard a scream, but then saw that Mags was a scary monster for you," he says with a chuckle. "Big scary Mags."

"I know, right? She scared the shit out of me." Her frayed nerves start to settle.

"I assume you are okay? Right? Why did you run out here?" Bridge clears the doorway so Juniper and Mags can come in.

"I just felt creepy and wanted to check the outside wall for a door. Never mind. It's silly."

"Hey, babe. Don't fret. Nothing is silly about this. We just found a secret video monitoring room in our house, that's bound to give us some creepy feelings." Bridge raises his hands in the air with his eyes open wide. "But we can use it. This is a good thing. Especially when I'm out of town."

"So, will you delete all the footage then?" Juniper hugs herself, despite the clear lack of danger. She rests her elbows on the island. If only she could relax about all this, like Bridge and Matt.

"Yup. Matt's already working on it. I totally understand why you want it all deleted. I mean, you expect you're alone only to find out you've been videoed. It's quite a violation, even if no one saw it." His eyes are kind and understanding. "Matt will only keep last night's recording."

Why was she the only one who seemed perturbed by this? "Yeah. Exactly." She scoffs with a frown. "I don't need some freak getting off on watching me poop."

Bridge smirks, then laughs. "There probably are people out there who get off on that. Freaks abound."

She gives him a harried look.

"Hey." He throws his arms around her. "Aw. Don't worry, baby. We've got it taken care of now. So don't worry. Tell me. How was work?"

"Fine. I had a little girl with cancer tonight. So sad. She's only six and getting sick from the poison pumped into her body. But she needs that poison to live."

"Oh, you went to a different floor?"

"Yeah. They were short on hem/onc, so they sent me there. They gave me her as a patient because she's one of the easiest, at the moment, which I found sad because she's pretty roughed up. Her mom's under eyes were so black. She looked so exhausted. She must be so sick with worry that she can't ever sleep. I know I wouldn't be sleeping if my baby were going through chemo." She slumps her shoulders. "I felt so awful for her."

Bridge kisses her on the top of her head. "This has got you pretty upset. And no wonder. I'm glad you don't work on that floor all the time."

"Me too, honestly, it's brutal." She sighs. "Guess I'll make myself a mug of tea. I mean, technically, I could probably have one glass of wine, but I need to get out of the habit anyhow in case I do wind up pregnant. Fingers crossed." She crosses her index and middle fingers on both hands and holds them up. Relief fills her as she starts to relax. Talking with Bridge always helps.

Bridge kisses her fingers. "For extra good luck. Now go get that tea and relax on the couch for a bit."

Matt crawls out of the hole in the wall. "Well. I believe I have successfully deleted it all, after downloading our fuck fest. I just mass deleted stuff. It really wasn't that hard." He raises his eyebrows. "Hey, do you have another flash drive so I can copy it for you?"

Juniper nods. "There's one in the desk drawer."

"That is that one. The one he's holding," Bridge says. "Do you know if we have another?"

"Well, we could add it to my photos one. I'll get it." Juniper opens the drawer next to the wine fridge and rummages around. "Geez. I know I left it in here. Where could it have gone? That's weird."

"Oh, well, duh. Let's just download it to the laptop." Bridge chuckles. "What the fuck are we thinking? We don't need a flash drive."

Matt laughs. "Well, color us morons."

Bridge starts up the laptop on the island as Juniper still rummages through the drawer. "Damn, I hope I didn't lose it. I mean, I guess I do have them on the laptop, too. These were just my backups, but I kept them for a reason."

"You guys need an external hard drive for backups," Matt takes a swig of his beer and runs a hand through his hair, sufficiently fluffing it. "Not just flash drives."

Juniper grins at him; he's definitely a computer nerd. He's a very sexy man, trim and slim, where Bridge is trim, too, but very broad-shouldered compared to Matt. He's still bulked up and thick, a remnant of his football days. She sighs deeply. She's feeling much calmer now that the videos of her in the bathroom are gone.

"We'll protect your pooping alone status, sweetheart." Matt's grin turns goofy. "Dang, I wish Sara were here so we could all have some fun."

"She could come over?" Bridge asks.

"Nah, she's got the kids. We've got no sitter lined up."

Juniper puts her mug of water in the microwave and sets it to two minutes.

She watches Matt as he watches Bridge download the sex footage from the flash drive to the laptop.

"I should get back home now. So, when are we doing this door?"

"How about Tuesday? I have plans to get together with a buddy tomorrow." Bridge wraps his arm around Juniper as she slides by with her steaming mug.

"Perfect. I can come after work."

"Maybe Sara could bring the kids and they could swim, play in the sand while you men work. We could have dinner." Juniper blows on her tea.

"That sounds great. The kids love the beach." Matt reaches inside his jeans pocket and pulls out his keys.

"Great. It's a date." Juniper hugs him, noticing his obvious boner as their lower bodies connect. "You'd better get that thing out of here before I attack it," she whispers glancing at his groin.

"I can't help it. You're too sexy." He grins wickedly.

"I heard that," Bridge says. He smirks. "I have one for you, though."

"Good. I need it. Right after this tea." Juniper and Matt give each other a peck on the lips. "Goodbye and thanks for destroying my house," she says.

"My pleasure. And. Jealous. But enjoy. See you both Tuesday."

"Bye, Matt," Juniper calls with a wave of her hand.

"Later. Thanks for your help, Matt." Bridge waves a salute.

"Bye. Have a good evening, you two. Fuck like rabbits for me, will ya? Cause I won't be able to with the kiddos."

# Chapter Twenty-Five

John paces his living room, trying to keep his vomit from flying out of his mouth. His heart is pounding, he's trembling, and he's short of breath. He's lost all control. He's doomed. Sweat has wet his hair, and his head hurts. His chest hurts. And fuck! This is the end! But it can't be. He needs this.

He tries to focus his vision. He spies Harold. He's playfully attacking a new feather toy John just bought. He's jumping and pouncing, landing with his paws on the feathers, which makes it bounce further down, and he then tackles the wiggling spot. Basically, he does this on repeat. It's calming to watch Harold play, but his panic rears its head again after a few minutes. John has now gone four hours without seeing Juniper since the men turned off the equipment. His breaths are erratic, oscillating between slow and rapid, and just fuck, he can't breathe. His need to see her is so grand that he feels he may die without it. Earlier, she was hyperventilating in a severe state of panic and upset; is she okay and safe now? Is she hungry? Is Bridge taking proper care of her? He feels so helpless, not knowing anything about her current well-being. The loss of seeing the intimate parts of their private world is wrecking him. Watching the two of them had become his life, other than eating, sleeping, showering, writing, and now, Harold, they had consumed all the waking thoughts he had, except for when working on his book. He's lost his own life. Tears are threatening to erupt again.

He's just miserable.

He must do something.

He shakes his hands as he runs back and forth across the living room.

"Fuck!"

He needs Juniper. He needs her face, her hands, her movements, her voice. I mean, he's got all the recordings of the past few months, thank goodness, but that's not now, that's not live, that's not really real. Those aren't her in the moment. It's like watching a movie again or rereading a book. Yes, he could catch new things, but now the past was basically fiction, not reality, and it made his stomach roll enough to almost hurl chunks. The nausea came as an overwhelming wave again, and he sat down on the floor, cradling his head in his hands. He began rocking himself and humming.

He must take action now. It's too soon. But his yacht is ready. It's fully stocked with supplies for at least three months. He just needs to drive Harold there and set him up on the boat. He wants to have Harold on the yacht for her. He's essential. Should he take Mags, though? He wants to, but will Mags allow it? He could try to snag Mags beforehand, too, if she's outside, but it will be tough to do when he takes Juniper if she's unconscious. He's hoping he doesn't need to sedate her, but he's fully aware he may need to handcuff her at the very least to force her a bit, just to get her away. He'd try reasoning with her first, though. Surely, he could do that. He's good with words. Very good, good enough that he could surely even convince a baby bird to abandon its shell early, so he should be able to convince Jumper to come with him, easy peasy.

He needs a solid plan. Bridge is leaving tomorrow. That at least he heard them talking about before Juniper went for work, so, yeah, thank goodness he got that necessary snippet before he got cut off from their world. No more real-time visuals. No more audio. No more seeing. It makes him just sick, and he throws up in his mouth.

He hops up and paces as he swallows it back down, increases his movements, and bites his lip. He manages to stop periodically to try to calm down his excessive panting. He's a big failure at it, and he feels faint. He forces himself to sit on the couch.

"Fuck. Fuck. Fuck. Fuck. Fuck." He shakes his hands as he chants. He keeps the words almost silent, then mutters them only in his head. He needs to cool it. The last time he screamed it, he terrified poor Harold, surely scaring him out of one of his nine lives. The poor kitty hid for an hour, and John had to coax him back out with the new feather toy. It's not Harold's fault. All this is Bridge's fault. Couldn't he have left it well enough alone? It wasn't harming them at all, not a single bit. Why, oh why did he have to break into the room?

"PLEASE," JUNIPER BEGS Bridge. "It's morning, you have the wood, let's do it." She strokes his cheek and shakes her foot in the extra sunshine patch on the bed that the skylight creates. Her mind keeps flitting to the thoughts of all she's done in this house where she was recorded. She admits that she now looks around, wondering if there's some other hidden camera documenting her life without her knowing it. She's being paranoid. She's told herself a million times it doesn't matter now, as Matt has deleted it all. But still. It bugs her, what an invasion of privacy. She's sure John was just being cautious when he built that room. He surely isn't a psychotic individual. Perhaps he had a stalker to watch out for. Maybe he got letters or messages on social media indicating he had a stalker, and he was just taking precautions, videoing each room of the house to protect himself. She shoves it out of her mind as she reaches for Bridge's hard cock. Sex will help her forget.

"No. Baby. We have a plan. I want to use that toy on you while we are out to lunch. We've planned this. Then we come home and fuck, and then I'll go to meet Trevor and Jack for dinner. It's a perfect plan."

"Mmmm. Perfect. Sure, other than I'm horny as fuck right now and I want this in me." She grabs for his cock again, but he swings out of the way, so she misses him. "You damn tease. You have that and won't share it with me." She pouts, her bottom lip sticking up in the air like a beacon of the pissed off.

"The plan."

"Please," she begs.

"No. We've been waiting to do this. Let's not waste it." Bridge gets out of bed. "I'll shower first. Then you can. Then we'll go for a nice walk in the park, with the toy in you, and me messing with you, deliciously pleasuring you in public." He grins wickedly. "Then we'll go eat. Me messing with you, edging you along. Baby, your orgasm will be so huge. Come on. Let's try this." He pats the bed. "You know I want to pound that pussy right now, more than anything. I want to shove this in you, but we have plans." He shakes his hard-on in his lounge pants. "Play first, pound later."

He smiles at her even though she's still giving him the pout. He disappears into the bathroom.

She touches her pussy and rubs it. She just wants to grab a toy out of her drawer and fuck herself. Bridge wouldn't know. Fuck, meaning...fuck, she's so horny. She leans over to reach into her bedside table drawer.

"No toys," Bridge calls from the bathroom.

"Damnit!" she screams, to which he responds with laughter. Can he fucking see her?

"Your pussy is mine for the day, the toy and I own you and we're gonna drive you wild," he calls over the sound of the shower. "You even touch those toys, and I'm gonna handcuff you and spank you with the flogger. Wait, I take that back, you might want that."

He cackles from the shower. "Then I'd end up ruining the plans because I'd fuck you."

She rolls to her side, her lips still in full pout mode. But then she grins as she realizes how to get him to act.

"Don't you be getting any ideas there, missy." He towels off, his cock still a steel bar perpendicular to his body.

She sighs and plops her arms on the bed. "Fine."

She showers after him, defeated, hell, he hadn't even let her see him naked for very long. She scrubs with a sugar scrub, and her skin feels luxuriously soft in the water spray. Bridge barges into the bathroom as she's drying off.

"Spread 'em." He holds up the little pink toy that looks basically like a mini whale. It dangles from his fingers.

She reaches for the whale, making her boobs jiggle. He pulls it away, and she lunges for it.

"Uh, uh, uh. I want to insert it. This was my pick for a game. Now lie down so I can insert this into you." He flares his eyes wide open at her. "Now cooperate or else."

"Or else what?" She sticks out her tongue at him, then crosses her arms under her breasts. When he simply stares back at her, she reluctantly sits on the ground and spreads her legs.

"Good girl," he says. He kneels, then pushes his index finger into her pussy. "You're already wet. So, you don't need lube. We don't need it falling out because you're too slick." He pushes the larger bulbous end of the toy into her pussy, and it slides right in without any effort.

"Well, duh, I'm wet. I told you I'm horny as fuck." She frowns. "Plus, I just took a shower, so my lips are moist."

He grins. "Then this is going to be a lot of fun." He pulls out his phone and touches the screen, then taps it several times.

The little toy has a very low hum, but Juniper can still hear it slightly, and holy hell, can she feel it, every vibration. She moans and twitches as Bridge adjusts the toy's settings and modes.

"I'll never be able to get ready if you keep this up, though." She writhes on the rug, grabbing at her clit. "Mmmmm, damn," she whispers, followed by a moan.

"Just testing it out. Go ahead and get ready."

She frowns deeper at him, then stands. She shoots him an annoyed look, then grabs her bottle of foundation.

AN HOUR LATER, JOHN watches as the couple pulls out of the driveway, but it seems neither sees John. Thankfully, he's safe. He considers his options. He could follow them, or should he stay and watch for when they return, so he can see when Bridge leaves? He brought Harold and a bunch more food to the yacht earlier, along with all his clothes and personal belongings for the upcoming months. He figures they will be gone a long time. Long enough to convince Juniper that they are meant to be together. She might even have a baby while they're gone. That would be awesome. He will just write on the boat, keep working. He can't think of this as kidnapping because he loves her too much, but many will think that. Even might call it that. He cringes. He doesn't want the world to see him as a criminal. She might accuse him of kidnapping her, which saddens him. He just wants a chance to love her. To help her fall in love with him. He wants to show her what a wonderful life they can have together.

They must be running errands or going out for lunch, or something. Sadly, without his live feed, he's in the dark. He hates it. He taps the steering wheel with his thumbs. Then, in a rush, he puts his car in drive and zooms after them to catch up. He's too curious what they are up to, so sitting in the car and waiting sounds too torturous. They stop at the drug store, and Juniper runs in. She's in there for about five minutes, and John is biting his fist, fighting the urge to run in there just to see her live and up close again. Patience, John, patience. Don't ruin this. It's a one-time chance.

She dashes out of the store, gripping her bag and purse, her beautiful hair flying up as she runs. She throws one hand up to her mouth, which is wide open in an O. She's moving weirdly, like a stiff zombie, staggering as she tries to run. Halfway across the crosswalk, she stops dead and crumples to the black top. Alarms blare in his head. What is wrong with her? John fears she's having a seizure. He glances over at Bridge, who is leaning against the car, phone in his hands, and he's...laughing?

What the fuck? He's laughing at her?

Bridge taps his phone as Juniper pushes one hand down her stomach toward her pussy. She starts to laugh as she straightens up. She throws her hand over her mouth, balls it into a fist, and shoves it in. She's walking, squeezing her legs toward the car, bending, twitching, writhing. The looks on their faces hit John like a slap. Shit. They're playing sexually in public. She must have one of those remote-controlled vibrators in her pussy, and Bridge is controlling it. Lucky fucking bastard. He watches, salivating, imagining himself doing that to her. His cock is packed full of blood as he fantasizes about teasing her, bringing her to the brink of orgasm, climaxing over and over again, pleasuring her so that when he does fuck her, her orgasm will be massive, and she will come hard, and her vagina will convulse on his cock inside her, milking all his come out. Then they'd lie spent on the bed, holding each other, and fall asleep. It will be heaven. He rubs his cock, but then stops as Juniper manages to get her orgasmic twitching self into the vehicle.

Fuck. He's desperate as fuck for more of her.

John smirks as he sees her thrash and writhe inside the car. She's getting all hot and bothered. He loves it when she gets like this. She lurches for Bridge, crawling on his lap. He watches as she attacks Bridge in a French kiss as he sits in the driver's seat. She's bouncing and grinding on him, her body bobbing up and down. She looks so hot, John almost comes in his pants. Bridge pushes her off, and the car takes off out of the parking lot.

John follows.

Bridge pulls into an Italian restaurant parking lot, and Juniper spills out of the vehicle door. She falters as she walks, still looking haphazardly out of control. Bridge is playing her like an instrument. But she's laughing and twitching, twisting with her mouth wide open in moans. She slumps against him in a giggle fest, and John smiles.

What a sweetie she is. Watching her relaxes him, and a lot of his panic has blissfully dissipated. See. He needs her. He's so much calmer now being nearer to her.

They disappear into the restaurant with Juniper still leaning against Bridge like a crutch. John peruses social media on his phone while they are in the restaurant, and time flies. After about an hour and forty-five minutes, they appear at the door. Bridge is carrying leftover boxes. Juniper is still faltering as she walks. She looks so floppy and animated.

John's heart freezes, and sadness consumes him as he realizes he won't be able to see them fucking this time, unless he sneaks in. But that's way too risky when he's about to take her. He still doesn't like that phrase. He means no malicious intent, only love.

He'll just have to sit this one out. It would have been the last time he watched them together. That loss hurts, and he releases a big sigh. But Bridge's dick isn't going anywhere near her pussy after, only John's will be. He will wait until she's ready to have sex, though. He's never going to force her. Ever.

"I need to win your love, Juniper, before you fuck me," he says to a picture of her on his phone. It's a still shot he swiped off a video of her smiling on the deck, sitting in the Adirondack chair, wine glass in hand, so relaxed and beautiful, the sun shining off her hair and skin. She looks stunning. It's one of his favorites.

He follows them home, staying far enough behind to not cause suspicion. He knows where to go now, so he doesn't need to follow so closely anymore.

JUNIPER DROPS HER PURSE and the plastic bag from the drug store on the counter. A pregnancy test spills out along with ovulation sticks. "You're killing me, Bridge. Killing me. I swear my pussy is dead. You've brought me to the brink of coming so many times, I've lost count. And I almost came that one time in the restaurant, you know, when I almost dropped my water glass."

"Oh, I could tell. That's why I stopped immediately." He wraps his arms around her shoulders. "Now I'm going to make you come with the real thing." He thrusts his hard-on gently against her belly. "But inside your wanton cunt, now that you're a blazing fire in there."

She giggles. "You'd better fuck me good and hard after all this buildup. I've been dripping for hours now. The crotch of my pants is quite wet."

"Bet you come in the first minute." He pulls her body to his so they can be in touch across every possible inch. "I want to make you come as many times as I can. How about seven? Nineteen? Thirty?"

She laughs and snuggles into his chest. "I won't complain, that's for sure."

"I want to see your body twitch, your eyes roll back, your body shake, your pussy convulse, all of it." He grips her body and whispers into her hair, "I can't get enough of you."

"Mmmm. I can't get enough of you either," she coos softly.

He lifts her chin so they can connect their gazes. "I live to pleasure you."

He takes her upper lip between his and lets it slip out slowly. He caresses her bottom lip the same way, his hand fingering her scalp, then messing up her hair as he deepens the kiss. She opens her mouth fully to connect with him, their lips smacking, the only sound in the room besides the light hum from the fridge, and the buzz of the toy from inside her.

"I'm gonna fuck you hard and you're gonna come harder. It's a promise I don't take lightly," he whispers in her ear before taking her earlobe in his mouth.

He travels down her neck, kissing her soft, supple skin on the way to her cleavage. He nudges the loose fabric of her shirt away from the top of her breast with his tongue, and he licks, then lightly sucks her skin as she moans. She tips her head and leans backward on his arm as he bares her breast with his other hand. He noshes on her nipple, devouring it with his mouth, stretching it with his teeth, and letting it slip out with a pert pop, releasing it back into shape.

She moans and rakes her hands through his hair as he suckles her hardened nipples. He nibbles on her right one, and she whimpers as ecstasy looms readily. She wiggles her hand into his shorts and grins as she finds his swollen head is wet with precum, so she strokes it down his shaft, then brings her hand back up to the tip again.

He groans. "Yes. Been waiting for that," he mumbles.

Their mouths collide in a smash. His hands migrate to her thighs, under her, lifting her up. She straddles his torso, wrapping her legs around him, her arms encircle his neck. He carries her as they kiss. He lays her down in front of the sliding glass door, the sunshine illuminating and warming her. She arches her back in the sunshine, and he runs a hand down her body the full length of her, from her neck down to her thigh.

"I'm eating you out while you have that toy in." He kisses her again.

She moans into his mouth, hungrily sucking his tongue.

He feels up her body, roaming everywhere, caressing her shoulders, arms, and chest.

She grabs for the hem of his shirt and snakes her hands under it to feel the skin of his chest and finger his hard nipples. She needs him more than he needs her.

He sits back on his knees and removes his shirt; his eyes are passionate and urgent. They speak too many words to even acknowledge.

She sits up and pushes his pants down to his thighs and takes the head of his cock in her mouth. Feeling ravenous, she takes him in deeper than usual. She rubs his engorged shaft with her hand as she keeps her lips wrapped around sucking him, caressing aggressively with her tongue presses.

He tangles his hands in her hair. Pulling a bit too hard, he squeezes chunks of it as she sucks him. He grips her scalp, and she winces slightly, so he lessens his pressure.

After a minute, he pulls himself out of her mouth and pushes her to lie back. She gives him an amused look. He's really turned on, and she loves it. Her breathing is ragged and quick, her chest rising and falling rapidly. She lets out an unabashed moan, raising her arms up and gripping the sides of her neck just for something to grab.

He takes her nipple into his mouth, mounting it with a force of suction. The air itself feels as if it will explode.

She threads her fingers through his hair as he sucks and plays with her, his other hand finding and digging into her wet pussy cleft. He quickly finds her clit and presses it, rubbing it, manipulating it between his fingers. She moans with his touch, her gasps growing robust when he gives her a few clit spanks.

He chuckles as he travels kisses down her belly.

She might be pregnant already, for all they know, but that's not stopping this.

He pauses and grabs a pillow from the couch. As she lifts up her pelvis, he slips the pillow underneath her mid-region, sufficiently raising her pussy up for him. Positioning matters. He takes her capris down to bare her mound, then slips his forearms under her thighs to grip the tops of them from underneath. Snuggly pulled into her, her pussy is closer to his mouth. He grasps her breasts and tweaks them.

At his first lick of her lips, she gasps sharply, his tongue grazing the vibrating tail of the toy sticking out of her vagina. Her moans swell and fill the air as he wiggles his tongue over her clit. She writhes in response, not hiding any desire for movement or sound, undulating to the pleasure. He drenches her with his mouth, licking, sucking, flicking her clitoris, squeezing her thighs as they are ever closer to clamping around his head.

She's breathless as soft whimper-moans birth from her mouth, her arms bend in response to the raw, helpless climb toward her climax. It won't be long now.

Bridge goes at her with more force against her clit.

"Ah, fuck, ah, fuck, yes," she mutters in a soft, sultry voice. "Yes. Yes. Yes," comes out of her parted lips. She palms her own breasts, heightening her arousal further. She's wild and erratic in her movements and sounds, so ready to tip over the cliff.

He rides her clit hard with his tongue, flattening it, mashing it, wiggling across, separating her folds. He pushes the button on the tail of the toy, and it vibrates louder. She cries out in a succession of poignant, angsty grunts.

Her arms draw to her body, and her legs start to scrunch up. She curls her chin to her chest. Her lips are pursed. She convulses, twitching, her upper chest bobbing against the strength of the orgasm as her vagina continues to contract. Bridge sticks his fingers in her pussy. Being extra stuffed, she climaxes and comes again in a long, drawn-out intense orgasm. Her vagina convulses four times, stops, then does two more squeezes, her body jerking with each one.

The agony of the long-awaited release is marked, yet sweet, and totally satisfying.

"Oh, uh, shit," she whispers as the scrunching of her body unfolds to a flaccid state. She comes down off the orgasmic high with waves of floatiness in her body. "So strong," she mutters breathlessly.

Bridge lightly licks her clit, and she winces. It's mega sensitive.

"More, babe. More." He gently suckles her clit and then lightly licks it. "Getting you through this intense patch. Want more for you."

"That. Was. Huge." Her chest is still heaving as she speaks. "Epic." She twitches. It's tempting to smack him away from her over-sensitive spot.

He keeps licking her as she regains her composure. "Love seeing you come undone like this."

"Get that cock in my pussy. Let me swallow you over and over again as we fuck." The word 'swallow' bounces around in her head like mental foreplay. The image of it is exciting.

She stretches and writhes against his firm hold of her thighs. He presses his fingers into her as he increases his licking. He's not letting up one single bit. Her panting ramps up.

"Mmmmm," she moans. "My pussy wants to kiss your dick, Bridge, deep inside me. Put it in, please. Fuck me like the slut I am."

It's hot to say it, and she loves how the word fires him up. She's his slut as much as she's truly one.

He ignores her pleas for cock and makes a stronger seal around her clit. He sucks harder. She bucks against him, grabbing the rug by the fistfuls at her sides, moaning, grunting, twisting her head back and forth. She's pinned as he firmly holds her ass to keep his face smashed into her pussy. Her only defense is to smack his head.

She squeaks, then squeals, and lets out a "Fuck!" that sounds more like an anguished scream. Her legs tuck, arms bending, her whole body twitches. Her top half lurches her forward, wrapping up his head as her vagina convulses.

He finally releases his suction. "Mmmmm, yes, baby girl, feel it, ah, so good, baby," he murmurs.

"Oh. Damn," is all she can manage at first. Then, after a full minute of lying limp, she says, "Fuck, that was unreal. You're amazing. I couldn't hold out any longer." She pulls on his shoulders, trying to haul him on top of her. "Now about that cock."

"Want to play hide the sausage, baby?" He chuckles.

"Those cheesy sausage lines always work on me," she murmurs as he slides on top of her, running his engorged cock along her soft tummy.

"I know. That's why I say them. I need to be cooked limp. Can you help?"

"I have the best recipe, and it will only require you to put it in the oven." She giggles as she reaches down to stroke his hard-on. "Can you handle that?"

"Um, yes, absolutely." He pulls both of her hands up over her head and holds them there. He reaches under the rug and pulls out leather handcuffs.

"Ah! You sneaky devil! This location was planned! You planted paraphernalia." She pouts with her lower lip out, but damn, is she proud to call him her man.

"Yes, I did. I confess."

"Pussies like to be pirated and pillaged and plundered. Shackle me," she murmurs.

He secures the handcuffs around her wrists and kisses down her arms.

"Ever want to try rope, kitten?"

"Yes, Pirate Captain Bridge, Sir. I'll be your prisoner any day," she purrs.

"Oh, I even got a Sir on that one." He devours her mouth in a kiss while pinching her nipple and tugging it. "Love you helpless," he murmurs against her flesh.

"You're going to make me useless this evening," she says, wiggling her secured arms.

"I'm going to be gone soon; I'm boinging you silly, so you just sleep and don't miss me." He snickers, then grunts as he thrusts his hard cock against her.

"Get yours, do it."

He plucks out the toy, which has run out of power. Tossing it aside, he then teases her pussy lips by moving his swollen head around his cock deftly spreading both their fluids. She writhes and wiggles against him as he pushes himself past her puffy flesh. They groan simultaneously at full penetration. He stays at a slow thrusting for only about twenty seconds before he speeds up, slamming into her and making the most deliciously exquisite squelching sounds. He holds her bound wrists above her head for more leverage and positions himself for mega fast jackhammers.

She moans and whimpers, shimmies herself under his control, lapping up every bit of aggressive passion he's giving her. It soaks into her sexual aura and feeds it just as her naked body is drinking in the warm sunshine of midday. It's a warm, hot frenzy of a fuck, and she willingly submits to all of it.

Juniper gives Bridge her eyes unhindered by anything. Their connected gazes as they're joined in making love bring them to touch each other's lust and souls at once. It's unmatched. She squeezes her vagina, inciting her climax. Her walls clench down on Bridge's cock, and he lets out his sexy growl. He collapses on her, sweaty, panting, spent.

They lay together, their bodies entangled, both breathing heavily in the silence. Juniper's face and body relax; the warm sunbeams are still streaming in.

Life is perfect.

A baby might be forming inside her, and their sex life is now the best it's ever been. They have this amazing house and friends with benefits. They have Mags. They get amazing beach house views every day of their lives. They seriously have it all. Nothing could make this moment better.

"I love you," she whispers into his hair, his head lying on her chest.

"And I love you." The words finally come from his mouth after about twenty seconds. "That was the best for me, after all that edging today. Damn delicious." He lifts his head to gaze at her.

"It was. You fucked me good and hard, you fucking sex machine. Do I get to be freed yet, oh, Sir Master, Sir?" She giggles, unabashedly facetious to her core. "You're heavy as fuck."

"Well, you need a tickle fest first." Bridge raises up on one arm and places his right hand above her armpit.

"No!" she shrieks. "Oh no, you don't. Don't you dare. You do that and I'm sneaking something in your brownies, putting extra fiber powder or a laxative in your sandwich, and in the edges of your pieces of lasagna if you do that to me." She widens her eyes at him. "I will get my revenge. I'm not kidding!"

"Okay, okay," he says with a sad look. "So, your revenge is me pooping well?" he asks with a snicker. "But just one can't hurt." He wiggles his fingers in her armpit as she wiggles and screams.

"Stop it, you motherfucker!" she belts out. "No!"

"Oh, I want to be a motherfucker." He rubs her belly and kisses it. "Baby, be there. We want you."

"Aw. I want that too," Juniper says with a tilt of her head. "Now get these cuffs off me." She wiggles her wrists at him. "Free me, you dastardly beast."

He smirks. "Oh, now I'm a 'dastardly beast,' huh? What's it worth to you?"

"It's worth my not lacing your food with copious amounts of laxatives, that's what." She scoffs and widens her eyes, then rolls them. "I'll do it! I'm a nurse, I know how much to add!"

He laughs as he releases her from the handcuffs. "We can't have me shitting that much. I'll stink up the whole house."

# Chapter Twenty-Six

John watches Bridge leave from his hiding spot behind the large bush in the front yard, near the side of the house. His hand is swelling from punching the wall in the gas station bathroom. That was really fucking stupid. He shakes his head, then takes a swig of vodka from his flask and replaces it in his shorts pocket. He wipes his lips and takes a deep breath. He needed a bit of liquid courage. Each step he takes toward the house makes his heart beat harder, faster; he's so fucking desperate for this to work. It's got to.

He glances around, hoping he won't see anyone watching him. He's good as far as he can tell, but he must hurry. He's got to be on top of his game of words to convince her to come with him. He's got to be a top-notch wordsmith. And now he will have to hide his hand from her, so she doesn't get scared. He stops and takes another swig of alcohol. Liquid lube to speak out his love to his love.

He steps up to the door that was his for so long and knocks. He waits. While he's reaching for the doorbell, Juniper opens the door.

She's a vision. She's wearing a sheer magenta swimsuit cover-up over a white bikini; her cleavage peaks out at the top like round orbs above the high-waist tie. Her hair is shimmering, shining, catching all the sun's rays. She's golden, somehow; her strands catch all the light, as if she's positively glowing. Her cheeks are blooming a nice pink sheen as if she didn't put enough sunscreen on the tops of them and sat on the beach all day, marking her a sun-kissed beauty.

He glances down. Her toenails are painted a coral pink on the sexiest pair of feet John has ever seen in his entire life. Her legs are toned, her thighs thick with muscle, but that taper in a lush curve joining her curvy hips. Her lips are plump and moist in the middle as if she just licked them in a circle. With bright, flirty, friendly eyes, she welcomes him in. He couldn't have written a more perfect woman for himself than Ms. Juniper Clovis. His heart pounds out of control, and all he wants to do is take her in his arms.

"OH, HI, JOHN. COME in." She steps back to let him enter. "What brings you here?" A twinge of something uncomfortable jerks wildly in her brain like a poked snake. It's not wasted on her that he's shown up twice at the house, and both times Bridge has been gone. She shakes her head, trying to shove that irrational fear out of her brain. Logic. Be logical, Juniper. It's just a coincidence. He's simply a kind man stopping by. She can't let paranoia get the best of her. "Shoes off, please." She points to the rug.

"Of course." He slips his shoes off and places them neatly on the rug next to her sandals. "Well, I've been thinking about stopping by to show you how to get into that room. I'm sorry it's taken me so long to return. I've been working on a new book, and I had a deadline. So, I've just been swamped." His face is set in a kind expression, with an almost innocent smile. "I'm like a dog with a bone once I'm on a roll."

Juniper's eyes drop to the obvious wood in his pants. Her heart flutters as she recalls how last time he stopped by, he was sporting a raging hard-on, too. She draws her arms back and resists the urge to flee by grounding herself in politeness.

"Oh, thank you. What timing you have. Bridge just busted into that room yesterday. He got too curious and just sledgehammered the wall open." Her heartbeat is jumping like a drumroll. She carefully says, "We didn't know you already had a security system."

John guffaws and shrugs. "Oh, the agent didn't tell you? That's odd. I told him about it."

Juniper shakes her head as her shackles are lighting up. "No, he says he didn't know." She takes a step backward toward the kitchen, trying urgently to dampen her rising panic. Just small talk, stick with small talk. She can't let her irrational thoughts take over.

He doesn't advance toward her. "I'm so happy you two are enjoying the house. I loved living here." He glances around. "Looks pretty much the same."

She stiffens, then draws in a sharp breath. "Um, yeah. We really haven't changed much."

"Is this a bad time?" he asks with a pleasant look on his face.

She shifts her gaze back and forth, then settles her eyes on the floor. The urge to get him to leave consumes her. It seems like an impossible task. She slowly raises her head to look at him in the eyes.

"No. It's okay." Just breathe. She considers rushing off to get a book for him to sign for Bridge, or maybe a trip to the bathroom. She's being stupid; there's no reason not to trust John, but she wants to text Bridge, or Sara, or her sister, or someone, but she's not quite sure what she would say. She's uneasy? She's nervous? Nervous about what? A man stopping by, a man whom she had asked to stop by?

She takes another step backward, and John's eyes turn pleading.

"Okay, good. I was near the area and thought it would be a perfect time to stop in. But I'm a bit late to save the wall, I guess." He snorts. "Anyway, how are you enjoying the exercise room?"

She relaxes her shoulders, and she musters a polite smile. See. She's worrying for nothing. "Oh, it's very lovely. We both like it very much. We use it about once to twice daily." She hugs herself. "It's certainly getting used."

"Oh, good. I see you've added a pole. Is that for some kind of exercise routine?"

The hairs on the back of her neck flare on high alert once again. How can he even see the pole? She quickly follows his line of vision and lets out a breath of relief as she realizes it's in his sight. Geez she's so on edge. She's struggling to be a good host with her damn gut churning, a slow burn of nausea swirls deep inside her abdomen. A sick feeling falls heavily upon her.

"Yes, kind of," she says as she reaches to steady herself on the edge of the island countertop. The granite is cold and smooth beneath her fingers. With her other hand, she plays with the sheer fabric of her cover-up. Maybe she can retract what she said and say it's a bad time, and he should come back when Bridge is home. However, she doesn't want to offend him. She attempts to smile, but can't quite do it.

"How nice," he says. "Hey, where's your cat? I just adopted a kitten myself, named him Harold."

Her face softens, and her nerves calm a bit. She feels like a crazy person with her oscillating emotions. "Oh, that's so wonderful. Cats make wonderful pets. Mags is probably sleeping somewhere. I'm not sure where she is at the moment. She loves to lie in the sun in the spare bedroom, so she's probably there. She's funny. She will follow the squares of sunlight around the house for her naps."

"Ah, how sweet. Harold is either asleep or being a maniac, attacking things." He laughs. "Being he's a kitten."

She giggles. Ah, this is better, talking about cats is good. "Yup. The true nature of a kitten. I remember those times well. Mags has maniac moments still, too. She gets the zoomies. But mostly she's a lazy butt and sleeps all the time. That's what they turn into as they age."

"Ah, yes. Well, Harold is very pesky and gets into stuff a lot. But he's very sweet, too, though. I'm so happy to have him. It's hard living alone. He's good company." He rubs his thighs with both hands.

"Yes, some cats go and hide, but we got lucky with Mags; she likes to be with us most of the time, unless she's napping, like now." She unfolds her arms and focuses on breathing normally. She raises her hands as she asks, "Hey John, could I bother you for an autograph? Bridge would just love it. I forgot to ask you last time you were here."

John grins and looks extraordinarily pleased. "It would be my utmost pleasure to do that for you, Juniper. I always love doing that for fans."

"Okay, let me go and find the one Bridge is reading right now. I think I know where it is." She takes a few steps toward the office. She walks with deliberate slowness, so she doesn't seem like a freak.

"Oh, it's not there, it's on the nightstand."

She freezes and glances at him sharply. What?

His face erupts in alarm and then reverts instantly to calm. He gives his shoulders a slight shrug. "I mean, that's where most people keep books they are currently reading, right?"

Juniper looks away from him, remaining motionless from confusion. Her heart crashes into a million splinters, beating out of control like a stampede. The blood drains from her face as panic fills every speck of her. This isn't possible. How does he know this? She walls off her brain from her heart in an instant; she won't let herself think the unthinkable. No. Nope. No. She shakes her head sharply. It's not possible. She turns her head and watches him, readying to move.

John gasps, shaking his head slowly. His face falls into guilt as his hands go into his pockets. He sighs, then says, "I didn't want it to go this way. But, you must know that I'm in love with you."

Juniper's legs give out, and she crumples, nearly falling to the floor, but catches herself by leaning against the living room chair. Turning partially, her confidence cracking, she scans the room. Alarms ring in her brain, her body is readying to launch, but she's flooded with helplessness. Like a baby deer in headlights, she swings her gaze to fully meet his once more. What she sees in his eyes sends chills down her spine. Tremors ring through every cell. He's fucking serious.

Her voice faltering, she says, "Wh-what? What did you say?" Strength drains from her from a slowly forming horrific revelation. It's all starting to make sense.

He tips his head back in a jolt. His eyes go wide. "I can give you everything you want. I can promise you that. Anything you want. Anything. Everything." He pauses and bends at the knee slightly as if he will kneel, but then he doesn't. "Juniper, my dear. Will you come on my yacht with me? We can bring Mags, and she can play with Harold every day as we sail the sea together."

Her panic explodes. "What the hell are you talking about? Sail the sea?" The carpet is soft beneath her soles, but she can't seem to get her feet to move toward the sliding door. She needs to get the fuck away from him, and fast. It's taking most of her energy to remain standing as she tries to fathom what his words really mean. Is he insane? Delusional? Her stomach churns; she feels like she might throw up. She twitches in a failed dash.

He flinches.

A weapon. She needs a weapon. Outrunning him will not be possible. She looks around but sees nothing close enough to her that will work.

Memories of all the mysterious things that have happened flood her. There was the person shaped something that flew by the window that night when Sara was over, the granola bar wrapper, the cognac that disappeared, the glass in the room—that glass was fresh, not old like Bridge thought. The room! The room recording the whole fucking house!

No, no, no. It can't be.

Doom chokes her as he stares. She needs to fucking do something. Memories of the story her co-worker shared flit into her brain. Her sister was jumped while jogging near a park's edge. Her attacker had a ski mask on and immediately shoved her down to the grass and began removing her pants. The woman began mooing like a cow and eating grass, making weird grunting noises. The attacker freaked out and left.

Be normal. Be weird. Just do something, Juniper!

Scraping up the last bits of her wits, she clears her throat. She won't make it out the door; he will surely catch her. She glances around her kitchen, then looks back at him, trying to keep a poker face. Ignoring the look of horror growing on his face, she says, "My throat is very dry. I need a drink of water."

Shaking, she forces herself to walk past him into the kitchen, heading for the cupboard to get a glass. She fills it too full of water from the fridge. If she can grab a knife or a frying pan before he reaches her, she might have a chance. She moves slowly, trying desperately not to spill any water. Playing along seems the safest thing to do.

He sighs, then he says, "Juniper. Please listen. I just want a chance to show you my love. A chance to win yours. I've been in love with you for months now, and I hope we can be a family together, with the baby."

Seized by panic, she drops the glass of water. It shatters against the tile floor, the water splashing everywhere.

Terror fills her. "What the fuck did you just say?" She takes a step away from the glass as she tries not to scream.

John raises his hands in surrender. "I know you wanted a baby, honey. So, I put the lube in the cupboard to increase your chances of pregnancy. I wanted to give you what you want." He grins as if he's giving her a gift.

A cry escapes her lips. "You put the lube? What do you mean?" She's the size of a pebble falling into the abyss of a canyon, significant only to itself as it falls, bouncing along the harsh, unforgiving walls of it. Helpless, without hands, it cannot grab onto the rocky edges that jut out to save itself, and it just tumbles down, getting hit as it spins in a downward spiral toward a place it can't walk out of...John's grasp.

She notices the zip ties in his hands. How did she not see them before?

He moves his hands toward his pockets as he shakes his head, his eyes going apologetic. "I'm not gonna hurt you."

"Oh, my gawd!" she screams and begins to back up. "You've been watching us, haven't you? Spying on us with that security system, all those cameras. That's why you didn't tell us; you were using it, you freak!" Her chest is heaving. Her mind is spinning.

"No. Wait. I only wanted to see you." His eyes are genuine.

She can't think. He's literally gone mad. She can't mask her fear any longer and shrieks.

"Ho, no, now hold on. It's not like that. I love you. I've loved you from the first moment I saw you. I want you to be safe. Be happy. Have a baby." He looks as if he might cry as he pulls his hands back out of his pockets, fingering the zip ties.

She stares at the zip ties in his hands, her panic reaching full red alarm. Her eyes flare wide as the most dark demonic thought hits her. "John. What did you do to that lube?"

He fiddles with the zip ties, bites his lip, then smirks, looking sheepish.

"What did you do?" she screams loudly, each syllable piercing the air.

He takes a step toward her, raising his hands up in the air. "You need to see into my heart, honey. Let me show you. My heart is so full of love for you. For the baby. And I don't even care if it's Bridge's. I mean, I hope it's not his, but really, I don't care if it's his or mine. I will love the baby as I love you, no matter what. You don't have to worry about that."

This can't happen. She doesn't want to be torn away from Bridge. She can't be. He's the love of her life.

She's shaking as she quickly looks around. She spies the odd statue on the counter. The sleek, perfectly narrow-tipped black statue stands on the island like it's a shrine. The one that she and Sara joked about looking like a skinny dildo or a slender log of smooth shit. It's the perfect weapon, and it's closer than the block of knives. She glances at the broken glass on the ground, and her brain ticks off the barriers he has to cross to get to her. She's thankful as fuck for dropping the glass.

"Tell me what you did." Her voice comes out grave, cold, and void of emotion.

He looks hurt as he scans the floor of glass shards between them. He makes no moves, but grimaces. "I was hoping you'd give me that beautiful beaming smile of yours and then we could pack up your stuff before Bridge returns home."

"Tell me what you did, you crazy fucker. And you tell me now. Admit what you did!" she hollers. She leans toward the island cautiously, her sanity hovering at the brink of madness. The entire world is in her throat, and she must swallow it to survive.

He shrugs and becomes jovial. Fucking almost cavalier. "I jerked off into it."

Her stomach shoots vomit up her throat, but she forces it back down as she lunges for the statue.

John charges at her, but he falters, yelling out as he stumbles over the shattered glass like a dragonfly that has lost a wing. His arms raise up, his eyes desperately pleading. "Please, Juniper. I love you. I really love you. I won't ever hurt you." He takes another step and cries out, hunching over. "Ow, fuck." He reaches for his foot.

She grips the statue until the blood leaves her fingers, but she's not fucking letting go for anything. She doesn't want to do what she needs to do. Her resolve wavers as something wild erupts inside her. The will to live.

"Please, don't," he pleads as he reaches for her.

She raises the statue, his statue, over her head, her beautiful soul now tarnished by a crazed flood of murderous blackness, and slams it down full force, driving its tip into his shoulder.

The statue glides in easily, stabbing him as easily as the sharpest knife would. A cry of anguish flies from his mouth as he falls to the ground, dousing the flame of his irrational hope as he crumples to the kitchen floor at her feet.

Snapping into action, she runs before he can grab her, stealing all his vile plans as she dashes. She dares a glance back. He's grunting, grasping at the air with two outstretched fingers toward her as she skitters toward the front door, the zip ties sticking up firmly still in his grasp like torches of failure.

Juniper keeps running. Her heart is beating harder than her feet are padding the ground as she runs for her very life. The stones embedded in the black top road bite at her bare soles with each step, but she plunders on, away from the horror she just witnessed, from the dreadful thing she just did. The fear of John being her baby's father is strangling her throat, constricting it so she can barely breathe. What she really needs is fresh air, even though she's out in it. She pants, she can't get enough of it into her lungs to rescue her from the atrocity she just endured. Tears make their bold way down her cheeks unchecked, streaking onto her neck as she flees.

She runs up the front steps toward her neighbor's house, almost falling but catching herself at each agonizing step. Before she even reaches the front door, she yells out, "Help!" She gasps through her sobbing. "Please, help me! I need help." She reaches the door and pounds on it with both fists. Wildly searching for the doorbell, she locates it just as the door opens.

"Juniper! Hey! Are you okay?" Dan looks alarmed.

She sighs. "Oh, Dan, thank God you're home." She can barely talk; her raspy breath is stealing all her ability to do so. "I..."

"Come in," he says. "Come in, please." He steps aside and waves her in. "What's happened?"

Juniper stumbles inside, bends over, and puts her hands on her knees. "Lock it," she gasps out.

His wife, Krista, appears looking worried and says, "Juniper, what's going on?"

"Attacker," Juniper says, gasping, as she collapses to sit on the floor. "A man. An author. In my house...he tried to take me. His name is John Penn." She lies down on the floor. "I'm gonna pass out. I need to lie down." She's hyperventilating, her panic finally subsiding a tiny bit.

"Call the police," Krista says. "I always felt something was off about that man."

Her vision tunnels to blackness.

JUNIPER WAKES UP IN a panic as an EMT is hovering over her, holding an oxygen mask over her mouth. She struggles to get away from him until her brain registers that she is okay now. Fuck. She'd fainted. She notices Krista and Dan are nearby, talking to a police officer. Her eyes migrate to another EMT walking up to her.

"She's awake," the man holding the mask says. "Ma'am. You're safe now. Just relax."

"Bridge," Juniper says into the mask. "Where's Bridge?"

Krista calls out, "Juniper. I called Bridge. He'll be here soon."

"Who is Bridge?" the man with the oxygen mask asks kindly. He's got such soft brown eyes, like molten chocolate stars that get all melty when pressed into a peanut butter cookie. Somehow he conveys safety.

"You have cookie eyes," she says dreamily. "Bridge. He's my husband," she whispers. She draws the oxygen deep into her lungs with a gargantuan breath.

"Good. Keep taking deep breaths like that," the cookie-eyed man says. "You're doing great."

She grins. "I know. I'm a nurse," she gasps out.

He smiles back. "Oh, good. Then you won't fight me anymore."

She shakes her head, a weak smile on her face. "I fought?"

"A little. But know you're safe now. The police are here, too."

"Did they get him? Did they get John?" She starts to rise and look around.

The man shakes his head. "I don't know, but I don't think so. Don't worry about that right now. I don't want you to fall into a panic attack again." He gently presses her to lie back down.

Juniper nods and acquiesces. She can feel another attack is imminent. She tries to calm down, but her brain isn't cooperating. Through all the fear, the absolute nightmare she just went through, she still feels helpless, even though she's away from John. The repulsiveness of not being able to stop the history of his sperm already being inside her without her consent is devastating and the rise of tears threatens. The loss of control from not being able to stop biology from happening is completely destroying her.

Her breathing rate ramps up again, and the world spins. She's doomed, unable to stop this potential train wreck that may already be underway inside her. Her tears sprout as it hits her that she's completely unable to prevent a tragedy from happening inside the universe of her uterus. She's been unfairly rendered a spectator to her own baby-making, unable to prevent a crime because it's occurring in a place and a time she can't even touch. It might as well be on the moon. John has stolen something precious from her. He has taken something beautiful and made it horrible, vile, and disgusting.

Her gasps increase as the depravity of it all plagues her. She's endured a rape without having been touched. John has ruined the wonderful hopes she had for making a baby with Bridge. He has taken her worldview and shaken it, scrambled it, punctured it, torched it, and killed it, leaving it strangling in the unknown with his devious act. He has rendered her mute, a victim, and someone void of action. She weeps, a sufferer of wicked circumstances, left wondering about what could be growing inside of her. Is it a baby created out of love? Or from hateful obsession?

Tears stream down her face as Krista comes over and strokes her hair, whispering, "It's all okay now, honey."

But it's not okay, and it never will be.

Juniper hears the police officer ask Dan, "Was she wearing this when she came to your door?"

"Yes, she was the same as she is now." Dan looks worried, too. He's always been kind to her, as has Krista.

Juniper lets the tears fall because she can't stop her gut from erupting in chaos. She's trying to keep her brain from falling into the insane realm of reality that John has just painted for her. Sure. She's safe on the outside, but not on the inside. Anywhere. She will never be safe again.

How is she going to tell Bridge?

# Chapter Twenty-Seven

Alexa cries out as Juniper brings her to her swollen breast to nurse. Her baby's eyes satiate as her hungry mouth finds relief in her nipple, sucking in an instant latch on. She's gotten so good at it now. Juniper smiles down at her, and again her heart softens at the sweet suckle of her baby girl that is by no means gentle at all, but voracious. It amazes her once again how such a little thing can have such a strong suck.

"Hungry for milk trucks again, huh?" Bridge peers over Juniper's shoulder. He looks proud.

"She's your daughter after all."

"You're just as tenacious as I am, maybe more so," he says with a loving smile as he caresses Alexa's arm. "She's quite hungry."

"Indeed."

The day they got the results is never far from her heart. They had cried tears of relief on and off for hours when they got those test results, and luckily, while John's DNA was all over the house, that damn mysterious cognac glass, and a hairbrush under the bathroom sink, which nicely provided the fodder for the paternity test, his DNA was not a match to Alexa's.

John is gone. He completely disappeared without a trace, but his yacht has been gone, too, so he is somewhere on the ocean where laws don't apply, sailing around without Juniper, without Alexa, and all on his despicable own. Without more proof, Juniper and Bridge were powerless to press charges because John had destroyed all the evidence by taking the laptop with the remaining videos, and the statue she stabbed him with. All that was left was what Sara and Matt had in their copy of the videos, but that wasn't enough by itself. They couldn't prove it was John who recorded them. The police had scoured both houses, and the only evidence of what happened was Juniper's word. But, since it was John's house prior, and he gave them everything in it, the things in the house were not enough to charge him either, because he'd already touched everything while he lived there. The fucker had even managed to take his contaminated lube bottle from the bathroom as he must have staggered out of their house that day. He was a smart fuck up, but clearly, he knew how to cover his tracks. No wonder the man wrote such fantastically devious and complicated novels; his brain was just wired that way. Even in pain, the man could pay attention to the details that would have convicted him. The evil villain managed to save his own ass even with a statue sticking out of his shoulder.

Juniper is safe now, however, despite it all. They had paid to have the house scoured for video cameras and sold every last piece of the dreadful equipment and furniture in case cameras were hidden inside. And to make things their own, they created their own story in the house, thereby erasing John's atrocities. They turned the security system room into a stunning nursery for Alexa. Now it's bright and cheery with pale pink, lavender, and yellow butterflies and full windows that allow the world into a once dark, secret room that had almost destroyed their lives. Now it is a beacon of light, of hope, a haven of love and growth. Now it is beautiful. But not more beautiful than their daughter.

Juniper may never shake the feeling of always being watched, but she's working on it, and each day she believes it a bit more.

"She's still going. She's really got quite the appetite. They seem fully drained and will need to make more. Her hunger is insatiable." Juniper chuckles as she cradles her sleeping babe. She strokes

Alexa's head, her wispy blond hair as soft as warm moss. "My sweetheart. My love." She hums as she watches Bridge head out onto the deck.

"I'm going to go get set up downstairs. Get the toys out for the kids and stuff," Bridge says.

"Great, thank you," Juniper says. "Sara texted, and they will all be here by four. We're just going to order pizza for dinner to make it easy."

"Nice. Perfect," says Bridge as he lets Mags out behind him. "She's coming with me, I guess." He laughs. "She likes me a lot more now with Alexa around."

"That she does. And I can't blame her." Juniper coos as Alexa stirs in her sleep and opens her mouth to feed on her breast again. The nursing connection to her baby is the most beautiful union of bodies she's ever experienced; the ability to feed her baby with her own body is unmatched in its glory and fullness. Alexa conks back out happily, and Juniper carries her to her bassinet, her now more flaccid, bare boob bouncing as she walks. She sighs as Alexa stays asleep as she puts her down.

The doorbell rings. She fastens her nursing bra as she walks and pulls her shirt down to prevent any nakedness from showing to anyone through the window.

It's a delivery.

She opens the door. The delivery man is young, with bright green eyes and a shock of blond hair standing straight up.

"Hi," he says, a cheerful expression on his face.

"Hi," Juniper says, wondering what Bridge ordered this time.

"Are you Juniper Clovis?" he asks.

"Yes, I am."

"This is a delivery you must sign to receive." He appears to enjoy the importance of his duty.

"Oh, okay, sure." She signs the little pad and hands the device back to him. "Thank you. Have a nice day."

"You, too." He waves and heads down the front steps.

Juniper shuts the front door and locks it. She carries the box to the island and cuts it open with the kitchen shears.

She opens the freed cardboard flaps and gasps as shock fills her.

It's a book entitled "Juniper's Jupiter Love" by Hahn Renn. "A romance novel for secret lovers the world doesn't know about," it says on the back. Inside the front cover, it's signed, All my love, in my past, present, future, and in heaven, Yours Always, Hahn Renn.

Juniper frowns as anger fills her. How dare he! What a monster! She wants to stab the fucking book with a knife. Burn it in a bonfire and bury the ashes in the sand. But she doesn't want it around that long. So, she wraps the hardcover book in a paper bag, seals it with packaging tape, and walks to the big garbage in the garage and throws it in before Bridge sees it.

She guffaws in disgust. "That shit ain't living here, only beach house views and love belong inside our walls."

THE END

# About the Author

Ruan Willow is an award nominated open door spicy romance author, sex blogger at https://ruanwillowauthor.com/ , sexuality and spicy romance fiction podcaster at the Oh F*ck Yeah with Ruan Willow Podcast, and an audiobook narrator/voiceover actor. She is also published on Medium, Frolic Me, and Theo Reads, plus in several anthologies. She loves spending time with family and friends, interacting with fans, cooking, sharing/chatting with and educating people about sex, reading, travel, being outdoors, swimming, learning about sex, podcasting, and more sex. Did you catch all the sex? She's giggling right now thinking about you reading all about sex. She values openness and talking about the natural act of sex. And. Yup, she loves to laugh!

Pen Names:

She writes spicy romance, open door, rom com, and menage as Ruan Willow, hotwife romance as Ruin Willow, taboo erotica as RuAnn Willhoe, and R.U. Ann for open door romantasy/horror/paranormal and dark romance fiction.

Ruan has been nominated for Best Erotic Writer by the ASN Lifestyle Magazine Awards 2025.

Images: Logo for Ruan Willow and R.U. Ann

# Thank you!

T hank you to all my family and friends who support me. I wouldn't be where I am without you. You are all the magic and the light in my life, the love that grows in my love. I am honestly thrilled and humbled by the supportive people in my life. Love you!

***To Fans:***

***Thank you for purchasing and/or reviewing this book!***

I peddle fantasies for the purposes of your enjoyment, entertainment, and expanding your sexuality and openness. Always remember that no fantasies are bad. You should enjoy your sexuality and your fantasy life as much and as often as you can.

Thank you for reading my book! I write for myself and for my fans. My fans are my main focus though, but of course, I want to like what I write too, and I thoroughly enjoyed writing this story.

In writing spicy romance, I'm always excited for the erotic journey! I'm personally on a path of sexual empowerment, enlightenment, and enjoyment. Thank you for reading this and I'm honored to be a part of your journey as well. I strive to spin stories where the characters get to enjoy lots of pleasure, and I hope you have also gotten pleasure from reading this book. Enjoy your own journey!

I am where I am because fans have responded to me and my content, so I owe everything to you! Thank you! Thank you! Thank you! You are a blessing in my life, and you give me more joy than you will ever know. I love interacting with all of you and I will never give that up.

My stories are open door romance, so they have a generous amount of sex in them, as I believe our relationships should have as well in real life. I hope you enjoyed this novel for what it is, literature that is in the spicy romance genre where sex is a part of the plot, storyline, and character development. It is very different from a closed door romance, and there are different levels of heat in the genre as well. Explore them all! I personally love open door romances because I want the full story of the relationship, not a partial one.

If you'd like more of my work, please see below for my list of published works on the following pages, visit my sexuality/sexual health/wellness podcast, find my audiobooks, visit my website, my Patreon, visit my profile on Medium, and my linktree with all my links at https://linktr.ee/RuanWillow

Thank you for purchasing this book, I'd love to hear your thoughts in an honest review on the site where you purchased the book from. I'd absolutely love it if you shared my book with others. It warms my heart profusely when I see someone who has taken the time to review/share my book. Love you all very much!

All my best, yours truly, with overflowing love from a full heart,

Ruan Willow, spicy romance author, sexuality/spicy romance podcaster, and audiobook narrator

# Ruan's other books
# and novellas:

All books:
https://books.ruanwillowauthor.com/
Collections:
Mallory and Derek Attend Secret Parties:
https://books.ruanwillowauthor.com/
malloryandderekattendsecretpartiesseries
Hotwife books:
https://books.ruanwillowauthor.com/hotwifebooks
Spring Break and Stranded with Her Best Friend's Brothers
Collection:
https://books.ruanwillowauthor.com/
springbreakandstrandedwithherbestfriendsbrothersseries
Servicing the Work Men, Her Filthy Hotwife Adventures
Series
https://books.ruanwillowauthor.com/
servicingtheworkmenseries
The Sex Challenge Series
https://books.ruanwillowauthor.com/thesexchallengeseries
The Getaway Series: age gap
https://books.ruanwillowauthor.com/ruansgetawayseries
Taboo books
https://books.ruanwillowauthor.com/
taboospringbreakandstrandedwithherbestfriendsbrothersplus6men

Check out the Audiobooks:
https://books.ruanwillowauthor.com/
audiobooksnarratedbyruan
Standalone by R.U. Ann:
In Scarlet's House, in ebook
https://books.ruanwillowauthor.com/inscarletshouse
In audiobook
https://books.ruanwillowauthor.com/
inscarletshouseaudiobook
Arching Hunger Series (open door HEA Romantasy)
https://books.ruanwillowauthor.com/archinghungerseries

# Anthologies and Award Nominations

Ruan has stories in the following anthologies:
He Will Obey (which was AWARDED THE 2020 SILVER PIGTAIL IN BEST ANTHOLOGY CATEGORY

The Femdom Coven (nominee for 2021 Golden Pigtail Smut Awards)

Inside of Ruan Willow (also available in an audiobook)

(this audiobook was a nominee for the 2021 Golden Pigtail Smut Awards)

Decadent Erotica An Anthology **3rd Place Winner in the 2022 Golden Pigtails Smut Awards for Dark/Taboo Category**

Nominations for the 2023 Golden Pigtail Awards include:
Servicing the Trash Man, My Filthy Hotwife Adventure
Dressing Room Domme
Anthology Ruan has a story Hearts and Flowers, Whips and Chains

Nominations in 2025 for 2024 books
Narration of Emma's Policy (finalist) (Book is no longer available).

Ruan has been nominated for Best Erotic Writer by the ASN Lifestyle Magazine Awards 2025.

ANTHOLOGIES: SEASON'S Teasings: Snowbound Seductions (finalist) and the charity anthology Not So Guilty Pleasures 45 Filthy Stories for a Cause (no longer available)

Ruan was nominated for Best Erotic Writer by the ASN Lifestyle Magazine Awards for 2025.

GOLDEN PIGTAIL AWARD Nominations for 2025:
John Gives His Wife Hot Adventures
The Arousal Package
The Drink Master
Anthology Summer Teases 2

OTHER ANTHOLOGIES:
Halloween Anthology: Trick or Tease II
Christmas/Holiday anthology: Season's Teasings: Snowbound Seductions
Summer Teases II
The Best Bi Erotica of the Year, Volume 2

# Other links/URLs:

Ruan Willow on Goodreads Ruan Willow Goodreads Author page[1]

Ruan Willow on BookBub https://www.bookbub.com/profile/ruan-willow

Sign up for Ruan's newsletter: https://subscribepage.io/ruanwillow

ARC copies are usually on BookSirens and StoryOrigin App. Check those sites for FREE ARC of books and audiobooks.

---

1. https://www.goodreads.com/author/show/21312130.Ruan_Willow